Sev kissed her in a way h~~e~~ perhaps shouldn't if N~~aomi~~ ~~was~~ going to keep her h~~ead~~

Side on, eyes open long enou~~gh~~ for them to know that what they were doing was breaking their rules.

Their legs were entwined, but now there was time for more. And so Naomi kissed him in a way perhaps *she* shouldn't. Three months of restraint had ended on the plane, but a different restraint ended this morning. She had never known a kiss like it. Their tongues swirled, mouth played with mouth. She took in his lower lip just to feel it between hers, they stroked at each other's mouths, caressed the other's tongue. Yes, she had never known a kiss like it—and she guessed after this morning she never would again.

Irresistible Russian Tycoons

Sexy, scandalous and impossible to resist!

Daniil, Roman, Sev and Nikolai have come a long way
from the Russian orphanage they grew up in.
These days the four sexy tycoons dominate the
world's stage—and they are just as famed for
their prowess between the sheets!

Untamed and untouched by emotion, can these
ruthless men find women to redeem them?

You won't want to miss these sizzling Russians
in this sensational quartet from

USA TODAY bestselling author Carol Marinelli—

available only from Mills & Boon Modern Romance!

The Price of His Redemption
December 2015

The Cost of the Forbidden
January 2016

And watch for Nikolai and Roman's stories…
coming soon!

THE COST OF
THE FORBIDDEN

BY
CAROL MARINELLI

Published in Great Britain 2016
By Mills & Boon, an imprint of HarperCollins*Publishers*
1 London Bridge Street, London, SE1 9GF

© 2016 Carol Marinelli

ISBN: 978-0-263-92096-3

Our policy is to use papers that are natural, renewable and recyclable
products and made from wood grown in sustainable forests. The logging
and manufacturing processes conform to the legal environmental
regulations of the country of origin.

Printed and bound in Spain
by CPI, Barcelona

Carol Marinelli is a Taurus, with Taurus rising, yet she still thinks she's a secret Gemini. Originally from England, she now lives in Australia and is a single mother of three. Apart from her children, writing romance and the friendships forged along the way are her passion. She chooses to believe in a happy-ever-after for all and strives for that in her writing.

Books by Carol Marinelli

Mills & Boon Modern Romance

The Playboy of Puerto Banus
Playing the Dutiful Wife
Heart of the Desert
Innocent Secretary...Accidentally Pregnant

Irresistible Russian Tycoons

The Price of His Redemption

Playboys of Sicily

Sicilian's Shock Proposal
His Sicilian Cinderella

The Chatsfield

Princess's Secret Baby

Alpha Heroes Meet Their Match

The Only Woman to Defy Him
More Precious than a Crown
Protecting the Desert Princess

Empire of the Sands

Banished to the Harem
Beholden to the Throne

The Secrets of Xanos

A Shameful Consequence
An Indecent Proposition

Visit the Author Profile page at
millsandboon.co.uk for more titles.

PROLOGUE

'YOU'RE ENGLISH?' NAOMI watched from the other side of a large polished desk as Sevastyan Derzhavin flicked through her résumé with little enthusiasm.

He'd already made up his mind that she hadn't got the job, Naomi decided. So it was now just a matter of going through the motions.

What she didn't know was Sevastyan never went through the motions.

Social niceties did not apply to him.

'I was born here and my father lives here in New York,' Naomi answered. 'So I'm legal…'

'I wasn't asking for that.' He shook his head 'I'm not really big on red tape. It was your accent that had me curious. How long have you been here?' He continued to look at her résumé and frowned as Naomi answered him.

'Twelve days.'

'You're staying in a hostel?' he checked.

'Just till I find somewhere to live, though that's proving harder than I thought it would.'

He glanced up and saw that she was blushing—she had been since the moment he'd called her name, or perhaps her complexion was just perpetually red?

'I thought that you said that your father lived—'

'His wife just had a new baby.' Naomi interrupted.

'I don't blame you, then.'

'Sorry?'

He stiffened.

It was the third time that she had said it.

'I don't blame you for not wanting to stay with him if there's a screaming baby.'

Naomi didn't respond but her slight swallow and blink told him that, very possibly, his comment was the wrong way around—that her father didn't want Naomi staying with him.

He had been about to tell her that they were wasting each other's time. Sevastyan didn't deal in emotion. Computers were his thing. Books too. Not people.

There was no point in dragging things out and so he would tell her that this wasn't going to work; that she could never be his PA.

And he would tell her why if she asked.

Naomi Johnson had one of those apologetic personalities that irked Sev.

One of the last English words he'd learnt had been 'sorry' and he rarely used it.

Naomi had said it twice even before taking her seat.

She had said sorry when he'd gone into Reception to call her in for the interview and she had knocked over her glass of water as she'd stood. Then, as she had taken a seat in his sumptuous Fifth Avenue office, he'd politely asked how her morning had been. Naomi clearly hadn't made out what he'd said and it had been 'sorry' again.

'It doesn't matter,' had been his irritated reply.

And now she had just said it again.

'I don't think it will work,' Sev said.

'Mr Derzhavin—'

'Sev,' he interrupted. 'I'm not a schoolteacher.' He looked up into serious brown eyes and, seeing her rapid blink, he reeled back a touch from his usual abrupt dismissal. She—Naomi—had clearly made a huge effort for the interview today. The hostel she was staying at was a dive yet she was here in a smart suit. It was a touch tight, Sev thought, noticing her curves. Her dark brown hair was neatly tied back and she looked...

Sev couldn't quite place it.

She reminded him of something, or rather someone.

He didn't really want to examine who or what it was, there was just, he decided, no need to be brutal.

'Look, Naomi, you're clearly qualified and for a twenty-five-year-old you have a lot of experience and you interview well but...' He watched her nervous swallow and found himself wanting to let her down gently. 'You've an extensive list of hobbies—reading, horse riding, ballet, theatre... It goes on. The thing is, the only hobby my PA can reasonably expect to have is me.'

'Felicity has already explained that to me,' Naomi said. Her first interview with his current PA had been thorough enough to leave Naomi in no doubt that the role would be a demanding one. Sevastyan Derzhavin's skills in cyber security were globally in demand. Apart from an impossible workload he was a rich playboy and had a little black book that was his PA's to juggle, along with his private jet and helicopter.

Yes, she had been told exactly what the role would entail. He was arrogant, emotionless, worked you to the bone but he paid through the nose for attention to duty.

Him.

From the bitter twist to Felicity's voice Naomi had soon guessed that there might be a more personal reason for the sudden vacancy.

'Even so.' Sev went to drop her résumé on his desk

and, Naomi was sure, terminate the interview and send her on her way.

'Would it help if I told you that I'd lied on my résumé?'

'Probably not.' Instead of standing, he leant back in his seat. 'Go on.'

'Well, I do like the ballet and theatre but it's stretching it to say that they're hobbies of mine and I haven't been on a horse since I was fourteen...'

'What about reading?'

'I'll read in bed.'

Sev opened his mouth to say something and then, very sensibly, he closed it.

God, he could so easily and so very inappropriately have responded to that. Clearly Miss Awkward had recognised the opening she had just given him because just as those full cheeks had been starting to pale, they had once again flushed pink the second she'd said it.

'Well, I can't command your time in the bedroom,' Sev said, and he hesitated again because, actually, he wouldn't mind doing just that...

He made a very abrupt verbal U-turn. 'I warn you— if I offered you the role then most of your waking hours would be devoted to me. Your time would be spent on a laptop, or the phone, sorting out *my* life. You wouldn't even have time to read your horoscope, it will be mine you turn to first.'

'I don't believe in them.'

'I bet you still read them, though?'

'Is that relevant?'

She was tougher than she had first looked.

Sev gave her an intense stare, barely noticing her full lips and round cheeks as her deep brown eyes drew him in.

And with that look Naomi revisited her need for the

role—twelve- to eighteen-hour days didn't trouble her, rather it was the company she'd be required to keep that did.

'I see you're engaged.' Sev glanced at the ring she wore before returning her solemn gaze.

'Again,' Naomi asked, 'is that relevant?'

'Actually, it is,' Sev tartly responded. 'Because you'd have to have the most understanding fiancé in the history of the world to put up with the demands that I would make on your time.'

'Well, my fiancé isn't here in New York with me, however...' Naomi hesitated for a moment and then decided that, no, if by some miracle he did offer her the role she wouldn't accept it anyway.

Twelve minutes ago her world had been complicated yet ordered.

Well, not ordered as such but twelve days ago she had arrived in New York.

Twelve minutes ago she had texted her father to suggest that they catch up for lunch after her interview.

She had just put her phone back in her bag and gone to take a drink of water when Sevastyan Derzhavin had walked out of his office and called her name.

'Naomi.'

He was beautiful.

Just that.

Dark haired, pale skinned, he had very long legs and despite the immaculate suit he looked as if he should be wandering out of a club or casino at 5:00 a.m. he was so rumpled and unshaven.

His tie was loosened, his grey-black eyes were a touch heavy lidded and he gave her not a smile as such, just a nod in the direction of his office and a vague, unrelated memory had popped into her head—she had remembered the time she'd gone to see her lovely familiar female doctor for a pap and a sexy-as-hell locum doctor had come out.

Naomi had flunked it and had asked the sexy doctor for a flu injection instead. And she'd flunked it again as Sevastyan had come out of his office and greeted her. As she'd stood, she had got all flustered and knocked over her drink. When he'd enquired, in a deep, Russian-accented voice, about her day, she'd been so entranced that she hadn't really heard what he'd said and he'd had to repeat himself twice.

With every question he'd grown sexier.

With every vowel he uttered she wondered if the chair she was sitting on might be battery operated. Somehow even her list of hobbies had led them to bed and so now all Naomi wanted to do was stand up and get the hell out of there.

I'm an engaged woman, she wanted to say. *How dare you make me feel like that?*

No, she didn't want the role.

'You don't speak a second language,' Sev checked.

'No.' Naomi shook her head. 'I don't.'

'At all?'

'Non,' Naomi said, and then laughed at her own feeble joke.

He didn't laugh, just stared back at her.

'You know,' Sev finally said, 'the English are lazy.'

'Excuse me?'

'I mean the English-language-speaking world.'

'Oh.'

'They rely on others speaking their language.'

'How many languages do you speak?' Naomi asked him.

'Five.'

Good, Naomi thought. She didn't have the job.

'Still, given that most everyone speaks English,' Sev said, 'I'm sure that we can work around it.'

Help.

'I just want to clarify that I'm only going to be in New York for a year,' Naomi said, giving him an out now and rather hoping that would be it, but he merely shrugged.

'You'd burn out long before then. I don't think I've ever had a PA last longer than six months. Three months...' He gauged. 'Yes, I think you would last about three months, though I'd hope for more.'

'Look...' Naomi flashed him a smile. 'I don't want to waste your time. Though your assistant was very clear that the hours were demanding I didn't realise that it would be quite so full on. I like my weekends...' She gave him another smile, which he didn't return. 'I'm actually here to get to know my father a little better and so—'

'You'd get weekends off.' Sev dismissed that obstacle. 'Unless we were overseas.'

'And also,' Naomi added, just to make certain that he didn't hire her, 'I don't really have experience in your field.'

'Experience in my field?' Sevastyan frowned and he knew exactly what she meant but he was enjoying watching her get flustered. 'I'm not a farmer.'

'I meant that I don't know much about cyber security.'

'If you did then you'd be my rival.'

She stood and held out her hand.

'I'm sorry, I—'

'Part of the package is an apartment overlooking Central Park. Well, once Felicity moves out. It's nice...' he mused. 'Well, I like living there.'

'We'd be in the same apartment block?'

It got worse and worse!

'It's huge. Don't worry, I shan't be knocking on your door to borrow a cup of sugar. It's convenient if there's an early morning or late-night meeting. And it saves time when we're travelling, which there's a lot of. Being in the same building shaves off ten minutes if I don't have to pick you up from another address and there's a helipad.' And then he told her what her wardrobe allowance would be, which should have had her cheering.

'No, really...'

Naomi wanted her life back.

She wanted a world where she had never seen this man. But Sev now wanted her.

She was as plump as forbidden fruit and, God, but he loved the word 'no'. He considered it a pesky firewall to get around or disable.

It really was a great motivator.

'Thank you for your time,' Naomi said, still holding out her hand, but he didn't offer his.

'Sorry,' she said again, only this time it didn't irk him. He simply sat in silence and watched her leave.

He picked up the next résumé and read through it.

Yawn, yawn, Sev thought, his mind still on the girl with the sad brown eyes.

Spaniel brown.

Like some puppy expecting to be kicked but hoping for love.

And a stray he did not need.

He headed out to call Emmanuel in.

The waiting room was empty.

'Felicity...' he called out to his PA, but her seat was empty too.

And her bag was gone.

There was her farewell message to him on the computer screen.

I FAKED IT!!!!

'No, you didn't.' Sev grinned but his smile faded as the lift opened and Emmanuel, presumably, dashed down the corridor.

'I'm so sorry that I'm late, Mr Derzhavin...'

Sev frowned. He recognised him. That's right, he had interviewed Emmanuel a couple of years before and now he was back for another go.

And he was five minutes late.

'Not the best first impression,' Sev said.

'I know but—'

'Let's not waste each other's time.'

'But...!'

Sev didn't wait to hear his excuses. Instead he headed back to his office and caught the last floral notes of Naomi Johnson. His mind made up, Sev picked up his phone.

Naomi was just checking hers when it rang and, given her recent text to her father, naturally she assumed it was him. He'd actually seemed impressed when Naomi had told him about the interview with Sevastyan. Maybe he was ringing to find out how it had gone?

'Hi, Dad, I was just—'

Her voice was all gushing and needy and not one she'd used on him, Sev thought. 'It's not your father. This is Sev.'

'Oh.'

He heard the sag of disappointment in her voice, which was a first for Sev—women were usually falling over themselves to get a call from him. 'Your boss.'

'Sorry?'

'Ha!' Sev said. 'We'll have to work on that one. Congratulations, Naomi, you've got the job.'

Naomi stood in the foyer and knew that she should end the call.

Simply hang up and get the hell out of there.

'I thought that I'd made it clear—' Naomi attempted, but Sev interrupted her.

'How about I sweeten the deal with quarterly trips home to the UK? I'm actually going there in November for a private visit. You can have a couple of weeks off. I'm sure your fiancé will be pleased to see you.'

Naomi swallowed but then frowned at his next question.

'Why didn't he come with you?'

'Excuse me?'

'To New York?' Sev said. 'Why did you come alone?'

'We trust each other...' Her voice was shrill because, bizarrely, at this very moment, Naomi didn't trust herself.

'I wasn't talking about trust, I'm just curious why he didn't come.'

Oh, he was like a shower of needles, getting into her skin. His question was one that Naomi had asked herself several times.

'He has an important job.'

'So do I,' Sev said, then he decided it didn't matter. A fiancé, and an absent one at that, was completely irrelevant to him so he deleted her fiancé from the file in his mind named Naomi Johnson.

Irrelevant.

'Come and work for me, Naomi,' Sev said, and Naomi closed her eyes and then opened them but she still felt giddy.

Breathless and dizzy just at the sound of his deep voice.

'Do we have a deal?' Sev asked.

She was playing with fire, Naomi knew, but then again

it was an internal one, and she doubted whether a man as suave as Sevastyan was, at this moment, self-combusting at the thought of her.

It was just a matter of keeping her private feelings in check and, Naomi knew, she was extremely good at that.

She'd been doing that for most of her twenty-five years after all.

She thought of telling her father that she'd scored such a prestigious job, that maybe, finally, she might see a flare of approval in his eyes.

It might be the new start they needed.

'Naomi,' Sev pushed. 'Do we have a deal or not?'

'We do,' Naomi croaked. 'When would I start?'

She hoped that he'd say a month, or even in two weeks' time.

Or Monday.

She just wanted a little space to clear her head before she faced him again but then came the deep of his voice.

'Turn around and get back in the elevator,' Sev replied, and then, like some expert quizmaster, he hit the stopwatch on her life. 'Your time with me starts now.'

CHAPTER ONE

NAOMI WOKE UP lying in a very warm, comfortable bed. She just stared out into the darkness and waited for dawn with butterflies dancing in her chest.

Last night she had called Andrew and had told him that they were over.

As expected, he hadn't taken it well at all.

But, then, he hadn't taken her coming to New York to spend time with her father well either. In fact, they had broken up the night before Naomi had flown out. The next morning he had turned up at Heathrow with an engagement ring, telling her that he would wait.

Now she didn't look back at that time with tenderness. She had been sideswiped, Naomi knew. It had taken these months apart to see that she had said yes under pressure and that she didn't need him to magnanimously grant her a year's leave of absence.

It was done and while she should feel relief and did, Naomi wasn't thinking about Andrew any more.

Instead the butterflies had turned into a flock of sparrows and she felt sick with dread at another difficult conversation she would be having at some point today.

With Sev.

Of course, Andrew had asked her if there was someone else and Naomi had hesitated for a beat too long before answering him.

No, there was no one else, she had told him, and that was the truth.

Sort of.

Naomi had been working for Sev for three months now and, yes, he'd tried it on a couple of times.

Once when they had been stuck in his jet for hours on a runway in Mali and he'd put down the book he always read on take-off and had suggested she might want to go for a lie-down.

With him on top.

Or she could be on top.

He was generous like that, he'd told her.

Another time had been in Helsinki when he'd come to her hotel suite to bring her up to date on a business meeting and to tell her that he'd changed his security code. Naomi had been making notes when Sev had declared himself permanently cured of his yen for blondes.

And had suggested bed.

Of course Naomi told him that, as flattered as she was by his offer, not only was she engaged, she would never get involved with her boss.

He was the least romantic person she had ever met.

And Naomi was completely in lust with him.

For all she had been told how cold he was, Sev didn't seem that around her.

Despite dumping Andrew, Naomi looked down at the ring on her finger and was grateful for the decision she had made last night to keep wearing it while she worked out her notice with Sev.

So, while technically there was no one else, Naomi would take all the help she could not to succumb to Sev's charms.

Oh, she'd love to sleep with Sev just to have slept with him.

It was the aftermath she did not need.

Or the absolute lack of aftermath on Sev's part.

Her phone buzzed an alarm and Naomi turned it off and then pulled back the covers and padded out to the kitchen and fixed herself a coffee.

It was a beautiful apartment, with thirteen-foot-high ceilings, mahogany doors and gorgeous fireplaces. Not that she used them. Instead she relied on the regular heating, worried that she'd burn the whole complex down.

Sev had the penthouse suite and he had been right—apart from the occasions when they prearranged to meet in the foyer their paths rarely crossed out of work.

The problem *was* work and very long days spent together and even longer trips abroad.

Or rather Naomi's problem was her feelings for him.

She took her drink back to bed and wondered if she was about to make the biggest mistake of her life by quitting her job, and then, as if in answer, her phone rang.

It was 6:00 a.m. on a Monday morning, but that meant nothing to Sev.

Naomi was available pretty much 24/7 and there was no space from him. There was little to no time to catch her breath from the roller-coaster ride, no time to slow her racing heart down and regroup.

'Hi, Sev.'

'What time is it?' Sev asked.

Naomi bit back a smart retort—oh, she could have said that she wasn't his personal talking clock but she conceded that he paid her enough for her to be one, if he so chose. 'It's six,' Naomi said. 'Six a.m.,' she added.

Just in case.

'Okay, can you cancel my morning?' Sev said. 'Actually, just cancel the rest of my day. I'll be back on board tomorrow.'

Oh, no!

Now she understood the odd question about the time. He wasn't even in the same time zone.

'Sev, where are you?'

'On my way back.'

'But from where? You're supposed to be meeting Sheikh Allem at eleven and then we're having dinner tonight with him and his wife. It's been booked in for ages, it's taken weeks to arrange.'

'I know all that.'

'So you have to be here.'

'What's the flying time from Rome to New York?' Sev asked.

Forget the time zone, Naomi thought. He wasn't even on the same continent. 'Just over eight hours,' Naomi sighed.

'So you see it's not possible.'

She could almost envisage him shrugging.

'Sev,' Naomi appealed. 'Allem rang last night to say how much he and his wife are looking forward to this visit. He's been so patient.'

Sheikh Allem had been. He had asked Sev to come to Dubai to review his hotel's security system yet Sev had been putting the visit off. Now he had flown with his wife to visit him.

They were friends more than business associates but Sev didn't need friends—he wanted Allem and his wife to back off.

They refused to get the message.

'Okay, okay,' Sev snapped. 'I'm on my way to the airport. When I get to the plane I'll ask the pilot to put his foot down or whatever it is they do. Look, I haven't a hope of getting there before three.'

'What should I say to him?'

'That's what I pay you to sort out,' Sev said. 'Just use your charm, Naomi.'

'It's all used up.'

'I have noticed,' Sev responded. 'You've been very…'

'Testy?' Naomi offered.

'I don't know what that word means.'

'Bad-tempered, irritable.'

'Yes, you have been very testy of late.'

'Because my boss keeps disappearing on me. Just what exactly are you doing in Rome?' Hell, she ran his diary, booked his flights, arranged his schedule and, Naomi knew damn well that he wasn't supposed to be there.

'You want to know *exactly*?' Sev checked.

Naomi closed her eyes. She knew, of course, that it would be about a woman.

And that was why she was being so testy. Naomi, more than anything, loathed confrontation, or rather she could not stand to be the one who brought things to the boil. In fact, she actually wanted Sev to fire her. It would be better than having to resign later today.

'I mean, why are you in Rome?' Naomi said. 'I'm just trying to work out what to tell Sheikh Allem.'

'Well, I guess it just seemed a good idea at the time.'

'And I guess that time was Saturday night.'

'You know me so well. I was at a party and—'

'I've changed my mind,' Naomi snapped. 'I don't need to know. I'll come up with something for Allem.'

'You're sounding very English,' Sev said. 'Work something out. Oh, and can you organise some flowers from me?'

Naomi closed her eyes.

'If you can send two dozen white roses…'

He really didn't need to tell her that—it was always the same routine with Sev.

On a Monday Naomi would arrange flowers for whoever he had seen over the weekend. Around Wednesday he might ask her to organise a hotel for the following one.

The next Monday it might be a case of more flowers but generally he'd lost interest by then.

'What's her name?' Naomi asked, as she reached for her pen. 'And what message do you want?'

'Actually,' Sev said, 'don't worry about the flowers. Apart from Allem, am I missing out on anything else?'

'Just a scheduled beginning-of-the-month meeting with me.' She had been going to tell him then that she was resigning.

Sev was silent.

'It's November,' Naomi said.

'I know that.'

'I'm just checking that you do.'

'Anything else?'

'No, everything was cleared for Allem.'

'I'll be there as soon as I can. Tell Allem…' He thought for a moment. 'Just tell him what you have to and if he acts up remind him he's the one who wants to see me.'

He didn't say goodbye, he simply rang off, and, no, Naomi thought, she wouldn't miss this part of the job—reorganising his schedule at a moment's notice and letting people down. At least that was how it felt to her. His clients didn't seem to mind in the least. That he was unattainable made him all the more desirable. The more elusive he was the more in demand he became.

'Bloody Sev,' Naomi grumbled, then sank back on her pillows to enjoy a rare lie-in.

There was no need to rush in now. She could work

here for a couple of hours, so she lay back and waited for sunrise and thought about what she was about to do.

Most would say she was mad to give up such an amazing job and all the perks that came with it.

For the past three months Naomi had been telling herself the same.

Yet she was fast learning that location, location didn't equate to happiness. A designer wardrobe and manicured nails and a fabulous haircut didn't magically put the world to rights.

On sight she had fallen for Sev.

Hard.

And, like her many predecessors, Naomi knew how futile hoping for anything other than the briefest of flings with him would be.

She should get out before she succumbed, Naomi had decided. She was already conflicted enough, trying to forge some sort of relationship with her father as well as ending things with Andrew.

A temporary fling with Sev she certainly didn't need, for though it might be temporary for him, an encounter of the sexual kind, Naomi knew, would add a permanent tattoo to her heart.

He wasn't cold at all. In fact, sometimes it felt as if he had been put on this earth with the sole reason to make her smile.

Which he did.

A lot.

He was inappropriate, yes.

But he was no more inappropriate than her own thoughts.

The chair in his office still felt battery operated.

His voice made her stomach curl.

And as for emotionless…

Whether he was or he wasn't, he brought out all of her emotions effortlessly.

The morning was arriving and it looked crisp and clear from the warmth of bed. Somebody must have been out with a paintbrush last night for Central Park was a rich palette of burnt reds and oranges and she wondered what it might look like to lie in bed in winter with the bedroom fire lit, looking out at the trees stripped bare and heavy with snow.

She wasn't going to be here to find out.

And she would tell him so today.

CHAPTER TWO

THE VIEW WAS just as impressive on Sev's part of the planet.

Not that he saw much of it.

He wore dark glasses and the tinted windows of the hotel's black Mercedes blocked out the midday sun as he called Naomi while being driven to his plane.

Sev looked out briefly at the sights of Rome as he was driven through the busy streets. He'd possibly get there quicker if he jumped on a moped but, though cross with himself for sleeping in and thus being so late for Allem, he wasn't about to go to such extremes.

Instead he had pulled out his phone and decided that Naomi would just have to fix things.

She wasn't best pleased with him but a moody PA he did not need so he snapped off the phone, relieved as his car pulled onto the tarmac near his waiting plane. What the hell had possessed him to call out his crew on a Saturday night to fly here when now he couldn't even remember her name?

It wasn't as if it was for sex that he'd gone to such extremes. Sex had been taken care of long before they'd boarded.

And it hadn't been about conversation—he wasn't particularly fluent in Italian.

Sev wasn't feeling very good about another reckless night and he certainly didn't need Reverend Sister Naomi's silent tsk tsk of disapproval.

Shannon, his flight attendant, greeted him and knew him well enough to wait and ask how he wanted his coffee before making it.

It varied.

'Long and black,' Sev said, taking off his jacket. 'With one sugar.' He took a seat but by the time he had Sev had already changed his mind and called Shannon back.

'A strong latte, two sugars.'

Maybe the milk would help his stomach but Sev knew he was, thanks to Naomi, suffering from a rare spasm of guilt.

He liked Allem and his wife and knew that they were in New York primarily to catch up with him as, thanks to the excuse of work commitments, Sev had declined their last two invitations to visit them in Dubai.

It had been Allem who had given him his first break.

Sev's past should mean he lived on the streets but he never had.

His grades at school had been outstanding and had meant he had received a scholarship to a very good school and then an internship.

It had been cell phones that Sev had been into then and he had come up with the design that Allem had run with.

Yes, Sev's cynical voice reminded him, that design had meant that Allem had made an absolute fortune out of his idea.

Yet Allem had then bankrolled Sev, allowing him to delve deeply into the cyber world. Now his genius sat in a range of one step behind or two steps ahead of the bad boys. This meant his services were in expensive demand from governments to law enforcement, airlines, royalty and show business. Sev fought his virtual enemies with talent and respect.

It was an endless, relentless game and one, more often than not, he won.

His success wasn't down to Allem—he owed him nothing, Sev thought, draining his coffee, as Jason, the captain, spoke and told him he was hoping to catch a tail wind and they should arrive just before three.

Shannon came to take his cup and any moment now they'd be on their way.

'Do you want me to fix lunch after take-off?' she offered, but Sev shook his head.

'I don't want anything to eat, I'm just going to go to bed. Don't wake me unless the plane is going down,' Sev said. 'Actually, don't wake me even if it is.'

He opened up his book, the one he always read during take-off, but not even that could distract him today.

Sev avoided friendships, he avoided getting close to anyone, yet Allem insisted on sticking around.

As soon as he was able to he made his way to the bedroom.

He stripped, had a quick shower and then got into bed but sleep eluded him.

That needle of guilt was still there so he called Naomi again.

'I can't sleep,' Sev admitted.

'Where are you now?'

'An hour out of Rome. Have you spoken to Allem?'

'Not yet. I've sent an email telling him that you've been delayed,' Naomi said. 'I'll call him closer to nine when I've worked out a reason why.'

There was a slightly tart edge to her voice.

'Go into my bureau,' Sev said. He had actually bought a gift for Jamal and Allem. 'There should be a polished box there you could wrap for me. You could give it to him as a little sweetener until I arrive.'

'Okay.'

'Is it there?' Sev asked, wondering if he might have left it in his apartment

'I'll look when I get to the office.'

'You're not in yet?'

'No,' Naomi said. 'Caught.'

'Caught what?'

'Having a lie-in.' Naomi said, but then hurriedly added, 'I'm up now, though.'

'Liar.'

'You trained me well,' Naomi responded. They were both in bed and both knew it.

'Go up to my apartment before you head into work. It might be in my desk there. If not, then it's in the bureau at work. It's got a statue in it.'

'Okay. So what lie do you want me to feed Allem?'

But Sev's mind was on other things.

Yes, he'd been feeling bad about Allem but knowing that Naomi was in bed, hopefully as naked as he, was, well, a bit of a turn-on.

She drove him crazy.

He could not read her.

It was like a weather report telling you it was sultry and hot and then stepping out to sleet and ice.

'Can I ask you something?'

'No,' Naomi answered. 'About Allem. What am I to tell him?'

Oh, that was right. The reason for his call.

'Just tell him there was a family emergency that I had to attend to. He's big on family. Tell him that my mother was taken ill and I'm on my way back from Russia.'

'Sev, is your mother alive?'

'Yes?'

'Is she sick?'

'She could be.'

He heard a slight noise as she sucked in her breath. 'You don't like the idea.'

'It's not for me to judge…'

'Oh, but, baby, you do,' Sev snapped. 'Over and over you do. And do you know what? I don't need it. I'm warning you—'

'Officially?' Naomi checked, more than happy for him to fire her now, even the dark rise of his voice turned her on.

'Unofficially,' Sev said.

God, but he even liked rowing with her.

Sev didn't row. Usually he simply couldn't be bothered to.

They both lay in tense angry silence but neither ended the call and then Sev said it again but his voice wasn't angry now.

'Can I ask you something?' No, he wasn't angry. His voice had that low edge to it that had her pull up her knees.

'Go ahead.' Naomi sighed.

'It's personal.'

She had guessed that it might be.

'I'm just curious about something.'

Somehow he didn't offend her.

Naomi was curious about him too.

She just lay there naked in bed, trying to imagine how that low voice might sound while making love to her, and she was terribly, terribly tempted to find out.

To just finally give in to the suggestive air they created.

'Ask away.'

'Well, I'm assuming, if you're engaged, that you must love your fiancé.'

She didn't answer.

'And fancy him.'

Naomi said nothing.

'So how do you...?'

'How do I what, Sev?'

'You've been in New York for three months and in that time I can't recall him coming over to see you.'

'He hasn't.'

'So,' Sev asked, 'how do you manage?'

Manage!

Oh, it was as basic as that to Sev, Naomi thought. An itch to be scratched, a line on his to-do list to be regularly ticked off.

'Sev,' Naomi crisply replied, when she would far rather dive under the covers and prolong the call, 'I'm giving *you* an official warning now.'

She hung up on him. Sev tossed the phone down in frustration.

Bloody Naomi, Sev thought as he lay there. He was hard for her and had been left hanging. And then he remembered why he'd come to Rome.

She had been brunette.

It was as simple and as messed up as that.

He was over Naomi and her moods.

Sev didn't need some sanctimonious PA sitting on her moral throne. She was there to run his life, not have him account for it.

Who cared what she thought?

He cared about no one.

Only that wasn't quite right.

God, but he hated this month already.

Sev *hated* November.

He always had and he always would.

In Russia it was Mother's Day at the end of November.

At school, the 'home kids', as he and his friends had called the students who'd had families, would sit and make cards for their mothers as the *'detsky dom'* kids stuck rice onto paper for, well, no one in particular.

There had been four at his table, they had been together since nursery school.

Sevastyan had always been the nerdy one, Nikolai had liked ships and then there had been the twins, Roman and Daniil, who were going to be famous boxers one day.

Some day.

Never.

'If you don't have a mother then make a card for someone you care about,' the teacher had suggested each year.

The *'detsky dom'* kids' cards had never got made.

A few years back Sevastyan had found out that he did have a mother, but he now knew that she wouldn't have appreciated a card with stuck-on rice anyway.

He'd send flowers, of course, but rather than rely on Naomi he would try to work out himself what to put in the note.

Each year it became harder to work out what to write.

Thanks for being there?

She hadn't been.

With love to you on this special day?

It wasn't a special day to her.

And there was no love.

November also meant that it was his niece's birthday.

Her eighteenth! Sev suddenly remembered.

He'd stop at Tiffany on the way to the office Sev thought, then decided not to bother.

Whatever he sent would just end up being pawned or put up on some auction site.

Yes, for so many reasons he hated November.

Sev closed his eyes but he still could not sleep.

He stared into the dark and could remember as if it were yesterday, rather than half a lifetime ago, hearing his friend quietly crying in the night.

These had been boys who had stopped crying from the cradle and so Sev had not known whether his friend would appreciate that he knew that he was.

'What's wrong?' Sev had asked. 'Nikolai, what has happened?'

'Nothing.'

'It doesn't sound like nothing.'

'Leave it.'

He had.

To Sev's utter, utter regret, he had.

In the morning Nikolai had been gone.

A week later his body had washed up and Sergio had come back with his bag, in it a ship Nikolai had been making out of matches.

Sev lay there and thought of his friend and his sad end.

And the thought of the others he still missed to this day.

On the twelfth of November, the day Nikolai had run away, Sev would be in London for yet another futile attempt to meet with his past.

He might give it a miss, Sev thought, but he was as superstitious as he was Russian.

If he didn't go, of course it would be the one year that Daniil showed up.

CHAPTER THREE

SHEIKH ALLEM WAS extremely gracious about the change in plans.

In fact, when Naomi had called him at nine he hadn't seemed in the least surprised. He'd told Naomi that he would come to the office at four but in the meantime, would she mind taking Jamal shopping?

'Of course.'

Naomi had dressed in a navy shift dress and flat ballet pumps and she headed up to Sev's apartment to check if the gift he had bought for Allem was there.

His apartment took up the entire floor.

She was often in there, packing his case, doing little jobs, showing through a designer because he'd decided he had changed his mind about a wall or a light or whatever it was that he might suddenly decide that he wanted changed. She basically took care of many details of Sev's life so that he didn't have to.

His maid was in there, changing the flowers and making sure everything was perfect for his return.

Naomi said hi and went through to Sev's study.

There was no polished wooden box that she could see in any of the drawers.

She looked on top of the desk.

There was no box there either, just a rather scruffy little ship.

It was odd, Naomi thought, picking it up and examining it. It was old and poorly put together, unlike anything else in the apartment.

She put it down again and then headed into his bedroom, deciding to take the opportunity to take a couple of fresh shirts to the office.

His bedroom was her favourite room.

Not because of him.

Well, maybe.

But it kind of fascinated Naomi.

The mahogany door she opened didn't close as the same thing.

Bored with the trimmings, he had made a few alterations to a heritage building and the other side of the door was ebony.

As were the rest of the trimmings.

Another maid was in there, changing the bedding on his big black wooden bed.

It was beautiful.

The view was amazing and the curtains were black on ivory with a dash of pistachio-green—the only dart of colour in the entire room, apart from the view.

Because it was the beginning of the month, Naomi took out her tablet and made a quick inventory.

He had one woman who shopped for his clothing, who Naomi liaised with. He had another who dealt with food and beverages.

His PA dealt with personal items.

She went to his dressing table and saw the cologne she had ordered last month from Paris. The container was still half-full but she made a note and then, joy, went to his bedside table and made another note of items that needed to be replenished!

She would not miss this part of her job in the least. In fact, she was so annoyed that she forgot to go through to the bathroom and instead took the shirts and headed into work.

Sure enough, in the bureau in his office was a gleaming wooden box and Naomi had a peek inside and frowned.

He'd bought it in Mali, she remembered.

And she'd wondered why at the time.

It was a fertility statue.

Naomi considered whether she should call Sev and tell him that this might not be the best gift to give the sheikh but what the hell, it was his faux pas and she was still cross with him and not in the mood for another little chat with a naked Sev.

Naomi wrapped the gift and decided that Sev could give it to him and deal with the consequences and she placed it back in the bureau. She then went to meet Jamal and spent a few hours shopping and chatting before Naomi saw her back to her hotel. She got a call from Sev's driver to say that his plane had landed but she came back to an office still devoid of Sev.

Damn.

Allem would be here soon.

She felt terrible, lying for Sev. Till today she hadn't even known that Sev had a mother. She knew everything and nothing about him.

He never spoke about family.

She was never asked to send presents or flowers for anyone other than girlfriends.

Naomi pulled up his account at the florist and looked at May.

No, judging by the messages sent that month, a Mother's Day bouquet hadn't been sent.

It was none of her business, Naomi told herself.

She just wanted to know some more.

She was alerted that Allem had arrived and Naomi greeted him. He was robed and wearing a *kafeya* and just so polished and well mannered she wondered if he was royal.

'His plane has just landed,' Naomi said, and fired Sev a text as they waited.

And waited.

Allem didn't seem to mind in the least.

'How long have you been working for Sevastyan?' Allem asked, as Naomi poured tea.

'Three months.'

And with her notice served it would be three months and two weeks. Naomi had absolutely decided that she was going to do it.

Finally Sev appeared, as rumpled as if he had flown economy to get here rather than on his luxury private jet.

Still beautiful, Naomi thought, but though she smiled a greeting it didn't quite meet her eyes.

His neck was a mess from his weekend of passion and she knew now why it had taken so long for him to get from the airport—from the bag he was carrying it was clear that he had stopped off at Tiffany.

Not for a second did she presume he'd stopped to buy something for her.

'I'm very sorry to hear about your mother,' Allem offered. 'How is she?'

'Touch and go,' Sev replied, and jiggled his hand. No, he didn't say sorry for being seven hours late. 'Let's go through to my office.' He led Allem through and as he closed the door he gave Naomi a smile of thanks.

No doubt he thought he had got away with it and Allem believed that his mother was sick—didn't he get it that Allem was just too polite to mention the bite marks on his neck?

Naomi was completely over this job.

No, she wasn't burnt out.

It was far more than that.

He'd lie about his own mother.

Sev was a bastard.

Felicity had told her that at her first interview.

Even Sev had warned her that he was on her very first day.

'I prefer computers,' he'd yawned, as he'd called on her, on her very first day, to handle a teary previous date who'd kept calling him on the office phone. 'No tears, no dramas.' He'd seen her cheeks redden. 'I'm not talking about porn.'

'I never said that you were.'

'I'm just saying that I prefer computers to people.'

Naomi thought back to her first day and now and the months in between and, really, even if she knew so many details about his life, she knew him no better at all. She didn't even know how he took his coffee.

It, like Sev, changed on a whim.

Sev closed the door on Naomi's silent disapproval and as Allem took a seat Sev opened up the bureau to see that Naomi had wrapped the gift for him.

'I got this for Jamal when I was in Mali,' Sev said and handed over the gift and watched as Allem opened it. 'I remember you saying that she likes statues and I…' his voice trailed off as Allem started laughing when he took out the ebony statue that had caught Sev's restless eye a few weeks ago. 'What's so funny?'

'Sevastyan, this is a most inappropriate gift to give to my wife,' Allem said, but with a smile. 'It's a fertility statue.'

'Really! Well, I want it out of this office, then.'

'Actually, Jamal will laugh when I tell her that you bought this with her in mind. You are in fact a little too late. I'm delighted to tell you that we are expecting a baby in March.'

Sev said all the right things.

Well, he tried.

Allem had been wild once, Sev thought.

Perhaps that was why they *had* got on so well.

They had used to hit the clubs wherever in the world they were.

But in the past couple of years it had been lengthy dinners with Allem and Jamal and whatever date Sev brought along.

Now, Allem spoke about morning sickness and how Jamal had lost weight and was a touch teary and Sev had to stop his eyes from crossing as Allem droned on.

'Though Jamal enjoyed shopping with Naomi and is very much looking forward to dinner tonight.'

Sev smothered a yawn.

'Will Naomi be joining us tonight?' Allem checked.

'Of course,' Sev answered. He knew better than to expect Jamal to come out for dinner without female company.

'So you and Naomi are dating?' Allem pushed the conversation to the personal when Sev would far rather that they spoke about work. 'I see she is wearing an engagement ring.'

'Well, it's not mine,' Sev snapped. 'What on earth gave you that idea?'

'It's just that you don't often bring your PA to our dinners.'

That was true, Sev thought. Generally he rustled up a date, promising her that if she would sit through the very tame dinner, he would make it up to her later that night.

It had been easier, though, to take Naomi lately.

She really was exceptionally good with his clients.

For all her faults, for all her little digs about his life-style, Naomi certainly knew how to smooth the feathers that he tended to ruffle along his decadent way.

Finally they got around to work and, yes, Sev agreed, he would need to come to Dubai. 'I really am booked out, though, Allem,' he explained. 'I need four clear days at least and I don't have anything like that until March.'

'Which is when the baby is due,' Allem said. 'Sev, I know you are busy but I have been asking for a while now.'

Sev nodded and pulled up his diary onto his computer screen.

This week he had to go to Washington DC and there could be no getting out of that. Next week he was heading off to London, which, despite earlier thoughts about not going, really was non-negotiable to him. But maybe he was growing a conscience—Allem had been asking him to come to Dubai as his guest for months, as well as do some work for him.

And he had been inexcusably late today.

'I'll get Naomi to reschedule some of my clients,' Sev offered. 'We can be there on Saturday.'

'Excellent.'

Naomi looked up when the two men came out of Sev's office. Allem was all smiles.

He came and thanked her for the tea she had made and for taking care of Jamal.

'We're looking forward to dinner,' Allem said.

'So am I.' Naomi smiled.

Instead of only seeing Allem as far as the elevator, which was as far as Sev usually went when saying farewell to clients, he was clearly going to see Allem to his car.

Were they friends? Naomi pondered.

They seemed such an unlikely mix.

'I shan't be long,' Sev said to Naomi on his way out, and, behind Allem's robed back, he made a gesture with his hand that was Sev language for *Pour me a cognac*.

Naomi went in to his office and poured him a drink but then, unable to help herself, she slid open the drawer and took out the bag. She looked at the pretty robin-egg-blue box wrapped in a white bow and tortured herself with images of engagement rings.

Was that why he'd flown to Rome?

Oh, God, the white roses were bad enough but she could not stand the thought of Sev actually getting serious about someone.

He had never bought anyone jewellery in all her time here; it had been white roses and that was all.

'Snooping?' Sev asked as he came, unheard by Naomi, into the office, and she was just too tired of it all to jump or even blush.

'I wasn't sure if you wanted me to wrap it.'

'You think you'd do a better job than Tiffany's?' Sev teased.

As she went to put the box back in the bag Sev held out his hand and she handed it to him.

'I think I've changed my mind about them.'

He tore off the bow, opened the box and stared for a moment then handed it to Naomi for her thoughts.

She'd rather not share them.

Silently she stared at the earrings—two heart-shaped, pink-diamond-encrusted studs.

They were gorgeous.

Seriously so.

'They're beautiful,' Naomi said, but Sev wasn't sure and he took back the box and looked at them again.

'I think that they're a bit too pink, but then again she's young and the guy who served me said that was what they all wanted at the moment.'

So, no white roses for Miss Roma, Naomi thought.

'You don't look very convinced,' Sev said, noting Naomi's lack of enthusiasm.

Just how hard did she have to act?

'Sev, they're stunning.' Naomi spoke, she hoped, with conviction. 'Any woman would be thrilled to have them.'

Especially from you.

She looked at the little frown line between his eyes as still he examined the earrings. This man who cared so little for other's feelings really did seem to care about this gift and its reception, Naomi could tell.

And so it really was time to leave.

'Okay, let's run through my schedule,' Sev said, snapping closed the box and leaving it for Naomi to re-tie the bow. 'It's changed. We're going to be flying to Dubai on Saturday and then from there straight on to London. I have to be there for the twelfth.'

'In the morning?' Naomi checked.

'No, no,' Sev said. 'I want to get there on the eleventh, just to allow for delays and things.'

Naomi raised her eyebrows—Sev was usually the delay.

'I know that you'll have to rearrange a few things but I can't not go to Washington and I really can't keep putting Allem off.'

'I get that,' Naomi agreed. 'Did he like the statue?'

'He loved it,' Sev answered, which only confused her more.

'Sev, could I have word with you?'

'Can it wait?' Sev asked. 'We've got to meet Allem in less than an hour.'

'No.' Naomi shook her head. 'It can't wait.'

If she didn't do it now then it would just get harder and, given they were going to be in Dubai, if there was going to be even a hope of finding her replacement she needed to get things under way soon.

'You'll have to watch me get changed, then,' Sev said, picking up the drink she had poured and taking a long sip as he started to undo his tie.

'Hardly a first.' She didn't take a seat, she was too nervous to, and so instead Naomi stood and leant on his desk.

Tie off, he pulled open a door to a dressing room and selected a fresh shirt with no thought as to how it had got there.

It wasn't his problem.

Sev peered into the mirror.

'I'd better shave.'

Naomi said nothing as he stripped off his shirt and dropped it to the floor and then walked over towards her to top up his drink.

He just walked towards her with no thought about the effect a half-naked Sev had on her.

That wasn't his problem either.

His skin was pale and on anyone else it might be too pale yet on Sev all it did was enhance his lithe, toned body and shadowed his chest to perfection. His arms were as long as his legs and his nipples were the same deep merlot of his mouth and just as tempting. His trou-

sers sat a little too low on his hips, just that fraction between notches on a belt, and those were the details she
fought not to notice as his hand reached for a heavy glass
and held it up to her.

'Have one,' Sev said. 'It's going to be a very long,
dry night.'

Sometimes they had a drink about now, especially if
they were going out for dinner, but Naomi declined with
a small shake of her head. Even if a cognac to settle her
nerves might be nice, she'd rather hold onto her inhibi-
tions than lose them around him.

This was going to be harder than she'd allowed for.

She loved her job.

Her career.

It just wasn't working.

Oh, there was a reason she could not abide certain
parts of her job. Had it been Edward, her previous boss,
or any of her bosses before Sev, this would be an unnoted
part of a long day—brief downtime before she headed
out for a dinner with his clients.

Instead she was trying to work out where to place her
eyes when they wanted to rest on him.

'If it's about this morning,' Sev said, lathering up his
chin, 'there's no need. You don't have to apologise.'

Her lips moved into an unseen but incredulous smile.

'We're reducing your use of the "sorry" word, remember?'

He really took the cake at times!

Yes, she could tell him he had been the inappropriate one this morning yet she was looking at his back and
fighting not to go over there.

Naomi was truly tired of fighting her feelings.

Feelings, Naomi knew, that could get seriously hurt.

And neither did those feelings allow her to do her job

properly. Naomi knew she had been surly this morning about his late arrival when, as his PA, she had no right to be.

'That's not what I'm here about, Sev.' Naomi cleared her throat and watched as Sev picked up the razor. 'I'm handing in my notice.'

She watched as the razor hesitated over his jaw but then he commenced shaving as she carried on with her little prepared speech.

'You said at the start that you'd be surprised if I lasted more than three months.' Naomi reminded him.

'I did.'

'And I've loved the work, I really have, it's just...'

He turned from the mirror. 'Naomi, you don't need to give a reason to leave.'

He could be so kind at times   awkward, embarrassing things like resigning he dealt with so well.

'Will you be sticking around to find a replacement?' Sev asked, as he carried on with his shave.

'I'll do what I can this week but if we're going to Dubai, it might be pushing it, unless you don't need me to go.'

'No, no,' Sev said. 'I need you to be there. I go to Washington the day after tomorrow...' He thought for a moment. 'I'll come back on Thursday night. If you can have at least two applicants lined up by then, that would be good.'

'Sure.'

She'd have little trouble. Applications to work for Sevastyan Derzhavin arrived in her inbox all the time. 'I'll go from Dubai to London and there we can part ways.'

'You're coming back to New York, though?' Sev checked.

'Oh, yes.' Naomi nodded. 'I want to have Christmas with my family here.'

'How's that all going?' Sev asked, turning back to the mirror and getting on with shaving.

'Good! I'm going there tomorrow night.'

'For dinner?'

'I'm babysitting,' Naomi answered. 'They're going to the theatre.'

Sev said nothing. He loathed how she jumped to her father's every wish. They could be in the middle of a meeting and if her father texted or called, even if she tried not to respond, Sev could feel the tension in her.

Then he chose not to say nothing. 'You like the theatre,' he pointed out.

'Not really.'

'It says that you do on your résumé.'

'And I told you that I lied about that.'

'Aren't you going to ask about a reference?'

Naomi nodded.

'I'll do that first thing tomorrow,' Sev promised.

He rinsed his face and then dried it, splashed on a load of cologne, took a sip of his drink and then put on his fresh shirt.

And that was that.

She'd resigned. It was done with.

And he'd barely so much as blinked.

CHAPTER FOUR

'ARE YOU GOING to get changed?' Sevastyan asked.

Naomi nodded.

His complete lack of reaction only confirmed that she was right to leave.

It was easy come, easy go to Sev, and that hurt a lot.

As she headed out of his office to get changed for their night out, only then did she remember. 'I haven't got my dress here,' Naomi said. 'I was supposed to pick it up from the cleaner's in my lunch break but I went shopping with Jamal and I forgot.'

'No problem.' He dealt with it as easily as the news that she had resigned. 'Do you have something at home ready to put on? We can stop on the way to the restaurant.'

Of course she had something at home—given her lavish clothing allowance—and they headed to her apartment. She rather wished he hadn't shaved or smelled so divine as they took the elevator to the tenth floor, where Naomi lived, rather than his penthouse.

'So?' Sevastyan asked on the way up. 'Where are we eating tonight?'

Naomi told him the name of a very upmarket Middle Eastern restaurant.

'That's not very imaginative.' Sev pulled a face. 'Won't they be sick of Middle Eastern food?'

'I doubt people get sick of their home cuisine,' Naomi said as she let them into her apartment. 'I had actually booked a French restaurant but Jamal is feeling a bit...' She chose not to tell Sev the news that Jamal had shared with her as they'd shopped. He was insensitive at the best of times and completely devoid of social niceties at his worst. 'She just wanted a menu she knows.'

'Fair enough.'

'Help yourself to a drink,' Naomi said. 'I'll just go and get changed.'

Sevastyan would have helped himself to a drink had there actually been anything decent to choose from. He opened her fridge and there wasn't even a bottle of wine in there.

He walked back out to the lounge room and saw the picture of a man presumably her fiancé, lying on the table by the phone.

How sweet, he thought with a brittle edge. She must look at him as she spoke to him on the phone.

Then Sev remembered he and Naomi's little near miss this morning and, though his question had been inappropriate, it had been a genuine one. Not just the sex. He knew he would never be close enough to anyone to get engaged but this jerk in the photo was.

It had been Naomi's birthday in October.

Sev hadn't known, he'd just known something was up, and when he'd pushed her, Naomi had told him she was upset that neither of her parents had called to wish her a happy birthday.

'I'm sure something nice will happen,' Sev had said. He had been sure.

Surely her fiancé was on a plane right now, about to whisk her off for one night.

And he wasn't thinking as a snob with a private jet.

Naomi had told him herself that her fiancé, Andrew, had an important job, so presumably it paid enough for a flight on your future wife's birthday.

Apparently not.

Sev had taken her to the theatre, which he loathed, and then dinner, which he'd enjoyed.

And then back to the same building, different floors by midnight.

Which had confused him.

He and Naomi...

It was something that needed addressing.

He was about to stick his middle finger up at the image of Andrew, but changed it to look as if he was scratching his ear as Naomi came out.

She was wearing a very elegant, fitted dark grey dress. However, she needed help with the zip and was carrying her shoes and a necklace as she attempted to get ready in two minutes flat.

'Do we have time for me to do my hair?' Naomi asked, slipping her shoes on.

'No.' He looked over to where she was struggling with the zip.

'Come here,' he offered.

She would really rather not but, choosing not to make a fuss, she went over and held up her hair. Sev went to the zip, but instead of pulling it the rest of the way up, he pulled it the rest of the way down. 'Whoops.'

'Sev!' Naomi sighed. They really didn't have time for his games.

But Sev was in no rush now that he was looking at her delicate pink neck; her hand was shaking a touch as she held up her hair and, no, he decided, he hadn't misread the sensual air he had sniffed back in the office. Naomi Johnson was as turned on as he—which was very.

Her back was bare, apart from the strap of her bra, and he was very tempted to undo that too.

She had a lovely back, Sev thought. Not that backs were generally his thing. He rather wanted to turn her around but instead he ran a light finger along her spine.

Naomi closed her eyes to the bliss.

'Hey, Naomi,' Sev said. His voice was a bit lower than usual and there was definite tension in the air. 'You do realise that now you've resigned, we can spend the next two weeks in bedded bliss.'

'I missed that when I went through my contract,' Naomi replied. 'Just how did you come to that conclusion exactly?'

'Well, you told me, when we were in Helsinki, that you would never sleep with your boss.'

'Actually,' Naomi corrected him, 'that conversation happened on the runway in Mali and I believe what I said was I didn't want to get involved with you.'

'Because you're engaged?'

It would never enter his head, Naomi realised, that someone might just simply not want him.

He was probably right, she knew, for she was fighting with herself not to turn around. Oh, she had been wise to keep her engagement ring on. Not that it warded him off. He had no scruples at all. His hand was now at the base of her spine, fiddling again with the zip, but then he got bored with even pretending that he was going to do it up.

Sev had wanted Naomi for a very long time. Only now that she had told him she was leaving, he seemed to want her even more.

He was more than used to his assistants resigning.

It had never troubled him at all in the past but now it did.

He had consoled himself, however, that now she was leaving they could leave a bit of the business behind and concentrate on pleasure, but Naomi had just closed the door.

He wanted it open.

'In Helsinki I told you I'd cured myself of blondes...' His finger moved up to the nape of her neck and he toyed with a stray dark curl.

Naomi stood there as he blew on her neck, or was that just his breath?

'I thought we had to be at the restaurant,' Naomi said. 'You said I didn't even have time to do my hair...'

'I'm not thinking about your hair now.'

Neither was she.

She was so tired of fighting it.

Maybe she would order her own roses once it was over, Naomi thought.

And it would be over.

Being crazy about Sevastyan was a terminal disease with no cure. She might just opt for some temporary pain relief, though.

He moved in closer behind her but not too fast. Sev didn't want her to startle to his hard-on and change her mind, but he could feel the shift in her.

'You've lost weight,' he observed, stroking the curve of her waist and moving a little higher.

'I know,' Naomi said, wondering how just the warmth of his hand on her skin could turn her on so. His hand had moved to the front of her body. Higher than her waist but lower than where she now wanted it to be. Her breasts ached, anticipating his touch. 'I thought that I'd be putting it on...' She halted her words—she was hardly going to tell Sev that with the amount of comfort eating she'd been doing lately, on top of the lavish dinners and lunches she shared with him, that should generally mean that she should be spilling out of her clothes. Instead they were hanging off her.

It was Sev who stopped the intimate moment. As his hand paused a tiny frown registered unseen on his brow. Why would Naomi think she should be putting on weight? he asked himself, and then he remembered the conversation he had just had today with Allem.

Yes, Naomi had certainly been moody of late.

Oh, God! Eternally superstitious, Sevastyan thought of the fertility statue that had been sitting in his office for weeks.

Was she pregnant?

Was that why she was leaving?

He glanced over to the picture of Andrew on the coffee table and then up went Naomi's zipper.

A pregnant PA he did not need and a pregnant lover he did not want!

'Come on,' he said in a gruff voice. 'We're already late.'

It was meant to be a very lovely dinner.

But in actual fact it was not.

It was one of those nights that you really wished you'd just stayed home.

Sev sat sulking and silent and it was Naomi who moved the conversation.

'It was cell phones then,' Allem said, turning to Sev, who was calling to the waiter for more water.

Naomi was quite sure there was a dash or three of vodka in his. He was in a horrible mood and she had no idea what had happened. One moment she'd been about to give in to three months of building desire but just as she had, Sev had changed his mind.

She would never understand him.

Thank God. Very soon, she could stop trying to

'Remember, Sev?' Allem prompted.

'I remember coming up with the design...' Sev shrugged.

'It would have stayed a design without my money behind it,' Allem pointed out.

'True,' Sev admitted.

'So how did you get your start?' Naomi asked, when she would have liked to kick him under the table for being so distant and rude.

It was like pulling teeth sometimes to get Sev to open up.

'You got a scholarship, didn't you?' Jamal asked, and Sev nodded. He hated, more than anything, talking about his past. That was the problem with people, they always wanted to talk—he'd far prefer a night in, cracking code.

'There was an old computer in the office where I lived,' he reluctantly explained. 'When I was thirteen they were going to throw it out...'

'Office?' Naomi frowned. 'Where you lived?'

'I mean the office at the school,' Sev said, and he shot Allem a warning look.

Allem knew a little, but Sev chose not to go into his past. It was too dark, too messy, and he'd moved far, far away from all that.

'I pulled it apart and...' He shrugged, dismissing the hours and hours he had put in to rebuilding it, scouring markets and dumps, finding parts, and then, when he'd got that one running, he had moved straight to the next.

And the next.

'The scholarship helped but really...'

It had been the hours and hours spent poring over machines and books.

Any book at first.

Fairy tales, romances, biographies and crime. Whatever the staff bought in, whatever he could find, Sev had read, often again and again. Then one day he had come upon a computer programming book that had become his first bible.

His fascination remained to this day.

He didn't say all that, though, even though everyone at the table would have loved to know.

'Remember you liked that princess...' Allem grinned. 'Do you know,' he said to Naomi, 'Sevastyan hacked into the palace webpage then told them the loopholes in their system and that he could fix them.'

'I used to do that in the days when clients were thin on the ground,' Sev conceded.

'And did you get anywhere with the princess?' Naomi asked, and Sev gave her a smirk. 'Stupid question.'

She looked at him, and he looked at her.

And both were hurt, not that either would admit it.

'When you come to Dubai...' Allem said, looking from one to the other and noting again the tension. He'd seen Sev's eyes follow Naomi when she had gone to the restroom and he could hear too the little digs at each other... It was the first time he'd seen this with Sev.

Always, if Jamal had been present, Sev had had a date.

Like Sev, he could never remember their names.

He liked Naomi and he wanted to see Sev happy for once.

'This time, we want to take you out on the water, both of you...'

'I'm not coming over for a holiday,' Sev said. 'You can take Naomi.'

Naomi rolled her eyes. 'Because I do nothing all day.'

'Just take a day,' Sev said. 'Get some sun.'

He thought of her smooth, creamy back and then he looked at her pale cheeks and remembered the day they had met, how they'd burnt just as they were starting to catch fire now.

He wanted Jamal and Allem gone. He wanted to go back to where he and Naomi had left off.

Right now he wanted to put his hand beneath the table and part her thighs and the oddest thing was he thought she might let him.

Not that he would.

Hell, did pregnant women even like sex?

Sev hadn't a clue.

'We would like to see a show while we're here.' Jamal said.

'Well, you're in the right place.' Sev was still looking at Naomi. 'You love the theatre. Maybe tomorrow we could all—'

'I've already got plans.' Naomi said quickly.

'What plans?'

'I've told you, I'm babysitting for my father.'

Sev said nothing.

It was far safer not to.

He wanted to point out that she'd upended her life, moved here to spend time with her father, and apart from a couple of babysitting jobs, looking after his kids while he and his wife went out, she never saw him.

Yes, it was safer to call for the bill.

Sev's driver first took Allem and Jamal to their hotel and then it was a quiet ride back home. As they walked up the stairs towards the foyer, Sev decided that he'd had a gutful of safe.

'Can you call your father and say you can't make it tomorrow night?'

'Why would I do that?'

'Why wouldn't you?' Sev asked. 'I'll pay for a nurse or something to look after the children.'

'A nurse?' Naomi blinked. 'Sev, what planet do you come from?'

'One without babies and children. A nanny, then.'

'I want to help out.'

'Help?' Sev checked as they walked to the elevators. 'More like be trampled over.'

'They're my sisters.'

'Half-sisters,' Sev said, and they stepped into a very small space with a whole lot of tension between them. 'And that daddy-o pie of affection isn't one that's divided equally when it's the second or third time around.'

'Don't go there.' Naomi had heard enough. 'Don't try and tell me how to handle my family when you'd lie about your own mother's health.'

At the tenth floor she went to get out of the elevator but he halted her. 'Naomi, I really do need someone to come with me.'

'Then find someone, Sev,' Naomi said. 'It's close to midnight. You called me at six this morning. That's eighteen hours that I've worked today. I'm not getting this coming weekend off. Surely I can have one evening to be with my family?'

Fire me now, her eyes pleaded.

Can we just get this over with? her mind begged.

'You can have tomorrow evening off,' Sev conceded.

Sev stood there in an unmoving elevator for a moment as she walked off.

Fine.

He'd find someone.

Sev didn't have to look very far.

He pulled out his phone and by the time he'd reached the top floor he was already calling her.

'Hey, Felicity, remember Allem and Jamal?'

His ex-PA knew them well and, what the hell, she was gorgeous, blonde and, bonus points, not pregnant with someone else's child!

CHAPTER FIVE

'So, HOW ARE THINGS with Derzhavin?' her father, Anderson, asked.

It had been a very long day in the office.

Sev had been brooding and silent and Naomi was very relieved that he was going to Washington early tomorrow and that she wouldn't have to see him now until Friday.

She wasn't in the mood to chat about him but, really, Sev was the main topic of conversation between herself and her father.

Naomi sat watching as Anderson gave Amelia, her tiny, four-month-old little sister, a cuddle and kiss before handing Judy the baby to settle her for the night.

Half-sister, as Sev would say.

Oh, she never wanted to be as cynical as Sev but she also wasn't the pushover that he thought she was.

Naomi knew why she was here in New York.

She wanted to give her relationship with her father a proper chance and it hurt to watch as Judy took the baby from her father's arms only for them to be refilled instantly as three-year-old Madison clambered onto his knee for her goodnight kiss.

Naomi had been younger than Amelia when her mother had gone back to the UK, taking her with her.

She had seen her father only once since then.

When she'd been eighteen the plan had been for her to come over for a month but her father's second marriage had been on the brink of collapse. The time she had scraped and saved for had been spent in a hostel, seeing the sights, and she had met her father just for the occasional lunch.

This marriage seemed a happy one, though.

'Derzhavin,' her father prompted, and Naomi gave a little shake of her head as she dragged herself back to the conversation her father kept pursuing.

'He's as difficult as ever,' Naomi said.

'Did you give him my business card?' Anderson checked.

'He's got his own attorneys, Dad,' Naomi said. 'I'm not going to be working there for much longer—I handed my notice in yesterday.'

'You what?' Anderson frowned. 'Why on earth would you do that?'

'The hours are impossible. Some days start at six and end at midnight and that's if we're here. It's even worse when we're overseas. We go to Dubai on Saturday and then it's off to London.' Naomi shook her head. 'And that's where I get off. I'm looking for my replacement this week.'

'But it's an amazing opportunity that you're letting go.'

'I'm not here to further my career, Dad,' Naomi said.

'Are you going back to live in London?' Anderson asked, as Naomi tried to ignore the little glance that took place between him and Judy.

'No, no.' Naomi shook her head. 'I've told you—I'm here for a year. I'm looking for another job, hopefully one that has more regular hours. It might take a while but I've saved quite a bit these past three months. I might take a few weeks off.'

'But what about the apartment?' Judy checked.

'I'm looking for somewhere,' Naomi said, 'though, I have to say, it's proving harder than I thought.'

They said nothing, or rather they suddenly noticed the time and said that they had to go and then told her to help herself to nibbles and that they wouldn't be too late.

'What are you seeing?' Naomi asked.

Anderson rolled his eyes and told her the name of the musical they were going to. 'Judy loves them.'

So do I.

And she could have been there tonight with Sev, Jamal and Allem.

Naomi felt like the hired help.

Or rather the free help.

She was that awkward extended family member that everyone grimaced when her name came up or the invitations went out.

But then she thought of her three little sisters, all so blonde and gorgeous and happy to see her. Especially Kennedy, the eldest. She was very sweet and so happy to have her big sister here.

'I like it when you come and look after us,' Kennedy said as Naomi tucked her into bed.

Even that hurt.

Naomi wanted to be here, spending time with them, getting to know them, not reading a note, as she tipped the last of Kennedy's bedtime drink down the sink, asking her to remember to turn the dishwasher on.

Perhaps she was expected to wipe down the bench tops, Naomi thought. Or fold some laundry.

Instead she went and sat on the couch and looked out the window to the rushes and the water beyond.

Long Island was so beautiful and they had a huge sprawling home. Oh, Naomi could understand that maybe they hadn't wanted her here when Amelia had first came along but now…

Yes, it was too far to commute for very long. But even if they had just said that she didn't need to rush to find somewhere to live and that she could have a couple of weeks here, it would have been enough for Naomi.

She thought about Sev and their row last night. She actually wasn't angry with him for what he had said, even if it had seemed that way to him.

Naomi was angry with her father.

Sev was right and Naomi knew he probably thought her pathetic but she wasn't.

She was here to find out for herself.

Growing up, she had felt like her mother's biggest mistake. Naomi was quite sure that her mother had set out to get pregnant in the hope of saving her marriage and blamed Naomi that it hadn't worked. Her childhood seem to have been spent waiting for the postman or phone calls that had never come.

He had paid child support and her mother had even resented that. Anderson had performed his legal duty towards his daughter and no more.

As a teenager Naomi had once picked up the telephone and called her father out on his shortcomings. He had listened and then listed his reasons for hardly getting in touch over the years.

He'd said that he hadn't wanted to cause friction between Naomi and her mother.

Work was another reason he had given.

Then there had been pressures with his then wife, who hadn't wanted to hear about his daughter in England.

That marriage had long ago broken up and now he was with Judy.

The excuses were running out but Naomi wanted to know for herself. She didn't want to rely on her mother's bitter, jaded opinion of her father.

And that was why she was here to find out for herself if he wanted her to be a part of his life.

Naomi turned on her tablet to read her horoscope, and laughed to herself as she thought about how she had lied to Sev at her interview…about many things.

'Tensions are at an all-time high tonight for all the star signs…' the astrologer warned, and Naomi read how some cosmic event meant that there was friction everywhere and arguments breaking out and, the astrologer advised, if you didn't have firm plans, then it might just be better to stay home.

Naomi rolled her eyes and checked the date.

Surely the astrologer was referring to last night, Naomi thought.

How wrong she was!

Her father and Judy were back just on midnight and, though they didn't shove her out the door when they came in, it was obvious that they would prefer she soon left. Judy kept yawning and saying how tired she was and there was no suggestion that Naomi have one of the brandies that Anderson was pouring and stay the night.

Or maybe she was just a little too used to Sev!

'I'll try and get over before I go to Dubai,' Naomi said as she did up her coat.

'Oh, but you'll be far too busy for that,' Judy said. 'Don't worry about visiting us, we'll still be here when you get back.'

'But it's your fiftieth birthday on Friday, Dad.' Naomi

looked at her father and then back to Judy, and she watched as their false smiles froze.

'How did you know?' her father asked.

'Because I always remember your birthday,' Naomi answered, and struggled to keep the edge from her voice because he hadn't remembered a single one of hers. 'What are you doing to celebrate?'

'Nothing!' Anderson snapped.

Judy guided her out to the hall and had a quiet word. 'He really doesn't want a big deal made about his birthday,' Judy said in a low voice. 'I think it's the middle-aged thing, what with me being so much younger. He just wants it to pass unnoticed so, please, Naomi, don't make a fuss and just leave it. We'll see you when you get back.'

The car was freezing and took for ever to warm up and then she got stuck on the bridge for ages.

Naomi turned on the radio for company and tried to sing along with a song, but who was she kidding? She was crying her eyes out. All she had ever wanted was a family. Parents who cared and said things like, 'Oh, my daughter Naomi is good at that.' Or who passed a shop window and thought, Naomi might like that. Maybe it was why it had taken so long to end things with Andrew. She'd kept hoping he'd turn into the real deal and she could make a family of her own. It hadn't and so she cried and continued to do so all the way back to her apartment. And then, just when the night couldn't get much worse, as she dashed through the foyer, there at the elevators she saw him.

Sev.

And he was standing there, getting very friendly with Felicity, her predecessor.

They both looked stunning. Sev was in a suit and a heavy grey coat. Felicity was all blonde and gleaming and Naomi, wearing jeans and flat boots, felt incredibly drab. She was tempted to turn and wait till they had gone, but that would make it more awkward if she was caught walking off. They were laughing at something but the smile faded from Sev's face when he turned and saw Naomi walking towards them. He dropped Felicity from his generous, given freely and regularly to any suitable female, embrace.

'Hi,' he said by way of an awkward greeting, but then he saw her red eyes. 'Are you okay?'

'Never better.'

It was the most excruciating elevator ride of her life. Felicity kept trying to get off with Sev and rubbing up against him like a cat wanting to be fed, and so when the elevator doors finally opened Naomi practically flew out.

She let herself into her apartment and found that, no, she didn't feel like crying now, she was furious instead.

Felicity!

She knew that he'd slept with her in the past and she knew he had simply gone out and replaced her tonight and not even with someone new.

Lazy bastard.

Hell, yes, she was angry. Naomi stripped off and got into her dressing gown and, rather than thinking of them bonking their brains out a few floors up, she went under the sink and pulled out a bottle of red wine.

New York was possibly the loneliest place in the world, Naomi decided.

It had been when she'd been here at eighteen.

Oh, it was the most beautiful busy city in the world but sometimes she felt as if it could swallow her up and make her disappear and no one would even notice that she had gone.

All she wanted was a home.

And then there was a knock at the door.

She ignored it. Maybe it was next door and they had forgotten where they lived...

There was another knock and then came Sev's voice. 'Naomi, it's me.'

Oh, this she so did not need.

If he'd forgotten his keys he could get the doorman and she'd tell him that.

'It's the middle of the night,' Naomi said, as she opened the door, but then she saw the slap mark on his cheek.

'What happened?'

'Felicity didn't like it when I told her she really needed to understand that when a man says no, he really means no...'

Damn him, Naomi thought, he could still make her laugh.

'She's gone home.'

'Sev, what are you doing here?' Naomi asked.

'I'm out of sugar.'

'No, really.'

'You've been crying.'

'Do I need a permission note for that?' Naomi asked, but instead of closing the door she stepped back and let him in.

'How's Daddy dearest?'

'I don't need another lecture from you, Sev.'

'Maybe you do.'

He looked at her swollen eyelids and red nose. And then he looked down at the wineglass she was holding. 'Is that wise?'

This from a man, Naomi thought, who had sneaked vodka at a dry dinner last night.

'I think I'm entitled to a glass of wine, given the day

that I've had,' Naomi said. 'Believe me, Sev, I've earned this.' She went to take a sip but he took the glass.

'I mean, should you be drinking if you're pregnant?'

Naomi was too taken aback to respond at first.

'Look,' Sev continued, 'I admit that it's taken me a while to get my head around it and I know that I've never had a pregnant PA before, but I'm sure we can work something out. I think there's a baby-minding centre downstairs somewhere and maybe we can look at cutting back on your travel.'

'Sev.' She found her voice. 'Why would you think I'm pregnant? Where on earth did that come from?'

'Isn't that why you're leaving?'

'I thought that I didn't need a reason to leave?'

'You don't. I was just trying to work out why you were,' Sev said, and then he frowned because it certainly wasn't something he usually bothered trying to work out.

People left.

People came and went in his life and he had learnt long, long ago to accept that as fact.

It just wasn't proving so easy to do that with Naomi.

'Why would you think I was pregnant?' she asked.

He chose not to mention the fertility statue in his office. 'Well, you're moody...' he looked back at her eyes '...teary and temperamental, and it's been going on for far too long for it to be PMS...'

'Would you like me to redden the other cheek?' Naomi offered.

'You yourself said that you've lost weight when you thought you should be putting it on.'

'I was referring to the amount I eat.' Naomi started to laugh. 'It's stress.'

'Do I stress you?'

She dodged the answer. 'Not everything is about you, Sev.'

Not quite everything.

'Phew,' Sev said. 'So you're definitely not?'

'Definitely not.'

'Then I think we should celebrate!'

'Celebrate?' Naomi checked. 'Celebrate what? That I'm not pregnant?'

'I can't think of a better reason.'

Clearly Sev was a lot more used to celebrating than she was because, having taken a sip of her wine and screwing up his nose, he promptly rang down to one of the restaurants on the lower level. Despite the hour, very soon there was champagne nestling in a bucket and a delicious platter of hors d'oeuvres that were far nicer than the nibbles that had been left in the fridge by her father and Judy.

He even lit a fire, which Naomi had been too worried to do just in case the apartment filled with smoke.

'I thought it was just for decoration,' Naomi admitted.

'I don't believe in things being for decoration,' Sev said. 'Here's to Naomi not being pregnant.'

'Here's to that,' Naomi agreed.

'How would he take it?' Sev asked, sitting down on the floor by the fire. Not thinking, Naomi joined him.

'Who?' Naomi said, distracted now because he was so bloody smooth they were on the floor by the fire and if she wasn't careful, they could well end up naked.

'Your fiancé?'

'Sev...'

'I'm just asking.'

'Well, I'm not discussing a hypothetical pregnancy that you conjured up.' She shook her head.

God, she was very glad she would never have to find out how Andrew might have taken that news.

It was so nice, though, to sit talking in front of the fire. Sev showed her how he could balance a champagne glass on his stomach, and given hers wasn't quite so firm and she was only wearing a robe Naomi declined when he suggested she try.

Though now she lay on the floor beside him.

It was silly, it was nice and then she remembered where and with whom he'd recently been.

'How was the theatre?'

'It was terrible,' Sev admitted. 'I hate the theatre.'

'You said you loved it when you took me.'

'Well, it was your birthday. If I'd said I hated it you wouldn't have gone.'

She thought back to that time. Not once had she guessed it had just been for her. Sev had said he'd had the tickets for ages. It was quite simply the nicest thing anyone had ever done for her on her birthday.

'Anyway, this one was particularly bad,' Sev said. 'It was all songs.'

'Well, it is a musical.'

'I hate them. Why can't they just talk? Imagine if I sang everything to you?'

She couldn't.

But then she did.

'You know how nice and sweet Jamal is?' Sev asked, and their brains must be hot-wired tonight because he then sang the same line in a deep baritone. 'You know how nice and sweet Jamal is…?'

They started laughing but then Sev, bored with singing, told her what had happened. 'When she realised that I hadn't brought you, sweet Jamal turned into an utter bitch. Honestly, she ignored Felicity and she was downright rude to me. She was even more badly behaved than we were last night and that's saying something.'

Naomi laughed and then she asked something she wanted to know. 'Are you and Allem friends?'

'Sort of.' Sev shrugged.

'How did you meet?'

'A chat room,' Sev said, and he saw her cheeks go pink. 'Not everything is about sex, Naomi. I had an idea for cell phones and, of course, I couldn't afford to do anything with it. I didn't tell him fully what it was but he was curious enough and rich enough to want to know more. He flew me to Dubai and we discussed it. It was odd. When you talk online you just talk business. Only when I got there did I realise he was a rich sheikh and he in turn found out that I was...' Sev shrugged. 'Well, put it this way, I hadn't flown before, let alone first class. A couple of months later he flew me here to work on a prototype. I've never really gone back.'

'At all?'

'A couple of times,' Sev said, but he was more interested in hearing about her.

'So, what upset you tonight?'

'My father and Judy were actually at the theatre.'

'You wish he'd offered to take you?'

Naomi nodded.

'Were he and your mother together for long?'

'They got married when my mum found out she was having me but they broke up when I was a few months old.' Naomi stared at the ceiling and the shadows dancing there. 'I think she got pregnant in the hope of forcing something between them,' Naomi said. 'And then spent the next twenty-five years regretting it.'

'You're not close to her, then?'

'No.' Naomi shook her head. 'She was very career focused. My school holidays I was palmed off to aunts or my grandparents. All I've ever wanted is a family, can you get that?'

He had wanted a family.

Growing up, it had been a secret dream.

A few years ago it had turned into reality but the plump, smiling woman he'd sort of envisaged his mother to be was, in fact, a skeletal alcoholic who wanted nothing to do with him.

And as for his sister!

Yet he had been about Naomi's age when the dream had died and he had realised that a childhood dream was all it had ever been.

'It's a childish want, Naomi.'

From anyone else it might have sounded mean, yet it didn't when it came from Sev.

'You want the dream.'

'I do.'

'You have a family,' Sev pointed out. He looked at Naomi. She was one of the home kids who had stuck rice on a card for their mother. One of the home kids he'd assumed had had everything.

He knew better than that now.

'Accept what is instead of trying to rearrange the formula.'

'It's not maths, Sev.'

'No,' he conceded, 'but maybe if you think of it more logically…'

'Aaaggh.' She banged her feet on the floor.

'Don't let people upset you, don't dwell on things so much.'

'I just want to give me and my father a chance. If you think about it *logically*, he doesn't know me. I'm giving us that chance. It's his fiftieth on Friday.' Naomi sighed.

'They were horrified that I'd remembered and then he and Judy kept telling me not to make a fuss about it.'

'Then don't.'

'I can't just ignore his birthday.'

'Of course you can,' Sev said. 'I do things like that all the time.'

'You're not normal, though.' Naomi smiled.

'What's his name?'

'Anderson.'

'Anderson Johnson?' Sev said, flicking through his mind like some search engine, trying to work out if he'd come across him before, but Naomi shook her head.

'No, my mother gave me her surname.'

'So what's his?'

'Anderson.' Naomi said, and she watched as his lips twitched into a smile.

'His name is Anderson Anderson?' Sev checked, and Naomi nodded.

'Thank God he's only ever had daughters, then…' Sev put on a formal voice. 'Allem, I'd like you to meet Anderson Anderson and this is Anderson Anderson, Junior…'

'Stop it,' Naomi said, though she was smiling.

Lying by a fire with Sev, her wretched night had been saved and she felt happy for once.

'So what's *your* father's name?'

'Pass,' Sevastyan answered. 'And, no, that's not his surname. I mean pass as in can we change the subject?'

She did, but only a little bit. 'What's your mother's name?' Naomi said. 'Am I allowed to ask that?'

'Breta,' Sev answered. 'Next question.'

She guessed he didn't want to dwell on them and so, given that he had invited her to, she asked instead about something else that had been bugging her. 'Why white roses?'

'You prove my point without me having to make it,' Sev sighed. 'Women read far too much into things that need no reading into at all. If I send red, they'd think love, if I send pink then its romance. Maybe I could try yellow, but I'm sure that they'd come up with something... White is just white.'

'Weddings,' Naomi said, and he shook his head.

'Oh, no, not me.'

'Virgins?' Naomi smiled but again he shook his head.

'Not by the time I send flowers.' He turned and matched her smile. 'Why can't women just get that I'm not going to be around for long? I don't want anyone for long.'

She just lay there as he spelt out what she already knew.

'Next question,' Sev said.

Oh, she had so very many questions but she settled for a rather tame one. 'What is your favourite colour?'

He was about to say that he didn't have one but then Sev decided that maybe he did and even if not, his answer might earn him a favour and he stared deeply into her eyes as he answered. 'Brown.'

'Oh, please.' She was so over his chat-up lines.

'It really is.'

'Faded, dried-up roses...' Naomi sighed.

'Lie between pages,' Sev said, and she thought about his words for a moment as she stared into his eyes.

They would lie between the pages, Naomi thought.

If she were ever the recipient of a bunch of roses from him then that's exactly where they'd end up.

'What's your favourite colour?' he asked.

'I don't have one,' Naomi said. 'I once dared to say green when I was sixteen and every year since then my mother buys me a green eye-shadow palette for Christmas.'

'You have to answer the question.'

'Black, I guess.'

'Technically, black's not a colour, it's actually the absence of colour...'

It was, Naomi thought. It was the delicious absence of colour that she would see any moment now, because his mouth was next to hers and when their lips met, black would be all she'd see.

It would be like sinking under anaesthetic, Naomi thought, but then he'd tear out her heart and use it like a stress ball, for a few hours, days, maybe weeks.

Right now she didn't care.

It was the lightest kiss, only their faces moved towards the other, and he tasted every bit as smooth and expensive as she had thought he might. They remained on their backs, eyes open. His mouth was very soft and his kiss tender for a whole six seconds.

He rolled onto his side and took over the kiss, just in case she changed her mind.

Naomi didn't and she saw her favourite colour as she closed her eyes.

Oh, she wished his kiss would disappoint her. How much easier would that make things if it did?

Instead, though, he kissed her harder and his champagne tongue slid in as skilfully as the hand that moved into her robe and straight to her breast that had ached for him since last night when he had suddenly terminated contact and pulled up her zip.

She struggled but only internally. Outside her head her body was utterly willing. Naomi could feel how hard he was against her thigh and from their deepening kiss her prediction was right—they'd very soon be naked on the floor.

'Naomi,' Sev said, as if he'd just struck gold.

He felt as if he had.

Yes, he'd imagined kissing her but they had been clumsy in his imaginings—a kiss to persuade, while this was so sensual and her mouth was just made for him. He moved on top of her, his elbows by the sides of her head. His erection pressed against her and he just looked down at her and pressed in again.

She was on the edge of coming just at that.

And he could feel it, the engine of her just revving, and his hand was down to his belt. Foreplay would have to be afterplay because Sev had to be inside her.

There was a frantic tussle that was deeply sexy. Her hands were trying to get her out of her knickers as he freed himself, and there wasn't even a thought as to protection. Sev even wondered if he'd get it in before he came as her hips pressed up into him.

And then she remembered that had she not come home when she had, he'd be a few floors up with Felicity now.

Sev was right, she would read more into things than she should if they made love.

Made love.

She'd just proved her *own* point without even having to make it.

God, she knew better than that.

It was like being stuck on the runway in Mali, Sev bored, with a few hours to kill and nowhere else to go.

'Stop.'

Oh, there was a word for girls like her, Naomi knew, but she didn't care if she was a tease. She would hold on to her heart and, breathless, still wanting, she halted things.

He looked right into her eyes as she denied him and then he rolled off and Naomi sat up.

He said not a word.

Sev stood and did up his belt and Naomi sat, unable to look up at him.

''Night, Naomi,' Sev said, his voice black. He went to go but then changed his mind and turned around and strode back.

'Is it because of him'?' He picked up her hand and examined the ring that she wore as a shield—how foolish to think a bit of gold could protect her from Sev. 'I wouldn't waste too many guilt trips on him. It's a fake.'

She thought he'd rumbled that the engagement was now a fake so it took a second to realise that Sev was talking about the stone in the ring.

Oh, she had so many other things to cry over but right now this would do. Only Sev didn't see the silent trickle of tears on her cheeks, he was too busy examining the ring, and though he didn't usually deal in feelings, he'd just been teased to the brink and he could be as much of a bitch as she.

'Did he get it out of one of those catalogues that you English have?' Sev's grin was malicious. 'Is he paying it off at fifty pence a week for the next twenty-four months?'

'Bastard!'

He was appalled when he saw her tears.

'Do you get a kick out of embarrassing me, Sev?'

'He's the one who should be embarrassed.'

'Will you please just go?'

'You know, I might be a bastard, Naomi, but at least I'm not a cheap one.'

No, Sev was a very expensive bastard, Naomi thought as she took off the ring and tossed it into the fire.

He could cost her her heart.

CHAPTER SIX

THANKFULLY, NAOMI DIDN'T have to see him the next day—whatever he was up to in Washington was classified and so she hadn't been required to go along.

Instead she woke at sunrise and lay in bed, embarrassed and cross with herself for what had happened last night.

Sev had had every right to be annoyed. She had been utterly willing and completely wanting.

She still was.

How could she tell him that it wasn't the sex part that worried her, it was afterwards?

Naomi had come to New York with the knowledge she might have her heart broken by her father. She really didn't need the added pain of Sevastyan Derzhavin and that, as he'd told her last night, was a guaranteed hurt.

She knew the appalling mixed messages she had sent, though, and she owed him an apology at least.

Naomi reached for her phone and then changed her mind.

Not yet.

For now she went into work and got on with the job of trying to find her replacement, as well as attempting to produce a file, as she had when she had left previous employers, outlining Sev's routines and preferences.

He was consistently inconsistent, though.

Even his coffee preferences changed from one cup to the next.

She scrolled through his diary, trying to establish some sort of pattern.

He travelled the world but his journeys were scattered.

The only thing that was regular was that he went to England once a year in November, Naomi noted as she scrolled through his past.

He called her a few times during the day but it was all strictly business. The disaster of the other night wasn't referred to, and though Naomi had a few questions for him they were mainly logistical.

'I don't think you can manage four full days in Dubai if you want to be in London by the eleventh.'

'Just sort it.' Sev's response told her that he'd far rather be concentrating on work than speaking to her.

And so she did her best to sort it and then got on with the first round of interviews for her replacement.

It was harder than she'd thought it would be.

Imagining them here, with him, and herself gone.

'You've interviewed for the role on two previous occasions?' Naomi checked, as she went through Emanuel's excellent résumé late on the Thursday afternoon. Tomorrow was her last day in the office and, despite her best attempts; she had only found one suitable applicant.

Hopefully Emmanuel would make it two.

'I have.' He nodded. 'The first interview went well but Mr Derzhavin was concerned that I didn't speak Mandarin. I do now. I've been attending night classes for two years and I also had a month in China to immerse myself in the language.'

He really wanted this job, Naomi realised, somewhat

startled when she thought of her own poor language skills and how Sev had said they could work around that.

There must be another reason, surely, that Sev hadn't employed Emmanuel, and she would do her best to find out what it was before she put him forward.

'And what happened at the second interview?'

'It never went ahead. I arrived late,' Emmanuel said. 'It's inexcusable at an interview, I know, but my dog had a seizure just as I was walking out of the door.'

'Did you tell Sev that?'

'I never got the chance.'

'And how's your dog now?' Naomi asked, but then wished that she hadn't as the tip of Emmanuel's nose went red and his eyes filled with tears.

'He had to be euthanised.'

Late on Thursday Sev rang to say he was home but could she pop out and get him some headache tablets?

'Why aren't there any?' Sev snapped. He paid for others to deal with these things and all he wanted to do was to go to bed.

'I forgot to check,' Naomi admitted, remembering when she'd done her monthly inventory but had baulked after checking the bedside table.

No, she would not miss this part of her job, Naomi thought as she knocked and then let herself into his penthouse suite.

He looked terrible. He was paler than usual and she could see his exhaustion. Naomi wondered why he was on his computer when surely he needed a break?

'How was Washington?'

'Cold.' Sev shrugged.

'Here are your headache tablets.' She put them down on the desk.

'Do you need anything else?'

'Nope.'

'About my replacement—I've narrowed it down to two applicants. The first interview is at midday. I think they're both—'

'I think,' Sev interrupted, 'that that can wait for tomorrow. I don't want to think about work.'

She let herself out and Sev punched out three headache tablets. No, it hadn't been a ruse to get her to come up. He was tired, had a headache and it was *still* November.

He was checking through his emails.

His mother's care level had been upgraded to high dependency. Another email informed him that the two gifts he had sent his niece had been delivered.

Sev had sent a small gift to Mariya's home but the main one he had sent to her school.

He didn't trust his half-sister at all.

Last year he had sent Mariya an antique necklace. It really had been a stunning piece but then, flicking through an auction catalogue a couple of months later, he had come across it.

The earrings he had bought not just with his niece in mind.

They were a touch more generic.

If she sold them on, he wouldn't know. He really didn't need a reminder as to how he'd been used.

The headache tablets did nothing and he woke the next morning and for a very long while debated whether or not he would even go in to work.

Of course he had to.

He walked and, unusually for Sev, stopped and bought a coffee before heading up to his office.

Naomi was in already, wearing the same suit that

she'd had for her interview, and it certainly wasn't too tight now.

He offered a brief good morning and then went into his office, closing the door. He sat staring at the door, picturing her behind it.

He'd miss her and Sev didn't like that feeling at all.

In fact, he was considering telling Naomi that he would prefer that she leave today rather than come with him to Dubai.

'Who's my first applicant?' Sev asked, when Naomi came in to ask how he wanted his coffee this morning.

'Her name is Dianne,' Naomi said. 'And then you've got Emmanuel at two p.m. They're both excellent'

'I'll decide for myself, thank you.'

'Do you want coffee?'

'I've already got it.'

He nodded to a take-out cup.

It felt like a snub.

It wasn't.

He just wanted it to be over and done with.

Sev sat thinking.

Okay, if one of the applicants was suitable and could start straight away, then he'd suggest that they do just that.

Midday came and Dianne arrived on time and gave Naomi a wide smile.

'He shouldn't be too long,' Naomi offered. 'Can I get you a drink?'

'No, thanks.' Dianne's smile stayed on and she took a seat as Naomi buzzed Sev to let him know the first applicant had arrived.

Naomi did her best not to look up as Sev came out of his office but, having shown Dianne through, he then came out of the office and over to her desk.

'You might as well go to lunch.'

'Sure.'

Naomi wasn't foolish enough to think Sev was going to be taking her out for a little leaving do.

She had hoped he might, though.

How she wished she could erase the other night. Well, not all of it, just the ending.

In fact, she wished now that she had slept with him.

Just to have known what could have been.

More than that, she wanted 'them' back, the little in-jokes, the easy conversation.

Now it was tense and awkward.

His voice was tart and she could barely look up and meet his eyes as he delivered his instructions for the rest of the day.

'Can you make sure my case is packed before you finish? I've got company tonight, I don't want you coming around after five.'

'Of course,' Naomi said. 'I'll go over now.'

'Before I go in...' he nodded in the direction of his office '...how soon did she say she could start?'

'She's available straight away.'

Naomi knew then that she wouldn't be going to Dubai.

Back to his apartment Naomi went.

For the last time, she was quite sure.

There were no maids there. They had clearly been in, though. His bed was made, Naomi noted as she took out his case.

She took out her tablet and pulled up the list she kept for Sev's packing. It would be hot and humid in Dubai and cold, possibly wet in London so she decided to pack a separate case for each. She packed his shirts and suits and a couple of casual options. And then she dealt with his toiletries.

How odd, she thought, that she could have such access to someone's life and still know so little about them.

And this really was it.

Naomi moved the cases through the entrance hall and had one final walk around. She was dreading going back to the office, to be told her services were no longer required.

But it was surely better this way.

She should have followed her instincts three months ago and said no to the job there and then.

Her heart had already known just how hard this would be.

Naomi didn't stop for lunch. Instead she went to the patisserie she had called earlier in the week and picked up the cake she had ordered.

It looked amazing.

A champagne-and-raspberry layer cake and, yes, she stopped and bought a bottle of champagne to go with it.

'Are we having your leaving party now?' Sev asked when Naomi came back from her lunch break carrying the champagne and cake box.

'You didn't need to go to so much trouble,' Naomi quipped.

Sev got up and followed her into the little kitchen where she usually prepared drinks and things for his clients, and when she put down the box he opened the lid and saw 'Happy 50th, Dad'.

'Naomi,' Sev warned. 'He clearly said that he didn't want a fuss.'

'People always say that,' Naomi said, putting the bottle in the fridge.

'Men generally mean what they say,' Sev said. 'Well, bastards do. When they say leave it they mean leave it. Take it from me and don't make a big deal of it.'

'It's just a cake.'

Oh, he knew that it was so much more than a cake.

It was her heart and her hope smeared between the layers and she was going to get hurt, Sev knew.

He knew exactly.

Not that he could tell her that without telling her about himself, which he chose not to do.

Not his problem, Sev decided.

'Everything's ready for Dubai tomorrow. The car's booked for six a.m.,' Naomi said. 'You fly at seven and arrive in Dubai for six on Sunday morning.'

'And I fly out when?' Sev said. He had heard she had taken herself out of the equation, he just had to officially tell her, that was all.

He just wasn't ready to yet.

'You leave Dubai at five a.m. on Thursday the twelfth and with the time difference get into London at eight a.m. the same day.'

'But I said specifically said that I wanted to be there by the eleventh,' Sev pointed out.

'And then you said you needed four full days for Allem and to just make sure you got into London early.'

'Not good enough, Naomi.' The day he hated the most in the world had just been extended by four hours! 'When I say I want to get there on the eleventh, you get me there on that date.'

'I can't rearrange time zones,' Naomi said. 'Believe me, I've tried.' She didn't want things to end on a row. 'I'll go and have another look at it,' she went on. 'If you leave Dubai—'

'Just leave it as is,' Sev snapped.

He hated the eleventh too.

If he could change one date, it would be that one.

He would have asked more questions, pushed for his

friend to speak or just stayed awake and made sure he was okay.

It wasn't a coincidence that Sev had hoped to meet Daniil on the twelfth.

That was the morning he had woken up in the orphanage to find the bed next to him empty. Nikolai's exact date of death was unknown but Sev had hoped, on what he considered the anniversary, to let Daniil know what had been lost that day many years ago.

'How did the interview with Dianne go?'

Sev shook his head. 'She's not suitable.'

'She was perfect.'

'Not for me,' Sev said. 'She had one of those nervous smiles.'

Naomi let out a tense breath but then she thought back and she smothered a smile of her own because, yes, Dianne had. 'Sev, you thought that I said sorry too much, remember? Surely you can give her a chance.'

'Nope.'

'Well, hopefully the second interview goes well.'

'I doubt it, it's his third application,' Sev pointed out. 'Why can't some people get that no means no?' He met her eyes then. 'I do.'

'Sev.' Naomi had never been braver in her life and he looked at her very red cheeks and saw the tears in her eyes. 'I want to apologise for the other night. I backed out...'

'You had every right to.'

And, no, he didn't want things to end on a row either.

He came over and he took her burning cheeks in his palms.

'It's fine.' He could see her tears. 'No crying over me,' Sev said. 'I've been thinking too.'

'About?'

'The catalogue comment.'

He trawled through his very impressive multilingual vocabulary and came up with that little-used word.

'Sorry.'

Naomi gave him a tired nod.

'I never meant to embarrass you. I was just...'

'I get it.'

'Did you give him hell?' Sev asked. He had happily noted she wasn't wearing the ring.

'No comment.'

And he looked into those deep brown eyes and he wanted to know more, he wanted Naomi to say that she'd dumped him.

Why did he need to know?

'Right.' He brought the subject back to work. 'In all seriousness, I'm less than hopeful about the next applicant. He was late last time.'

'Because his dog had a seizure.'

'Well, that doesn't bode well! So, if I employ Emmanuel, then I've got to arrange my schedule around my PA's epileptic dog.'

'He was euthanised.' Naomi sighed. 'Sev, the man's spent the last two years learning Mandarin on your casual suggestion. At least give him a fair go.'

Sev didn't want to give him a fair go.

And, despite his musings this morning, he didn't want her gone.

He loathed that she was leaving.

A while later his intercom buzzed and Naomi informed him that Emmanuel was here. She remembered her first interview with him, standing up and knocking over a glass at her first sight of him.

He still had the same effect on her. Sev turned her to jelly on the inside.

'Emmanuel.'

Sev's deep, rich voice still entranced her.

And he was still beautiful.

Just that.

Sev gestured with his head to his office and Emmanuel stood, took a deep breath and then followed him in.

'So,' Sev said, 'we meet again.'

Emmanuel interviewed like a dream.

'Why do you keep applying to work for me?'

'I want to work with the best.'

'And are you aware of the hours?'

'Naomi was very thorough—she told me there can be eighteen-hour days.'

'Several in a row at times'

'I'm an insomniac,' Emmanuel replied.

He had an answer for everything.

'When could you start?' Sev said.

'Now.'

'Is that fair to your previous employer?'

'I'm actually between roles,' Emanuel answered. 'I saw that, more often than not, you seem to hire around the three-month mark.'

'Most of my PAs burn out after three months.'

'I'm not like most,' Emmanuel said. 'I've been doing some temporary work in the interim. I wanted the opportunity to explain, in person, why I was late last time.'

'Your dog.'

Sev had enough trouble relating to people let alone grasping pets but, no, he didn't expect the guy to step over his dying dog to get here for an interview.

'How many languages...?' He glanced again at the résumé at the same time that Emmanuel answered.

'Four.'

He should have said *quatre*, Sev thought, remembering how Naomi had answered his question.

It was the only teeny fault he could find.

'Naomi will be in contact.'

Sev sat sulking in his office for the rest of the day and when he came out at five she was putting on her coat, guessing he was about to tell her that her services were no longer required.

Emmanuel had given her a thumbs-up when he'd come out of the office and had also told Naomi when she had first interviewed him that he could start any time.

It was just a matter of Sev telling her now.

'How was Emmanuel?'

'Useless.' Sev shook his head. 'There's a reason I've turned him down twice…' He looked at Naomi's bewildered expression. 'Have you got another job to go to?'

'I've got a couple of things in the pipeline.'

'Have you got somewhere to live?'

He saw her swallow.

'Why don't you stay on till you've got another job or I've got a suitable replacement?'

'No, thanks,' Naomi said.

'Naomi, you haven't been able to get an apartment. I heard you this morning on the phone—'

'I'll be fine,' Naomi interrupted. 'It's not as if I'm going to end up homeless. I've got family here after all.'

It dawned on Sev then that this little dark horse was pushing for Daddy-o to finally step up to the plate. Bingo!

That's what she did!

Sev was finally working her out.

He knew that she'd tried to get fired that morning when he'd called her from the plane and she'd given him attitude—Naomi didn't want the confrontation of resigning.

And she was pushing for her father to be the one to tell her that no, he simply didn't want her in his life.

He watched as she headed into the little kitchenette and came back carrying the cake.

'Do you want me to come to your father's with you?'

Sev saw her blink and so did he—as surprised as she was by his offer.

'Er…why?'

'I don't know.' Sev shrugged. 'I wouldn't mind a drive.'

'No, thank you.'

It was her last time here in this office.

She was walking out on a dream job, and a boss that couldn't be called a nightmare but he certainly woke her up deep in the night.

'Will you be coming back to get your things?'

'I took them all yesterday. Sev, I gave you notice, I've done everything I can to find a replacement…'

'Yep.'

He didn't want her to go.

'I'll see you in the morning,' Sev said, and he watched her shoulders sag briefly. 'I need you in Dubai. You agreed to stay for that—there's a lot of work I have to cram into four days.'

'Of course.' Naomi nodded. 'Have you done my reference?'

'I'll do it.'

He'd been saying that all week. Yes, she may only have worked for him for a short while but Sev's name on her résumé would open doors in her future.

Not that she could stand to think of that now.

Oh, she didn't want to leave but neither could she bear working alongside him and running his love life for even a moment longer.

'Good luck with your father tonight,' Sev said. 'Don't build up your hopes.'

And that was it.

He headed to his desk.

Naomi waited, just for a second. She *had* built up her hopes.

She wanted something from him, something she could keep, just something to show she had mattered a little to him.

He crushed them.

No bunch of flowers appeared, no rummaging in his drawer for a gift.

Sev was back to his computer and he didn't even look up as she walked out of the office.

It was a long and difficult drive through peak-hour traffic.

She wasn't expecting much from her father.

Naomi hoped, though, for coffee and cake, they could keep the champagne, she just wanted a little glimpse of family life.

It was Thanksgiving soon, and he and Judy had made no move to invite her.

And then it was Christmas, and they hadn't made any mention of that either.

Naomi had already bought presents for all of them.

They were wrapped and hidden in her wardrobe, though why she bothered to hide them Naomi didn't know because her father had never been over.

She was tired.

After the cake she would drive back and then pack for Dubai and London.

Naomi wasn't even looking forward to going home.

She'd texted her mother her dates and times and she hadn't even replied.

And as for Andrew...

That hadn't been love.

Naomi had been, she now knew, in love with the idea of being in love, or rather someone loving her.

Andrew hadn't.

He'd controlled.

As for Sev...

Naomi's eyes filled with tears but she blinked them back. As she neared her father's home there were cars everywhere so she parked a bit away and watched as a couple did the same and got out.

They were holding a gift and walking towards the beach.

So were a small family.

'Anderson's so lucky with the weather...'

She just stood there.

And then, when perhaps it would have been wiser just to get back into the car and drive, instead she followed the people heading for the dark beach.

And there, on a cold clear night, were gas burners and music and a party happening.

One she hadn't been invited to.

The seagulls would have the most wonderful feast because she dropped the cake on the sand and turned and ran.

She just ran to her car and reversed it out and drove.

A party and he hadn't even invited his own daughter!

Naomi was too hurt even to cry.

What the hell was she even doing in New York?

CHAPTER SEVEN

How HAD THINGS gone with Naomi and her father?

As Sev reached over to turn off his alarm, it was the first thought on his mind.

It was only because he knew, better than most, what she might be going through that he was concerned for her, Sev told himself.

He lay for a moment before he got up, thinking about the days ahead. He wasn't particularly looking forward to Dubai but he had put it off for a while.

Allem was always asking him to come, not just to work but for a holiday. His first time there had been Sev's big break and he hadn't really known it at the time.

He remembered getting his first itinerary and seeing that there would be a stopover in London.

Daniil lived near London.

He had written to Daniil and suggested that they meet outside Buckingham Palace on Nikolai's anniversary. Daniil had been adopted by a rich family and now went by the name of Daniel Thomas. Sev had guessed, rightly as it had turned out, that he wouldn't show up.

Why did he still go to London each year?

Why did he still hope that somehow Daniil might appear when logic dictated otherwise?

Last year he had cancelled the flight but at the last minute had changed his mind.

Literally the last minute.

He had made it to Buckingham Palace on the stroke of midday.

Of course his old friend wasn't there.

Sev thought of another flight he had made when the money had started to come in.

He had returned to Russia full of hope at the thought of meeting his mother.

The memory of that was not one he wanted to dwell on and rarely did. Certainly he never spoke about it with anyone else.

That was why he had awoken thinking about Naomi, Sev decided as he hauled himself as he out of bed and into the shower.

He knew *exactly* how it could be.

Apart from the slight date mix-up with the Dubai-to-London dates, Naomi had arranged things well. All that he had to do was shower and dress. He chose black jeans and a top but couldn't be bothered with shaving.

It was one of those cold mornings that gave the first real indication of the harsh winter ahead and Sev sat in the back of the car and closed his eyes, waiting for Naomi to get in.

Usually they met in the foyer but this morning she wasn't there.

'Where's Naomi?' he asked as his driver got in.

'We just put a load in the trunk and they're just bringing down the rest.'

Sev didn't give it too much thought at first as he was used to women having way too much luggage. When he stopped to think about it, though, it was unlike her.

Like Sev, Naomi travelled light.

Then he heard her voice and when he glanced out of the window she was speaking to the doorman and a lot more bags and cases were being put into the trunk. Not only that, there were some very large parcels with Christmas wrapping on a trolley that, from what Sev could make out, Naomi was leaving with the doorman.

Then he watched as she handed over her keys and a large wad of cash.

Sev said nothing as she got into the car.

She was dressed in a smart black dress with black boots and a neat coat and had a small case, no doubt with a change of clothes for Dubai. She had even put on lipstick, yet she was also terribly white with dark rings under her eyes and on the very verge of tears—so he knew her father must have hurt her and badly.

Bastard!

He felt like telling his driver to take them to Long Island where he could happily haul Anderson Anderson out of his bed but, Sev knew, that wasn't going to help matters.

'How was last night?' he asked instead.

She flashed him a look and then shook her head.

'What's going on, Naomi?' Sev asked. 'Why all the cases?'

'You can take any excess baggage out of my wages,' Naomi snapped.

'Naomi?'

'I'm not coming back here,' Naomi said.

'What the hell happened last night?'

'I don't want to talk about it.'

'Tough!' Sev said, but then he decided it might be best to leave it for now. She really did look terrible and, despite the heating in the car, she was shivering. He wanted to pull out a rug and wrap her in it, or to open the bar and pour her a brandy but he could just imagine her comment if he did so at this time of the morning.

Sev also had the strong feeling that if he pushed Naomi to speak too soon she might just get out of the car at the next set of lights and not even come with him to Dubai.

It would be warmer there.

It was another illogical thought but suddenly he wanted her to be warm and lying in the sun.

They would talk on the plane, Sev decided.

She couldn't avoid him there.

One of the very many plusses of owning your own jet was that there were no queues or lines to deal with. Instead they were driven straight onto the tarmac and there stood Jason, the captain and co-pilot, along with Shannon and another flight attendant.

They boarded and the captain briefed him about flying times. Sev nodded and took off his coat and handed it to Shannon.

Naomi did the same but unlike Sev, who went straight to his seat, Naomi still had some work to do—touching base with his flight crew.

'Come and sit down,' Sev called.

'I shan't be long.'

'I said come and sit down.'

They sat face-to-face in heavy leather seats. The engines were already going and the cabin crew were preparing for take-off.

Sev had declined a coffee, he would have one once they were in the air. He looked at Naomi, who was staring out of the window. There was no point trying to talk to her now, Sev decided, so he took out his book.

He couldn't concentrate, though, and looked over at her.

Naomi could feel his eyes on her as she looked out

at the dark sky. They hurtled along the tarmac and then the plane lifted.

She didn't care if he could see the tears filling in her eyes as she looked down at the Manhattan skyline and remembered her first flight here and all the hope that had filled her heart when she had arrived at eighteen, only to be let down.

The same hope had been present the second time around.

What a fool she had been, Naomi thought.

'You will be back,' Sev said.

'For what?' Naomi asked.

Another round of rejection was the last thing she needed.

Coffee was served—white and sweet for Naomi and a long black for Sev with no sugar today.

There were pastries also and Sev was on his second while Naomi was still nibbling the edge of her first and he could wait no longer to find out.

'What happened last night?'

'I've already told you,' Naomi answered. 'I don't want to talk about it.'

'Well, I'm sorry to pull rank but, given you're leaving the apartment with no notice, I think I have every right to know, and furthermore—'

'I have given you notice,' Naomi interrupted him. 'The only thing that has changed is that I shan't be returning to New York after London. And if you're worried about the apartment, that's already been taken care of,' Naomi said. 'I've brought what I could with me and the rest I'm having shipped home. I've cleaned up as best I can behind me and I've left money for it to be serviced.'

They both knew he couldn't give a damn about all that.

'What about the Christmas presents?'

Naomi closed her eyes.

'It's not even December,' Sev pointed out. He couldn't fathom why she'd had them bought, wrapped and ready.

'I like to be organised.'

'You didn't have to get me so many.' He gave her foot a little kick and Naomi gave a pale smile.

He knew they were for her half-sisters.

'Do you want me get someone to deliver them?'

'Please,' Naomi said. 'If my dad or Judy doesn't come and collect them.'

They wouldn't. Sev was quite sure of that.

'Well, your mum will be pleased to see you.'

He watched those lips stretch and not into a smile. They pushed downwards to suppress tears. He wasn't being a bastard, he was trying to gauge her.

'What happened last night?' Sev asked again.

Still she didn't answer him. Instead she went into her bag and took out two headache tablets and swallowed them down. He could see her hand was shaking as she lifted her glass of water.

'Did you get any sleep?' Sev asked.

Naomi shook head. 'Don't worry, I'll have a doze while you're asleep and I'll be fine by the time we get to Dubai.'

'Go to bed,' Sev said.

'I don't think so.'

There was only one bedroom on the plane and she wasn't in the mood for sharing.

'Go to bed,' Sev said again. 'We're going to hit the ground running once we get to Dubai and right now you look like death warmed up. You represent me, remember.'

It was the only way he might get her to comply.

Shannon came to ask what they would like for breakfast but even the quarter of a pastry she'd had already had Naomi's stomach turning.

She really was exhausted to her very bones. Not only had she spent last night packing and cleaning up the apartment, the previous one she'd had little sleep, nervous, not just because she would be turning up at her father's but that it was her last day in the office.

'What are you doing?' Sev's voice was irritated as Naomi pulled out her tablet, clearly about to start work.

'I'm just going through last night's emails for you.'

Sev answered the questions the emails posed with a clipped yes or no. But finally she gave up pretending that she was okay.

'I might actually lie down, if you're sure.'

'Please do,' Sev agreed. 'You're so white you've got me starting to believe in ghosts.'

Her smile was equally pale as she stood. 'I'm sorry about all of this.'

'I doubt you have anything to be sorry about regarding last night,' Sev said. 'Surely you know me well enough to—'

'Know you!' Naomi angrily interrupted. She wasn't cross with Sev, she knew that, but he was human, he was close and unwittingly perhaps he had hurt her too and so he got a glimpse of what she was holding inside. 'I don't know the first thing about you.'

'What the hell do you mean? You've been running my life for the last three months.'

'Oh, I might know your schedule and your pillow preference for hotels but I know nothing about you, Sev. You tell me precisely nothing, so don't expect me to pour my heart out. You have no idea what I'm going through.'

'You don't know that.'

'What would you know about families? You don't even send your mother flowers for Mother's Day…'

'Hey! Hey!' Sev reared.

'Well, it's true—I've been trying to sort out your diary to hand over. You care about no one, Sev, so don't go offering advice.' She couldn't go on…she had said too much already. She turned and headed to the bedroom, deciding she would apologise to Sev later. Right now she was too spent to feel embarrassed or apologetic.

Again.

She looked around the bedroom. It really was amazing. The trim was ebony, like his bedroom at home, and there was a shower and everything. She could be in a luxurious five-star hotel right now rather than miles up in the sky.

Naomi stripped off her clothes and headed for the shower, though more to see if it would warm her up.

It didn't.

Shivering, she wondered what she should wear to get into bed, but was too tired to work it out so instead she climbed naked into the luxurious sheets and lay there, listening to the hum of the engines and willing sleep to come.

She would love to roll over and bury her face in the pillow and sob but, given Sev was outside, that would just have to wait until she was safely in a hotel room.

So for now she lay and stared up into the darkness, dizzy from being so tired and watching fragments of her heart floating in the air and wondering how to put them all back into one piece.

How to start over again, knowing that her father really wanted nothing to do with her.

That wasn't all of it.

How did she move on, knowing that after Dubai she would never see Sev again?

Sev took one look at the lovely breakfast Shannon served him and pushed the plate away.

He had a large cognac instead.

The colour of sad brown eyes.

He should leave her and let her sleep, Sev thought.

He couldn't.

Sev was quite sure that on the other side of the door she was crying.

He reclined the leather lounger and closed his eyes but, no, he couldn't leave her alone.

Naomi heard a knock at the door but he didn't wait for an answer. She turned and looked at his outline as he stood in the doorway.

'I thought the deal was I got to sleep...'

'I just wanted to check if you were okay.'

'I was almost asleep,' Naomi lied.

'Can we talk? Sev asked.

'No,' Naomi said. Then she hesitated. 'I'm sorry for what I said about Mother's Day.'

'You were wrong.' Sev spoke from the doorway. 'I do send flowers. Mother's Day in Russia is at the end of November but I take care of the delivery myself.'

She just lay there.

'Are you blushing?' he asked.

'I've run out of blushes.'

'Come on, Naomi,' Sev said. 'What happened last night?'

She looked at his outline in the doorway and decided it was easier to admit what had happened when she couldn't see his reaction. And so she told him.

'I wanted to find out how he felt about me and if there was anything to build on.'

'And?'

'Now I know.'

Those three little words told him enough so he went over and sat on the edge of the bed. Naomi felt the mattress's indent and was about to tell Sev that if he didn't get out of the bedroom she would, but then he took her hand.

'I know how you feel.'

'Believe me, you don't.'

'Ashamed, unwanted, a mistake...'

He'd picked her top three.

Now she cried.

'It's okay,' Sev said, and his other hand held her shoulder.

She didn't think the tears would ever stop.

And she felt embarrassed.

So, so embarrassed.

Not with Sev, not that she'd broken down; she felt embarrassed for her big fat face eagerly smiling at her father. Embarrassed at the secrets they had gone to such lengths to keep, just to keep her away. And ashamed by the looks her father and Judy had given each other as they'd worked out ways to keep her locked out of their lives. 'I thought that when he got to know me...'

'I know.'

'That when he saw me...'

'I know.'

It was himself she had reminded him of at her interview, Sev thought as he held her.

'*How* do you know?' Naomi asked.

'Because it happened to me.'

CHAPTER EIGHT

SEV NEVER TOLD anyone this.

Ever.

It was one of those private pains that for Sev had been better dealt with alone.

He just didn't want Naomi to have to deal with it alone, though, and so he worked out how best to tell her what had happened to him.

'You're right I don't let others know about me very much...well, not the private stuff...'

'I beg to differ—I order condoms for you. I've dumped two women on your behalf...' She tensed at his emotional approach, trying to keep things light, to somehow keep back because, even though she had spent three months wanting to know more, suddenly he felt too close.

It was going to be hard enough already—saying good-bye.

What would it be like to know more about him and then be apart?

'You don't have to tell me.'

'I will, though.' He looked at her sad brown eyes, which had always melted him, and he knew why now.

He had spent his adulthood avoiding feelings yet lately he felt like a Bunsen burner had been turned on under his emotion button and he just wanted her to feel better, or rather not so alone in this.

He lay on the bed beside her, on his back, and unlike in her apartment it wasn't a smooth move. Yes, she was naked under the sheets, but it mattered little. This conversation was way more intimate than sex and the closest he had ever been with another.

Sev turned his head to face her. 'Do you remember when I spoke about the computer in the office at home and you picked up on it?'

'The one at your school?'

'You were right,' Sev said. 'There was an office where I lived. I was raised in an orphanage.'

She just looked back at him.

'I didn't know if I had parents.' He couldn't properly tell her a little without telling her a lot. 'There were four of us who grew up together,' Sev said. 'We were as good as brothers and we spoke about everything but never that.'

'What?'

'That dream, that hope of being a part of a family.'

He saw her mouth move as if she was about to cry again.

'I get it,' Sev said. 'Daniil and Roman were twins and so, though we were all close, they were true brothers. Then there was Nikolai and I. He felt like my twin—we were the other person in the other's world and we looked out for each other. All four of us said that we didn't care who our parents were and that we didn't care if no one chose to adopt us. I said it all the time but I know I was lying and, looking back, I guess that they were too. Daniil finally did get adopted. He said he didn't want to go but, I'm sure, only because it meant leaving Roman.'

'They split up the twins?' Naomi asked, and Sev nodded but he tried not to dwell on it and to tell Naomi only what was relevant.

'Before that, though, I was good at reading and I would read stories to them at night. We laughed at them but in my head my mother *was* a princess and it was safer that we were apart. Well, I thought that till I was about seven. Then I decided my parents were poor and couldn't afford to feed me but they cried at night for me, or at least on my birthday. I would make up in my head that they were waiting till they could afford to come and get me. I made up so many reasons as to why we were kept apart.'

'I did that too,' Naomi admitted, and she rolled onto her side and faced him. 'I thought it was distance, or work pressure. And he fed me excuses as well—that it was my mother's fault, or his wife who stood in the way...' She looked into Sev's lovely grey eyes.

'A few years ago I found my mother. She had worked as a prostitute and was in a home. I also found out I had a half-sister called Renata, who was quite bit older than me. I didn't know what to do.'

'You didn't know whether to make contact?'

He could see the confusion in her eyes and he knew he had to explain better, and that meant going back, which he hated doing.

'Sev?'

'Okay,' he sort of snapped, but he was actually having to drag it out and make himself out a fool. And then he remembered her tears—the thick, heavy tears she had shed—and he pushed on.

'You think I am rude and antisocial?'

'I wouldn't say that exactly.' He could be a little too social at times, but she gave him a small nod because, yes, he could ignore the niceties at times.

'Well, had you known me a few years ago you wouldn't

hesitate to answer that question. I lived in an orphanage till I was fifteen, then a boarding school, which was hell if you were on a scholarship. So I'd always go to my books and computer. Then I went to university and my room was a quarter the size of this. I studied maths and the people I studied with were the same. I got an internship and was doing really well, but I still rented a room in a house with five guys who were as computer crazy as me.'

Naomi frowned, unsure where this was leading.

'We didn't talk much, we didn't eat together. On weekends I'd go to a bar and hook up, which was the best bit of the week. On the Monday it all started again. Then one day I got an offer to go to Dubai to discuss a design.'

'Allem?' Naomi checked, and he nodded.

'I'd never flown before and Allem flew me first class.'

'Wow!'

'No,' he corrected. 'It was excruciating for me. The whole trip pushed me out of everything I had ever known. I had never eaten with a family before or received a gift but Allem and I did get on and he taught me a lot of things. And so when I found out I had a family I went to Allem. He is good with his family so I asked his advice. Allem said not to be too pushy, to take a gift and some flowers, to understand my mother might be embarrassed or upset at first. I did everything I could to make our meeting go smoothly. I asked the staff at the home to tell her I was coming so that it wouldn't be a shock and then I turned up on time.'

'What happened?'

'I was nervous.' He took her hand and placed it on his chest. 'Thump-thump-thump,' Sev said, at a rate far more rapid than his current heartbeat. 'I walked in and

I was surprised. She was very thin and for the first time I saw someone who looked like me. I recognised her.'

'How old were you when you went to the orphanage?'

'Two weeks old, yet I felt as if I recognised her and I'd never felt that before in my life. I forgot to be calm and I went to embrace her but she pulled back.' He thought about that moment for a while and then he told her the rest. 'She looked at me and said, "I didn't want you then and I don't want you now."' Sev looked at Naomi and said it in Russian just so she could try those words on for size. 'Then she must have seen the suit and the flowers and the gift I had bought and she asked if I had money, which I did by then. Now she is in a nicer home and drinks better vodka but she didn't want me then and she still doesn't want me now.'

'Maybe she—'

'No.' He would not make up excuses or fairy tales again. Never. 'Do you know what? I'm grateful for those words. I really am because I knew there and then where I stood and it would seem that you know now too.'

Naomi nodded.

'It's better to know than to dream.'

'I don't know if I agree.'

'What happened last night?' Sev asked again, and now she was ready to tell him.

'When I got there I saw people heading to the beach and I saw that they were having a party for his fiftieth.' Naomi said. 'I just dropped the cake and ran.'

'Did they see you?'

'No.' Naomi shook, not in answer to the question, more in confusion. 'I don't know, maybe it was a surprise party and—'

'No.' He would not let her have hope. 'If it was a surprise, why wouldn't his wife have asked you to come?'

'Stop it.'

'You need to be tough,' Sev said. 'You need to worry only about yourself from now on.'

'Is that what you do?'

'Absolutely.' Sev nodded. 'I don't care for anyone, I don't *want* to care for anyone, and I don't want anyone ever to rely on me.'

'So you don't care for your friends?' She didn't believe him. 'What about Allem?'

'Oh, Allem says that he wants to be friends and all this talk about me coming for a holiday and taking us out on the water…' Sev shook his head. 'He wants me to call him more and to talk about things other than work.'

'Yet you don't?'

'Not really. He's married now, things are different. I ask after Jamal and I go out to dinner…' he nudged her '…even the theatre, but I know it will change again. Come March they will have the baby. Just stay back from people, Naomi.'

'I'm not like that.'

'Become like that, then,' Sev said. 'I work on it. Sometimes I get drawn in, but I generally choose not to.' He looked at her. 'Take only what you need from people and give no more than you're willing to lose.'

'That sounds selfish.'

'No, it's not. I don't care for family, or deep friendship. I don't want romance and sex is still the best part of my day or week.'

'People get hurt,' Naomi said, thinking of the tears of some of the women she had dealt with but more thinking of herself. 'That's what I was worried about when I said no to you.'

'What? That I was going to turn into some raging monster?'

'Emotionally hurt,' Naomi sighed. Sev wasn't even from Mars, more like the next galaxy.

'From the start I make it very clear sex is all I want. As I said, only gamble with what you're prepared to lose. You *can* choose not to throw your heart in the ring. Expect nothing from anyone…' he gave her a smile '…while demanding excellent service.'

'I don't get it.'

'Take your father, for example. Tell him that if he wants a relationship with you then he has to be the one to make a continuous and sustained effort.'

'But he won't.'

'Then you know.'

'I might never see my sisters.'

'So?'

'I don't want to be like that.'

'It hurts less,' Sev said. 'Call him now and tell him you're gone and tell him why and then see what happens. Do it now—I'll be beside you. Grow some balls, and if you think you can't then borrow mine…' He took her hand and led it to his, and he did so without thinking.

They were on a bed together and he took her hand and placed it there and then he muttered something and went to push her hand back.

Naomi kept it there.

'I didn't come for that,' Sev said.

'I know.'

'I was just making a point.'

'I get that.' Yet her hand remained.

He was semi-aroused, she could feel that.

So was she.

That little trip for Naomi had happened not by the guidance of his hand but earlier, when he had been talking about not throwing your heart in the ring. Naomi had lain there listening but her mind had wandered too. A part of her regret for the other night was that she'd denied herself also.

She wanted Sev, she wanted those lips back on hers, and to give in to the want that had never left since the day they had met.

Could she, as Sev had suggested, take her heart out of the ring?

And as her hand moved over his crotch, Sev conceded to himself that, even though he hadn't come in for that, he had become turned on, which was why his hand had led hers there. Not consciously, more just a natural extension of the feeling between them.

'Naomi,' Sev warned as she continued to explore him. 'I won't let it go down a third time.'

'Third?' Naomi frowned.

'You were hot and naked under those sheets that morning when I called you from Rome,' Sev said. 'Do you want me to remind you of the second time?'

'No.'

'I'm not making a move on you again,' Sev said, and she felt him harden further to her touch. 'You want it, Naomi, then you come and get it.'

He was the most arrogant person she had ever met. He slapped her hand away and sat up, but only long enough to take off his top, which he threw down on the floor, and then lay back.

She had seen the top half of his body many times, usually when he wore a face full of shaving cream, but now he was very unshaven and he lay on his back, looking up at the ceiling, and that body was hers to explore.

If she so chose.

No kiss.

No turning towards her.

No making this easy.

'I mean it,' Sev warned. 'You can make the moves now.'

'What, you're just going to lie there?'

'Yep,' Sev said. 'I've tried being nice and look where it got me. It's your turn to seduce me.' He stretched and closed his eyes. 'If not, I'm going to sleep.'

Naomi lay there on her side and looked over and conceded that she had probably used up rather a lot of chances with Sev.

She went to his mouth and kissed him but Sev did not kiss her back. It was a surprising turn-on, just working his relaxed mouth, tasting cognac at 7:00 a.m., and he was as bad as he was delicious.

Naomi kept waiting for him to reach for her, to respond, but he didn't, he just allowed her to do what she would.

It was an incredible turn-on and she kissed him deeper, sexier, using her tongue to try and get him to respond, but only the deeper breaths from Sev gave any indication of a response.

Two indications, Naomi amended as she knelt back on her heels and planned her next move. She could see him straining beneath the denim and this time *she* went for his belt.

He made it about sex.

Just about sex.

It was incredibly freeing.

And to see this once apologetic person relaxed in herself was surprising for Sev.

When he opened his eyes there was just enough light in the dim cabin that he could see her feminine outline. Combined with the recent feel of her naked breasts on his chest, he was fighting himself not to reach out and touch her.

He loved the bold her.

She dealt with the belt and zip and her hand slid in, feeling him hard and waiting, and his silken pubic hair made her throat close up. Naomi tugged at his jeans and Sev rebuked her.

'I was going to do you fast that night,' Sev said, lifting his hips just enough so she could strip off the bottom half of his clothes.

He gave her nothing except his deep voice but it was more than enough to turn her on, especially as he was naked now and fully erect. He was talking to her in a way she'd never heard. Oh, she'd had the odd reprimand, they had occasionally tipped into a row, but now it ended in bed.

'I was going to take you fast and then I was going to make up for the lack of foreplay…but you said no, that I had to go.'

'Okay…' She didn't need reminders but maybe she did because she was rocking on her heels as she took him in her hand.

'And,' Sev continued his sensual berating of her, 'you think I just wanted a quick come when I was on the phone that time, but then you've never been spoken dirty to by me. You have no idea what you missed out on that morning…'

He said something in Russian, something filthy. It had to be, because her hand tightened her grip on his cock and she tightened inside. Naomi was possibly following orders, because she was climbing on top of him to sit on his thighs.

'Condom,' Sev said. 'Then I want you to get on and…' He switched back to Russian and Naomi, a touch frantic, reached for the bedside table but, no, she didn't deal with his in-flight toiletries!

'Where?'

'By the shower.'

'You're a bastard, Sev.'

'Yeah, but you're going to go get them,' Sev responded. 'And put the light on on your way back.'

He didn't make her beg; he made her eager.

Sev made her want of him clear because she stood in the bathroom and saw a face in the mirror that had forgotten tears. She had never seen herself wanton. Naomi located the necessities and was back in a matter of seconds with her breath coming too rapidly.

'Lights,' Sev reminded her just as she reached the bed, which meant she had to turn around.

'Walk slowly,' he said, once she had turned the lights on and his eyes feasted as she did so. He could see how aroused Naomi was. Her face was flushed, her nipples erect and her eyes, when they met his, were glittering.

There was such a prickle of anticipation from her head to her toes that when she touched his cock, she thought there might be a spark of electricity, but instead it was warm and moist, only not moist in the way Sev wanted.

'Wet it first,' Sev said.

'I thought I was the one doing the work.'

'Do as you're told.'

She laughed, at herself, at any thought that Sev had come in here to make love to her, and it helped that this was not what that was.

She lowered her head, knowing it would be sexual bliss. Taking charge once more, he positioned her so that she straddled his face. He didn't touch her, or reach to taste her, but that only served to incite her desire. She was moaning to the taste of him, the need for the intimate touch of him which he persisted in denying. Then, as she took him deeper into her mouth, he pulled at her hips and halted her again.

'Turn around.'

He, rather than the motion, made her feel dizzy.

She sat on his thighs, giddy and more turned on than she had thought it possible to be.

Sev tore open the wrapper and held it out to her. 'Put it on.'

'Are you going to say no to me at the last moment?' Naomi wondered aloud.

'Why would I say no to you?' Sev asked, watching as she rolled the condom down his thick length. 'Now get on.'

Oh, he was more than making sure that yes meant yes.

Naomi went to do that. She lifted her hips and he suddenly spun her around and pinned her on her back. Now Sev was on top.

And they were back, exactly where she had said no to him, except they were naked and he was sheathed.

Naomi was arching into him and, just as she had been that night, about to come.

'Oh, no, you don't,' Sev warned. 'You don't get to come without me...' He drove into her, right into her orgasm, and she had never known anything close to it. To be taken so strongly while already coming.

She couldn't even cry out as all her energy gathered around him and the only part of her brain that worked was begging for him to come but he didn't. Sev thrust into her with such intensity that even as her come receded it never fully left. Her life felt as if it had been pale till that point. Naomi's lungs remembered they were supposed to be breathing and she dragged in some air and then found her mouth near his ear.

'Sev...' There was almost a need for him to stop—his rapid, deep thrusts were so consuming, but then he moved up onto his elbows and slowed down but it was no less intense.

Slow and deliberate motions that kept her in this tense sense of gridlock, with an open road ahead, but then, when her urgency increased, so did Sev's speed and he brought her back to boiling, at his whim.

'There,' he said, as he started to come.

'*Krasavitsa*,' Sev said, as he reached his climax, and Naomi let out a shout of pleasure. The lights seemed to go out in her head as he took her to a place she had never been.

Yet he was there with her.

'I think,' Naomi said, as he collapsed on top of her and they lay breathless, 'that you just took my virginity.'

He laughed, understanding that, until now, possibly she hadn't had such sex before.

'I think,' Sev said, 'that you just took mine.'

CHAPTER NINE

'WHAT HAPPENED TO the others?'

They had slept a little, spoken a bit and filled the remaining time with the other. Now, a couple of hours from Dubai, her head felt clearer than it had in three months yet she was curious to know more.

'No idea.' Sev shrugged.

'Have you looked them up?'

'Why?' Sev's voice was scathing. 'So we can speak about happy times?' He relented a touch. 'Daniil is some big-shot businessman now. I wrote to him once but he never got back to me.'

'Roman?'

'I don't know. He was always in trouble, especially after Daniil left for England. I just focused on school and getting the grades so I could get a scholarship and get the hell out of there.'

'Nikolai?'

'Dead,' Sev said. 'When he was fourteen he threw himself in a river.'

There was no elaboration, no emotion, he just told her how it was.

'Why?' Naomi asked, but Sev didn't want to talk about that.

Shannon buzzed and asked if they wanted breakfast.

To Naomi's embarrassment Sev said yes and a little while later she sat up as Shannon brought it in.

Champagne and orange juice was very nice but what made Naomi tear up was a cake and it had her name on it.

'I hadn't told Shannon I was leaving.'

'I called her yesterday.'

So he had made an effort.

'This is your leaving party,' Sev said. 'Though I didn't think we'd be eating it in bed. I'm very glad that we are.'

'We could have done this on the way to London,' Naomi said, but Sev shook his head.

He'd be in no mood to party on the way there, whether or not they were in bed, as it would still be November the twelfth.

He looked at Naomi.

There would soon be another reason to loathe that date.

'Do you have a job to go to in London?'

'My old boss emailed me a couple of weeks ago to say that his current PA isn't working out. I dismissed the idea at the time...' She looked at Sev. 'What you said about working for you still...'

'Naomi.' Sev was as blunt as he needed to be. 'It would be very foolish to come back to New York because of what happened today.'

'I know it would.'

It felt strange to be so honest and to speak with someone who was so direct. And yet, again, words that might cause offence when said by others didn't when they came from Sev.

She knew where she stood. Or rather where she lay.

'I think,' Sev said, 'that when we get to Dubai you should ring Emmanuel.'

'I thought he was useless?'

'He'll do,' Sev said. He certainly wasn't going to tell Naomi he had only said that in the hope she might stay.

Yes, he didn't want her gone, but for her to return solely for him, Sev knew, would be cruel.

'Do you know what you need?' Sev asked.

'What?'

'A holiday.'

'If I want my old job back I'll probably have to start straight away. I might see if I can take a few days, though.'

'No, I mean a proper one. How about we have a holiday before you go back to London? Both of us?'

'We're going to be busy.'

'No, we're not.'

'You told Allem that you're going to have to squeeze two weeks' work into four nights.'

'That's just so I can bill him adequately.'

'But the work still has to be done.' Naomi frowned.

'Most of it already has been.' He looked at her and smiled. 'Can you keep a secret?'

'Yes.'

'It will take me a couple of days… And before you say I'm overcharging, I'm not. He's paying for my knowledge, not the actual labour. And,' Sev added, 'I'd end up with far too many clients if I didn't pace things. So,' he said, 'how about it.'

'A holiday?'

'A proper one,' Sev said, and then he gave her another tiny glimpse of insight. 'I've never had one before.'

He'd travelled the world many times over and yet he'd never taken a break.

'I don't know…'

'Think about it,' Sev said, and got out of bed and went to the shower.

Naomi did think about it.

She had been scared that if she slept with him she might fall deeper and, of course, she had.

Only she wasn't scared now.

Naomi was sure of her feelings for him.

Oh, it would be a very foolish woman to expect more from Sev.

It didn't stop her wanting more, though.

And some might consider her foolish for upending her life to give herself and her father a chance, but even if it hadn't worked out, she was glad that she had.

'How about it?' Sev asked, as he took the towel from his hips and started to dry his back while facing her.

'How about what?' Naomi smiled.

'The holiday.' Sev grinned. Really, she was nothing like he'd thought she'd be, and he had thought about it a lot!

'Oh, that!' Naomi just lay there looking at him, but her mind was already made up.

No, she wouldn't throw her heart in the ring and she would hold back but, yes, she would open it up enough for potential hurt. There would be no declarations of her feelings and no asking Sev for more than he was prepared to give.

And she would walk away with her head held high.

At least she would have given them a chance.

'I need an answer.' Sev was still drying himself.

'Yes, please,' Naomi said, looking at his hardening manhood. She laughed as he threw down the towel and got back into bed.

'I wasn't asking about that!'

CHAPTER TEN

DUBAI WAS, AS PROMISED, humid and hot, but they were whisked straight from the plane to a stunning hotel complex that was icy cool and very elegant.

Allem proudly showed them around.

It was beyond luxurious.

There were private beaches and pools and Naomi could only guess what the rooms must look like.

'We host a lot of foreign delegates as well as royalty,' Allem explained. 'I never want their privacy or safety to be compromised as has happened at some other hotels. Last month one of our main rivals had their accounts system hacked into,' Allem told Naomi. 'Some very personal information was revealed, which is why I have been pushing for Sev to come and update all our systems. While I employ the best IT staff, I would prefer—'

'It will be fine,' Sev interrupted. 'I'll meet with them but I'll check it myself.'

It was clear Allem really only trusted Sev to have full access to everything.

'I'll return on my way back from London so if there are any glitches I can work on them then.'

'We'll see you both again.' Allem beamed but Sev shook his head.

'Just me. Naomi has resigned. I'll have a new PA,

but he shan't be starting for a couple more weeks. Any problems, just contact me directly, Allem.' He glanced over at Naomi. 'I'll be fine now. I'm going to meet with the IT team. I should be back around two. Just take the day and relax.'

'I hope you will enjoy your stay,' Allem said, 'and I trust that you both will be comfortable. Anything at all that you need, just say.'

'Thank you.'

He stood there as she walked off.

'Why did Naomi resign?' Allem asked.

'I've no idea,' Sev admitted.

He still didn't know. Yes, sex might make things awkward in the end but they were far from awkward now.

'You're finishing at two?' Allem checked.

'I decided to have a bit of a holiday, that's why. If anything doesn't get done, I'll be back after London. It will give me a few days to tweak things as well.'

'You must let Jamal and I show you around. We can go out on the water—'

'No, no,' Sev interrupted, and made no apology for turning down Allem's kind invitation. 'We're just going to relax. Naomi might be starting a new job pretty soon.'

'Oh, so you're both having a break? I see that Naomi is no longer wearing her ring,' Allem commented.

'No.'

'I've put you in adjoining suites.' Allem had remembered Sev's request from the last time he had been there.

Sev liked company.

Just not all the time.

Times, though, had changed.

'No need for adjoining suites,' Sev said. 'Move Naomi into mine.'

By the time Naomi had arrived at Reception, Allem

had made a call and, unknown to her, the arrangement had already been made.

Naomi was checked into a room that was more sumptuous than any she had ever stayed in, or could even had imagined staying in.

The furnishings were amazing, from Persian rugs to vases filled with exotic flowers.

The Persian Gulf stretched out before her and there was an alfresco area with its own pool and spa.

And then she found out why. This wasn't Sev's PA's suite, she realised as the cases she had packed for Sev were delivered and the contents put away, and it was a little closer than she had expected him to be over the coming days.

They had travelled together a lot.

It felt strange, knowing that there wasn't a door that could be closed between them, and for the first time since making her decision Naomi had doubts.

This *was* going to hurt.

She did her best to push their imminent parting out of her mind.

For an hour or so she dealt with work but then she looked through one of the brochures in the suite and decided that, no, they would not be eating in a restaurant tonight and made some reservations.

It was her holiday too!

She enjoyed a morning at the spa and was lying on a vast bed, looking out at the Persian Gulf, when the door opened around three and Sev came in. 'It took longer than I thought but his guys will be working on it round the clock tonight and I'll be back onto it tomorrow. For now we can relax.'

'I thought that we'd have separate rooms.'

'Why?'

'I just did,' Naomi said. 'Come on, you need to get changed.'

'Why?'

'We've got a date with the desert. Camel riding, a meal and belly dancing, and then star-gazing till midnight.' Naomi smiled. 'My treat.'

'You're kidding me?'

'No.' Naomi shook her head. 'I'm not.'

'I don't do that sort of stuff.'

'Well, I want to.'

'Allem will arrange a private tour—'

'I told you,' Naomi said, 'this is my treat. If you don't want to go, that's fine. I think the transport drops us back here about one. I wanted to book the overnight trip but I wasn't sure what time you'd have to work tomorrow.'

It turned out to be the nicest, maddest, most beautiful thing that either he or Naomi could have done.

The desert was stunning, especially looking at it as you rode a camel. The group they were in made a lazy procession as the sun slid down the sky and it was like being bathed in liquid gold.

The magic didn't end there. They arrived hungry at camp to the smoky scents of dinner. They sat on rugs and ate, and their group were all amazing. Some were backpackers, there was a couple on their honeymoon and another here for their wedding anniversary. The shisha pipe came around and Naomi had her feet painted with henna as she ate the best dates she had ever tasted. Then they watched the belly dancing and, as Naomi had known it would be, it was wonderful.

Sev thought so too.

Usually his view was an office, or hotel window, or looking out from his plane.

Now he breathed in the warm night air and that night,

amongst strangers, they lay on their rugs and looked up at the stars as a guide pointed out constellations and star clusters.

'That was amazing,' Sev admitted afterwards, as they still lay looking up at the stars. 'Emmanuel won't be nearly as much fun.'

'He might be once he's resigned.' Naomi smiled and looked at him.

'Did you call him?'

'Yes,' Naomi said. 'He's completely thrilled. He offered to come out to Dubai to transition…'

'You said no to that, I hope. I know the bed at the hotel's big but I'm not sharing with him too!'

'I said no, that there's no need for him to come here at this stage, though you might want him after London.'

'No.' Sev didn't want to think about London, or the trip back here afterwards.

'Anyway, I said that I'd be in touch with dates shortly.'

And Sev got back to looking at the stars. He knew then that she was leaving for sure.

Naomi wouldn't change her mind and come back and work for him; she simply wouldn't do that to Emmanuel.

'What about your father?' Sev asked. 'Did you call him?'

'No.'

All too soon it was over and Sev actually wished that Naomi had booked the overnight trip. They headed back to the hotel and it would seem the fairies had been in while they'd been out—a sunken bath had been run and there were petals floating on the surface of the water. The lights were dimmed and there was champagne on ice. Even Sev blinked.

'I think we've got the honeymoon suite.'

They had.

And, yes, it was like a honeymoon.

Except at the end of it they would be parting ways.

Over the next few days Sev worked harder than he ever had just to give them more time to do the things Naomi wanted to do, like parasailing, long lazy lunches and dinners taken on the beach, and slow walks afterwards.

The moon was so big and yellow, as they walked, that it almost looked like the sun had stayed up too long.

'I called my father,' Naomi told him. 'I just wanted it over and done with.'

'And?'

'I didn't say I knew about the party. I just said that I hadn't been able to find a new job or somewhere to live and so I thought it might be better to stay in London rather than come back.'

'What did he say?'

'That he was sorry we didn't get a chance to say a proper goodbye. I honestly don't know if he meant it.'

She looked at Sev and wondered how their goodbye would be.

'I'm going to stay in touch with my sisters, though.'

'Why?' Sev asked.

And she looked at a man who just didn't care and wondered when her heart would get the message—he never would!

'Did you ever contact your sister?' Naomi asked.

'Yes,' Sev said. 'Renata. She's ten years older than me, a single mum with a daughter...'

'Your niece?'

Sev shrugged.

'I guess.'

'Don't you care about them?'

'Nope.' He saw the flash of confusion in her eyes, and

he was damned if he'd tell her why. 'You rely on others for your happiness too much, Naomi. You just hand out that heart and you wonder why it comes back broken. I'll tell you what happened. I did look up my sister and I was welcomed into their home and I met my niece, Mariya. Then I came back to New York and for a couple of months we spoke most weeks. Then I got a phone call. Renata told me that Mariya was sick, very sick with a very rare form of cancer.'

'Sev!' Her eyes actually filled up. She might not know her sisters well but with the thought of one of them being so ill and so far away, she could understand his pain.

'I was devastated. I'd only just found a family and I asked if there was anything I could do. Renata told me about a treatment that was available in America. It was Mariya's only chance…'

He could see the concern in her eyes.

'She only had a few weeks to live. She was too weak to come to the phone. I offered to pay for the treatment, to bring her over to America. I was going to send the jet and sort out medical team to fetch her but…'

He looked into those spaniel eyes that would trust in others for ever, no matter the hurt they caused, and when Sev hesitated, she assumed the logical conclusion.

'It was too late?'

The logical conclusion if you had a warm heart.

His had grown cold for so many reasons.

'Hey, a bit of advice, Naomi, never, ever respond to an email asking for your bank account details.'

'I'm not with you.'

'I asked Renata for the clinic's name so I could send funds.' Naomi still frowned and it annoyed him. It scared him just how much she trusted and how easily she could be hurt.

Had been hurt.

Could very easily still be.

'Renata wanted me to send the funds directly to her.' Naomi swallowed.

'Mariya was never sick,' Sev explained. 'There never was any cancer. So you see now why lying about a family member's health comes easily to me. It must be hereditary.'

'You're sure it was a scam?'

'Quite sure,' Sev said. 'I now have nothing to do with Renata but I've sent gifts for Mariya, though they end up auction sites.' He was brutal then. 'Don't go looking for hurt, Naomi. It's the best advice I can give.'

'We're not all like that, Sev.'

'I'm not talking about women,' Sev said, thinking she was referring to his mother and sister, but Naomi was one step ahead of him.

'I know you're not,' Naomi responded. 'You've ruled out the entire human race.'

CHAPTER ELEVEN

SEV STILL HAD to work but, Allem noted, he looked more relaxed than he had ever seen him. 'What are your plans for London?' Allem asked, as Sev took him through the changes he was making to the system.

'Just…' Sev shrugged. He never told anyone that he went there in the hope of catching up with Daniil.

'Will you be meeting Naomi's family?'

'No. Allem, Naomi and I aren't going anywhere.'

'But why not? It's clear you two have strong feelings for each other. It was obvious at dinner but it's fact now.'

'Can we just concentrate on work?' Sev snapped, but for once it was Sev who was distracted.

Sev dealt in facts and Allem was right.

Their walk on the beach and what Naomi had said about him mistrusting the human race had rattled him. Sev knew he had many reasons not to trust in others, except none of them applied when he thought of Naomi.

Tomorrow would be their last full day in Dubai. They had spent the morning in bed and then the pool and Sev, who was usually only too happy to head into work, hadn't wanted to leave her. The day after tomorrow they would be boarding his jet and then Naomi would be gone. There was a part of him that was relieved—he would restore factory settings on his heart and get the hell on with his life.

'Jamal and I knew within a week of meeting each other that we would be together. Our families weren't happy about it at the time but I knew that she would be the woman I would marry.'

'Allem,' Sev warned. 'We don't all want a wife.'

'Sevastyan—'

'Leave it.'

'I don't want to leave it. Why would you not fight for her?'

This, Sev thought, was the reason he didn't want friends. He had boundaries and Allem was overstepping them, and it needled at him.

'Sevastyan.' Allem said again. 'How long have we known each other?'

'Long enough,' Sev said through gritted teeth.

Allem did not take offence.

Oh, he had taken offence when they had first met. Many times.

Most people, when they stepped off a first-class flight, would be pleasant and relaxed.

Sevastyan had arrived in Dubai looking grey.

He had refused basic pleasantries and had struggled through a lavish meal that had been prepared and then he had, on retiring, put outside the door, unopened, the gift that had been placed in his suite.

Yes, Allem had been offended.

He had knocked to enquire if the gift did not suit this very difficult guest.

'Do you remember when I knocked on your door and asked why you had placed the gift outside your suite?' Allem asked.

Sev actually let out a low laugh at the memory.

'You thought it had been placed in the wrong room.'

'Because I'd never had a gift.'

'And then you asked if we could get out?' Allem reminded him. 'We went for a drive and to a bar.'

Sev stopped smiling when he remembered that night.

He had never been out of Russia before. The flight had been awful, the constant attention from the flight attendants had unsettled him. Then he had got to Allem's and he had never been a guest in someone's home, especially such a palatial one, and he had been completely overwhelmed.

They had ended up in a bar, one that was far nicer than the ones Sev had been used to frequenting.

'You told me that night where you had come from.'

'Allem,' Sev pointed out, 'I've come a long way since then.'

'You have,' Allem agreed. 'Through your own hard work.'

And some help from a friend. Yes, Sev admitted then that Allem was one.

'Allem?'

Sev gave up trying to work.

He had a question.

Several, in fact.

CHAPTER TWELVE

DUBAI, NAOMI DECIDED, was amazing.

Or was it that she was on holiday?

Her job meant that she had seen many beautiful places but these past couple of days had been so relaxing, exhilarating and wonderful.

Or was it the company?

She didn't try to work it out.

She woke mid-morning to a note from Sev telling her he would be working with Allem till late to give them a clear day tomorrow.

Their last day.

No, she didn't want to think about that and so she had a lazy breakfast in bed, going through brochures and trying to work out, from the many choices available, just what to do with her day. Just when she had decided on shopping she took a call from Jamal, who said it was her turn to take Naomi out.

Naomi found herself laughing as she got ready, thinking back to the day she had met Jamal, when she had been priming herself to hand in her notice.

So much had changed in that short space of time and so much would change again very soon.

'Allem just called,' Jamal said as Naomi got into the

car, as arranged. 'They will be working till late, which gives us plenty time.'

Oh, Jamal knew how to shop.

And her driver patiently took her purchases back to the car.

They went into several boutiques, though Jamal steered away from the names Naomi knew. 'I dress more traditionally,' Jamal explained, 'and so I favour local designers.'

Naomi could see why.

The fabrics were stunning, the lines exquisite and Naomi found herself trying on dresses that she never usually would.

'Try this one,' Jamal suggested. It was in a grey silver and long, and should have been completely over the top, but with the delicate henna flowers on her feet and with her hair down it somehow worked.

'I'm not sure,' Naomi said. Oh, she loved it but it wasn't anything like she usually wore.

'It's perfect on you. Let me get it for you,' Jamal said.

'Jamal.' Naomi shook her head. 'Please, don't offer. I find it awkward.'

'Of course.' Jamal nodded.

'I just want to like what I like.'

Jamal smiled and gave another nod. 'It's very beautiful, though.'

It was, and, the lines having been drawn, Naomi made one purchase to Jamal's ten.

'I've no idea when I'll ever wear it.'

'Tomorrow,' Jamal said. 'Allem and I want you both to come for dinner. You can wear it then.'

'For dinner?' Naomi laughed because this dress seemed over the top for dinner with friends but then realised that Jamal was completely serious.

'We want to say goodbye properly; it is so nice to have Sevastyan here. We want him to come to our home so dress up, Naomi. I shall.'

They had their hair done and really it was just a lovely day and topped off by high tea, where Naomi ate date-infused scones topped with rosewater jam. It was the holiday she had never really had.

No, it wasn't just that she was with Sev, but the amazing city, the wonderful company and taking the time to do fun things.

She even bought camel chocolates for her sisters and mailed them there and then.

Yes, she understood what Sev had said and why he had chosen to pull away from his family; she just wouldn't be pulling away from Kennedy and her other little sisters.

She imagined the two older girls' excitement when they opened their little parcels and, Naomi decided, staying around for them, even if from far away, felt like the right choice to have made.

Given Jamal and Allem's news, they found themselves in several baby boutiques and it was fun to see Jamal so excited.

'We had two years of trying,' Jamal said. 'I was starting to really worry and Allem was so good to me, he said it was me he wanted.'

'He's a very nice man.'

'He's so kind,' Jamal said. 'So romantic. Is Sev?'

Naomi just laughed. 'That would be a no.'

When surely they should have been finished, there was one thing more to do. 'I want look at rugs,' Jamal said. 'We will wait till we know what we are having before we choose but I'd love your thoughts.'

'I always wanted a Persian rug…' Naomi admitted, looking around.

'Not these,' Jamal said. 'We want to look only at the handmade.'

Oh, this baby would have everything!

They were exquisite and so expensive but, really, Naomi thought, when would she ever get a chance like this again? She was here in Dubai, shopping with an expert, because Jamal certainly knew her rugs.

'That's beautiful,' Jamal said, when she saw Naomi running her hand over one. The colours were amazing—a pistachio green, cream and black. Jamal parted the rug and checked the knots to see that it really was handmade but, really, it was so intricate and lavish that you couldn't doubt that it was.

It cost way more than Naomi could justify but it was far more beautiful than her conscience had allowed for and Jamal could see that she was wavering. 'Do you want me to bargain for you?' Jamal said. 'It will be half that price.'

'No.' Naomi shook her head. It was ridiculous but she could feel her eyes starting to sting so she quickly turned so that Jamal couldn't see. 'No, thanks. Come on…'

It was a tiny moment in a wonderful day and yet it stayed with her long after it had passed.

Naomi got back to the hotel, had a light dinner and then lay on the bed, trying to work out how she felt.

'God, it took for ever,' Sev said when he came in.

'Are you finished?'

'I have to go in at lunchtime and speak with the head of IT. Allem was right to get me in. How was your day with Jamal?'

'It was great.'

She went to get off the bed but he stopped her. 'Stay there, we've got to be up early tomorrow. We're going on a hot air balloon ride,' Sev said, as he started to undress. 'We've got to be there at five so we'll have to be up at four.'

'A hot air balloon ride?'

'It's supposed to be amazing. You go over the desert, you can see gazelles and…' Sev shrugged. He was suddenly far more interested in devouring her body.

It would have been a crime not to respond. Sev was as beautiful as the first time she'd seen him and the sex that night was as good as ever.

She had held on to a part of herself, though.

From day one in his bed she had.

Her heart might be in the ring but she'd never let him know that.

And afterwards, Naomi actually wished that they did have separate rooms. Her mind was too busy and there was no chance of falling asleep. She lay staring into the darkness as Sev slept and imagined the rug rolled up in her mother's spare room till she found somewhere to live.

How could you buy a rug when you didn't know where you were going to be living?

Then she pictured it by the fire on the floor of her apartment that she'd just let go in New York and it would have looked amazing.

And then she did a really stupid thing and imagined it on the floor in Sev's bedroom.

Its preferred home.

It went with the drapes, Naomi realised as she pictured it in her mind.

How long could she pretend that she wasn't in love with the man who lay next to her?

Naomi lay there, hit by a wave of homesickness so violent she could have packed her case right now—there was a need to go home.

She just didn't know where that was.

CHAPTER THIRTEEN

SEV WOKE TO his alarm and tried not to think of the date.
So he lay there in the darkness, trying to motivate himself to get out of bed.

'Naomi?'

She woke to the sound of Sev saying her name and it
was just as beautiful as the first time she had heard it.
His hand was stroking her breast and he was tucked into
her back. 'We have to get up.'

They did.

Bloody Allem and his ideas, Sev thought. He didn't
want to go up in a balloon and be happy today.

Not today.

Or tomorrow.

These were the days he dreaded all year in their lead
up.

Nikolai's last day.

He did not want to think about it.

'Sev—' Naomi started, but he interrupted her.

'Come on,' he said. 'If we want to get there in time.'

'Can I tell you something?'

He was right up behind her and she had never felt
more comfortable in her life, warm, turned on. Tomorrow they would be up at the crack of dawn to get on the

flight to London and she wanted to stay here and linger this morning.

'Tell me,' he said, but Naomi lost her train of thought as his hand lifted her hair and he kissed the back of her neck as he had wanted to do the night when he had played with her zipper.

His hand moved down from her breast to her stomach.

'Remember when I thought you were pregnant?'

Naomi smiled in the dark. 'I do.' Sev completely confused her—he'd turned down Emmanuel because he didn't speak Mandarin and Dianne for a nervous smile yet he'd offered her day care for her baby and to cut back on travel!

He was hard and she wished the little circular movement his hand made low on her stomach would never end, Naomi thought, even if she wanted his hand to move lower. So heavy was her arousal that she didn't want him to roll away and put on a condom, and her bottom pressed back into him. 'I'm on the Pill, Sev.'

'Thank God for that.'

He slid in unsheathed and let out a long sigh as the slippery warmth gripped him and they both ignored the sound of the snooze alarm.

'Sev...' 'They were both on the delicious edge. On the edge of desire, on the edge of coming, on the edge of over.

'Come on, baby.' He was moving faster and deeper, bringing her to the rapid high that he easily procured.

And so she told him something that she'd been trying to say since he'd come back last night—a simple truth.

Not *the* simple truth—after all she had promised no declarations—but she voiced another one. 'I don't want to go on the balloon ride.'

Naomi was starting to come, which he'd been pushing her to do. As her deep orgasm gripped him tight it drew Sev not just deeper into her but further away from thought.

Now the pre-dawn sky was a rich navy and a quickie was no longer enough. Sev didn't want to come down and face the day he dreaded, or go up in the air. He would rather be lost in the two of them.

And Naomi waited—for the delicious trip of him, for the intense pleasure to be topped. And it was, only not in the way she had anticipated.

He pulled out and Naomi thought, *What? What?*

Then he turned her over.

'Sev?'

The alarm went again and he turned it off, and Naomi tried to get her breath as he faced her.

'We're not going up in a balloon.'

They stayed down on delicious earth.

He kissed her in a way he perhaps shouldn't if Naomi was going to keep her head.

Side on, eyes open for long enough to know what they were doing was breaking their rules.

Their legs were entwined, his cock nudged at her stomach, but now there was time for more. And so Naomi kissed him in a way perhaps she shouldn't. Three months of restraint had ended on the plane, but a different restraint ended this morning. She had never known a kiss like it. Their tongues swirled, mouths played with mouths. She took in his lower lip just to feel it between hers, they stroked at each other's mouths, caressed the other's tongue. Yes, she had never known a kiss like it and, she guessed, after this morning she never again would.

Naomi tasted love for the first time and she gave it back. She kissed him deep and slow, then his face, ear and down his neck. She breathed in the scent of him and savoured the taste of his skin on her tongue and lips as his hands roamed her body and read her like Braille.

He played with her breasts and then tasted them, lowering his head and his body too, so that his erection was on her thighs and they were rocking against each other as her hands went into his hair.

He took her nipple deep in his mouth and it felt like too much but not enough and then, in one motion, he lifted his head and found her mouth as his body came and fully joined hers.

Side on again, eyes open again, she looked right at him as he took her deep and slow.

If it was possible to be comfortable in scalding skin then she was. They were barely moving, face-to-face, with limbs entwined, both wanting the other's mouth but preferring eye contact.

They moved as one, changing tempo without thought, glad of sunrise just because they could take in the other's features.

Then they kissed, until each of Sev's thrusts became all-pervading, spreading through her body and then concentrating at her centre. He watched her lip turn down but not from tears. Sev felt her not just around his cock but it was as if her whole body tightened and they said nothing.

Yet.

Neither dared.

He released and she took and then took some more.

'Krasavitsa...'

She didn't want to know what it meant but he told her.

'Beautiful woman.'

She couldn't know he'd never said it to another.

CHAPTER FOURTEEN

FOUR THOUSAND FEET in the air would have been far safer.

Morning had more than broken, it was nearly midday when they woke up to Sev's phone and Ahmed, the IT guy, asking where he was.

Sev couldn't, Naomi noted, even look at her.

That was okay; she couldn't really look at him.

'I'm not sure how long I'll be,' Sev said.

'That's fine,' Naomi said.

Take your time! she thought.

Oh, there had been no declarations and after he had gone Naomi lay there, trying to convince herself that what had happened this morning had been no different from other times.

Liar.

And it wasn't just she who had broken the stated rules.

Sev had made love to her that morning and she knew, from the tension that now existed between them, that both of them regretted it.

For whatever reason he didn't want to get too involved or too close.

She did.

Worst of all, he'd let her glimpse what it could be like.

Sev went through all the changes with the head of IT but all day he found himself glancing at the time and thinking.

He remembered finishing school and taking the bus back to the orphanage with Nikolai.

He had been quiet.

That had suited him fine as he'd liked to do his homework on the bus and then read or study at night.

And then dinner.

Sixteen years ago they had lined up with their plates.

Now it was their last night in Dubai and it was to be spent being wined and dined by Allem.

'I'd rather it was just us tonight,' Sev admitted, as he dressed in his suit.

'And me,' Naomi admitted, but then she changed her mind. If it was just the two of them she might push for deeper conversation and demand answers about them.

Maybe there *was* safety in numbers.

'I'll call and tell him.'

'Sev!' Naomi halted him. 'No.'

'You just said you'd rather it was just us.'

'What we say and what we do are different things. He's gone out of his way to ensure that we have a good time. You can't just cancel on him.'

Oh, but he wanted to.

For more reasons than Naomi knew.

She put on her gorgeous silver dress and flat sandals and as Sev helped her with the zip there were no games this time.

'Come on, then,' Sev said.

No *You look nice*, or *Wow, I love that dress*.

And Naomi felt a burn of anger start to build.

She felt like emailing Emmanuel and asking him to order two dozen white roses.

It was that time, with Sev, she knew.

That time when the gloss had worn off and his interest waned.

She knew little of him but his routines she knew well.

'Naomi!' Jamal greeted her warmly and so too did Allem, but though the greeting was effusive and the dinner was magnificent there was tension in the air that Naomi couldn't read.

Sev wasn't at his most sociable but Naomi now knew Allem and Jamal accepted that.

There was something going on that she was not privy to, Naomi was sure.

'I had the chef make your favourite dessert, Sev,' Jamal said.

It was *sahlab*, a thick creamy milk pudding flavoured with orange blossom and rosewater. Topped with pistachios, it was delicious and light and Sev did comment.

'It's very nice.'

But then he glanced at his phone and, had the table been high enough to do so unseen, Naomi could cheerfully have kicked him.

Coffee was served and the shisha pipe came out. 'Would you like to see the nursery, Naomi?' Jamal asked.

Naomi smiled and nodded and as the women excused themselves Naomi thought back to their night in the desert and how light and easy life had seemed.

It was very different now.

Even Jamal seemed a touch strained, though she didn't comment or share her thoughts with Naomi.

Allem did with Sev.

Just as soon as the women were safely out of earshot, he turned to his friend.

'She said no?' Allem checked.

'I didn't ask her,' Sev admitted. 'Look, she's got some guy in England, maybe when she sees him...'

'Come off it, Sev.'

'I think he might be the safer bet.'

'You are being ridiculous.'

'No.' Sev shook his head. That morning had shaken him, that level of being with another person, feeling so close to another person, was one he wasn't sure he ever wanted to repeat.

'You didn't go up in the balloon?' Allem frowned.

'Nope,' Sev said, and tried not to think of what had happened. Instead he quickly changed the subject. 'I've spoken to Ahmed and I've told him I'll be back later next week. He seems to have a good grasp of the changes —'

'Sev, I don't want to talk about work tonight. Yesterday—'

'Was yesterday,' Sev interrupted. 'I've been thinking about things and while it's been a great break and we've both had a nice time...' They stopped talking as Jamal and Naomi came down the stairs.

'I'm sure Sev can rig up a system for you,' Naomi was saying.

'What was that?' Sev checked.

'Jamal is worried that the nursery and nanny's wing is too far from where they sleep.'

'I want to know if the baby cries,' Jamal said. 'I don't want to leave everything to the nanny.'

'Oh, please,' Allem said. 'We have the best security; we have monitors and cameras and, yes, of course we'll hear if the baby cries.'

About now, Sev thought.

About 11:00 p.m., sixteen years ago, the most important person in his world had cried.

And he'd heard him.

And then had rolled over and fallen back to sleep.

He thought of Nikolai.

No. Whatever he might have felt yesterday had long since passed. Sev did not trust himself to be the caretaker of another heart.

CHAPTER FIFTEEN

THEY'D STAYED ONE day and one night too long, Naomi thought as both her and Sev's alarms went off.

Three days and nights would have been enough and they could have ended it well.

She could have walked away having given them a chance but with her dignity intact.

Now she was doing her best not to cry.

Sev was right. Had she not messed up the schedule they'd be in London now and would already have parted ways.

Instead they lay in bed, barely touching and hardly talking.

Sev was thinking.

He had listened to Allem.

And he knew he couldn't ask her to come back to New York on a whim.

He'd bought a ring, yet he didn't know how to give it to her.

He scanned through his mind for even one example of a half-decent relationship that had survived the test of time.

Nyet.

Maybe Allem, but that was mainly business.

Anyway, he didn't have the space in his head for romance and maybes today. Instead he remembered what was.

Waking at five.

An hour earlier than usual but he and Nikolai had been on kitchen duty.

Sev had seen that the bed next to him had been empty.

Straight away he'd felt dread.

The first thing they'd usually done had been to make their beds.

It had been the very first thing that they'd done every morning without exception and yet Nikolai's bed had been unmade.

'We need to go,' Sev said, but he didn't need to. Naomi was already climbing out of bed.

She had packed yesterday.

For both of them.

Oh, as much as she might have pretended to herself that this was a holiday she was still on his payroll...for a few more hours at least. They drove to the airport and Naomi realised that this was finally it.

They boarded his jet and sat in silence.

Neither dared suggest bed.

Parting was already going to be hard enough.

'Where's your book?' Naomi asked, for something to say and because he always read during take-off.

Sev didn't answer her.

It was time to be practical. 'If I write up a reference,' Naomi asked, 'will you sign it?'

'I'll do one for you now.'

He took out his computer.

'How long did you work for me?' Sev checked.

'Three months.' Naomi sighed. He didn't even know that.

'I meant, how long do you want me to put that you have worked for me?'

'Just put the truth,' Naomi snapped.

Sev actually smiled. She was the only person he knew who growled as they asked you to write a reference for them.

'Testy?' Sev checked.

'Tired,' Naomi corrected.

Sev typed for a couple of moments and then flicked the result over to her computer. 'Let me know if you want me to change anything.'

Naomi opened the file and read it.

To Whom It May Concern,

Naomi Johnson has worked as my personal assistant for three very long months.

Initially when I interviewed her I decided she wasn't suitable for the role—she said 'sorry' a lot and that irritated me—but then I decided to give her a try.

I have regretted that choice at times.

Naomi Johnson was moody, didn't like ordering flowers and she was, I have to say, obstructive on occasion. Now, though, I understand that her belligerent attitude was because she wanted to have sex with me.

And I did with her.

I wish we hadn't waited so long but I'm also glad that we did.

In summary, Naomi Johnson is the best PA I've ever had, the nicest person I've known, and I feel a bit sick typing this because, though I don't want her to leave, I honestly think it's for the best that she does.

Sevastyan Derzhavin

PS I shall write you a real one now.

Naomi read it without comment and, as nice as it was, it made her feel cross too. For all they had found, he would let her leave, and while she might know him better, she understood him less.

It was a long, lonely flight.

Sev did write her a real reference.

One that was so good it had Naomi question if she should go back to her old job.

This could open doors.

She wanted to be walking through his, though.

The hardest thing ever, far harder than leaving her father behind, was to walk off the plane and to his car. She had sworn she wouldn't break down in front of him and that was a promise to herself that was getting more difficult to keep by the minute.

'I think my mother may have come to meet me,' Naomi said. 'Can your car drop me off at Arrivals?'

Sev didn't like that idea. He had thought he would be taking her home but instead his driver took them the relatively short distance to Arrivals.

'Leave your bags,' Sev said. 'Go and find your mother and then I can take you both home.'

'There's no need,' Naomi said. 'We can make our own way home.'

'No, my driver—'

'My mother has a car,' Naomi interrupted. 'We're hardly going to travel in separate vehicles.'

So this was it.

They stood as a trolley was loaded with her things, shivering in the damp morning air, and though Sev knew he was doing the right thing by her—that she would be far better off without him—it was harder than it had ever been to say goodbye to another person.

Usually his PAs left and, as long as he had another in place, he had given it little thought.

It was the same with lovers.

There was always another.

Family.

Ah, don't go there.

Friends.

Sev watched as the last bag was loaded onto the trolley.

Friends were the reason he was here in London, no doubt to sit waiting and to be let down all over again.

She turned and looked at Sev, the most beautiful man in the world, who had made love to her like he adored her. A man who had taken her heart and pocketed it like a piece of loose change.

'Thanks for everything, Sev.' She was able to look him in the eye. 'If Emmanuel needs any information—'

'I'll call you if there are any issues,' Sev interrupted.

'Please, don't,' Naomi responded. She didn't want to hear that voice pulling her back under his spell again. 'Emmanuel can email me. Anyway...' she took out her phone from her pocket '...this is yours.'

He had switched her over to a work phone on the day that she had started.

'Keep it,' Sev said, because it was far more than a work phone that she was handing back, it was a safety net should he change his mind, a line of communication she was severing.

'I don't need it,' Naomi said.

She didn't.

The very last thing she needed as she moved on with the next stage of her life was a phone that might ring, a text that might bleep. Oh, her heart would soar, Naomi knew, and it would no doubt be him, asking where some file was, or had she responded to…?

Or…

She looked into his eyes and she had no doubt, no doubt at all, that he might be cruel enough to call her deep into a long night, to toy with her heart just because he was bored.

'Here.' When he didn't take it she popped it into his top suit pocket and he just stood there.

'I've got your private number,' Sev warned.

'I'm changing it,' Naomi said.

It was the very first thing she would do.

And she would only open emails that came from Emmanuel.

Screw you for letting me leave, she wanted to shout, but didn't.

'What will you do?' Sev asked.

'Do?' Naomi frowned. 'I'll get back to the real world.'

One without castles in the sky.

One without a morning being made love to at sunrise followed by a cold grey goodbye.

He went into his coat and pulled out a slim package and handed it to her. 'Your leaving present.'

He just hurt her again and again.

Naomi didn't want a leaving present; she wanted him.

'I'm going to miss you,' Sev said.

'Not that much,' Naomi replied.

After all, he was letting her leave.

Her trolley was one of those that moved to the left and Naomi steered it badly, wishing that the automatic door would open more quickly, instead of leaving her standing a few seconds too long.

A terrible few seconds because she did turn around, just in time to see his car sliding off.

No lingering stare, nothing.
Sev had got back into his car and got on with his life.
Now it was time for her to do the same.

CHAPTER SIXTEEN

HE WOULD MISS her *that* much.

So much that, even if today could never be an easy one, it could be less unbearable.

'Pull in here,' Sev said to his driver.

He was trying to dissuade himself from going after her. The kindest thing would surely be to let her get back to her life, rather than hazard her with his first adult attempt at a relationship.

His phone buzzed and, rather than get out of the car, he checked it.

And then hope came back to his heart.

There was his niece, Mariya, smiling into the camera and showing off the pink earrings that he had bought for her eighteenth birthday. There was message beneath.

I told Ma that the earrings were from Zena, my friend at school. She thinks they are cheap and so I can keep them. Thank you Uncle Sevastyan.
I love them very much.
I love you too.
Mariya

The words were followed by two pink hearts, and for all that was wrong in the world there was still something right.

Every year he had sent his niece a gift but this year he had sent two.

One to her home.

The other, the earrings, to her school.

He cared not if they had been lost.

He cared a lot more that they had been found.

If he could just get through today... Sev thought.

If he could explain to Naomi the disappointment of Daniil not showing up and the black memories of this day...

Sev doubted he could, not today.

But something inside him doubted she would mind.

Was that love?

Where you wait with patience, where you hold on till the other is ready?

Maybe it was time to find out.

Arrivals at Heathrow was hell. It was all families and happy couples and tender reunions. Had she had her phone on her then Naomi would have texted her mother to see if she was here and ask her to meet her outside. But Naomi's old phone was in her case.

So she stood, scanning the crowd, deciding that her mother hadn't got her message, or, if she had, that she'd decided not to come.

Yes, it was a lonely morning and as she turned to head off, tears in her eyes, Naomi hit a solid wall, one her heart recognised because the tears she had held back started to fall as she was held in his arms.

'Too much,' Sev said. 'I will miss you too much if I let you go back now.'

He kissed her and she hated herself for kissing him back. It was a sizzling, passionate kiss, one where he moved her from the crowds and Naomi found herself pressed to a wall and she could almost taste the blood from the bruise of Sev's mouth.

He offered her nothing, an extension perhaps, and she loathed herself that she would take his crumbs.

But she would.

And she loathed herself that on a freezing morning he pulled her into his coat and he was hot and hard for her, and for all the pain of goodbyes to come she still wanted him.

He wanted away from the crowds, he wanted sex and then maybe to talk. And she wanted him—that trip in her that he recognised on sight, that shift where her body turned over to him was there.

'Airport hotel?' Sev asked.

'You are *such* a bastard!' She laughed, she cried, she was about to say yes.

'What the...?' Sev started, but he never got to finish. Instead he was literally hauled out of her arms and swung around.

All Naomi said was a flash of red and then a fist and then the sight of Sev flying back against the wall where she stood, but like being against the ropes in a boxing ring he propelled himself outwards.

'No one else?' a man shouted, and her mind was still spinning from the kiss and its rude interruption, but then she saw who it was.

'Andrew?' Naomi looked up and saw red foil heart balloons floating up to the roof and realised he must have come to meet her.

And so too did Sev.

He had come out fighting and, given the life he had led, that he would floor this guy was a foregone conclusion.

But then he heard who it was.

The next fist to his gut he took.

But then, when Naomi tried to come between them, shouting to Andrew that he had no right and Andrew responded with words Naomi did not deserve, Sev saw red—only they weren't heart-shaped balloons.

Sev went to floor him but four strong arms were holding him back—Security had arrived and, looking around at the stunned travellers, Sev tried to keep his breathing even, telling himself to calm down, that an airport, and being sober at that, was no place to fight. He was also telling himself that had Naomi been his fiancée, he'd have been just as furious as this guy was.

'I'm fine,' Sev said to Security.

'You're sure about that?' one responded.

'Sure.'

'Because—' It was the security guard who didn't get to finish their sentence this time because, unlike Sev, Andrew was unrestrained and still angry as he took his cowardly chance.

Naomi let out a scream as Sev's head was violently hit and knocked backwards.

The security moved quickly to restrain Andrew, leaving Sev to fall to the floor, and her quiet homecoming disappeared in a blur of police and then paramedics.

'No need...' Sev slurred, when they insisted on taking him to the hospital.

'There is, Sev,' Naomi said. 'You were knocked out.'

'For how long?' one of the paramedics asked.

'Three minutes.'

They had been the longest three minutes of Naomi's life.

She hadn't looked up, she hadn't cared that Andrew was being arrested—all she'd been able to think of was Sev.

Which wasn't a first—for the past four months almost all she had been able to think of was him.

Who was she kidding? Naomi thought as she got into the ambulance he had been stretchered into and the doors were closed.

As if a brave goodbye could change anything.

Her heart belonged to him.

Even if she was terrified and terribly worried it became apparent, about ten seconds into their arrival, that Sev, though terribly vital to her, was rather way down on the list of priorities.

The triage nurse checked him and Naomi wished she had a little triage desk in her heart.

She did have one.

On the day they had met it had spoken to her and strongly suggested that this man was trouble, that if she let him in, even a little way, she'd surely regret it.

Only she didn't.

'What the hell is this place?' Sev asked an hour or so later, when he was dressed in a gown and had come to better but was still groggy and growing increasingly irritable, which the nurse said wasn't a good sign.

He'd been irritable for a few days, Naomi wanted to point out.

'Why didn't you get them to take me somewhere private?' Sev demanded.

'The paramedics don't care if you're a billionaire,' Naomi said. 'They took you to the nearest hospital.'

'And now we'll be here for the next fortnight, waiting to be seen. I don't need hospital.'

'You need to be stitched.'

There was a huge gash over his left eye and it had closed over. He kept going to sleep, only to wake up angrier every time he woke up and demanding to know the time.

'It's eleven a.m.,' the nurse said. 'You're just waiting to go around for an MRI.'

'I don't need an MRI.'

'You're drowsy.'

'Because I haven't slept since…' Sev looked up at the peeling ceiling and he recognised it well, or rather he recognised that type of ceiling and he remembered Nikolai and that he had to meet Daniil.

'Where's my phone?'

'Here,' Naomi said. She had picked it up when he'd dropped it in the fight but as she handed it over it turned on and Naomi let out a shocked gasp.

There were the earrings he had bought from Tiffany's but the girl who was wearing them was in school uniform.

'Hell, Sev,' Naomi shouted. 'When you said she was young…!'

'It's my niece, Mariya,' Sev said. 'I got them for her eighteenth birthday.'

'Oh.'

And Naomi sat back on the plastic seat, as Sev lay squinting into his phone.

'Last year I sent a necklace and it was sold online by Renata. I don't know if Mariya even saw the necklace so I sent these to her school.'

Naomi sat there, thinking. It was a very smart uniform that Mariya was wearing.

Private-school smart.

And, no, she could live for a hundred years and not fully know him.

Yet she was starting to work him out.

'You sent that money, didn't you.'

'Sorry?'

'The money for Mariya's treatment.'

'Of course I did.'

'Why?' Naomi asked. 'Why would you do that when knew you were being scammed?'

'As I told Renata, she would have had the money anyway. I always wanted my niece to have a good education and for my sister to have nice things.'

Then he corrected himself.

'Half-sister. She has the money but we don't talk any more.'

Now Sev's body demanded sleep again but there was somewhere he needed to be.

'Naomi, I need to get to Buckingham Palace...'

'It will still be there tomorrow,' the nurse said as she checked his blood pressure.

'But I have to be there at midday.'

Naomi was starting to seriously worry about his head injury now—there was no place that Sev ever *needed* to be. This was a man who could arrive eight hours late for a meeting with a sheikh without making so much as an apology.

He never got upset or agitated and yet he clearly was now.

'Sev, you have to have this scan.'

'I don't have to do anything, apart from get there.'

''What's so important that it can't wait?'

'It doesn't matter.'

Sev lay there and decided that as soon as the nurse and Naomi left he would disappear.

'Can you go and get me a drink?' He turned to Naomi.

'We're keeping you nil by mouth for now,' the cheerful nurse said, and then left them.

'I'm sorry,' Naomi said, and he gritted his teeth as she went to apologise for her ex-fiancé.

'Don't start apologising,' Sev said. 'I thought I'd got that far with you at least. It isn't your fault if your fiancé—'

'My ex.'

'What?'

'I dumped him.'

'Er...when?'

'The night before I resigned.'

'And you didn't think to tell me? I let him hit me...'

'I know you did.'

And then he put Andrew in the file he had first assigned him to—irrelevant.

'I need to be somewhere, Naomi.'

'You can't leave yet.'

He bloody well could. Sev sat up and Naomi decided there was nothing sadder than seeing someone so strong and determined rendered incapable.

He squinted at the drip and that clever brain was foggy as he tried to work out how to get it down, and then he looked at the curtain that separated them from the world.

'Where's my wallet?'

'In the safe.' The cheery nurse was back. 'So I suggest you lie there.'

She had never seen such defeat on someone's face.

And then she watched as he came up with a solution and those grey eyes turned to her.

'Can you go there for me?'

'To Buckingham Palace?' Naomi frowned. 'Sev, I think you might be a bit confused.'

'I've never been less confused,' Sev said. 'I go there each year and I cannot miss being there.'

'Why?'

'In case Daniil shows up. I wrote to him a few years ago and asked him to meet me at midday on November the twelfth and he never showed.'

'You think he might now?'

'No,' Sev admitted. 'I just don't want to miss out on the slim chance he might.'

'Okay,' Naomi said. 'What does he look like?'

'I haven't seen him since he was twelve. Black hair, tall…'

It wasn't an awful lot to go on.

'He's Russian,' Sev added.

'I'd worked that one out.' Naomi said. She could feel herself being dragged back into the vortex. A couple of hours ago he had been willing to take her to the airport hotel, Naomi reminded herself.

She deserved more than that.

'I'll do this, Sev, and then I'll come back and let you know what happened, but then I'm going home.'

And so she sat in the rain by the fountain and watched the world go by.

She was so angry with Andrew, so angry with Sev too, for prolonging the agony.

They should be over with by now.

She should be unpacking her case, instead of sitting on the ledge of a cold stone statue.

It was hopeless.

There were a few tourists, all huddled under their umbrellas, and some people walking around. How the hell was she supposed to pick out a man with black hair from the hundred or so other men with black hair? She saw a blonde woman smiling brightly, clapping her hands, and she had that sort of determined look that the rain didn't matter and that she was here for the duration.

So too, it would seem, was Naomi.

It was after one when she finally gave in.

There was no one—no one at all.

She gave a thin smile to the blonde woman, who was looking around too, and then Naomi watched as she went over to a man.

A moody-looking resigned man who shrugged and started to walk off, but the woman argued with him, pulled at his coat.

And, yes, he was tall and had black hair and so Naomi made her way over.

'Daniil?'

She could look the biggest fool ever here, Naomi knew. 'Daniil?'

'I told you!' The blonde woman exclaimed. 'Sevastyan?'

'Well, if it is, then you've got a lot better looking,' Daniil said. Naomi started to laugh as they were all so stunned and sort of staring at each other, not really knowing what to do.

'I'm Sev's PA. He wanted to be here—'

'I am here.'

Naomi turned and there was Sev, as white as putty but stitched, and she watched as the two men shook hands.

No, it wasn't a tender reunion. Maybe Sev just didn't go for that type of thing.

They spoke in Russian with guarded voices and Naomi looked at the other woman.

'I'm Libby.' She smiled, rubbing her hands together from the cold.

Naomi saw her rings. 'You're Daniil's wife?'

'Yes!' Libby nodded. 'It feels strange, saying that. We just got married yesterday.'

'Congratulations,' Naomi offered, and then she looked back at the two men and she would never understand Sev because he concluded the conversation and walked back over to them.

'It's good to meet you, Libby,' he said. 'Congratulations on your marriage.'

'Thank you.'

'It's good to be back in touch with Daniil but right now you two need to get on with your honeymoon and I need to get to the hotel.' He looked at Naomi. 'Come on, we ought to go.'

He shook hands again with Daniil.

Was that it?' Naomi pondered as Daniil and Libby walked off. All those years together and then all those years apart and yet they'd chatted for all of ten minutes.

That was who Sev was, though, Naomi realised, cold and dismissive.

It was she who had refused to accept that.

'You have to watch me,' Sev said, and handed her a head-injury leaflet. 'They wanted to keep me in and only let me go on the proviso that I'm checked every hour until morning.'

'Get a nurse, then.'

'No, I don't want some stranger watching me sleep. If I did, I'd have stayed in the hospital.'

'Well, tough, I don't work for you any more.'

'Fine.' He hailed a cab and climbed in.

And he would, he bloody well would, Naomi thought, he'd just go and sleep alone.

'One night,' Naomi said, getting into the taxi. Looking at his grey complexion, Sev wasn't asking her there to seduce her.

That much she knew.

Naomi dealt with check-in and when they got to his suite Sev didn't even fully undress, he just kicked off his shoes and socks and then went to deposit his hospital bag with his wallet and things in the safe.

'What's my code?' Sev asked.

'I'll do it,' Naomi said.

'I can manage,' Sev said, and punched in the numbers. Once done, he went and lay on the bed and Naomi closed the drapes and just sat.

'How was he?' she asked. 'Your friend?'

Sev shrugged.

'He asked me what had happened with Roman,' Sev said. 'I told him that I don't know anything. I got a scholarship at fifteen and left then.'

'What about the other one, Nikolai?' Naomi asked. 'Did he know?'

'What? That he had died?' Sev easily said what she had struggled to voice. 'Daniil had already found that out—apparently he was being abused.' There was no emotion Sev's voice, just the exhaustion of a very cruel life. 'I didn't know that.'

'I'm sorry.'

'I let him down,' Sev admitted. 'He was crying one night and I didn't know if he'd want me to say anything. The dormitory was not very private at the best of times. So I let it go, pretended I hadn't noticed. Then he cried again and I asked him what was wrong. And he told me to leave it. I did. The next day he'd run away. They found him a week later, and his bag with this ship he'd made by the river.'

'The one on your desk at home?'

'Yep. It's not much to show for a life,' Sev said, slowly drifting off into an exhausted sleep.

Naomi woke him every hour, just enough to be sure that he was okay, but by 7:00 p.m. she was exhausted too and she watched as he woke up.

Sev tried to guess the time.

Then the month and year.

And then he tried to work out their location.

'You're in London.' Naomi said.

'So I am.'

And he remembered again that before such a violent interruption they had been heading to the airport hotel...

'Come to bed.'

'No, thank you.' Naomi said. 'I'm supposed to watch you till morning, according to the leaflet, and then I'm going to go.'

'Where?'

'Home,' Naomi said. 'Well, to my mum's for a couple of weeks and then I'll find somewhere...'

Somewhere.

It was a horrible word at times.

Somewhere to get over you.

'My head hurts,' Sev said.

'You're due for some painkillers.'

'Not that head.'

She didn't want to laugh but that was the problem—he could turn her smile on even when her heart was in shreds.

'Come to bed,' Sev said. 'God, the day I've had, I need a shag.'

'Well, seeing as you put it so nicely.'

He had the nerve to ignore her sarcastic response and pulled the covers back.

'Not a chance.' Naomi turned and looked at him and his lazy heart that had let her leave. 'If Andrew hadn't hit you, we'd be over with now.'

'Wind back,' Sev said, as if she was some bloody computer. 'I'd suggested that we go to the airport hotel.'

'You're *so* romantic.'

'No, I'm not.'

'I'm going to order dinner,' Naomi said. 'Do you want anything?'

He didn't.

As Naomi went into her bag to get the tip ready she saw her leaving present. She would wait till he was asleep to open it.

There was a knock on the door and in came her dinner.

'Good,' Sev said, and sat up. 'I'm starving.' And he saw her blow out an angry breath and then wheel the silver trolley over to him. 'I was joking,' Sev said. 'Enjoy your meal. I'll have a glass of champagne, though...'

'You can't drink with a head injury,' Naomi said. 'According to the leaflet.'

'That's not very nice of you.'

'I never said I'd be a nice nurse.'

She ate the most delicious steak ever, with truffle butter, and she drank champagne and watched his wry smile as he heard her top up her glass.

'You are a cruel tease.'

'I know,' Naomi said.

'Go into my jacket,' Sev said. 'Daniil gave me a copy of a picture.'

She went to his jacket and sat down to look at a photo of four young boys from a lifetime ago.

'Daniil's an identical twin.'

'Yep.'

How cruel, Naomi thought. It had been bad enough knowing that twins had been split up, but that they were identical made it seem somehow worse.

'He can't find Roman. From what Daniil has been able to find out, it would seem that he shacked up with Anya for a while after he left the orphanage and then left—'

'Anya?'

'The cook's daughter. Daniil said that she's a famous ballerina now.'

Naomi looked back at the picture and at Nikolai. Well, it had to be him because other boy was Sev.

'You were a nerd.'

'I was,' Sev said. 'I am.'

The sexiest nerd in the world, though.

CHAPTER SEVENTEEN

SEV FINALLY WENT to sleep and Naomi put the tray outside the door and then, when that didn't wake him, she took out her present and quietly opened it.

His book?

Why?

It was old and tattered and the one that he always read on take-off.

She'd made a joke once about what a slow reader he was. That had been in Mali and that had been when he'd put down the book and, er, suggested that she might need a little lie-down under him.

'Or on top.' Sev had grinned. 'I'm generous like that.'

It had been the most direct offer of sex she had ever had.

Hell, she'd been tempted but had told him off and Sev had got back to his book.

She opened it and frowned. It was all in Russian but as she turned the pages she saw some pictures, just black-and-white ones but it took just a few moments of looking to realise it was a book of fairy tales.

He'd read them to his friends, he had told her that.

She saw a photo of a wolf that had a woman draped over it and she looked at this beautiful, complex man, who was glib and dismissive and yet sat reading old fairy tales on take-off.

A man who said he didn't want relationships yet had spent five years standing outside a palace in the hope of finding a friend.

And she saw it then. Pain. Not the pain of his head injury, she was sure, just the agony of so many losses that were etched on his face.

And she understood a little more how hard today must have been. No, there could be no effusive greeting after so much hurt.

And she knew why the men had stood back from each other, how they'd had to stay distant to stay standing.

Who could blame him for 'needing a shag', as he'd so nicely put it today?

And who could blame her for wanting him?

Naomi put the book beside the bed, undressed and got in.

She was, Sev thought, like a pillow, but better than, and he rolled into her.

'You're a nice surprise,' Sev said, and ran a hand along her body and felt her naked. 'That's an even nicer surprise.'

He just breathed her in.

'Both heads hurt,' Sev said.

She hadn't expected a gymnastic event as they shared a kiss, a long slow one, but face-to-face sex was something she couldn't deal with again. Not the sort where you looked at each other and your eyes made promises that by daylight you could not keep.

So she went down on him but on the way she took in those Merlot-coloured nipples and that flat stomach that had always tempted her.

And so to her favourite part and she took her time because it must be the last time.

He stroked her as lazily as if he were stroking a cat and turned her on just as easily as he always did.

There was little noise, just the sounds they made and that moan he gave that signalled the end, and he spread his fingers inside her and stretched her as he came.

It hurt, but it was amazing to come to his palm as she swallowed him down, and then he pulled her up to lie with him.

'I'll return the favour tomorrow,' Sev said.

Favour?

He made her too angry to sleep at times.

A favour.

An itch.

That was all it was to him.

As Sev dozed she took down the book from the shelf and started not to read it, it was in Russian after all, but to turn the pages.

'Remember your interview when you said you'd read in bed?' Sev asked sleepily.

'Ha-ha...'

'What are you reading?'

'My present,' Naomi answered. 'Sev, why would you give this to me?'

'Because you still believe in them.'

'And you don't?'

'The dark bits,' Sev said. 'I don't know what I believe today. It's a bad day.'

'How can it be a bad day when you're back in touch with your friend?' Naomi asked.

'Because today is Nikolai's anniversary, or rather it is the day when we found out he was missing. Yes, I saw Daniil and one day, tomorrow maybe, we will be so glad to be in touch, but for today, I know, he misses his twin and that he wishes it could be me...'

'No.'

'Yes,' Sev said, 'because today I wished it was Nikolai that I stood and spoke with. To apologise, to go back...'

'To what?'

'He cried that night. I can't remember him crying before that, not once. I can't remember any of us crying. And when I heard him I just didn't know what to say. I didn't know if he'd be embarrassed. I thought we could talk on kitchen duty the next morning and then I couldn't ignore it and so I asked what was wrong and he said to leave it. I did. I left it be. The next morning he was gone. Naomi, I rolled over and I was all he had and yet I rolled over and went to sleep.'

'Like this?' Naomi said, and she closed her eyes.

'Don't joke,' he warned.

'Oh, I'm not joking. You just said you lay there thinking how embarrassed he might be that you could hear him, that you couldn't remember any of you crying...so were you thinking those things when you *let it be*? Or did you roll over and try to work out what the hell to do?'

'I was going to talk to him on kitchen duty. I should have handled it differently.'

'Who knows?' Naomi said. 'Maybe he wanted to just cry and not have the whole dormitory wake up. Were Daniil and Roman there?'

'No,' Sev said. 'Daniil had been adopted by then and Roman had been moved to another area. I told you,' Sev said, 'I'm crap at emotion.'

'Not really,' Naomi said. 'When I was upset on the plane you were very lovely to me. You told me stuff you didn't want to.' She thought for a moment. 'The night of my father's party, when I was upset, you came to see what was wrong.'

'And made things a whole lot worse between us.'

'Oh, I think that might have been me.' Naomi smiled.

They just lay there and it was Naomi who rolled over as she had never felt more tired.

'Go to sleep.'

'I'm supposed to check you every hour.'

'Go to sleep,' Sev said. 'I'll set the alarm.'

Yet he knew he didn't need to. If something happened she was there, half awake, half asleep, as he had been that night.

Naomi was right.

Sev had lain awake for hours, trying to think of how to best broach things with Nikolai the next day.

And, whether he'd handled that night badly, at the very least he had learned from it.

Sev would not leave her alone and crying.

He hadn't, in fact.

CHAPTER EIGHTEEN

'WHAT TIME IS IT?' Sev asked.

Naomi opened her eyes to the familiar question from him and glanced at the bedside clock.

'Six,' she said and then added, 'A.m.'

Just in case.

But she wasn't paid to be his speaking clock any more, and so she made herself do it.

Made herself sit up and get out of his bed.

She went and had a shower.

She didn't want him.

Oh, she loved him, she was crazy about him, but she didn't want him.

It was the biggest revelation of her life.

No longer did she want someone who so clearly didn't want her. Or, if he did, then he wanted her just a bit and she wasn't prepared for his crumbs. For sex when he felt like it, for conversation when it suited him.

It wasn't just Sev she was saying goodbye to but a lifetime spent waiting for the cavalry to arrive for her.

It just had.

It was her.

'What are you doing?' Sev asked, as she got dressed.

'I watched you last night.' Naomi said. 'That was what we agreed to.'

'You did a bit more than watch me,' Sev said. 'Do you sleep with all your patients, nurse?'

And she laughed.

He would always make her laugh, even with a broken heart.

'I am going,' Naomi said.

'Why would you leave when things are just getting interesting?'

'They got interesting for me a few months ago, Sev. I'm not waiting around for you to decide how much I mean to you, or if you might keep me around a while longer. I'm not tiptoeing around waiting for you to change your mind one day, or not.'

He had never been more proud of another person.

Never.

And, Sev knew, because he'd been thinking all night, that this he could now do.

November had always been his most hated month.

Her leaving would make it hell for ever.

'Could you get something from the safe?' Sev asked.

'Get it yourself.'

'I'm sick,' Sev said, and tapped his closed eye and the mess her ex-fiancé had made of his face. 'Do you think I'll scar?'

She picked up her case but he had pushed her guilt switch so Naomi did stop at the safe on the way out.

'You're not very good at your alphabet, are you?' he commented.

She was in no mood for his games.

'N is the fourteenth letter,' Sev said, just as she went to key in one, four.

And A was the first, Naomi knew as she typed in one.

'You're my secret code,' Sev said. 'You're the key that opens the door.'

'What are you doing, Sev?'

He had changed his code a few weeks ago…

'In Helsinki,' Sev answered her thoughts. 'I've been crazy about you since then.'

'Why didn't you tell me?'

'I tried,' Sev said. 'I told you then I was cured of blondes.'

'And so you took yourself off to Italy!' Naomi snarled.

She had been so jealous of Miss Roma but, then again, maybe that was more because she had thought the earrings were for her.

And then she had to smile.

'Mali,' Sev reminded her. 'I wanted you then.'

'You have the worst chat-up lines.'

'They usually work just fine.'

Yes, Naomi conceded, they probably worked just fine when it was only sex you wanted.

She wanted more.

"What's in the safe, Naomi?"

There was a black velvet pouch.

Real velvet, and she was nervous about opening it because she could not stand for hope to be dashed again.

She opened the pouch and into her palm fell the most exquisite piece of jewellery she had ever seen, but she quickly looked away.

'I bought this for you in Dubai. I was going to tell you to dump that loser and then I decided against it.'

'You regretted buying it…'

'We are so going to work on your self-confidence,' Sev warned. 'No, I felt I had no right to be moving on with my life near the anniversary of my friend's death. Neither was I sure I could make you happy. I'm very sure I can now.'

He always had.

Despite the heartbreak of loving him, Sev had always made her smile.

'Marry me.'

'Sev!' He didn't have to go that far!

'Naomi Derzhavin.'

'Sev, please don't joke.'

'I've never been more serious in my life,' Sev said. 'Come here.'

She walked over in her coat and sat on the edge of the bed.

'I want you to be my family,' Sev said. 'I want us to make each other happy and we do. I want my book by our bed…' She looked at the ring. 'I know I need to open up and I'll try.'

Naomi looked into the eyes of a man who didn't need to change,

Well, maybe a bit.

But he could be as depraved as he liked just as long as it was with her.

'It's a very rare, natural black diamond,' Sev said, and now she let herself look. In the intricate setting there were also white diamonds. 'The metal is platinum with rhodium plate,' Sev explained. 'I chose rhodium for its rarity and strength but it's not very malleable…' Naomi smothered a smile—he'd be taking her through the periodic table soon.

Sev looked at the ring.

There was no doubt as to its beauty.

No doubt as to its recipient.

His doubt had been in him.

Not now.

'Do you know why I chose black?' Sev said.

Of course Naomi did. 'Because it's my favourite colour.'

'At first,' he said, 'but there were a few to choose from and then I found out this stone's name—Unseen Star. You might be an unseen star for some but never by me.'

'You *are* romantic.'

'I'll try to be,' Sev said. 'But I'm a bastard too—I think we can both safely agree that this blows Andrew's ring out of the water.'

'It does.' Naomi smiled.

He put it on and, honestly, it was amazing.

She had never cared for jewellery much but any woman would love this ring.

Especially when given by him.

'It was supposed to go well with that silver dress that you had on the other night.'

And Naomi remembered Jamal insisting that it was perfect when Naomi hadn't been sure. 'Jamal and Allem knew?' She frowned. 'Even about the ring?'

'Naomi,' Sev said, 'I asked Allem for advice...'

He did love her.

She knew it for sure then.

'I listened to Allem but it wasn't me. I needed to do this myself and I needed to get certain dates out of the way before I got to be happy.'

They shared a lovely kiss.

Sev naked, she in her coat, but not for very long as he was already slipping it off. 'You can't say no to me. Jamal and Allem have already got us an engagement present.'

'Was that what was wrong with them the other night?' Oh, she understood now! 'I thought they were a bit off.'

'You were supposed to arrive wearing the ring! Allem had said I should take you up on a balloon and propose. Naomi, can you really see me coming up with that?' Sev asked. 'Me?'

'No!' She couldn't and she was actually glad of that. 'I didn't want to go up in a balloon either.'

'See how suited we are.'

'Do you want to know what our present is?' Sev asked. 'It's a rug. And, by amazing coincidence, when Allem sent me a photo of it, I saw that it goes with my curtains. How lucky is that?'

She was as red in the face as when first he'd met her but she was laughing now.

'You are tragic, Naomi.'

'I know!'

'One piece of housekeeping,' Sev said, before he slipped the ring on her finger. 'If you ever flirt with another man when you're wearing this, the way you flirted with me—'

'Er...Sev,' Naomi interrupted. 'If we look back over the last few months, I think my behaviour is the pale one and that was fake and this isn't. And,' she added, 'I didn't flirt with you.' She'd always been holding back. 'You haven't seen me flirting.'

'Yet,' Sev said.

He couldn't wait.

Finally November felt better.

The world felt better for both for them.

EPILOGUE

'You look beautiful, Naomi,' Anderson said.

She had her father's approval.

Naomi just didn't need it now.

For six months she had had Sev's love and that made her stronger and the world all a touch clearer.

Together they had decided on London for the wedding. That was her home and, even if she wasn't particularly close to her mother, Naomi had felt a New York wedding might seem a snub.

It also meant Daniil could be there as his wife, Libby, was heavily pregnant.

Sev and Daniil were in regular touch now and slowly the past was being uncovered, which was painful at times but something both men felt they had to do.

In the six months since their engagement, Anderson Anderson had courted Sev—taking him along to his golf club and proudly introducing his future son-in-law, and for her, Naomi knew, Sev had gone along with it.

Sev did things for her that she never could have expected. He made her happier than she had ever thought she could be and so, today she was doing something for him.

Something that was also for her.

Anderson had brought Judy and Naomi's little sisters

to London. Kennedy was her bridesmaid but the others were all there in the church. Now Naomi stood in a hotel room and she knew that her father, who had never hopped on a plane for her, was here only because of Sevastyan and the contacts that name would gather when dropped.

It was father-and-daughter time.

Kennedy was safely in the car with Naomi's other bridesmaid, a friend who, unlike her father, had been there since schooldays.

'We'll have another celebration when we get home,' Anderson said. 'Judy's family and our friends and colleagues—'

'No,' Naomi interrupted. 'I doubt there will be another celebration. If there is then it will be a quiet affair.' She took a breath and looked her father straight in the eye. 'And I won't tell you about it. I'll forget to invite you, just as you did to me on your fiftieth birthday party.'

Anderson had the decency at least to look uncomfortable.

'It was a surprise party,' he attempted.

'I don't think so.' Naomi shook her head. 'And even if it was supposed to be a surprise, why wouldn't Judy invite me? It wasn't as if she didn't have the opportunity— I was there that week, babysitting for you. Anyway, I thought it was your second wife who had an issue with me, or that was the excuse you gave.'

'Let's not do this on your wedding day,' Anderson suggested. 'I don't want you upsetting yourself.'

'I'm not upset, though,' Naomi said. 'I was then. I came to bring you a cake and you were having a party with the people who meant something to you.'

'Come on, Naomi. Not today.'

'Yes, today,' Naomi said. She stood in her wedding dress and was far from the blushing bride. 'You gave me

away a long time ago,' Naomi said. 'There's no need for
you to do it again today.'

'It will look—'

'Yes,' she interrupted, 'it will look a bit odd if you go
to the church now and sit with your wife and my sisters,
but that's what you're going to do. You're a guest at my
wedding, that's all you are to me. But I do love my sisters and so, for appearances' sake, I'll be polite to you,
but never, ever pretend that you love or care for me...'

'I do,' Anderson said, and he meant it. 'Now that I've
got to know you.'

'Well, your timing's crap,' Naomi said. 'It's going to
take a very long time to convince me. For now, I'll see
you at the church.'

Sevastyan stood in the church next to Daniil.

'Nervous?' Daniil said.

'I'm curious to see the dress,' Sev said.

He doubted if she'd wear black, even if was her favourite colour. His bet was on brown, the colour of faded
roses and the colour of her eyes.

He turned and saw Anderson Anderson coming up
the aisle and taking a seat by Judy.

'God, I love that woman,' Sev said, as he realised
Naomi had sent her father away.

He looked at his side of the church and saw a very
pregnant Libby sitting with Rachel, her friend.

Anya had taken time off from the ballet she was pre-
forming in and gave him a smile, which Sev returned.

Mariya was here, wearing the earrings he had bought
for her, and her mother, Renata, was here too.

He smiled at Mariya, but not her mother. Sev just offered a nod of acknowledgement to her.

It still hurt but it hurt less and less.

And there too was Allem with Jamal, who had flown in from Dubai with their newborn just to share in this day.

That meant a lot.

Emmanuel was here.

But then again, Emmanuel had been everywhere—ensuring the wedding was perfect. God, was that guy efficient. He should have hired him years ago, Sev thought.

But then he'd never have met Naomi.

Sev had never thought that he'd be marrying in a church, let alone with people he cared for on the groom's side.

No, he wasn't nervous, at least not until he heard Daniil's always calm voice suddenly shocked.

'Bozhe moi!'

Oh, my God!

Sev looked towards the back of the church and saw a face he would recognise for ever, no matter his age, and watched a man trying to slip quietly into the back pew.

'Nikolai!'

Tradition forgotten, Sev simply left the altar and, along with Daniil they walked swiftly towards the friend they had thought lost for ever.

'You drowned...'

'No.' Nikolai shook his head.

'I don't understand...'

'Not now,' Nikolai said. 'Later. Today is about your wedding.' The music changed and people stood but Sev stood there, still stunned.

'I thought...' He had always thought it was his fault. That had he turned around that night, his friend might have changed his mind. It was too early to sink in that Nikolai was here in the flesh but finally he had the chance to apologise. 'I'm sorry I ignored you that night. I should have asked more...'

'*Nyet,*' Nikolai said. 'You have nothing to be sorry for. Go and get married.'

Naomi stood at the entrance to the church and saw that two had finally become three. Daniil must have found Roman, she thought as Sev looked over.

Yes, Sev knew that he should get back into his place but he wanted to share the news with Naomi and so, as Daniil led Nikolai to sit with his wife at the front, Sev walked over to his future wife.

'Nikolai is here.'

'Nikolai?' Naomi frowned. 'But I thought…'

And she looked at a man some considered had little emotion and saw tears of gratitude in his eyes, and knew she could put anyone who thought that right.

'I'm so happy for you,' Naomi said. 'How do you feel?'

'Relieved,' Sev admitted, and then he looked at Naomi properly.

Nikolai's presence was an extra gift,

Sev trusted himself even more now.

'You look…' He just held her hands and looked down.

Her dark hair was tied back as it had been on the day they'd met and the dress was white. It fitted like a glove and showed off her creamy bust, and she held a huge bunch of white roses.

They meant something now.

And these very flowers would one day lie faded between the pages of a book and she would cherish them for ever.

He smiled because, yes, white was for weddings and white really showed off those unseen stars.

The ring and Naomi.

And then she smiled, and showed him that she could indeed flirt because that smile told him they would be playing virgins tonight.

Sev then kissed the bride.

A thorough kiss that was so loaded with passion and promise that she almost dropped the bouquet.

'Dearly beloved....' the vicar said, and then coughed.

They stopped and only then did they remember where they were.

'Let's go and get married,' Sev said.

Naomi did not walk down the aisle alone, she walked hand in hand with Sev, both smiling.

Their vows were beautiful and heartfelt and again Sev got to kiss the bride.

At a more appropriate time.

Back at the hotel as husband and wife, her father toasted the bride and groom.

Naomi was very pleased she'd found the nerve to say what she had to Anderson when she saw her father checking his phone as Sev gave his response and toasted the bridesmaids.

Then Daniil gave his speech.

He thanked everyone and said all the right things, and then he thanked those who had come from afar and those that were not here, and then Daniil got to a part that had Naomi's heart rise in her throat.

'Sev looked out for all of us. He would try to halt an argument or tell us when to pull back. He would also read to us,' Daniil said. 'Remember, Sev? Sometimes it was a book on cooking that he had found, or gardening. One time a carer had left a sexy book...' And they all started to laugh as Daniil explained how the boys had kept getting him to read it again.

'And then there were fairy tales,' Daniil continued. 'We used to laugh at them—a black laughter, but we all hoped, I think.'

Naomi remembered what Sev had told her on the flight when he had admitted he had lied about not wanting a family. Her hand went into his as Daniil admitted he had felt the same.

'Who would have thought…?' Daniil started, but then halted, and as Naomi looked up she knew why. There could only be one reason that Libby was walking out during her husband's speech at a wedding.

Daniil's new family was about to get bigger.

Oh, there were so many happy endings today.

'Wrap it up, Daniil,' Sev suggested, given that there was somewhere else his friend needed to be.

'Naomi and Sevastyan!'

That was all that was needed to be said tonight.

Naomi had never thought that she could be so happy—dancing with Sev and surrounded by people she loved.

There were also the people she cared about but didn't necessarily love, but only because they had not loved her.

Sev did.

He told her so every day when he woke her and every night when they went to bed and she told him the same.

It had taken both their lifetimes so far to find out how it felt to be loved and to be the most important person in the other's world.

'Happy?' Sev checked, as they danced.

'Very.' Naomi nodded, though she was starting to wilt. She wanted to tell Sev what had happened between her and her father and of course to find out more about Nikolai.

'Can we go up?' Sev spoke into her ear.

'Up?' Naomi checked.

'To our suite?'

'It's not even ten o'clock.'

'I don't care what time it is,' Sev said. 'I'm done with other people.'

'You can't leave your own wedding at ten.'

'I can.' Sev shrugged. 'Everyone is having a good time. Jamal and Allem have gone up to settle the baby. Daniil and Libby are at the hospital. Your mother is drunk...'

He just reeled it off in his matter-of-fact way that made her smile.

And he was right.

It had been a blissful day and, no, they didn't need to stay.

'The only person I want to really speak with is Nikolai, but that can wait,' Sev said. 'I've a feeling that conversation might take some time. Anyway, he seems busy with...'

'Rachel,' Naomi filled in the name. 'She's Libby's friend.'

'Well, Rachel is taking exceptionally good care of him while her friend has her baby.'

She was!

'One more dance,' Naomi said, as the music changed to sexy and slow and Sev pulled her in.

'One more dance,' Sev agreed, and then he told her something he had found out today.

'You know Daniil said I read them an erotic book?'

She nodded.

'That's where I knew that word from—*"krasavitsa".*'

It really wasn't very fair to use the word he often did when he came when they were in the middle of the dance floor.

And it made her stomach pull in on itself when he told her then that he'd only ever said it to her.

'We're going to say goodbye now,' Sev said, and a little

frantically she nodded. 'Then we're going to get into that elevator.' And then, like some expert quizmaster, he hit the stopwatch. 'The honeymoon starts now.'

* * * * *

'All it would take is one little kiss.'

Miranda coughed out a laugh, but even to her ears it sounded unconvincing. 'Like *that's* ever going to happen.'

He was suddenly close. Way too close. His broad fingertip was suddenly on the underside of her chin without her knowing how it had got there. All she registered was the warm, branding feeling of it resting there, holding her captive along with the mesmerising force of his bottomless dark gaze.

'Is that a dare, Sleeping Beauty?' he said in a silky tone.

Miranda felt his words slither down her spine like an unfurling satin ribbon running away from its spool. Her knees threatened to give way. Her belly quivered with a host of needs she couldn't even name. She couldn't tear her eyes away from his coal-black gaze. It was drawing her in like a magnet did a tiny iron filing.

But finally a vestige of pride came to her rescue.

Miranda dipped out from under his fingertip and rubbed at her chin as she sent him a warning glare. 'Don't play games with me, Leandro.'

The Ravensdale Scandals

Scandal is this family's middle name!

With notoriously famous parents, the Ravensdale
children grew up in the limelight. But *nothing* could
have prepared them for this latest scandal…
the revelation of a Ravensdale love-child!

London's most eligible siblings find themselves
in the eye of their own paparazzi storm.
They're determined to fight back—
they just never factored in falling in love too…!

Find out what happens in
Julius Ravensdale's story
Ravensdale's Defiant Captive
December 2015

Miranda Ravensdale's story
Awakening the Ravensdale Heiress
January 2016

And watch for Jake and Katherine's
Ravensdale Scandals…coming soon!

AWAKENING THE RAVENSDALE HEIRESS

BY
MELANIE MILBURNE

Published in Great Britain 2016
By Mills & Boon, an imprint of HarperCollins*Publishers*
1 London Bridge Street, London, SE1 9GF

© 2016 Melanie Milburne

ISBN: 978-0-263-92096-3

Our policy is to use papers that are natural, renewable and recyclable
products and made from wood grown in sustainable forests. The logging
and manufacturing processes conform to the legal environmental
regulations of the country of origin.

Printed and bound in Spain
by CPI, Barcelona

An avid romance reader, **Melanie Milburne** loves writing the books that gave her so much joy as she was busy getting married to her own hero and raising a family. Now a *USA TODAY* bestselling author, she has won several awards—including The Australian Readers' Association most popular category/series romance in 2008 and the prestigious Romance Writers of Australia R*BY award in 2011.

She loves to hear from readers!

MelanieMilburne.com.au
Facebook.com/Melanie.Milburne
Twitter @MelanieMilburn1

Books by Melanie Milburne

Mills & Boon Modern Romance

At No Man's Command
His Final Bargain
Uncovering the Silveri Secret
Surrendering All But Her Heart
His Poor Little Rich Girl

The Ravensdale Scandals

Ravensdale's Defiant Captive

The Chatsfield

Chatsfield's Ultimate Acquisition

The Playboys of Argentina

The Valquez Bride
The Valquez Seduction

Those Scandalous Caffarellis

Never Say No to a Caffarelli
Never Underestimate a Caffarelli
Never Gamble with a Caffarelli

The Outrageous Sisters

Deserving of His Diamonds?
Enemies at the Altar

Visit the Author Profile page at
millsandboon.co.uk for more titles.

To Holly Marks.
Thank you for being such a wonderful fan.
Your lovely comments on Facebook
have lifted me so many times.
This one is for you with much love and appreciation.
xxxx

CHAPTER ONE

MIRANDA WOULDN'T HAVE seen him if she hadn't been hiding from the paparazzi. Not that a fake potted plant was a great hiding place or anything, she thought. She peeped through the branches of the ornamental ficus to see Leandro Allegretti crossing the busy street outside the coffee shop she was sheltering in. He didn't seem aware of the fact it was spitting with rain or that the intersection was clotted with traffic and bustling with pedestrians. It was as if a transparent cube was around him. He was impervious to the chatter and clatter outside.

She would have recognised him anywhere. He had a regal, untouchable air about him that made him stand out in a crowd. Even the way he was dressed set him apart—not that there weren't other suited men in the crowd, but the way he wore the sharply tailored charcoal-grey suit teamed with a snowy white shirt and a black-and-silver striped tie somehow made him look different. More civilised. More dignified.

Or maybe it was because of his signature frown.

Had she ever seen him without that frown? Mi-

randa wondered. Her older twin brothers, Julius and
Jake, had been boarding school buddies with Leandro. He had spent occasional weekends or school holidays and even university breaks at the Ravensdale
family home, Ravensdene, in Buckinghamshire. Being
a decade younger, she'd spent most of her childhood
being a little intimidated by Leandro's taciturn presence. He was the epitome of the strong, silent type—a
man of few words and even fewer facial expressions.
She couldn't read his expression at the best of times.
It was hard to tell if he was frowning in disapproval
or simply in deep concentration.

He came into the coffee shop and Miranda watched
as every female head turned his way. His French-Italian
heritage had served him well in the looks department.
Imposingly tall with jet-black hair, olive skin and brown
eyes three or four shades darker than hers.

But if Leandro was aware of his impact on the female gaze he gave no sign of it. It was one of the things
she secretly most liked about him. He didn't trade on
his appearance. He seemed largely unaware of how
knee-wobblingly gorgeous he looked. It was as if it
was irrelevant to him. Unlike her brother Jake, who
knew he was considered arm candy and exploited it
for all he could.

Leandro stood at the counter and ordered a long
black coffee to take away from the young, blushing
attendant, and then politely stood back to wait for it,
taking out his phone to check his messages or emails.

Miranda covertly studied his tall, athletic figure
with its strongly corded muscles honed from long hours

of endurance exercise. The broad shoulders, the strong back, the lean hips, taut buttocks and the long legs. She had seen him many a time down at Ravensdene, a solitary figure running across the fields of the estate in all sorts of weather, or swimming endless laps of the pool in summer.

Leandro took to exercise with an intense, single-minded concentration that made her wonder if he was doing it for the health benefits or for some other reason known only to himself. But, whatever reason it was that motivated him, it clearly worked to his benefit. He had the sort of body to stop female hearts. She couldn't stop looking at him, drinking in the male perfection of his frame, her mind traitorously wondering how delicious he would look in a tangle of sheets after marathon sex. Did he have a current lover? Miranda hadn't heard much about his love life lately, but she'd heard his father had died a couple of months ago. She assumed he'd been keeping a low profile since.

The young attendant handed Leandro his coffee and as he turned to leave his eyes met Miranda's through the craggy branches of the pot plant. She saw the flash of recognition go through his gaze but he didn't smile in welcome. His lips didn't even twitch upwards. But then, she couldn't remember ever seeing him smile. Or, at least, not at her. The closest he came to it was a sort of twist of his lips that could easily be mistaken for cynicism rather than amusement.

'Miranda?' he said.

She lifted her hand in a little fingertip wave, trying

not to draw too much attention to herself in case anyone lurking nearby with a smart phone recognised her. 'Hi.'

He came over to her table screened behind the pot plant. She had to crane her neck to meet his frowning gaze. She always felt like a pixie standing in front of a giant when she was around him. He was an inch shorter than her six-foot-four brothers but for some reason he'd always seemed taller.

'Are the press still hassling you?' he asked, still frowning.

Of course, Leandro had heard about her father's scandal, Miranda thought. It was the topic on everyone's lips. It was splashed over every newsfeed or online blog. Could it get any more embarrassing? Was there anyone in London—*the entire world*—who didn't know her father had sired a love child twenty-three years ago? As London theatre royalty, her parents were known for drawing attention to themselves. But this scandal of her father's was the biggest and most mortifying so far. Miranda's mother, Elisabetta Albertini, had cancelled her season on Broadway and was threatening divorce. Her father, Richard Ravensdale, was trying to get his love child into the bosom of the family but so far with zero success. Apparently Katherine Winwood had failed to be charmed by her long-lost biological father and was doing everything she could to avoid him and her half-siblings.

Which was fine by Miranda. Just fine, especially since Kat was so beautiful that everyone was calling Miranda 'the ugly sister'. *Argh!*

'Just a little,' Miranda said with a pained smile. 'But

enough about all that. I'm so sorry about your father. I didn't know about him passing otherwise I would've come to the funeral.'

'Thank you,' he said. 'But it was a private affair.'

'So, how are things with you?' she said. 'I heard you did some work for Julius in Argentina. Great news about his engagement, isn't it? I met his fiancée Holly last night. She's lovely.' Miranda always found it difficult to make conversation with Leandro. He wasn't the small talk type. When she was around him she had a tendency to babble or ramble to fill any silence with the first thing that came into her head. She knew it made her seem a little vacuous, but he was so tight-lipped, what else was she to do? She felt like a tennis-ball machine loping balls at him but without him returning any.

Fortunately this time he did.

'Yes,' he said. 'Great news.'

'It was a big surprise, wasn't it?' Miranda said. 'I didn't even know he was dating anyone. I can't believe my big brother is getting married. Seriously, Julius is such a dark horse, he's practically invisible. But Holly is absolutely perfect for him. I'm so happy for them. Jasmine Connolly is going to design the wedding dress. We're both going to be bridesmaids, as Holly doesn't have any sisters or close friends. I don't know why she doesn't have loads of friends because she's such a sweetheart. Jaz thinks so too. You remember Jaz, don't you? The gardener's daughter who grew up with me at Ravensdene? We went to school together. She's got her own bridal shop now and—'

'Can I ask a favour?'

Miranda blinked. A favour? What sort of favour? What was he going to say? *Shut up? Stop gabbling like a fool? Stop blushing like a gauche twelve-year-old schoolgirl?* 'Sure.'

His deep brown gaze was centred on hers, his dark brows still knitted together. 'Will you do a job for me?'

Her heart gave a funny little skip. 'Wh-what sort of job?' Stuttering was another thing she did when she was around him. What was it about this man that turned her into a gibbering idiot? It was ridiculous. She had known him *all* her life. He was like a brother to her…well, sort of. Leandro had always been on the fringe of her consciousness as the Ideal Man. Not that she ever allowed herself to indulge in such thoughts. Not fully. But they were there, like uninvited guests at a cocktail party, every now and again moving forward to sneak a canapé or a drink before melting back against the back wall of her mind.

'My father left me his art collection in his will,' Leandro said. 'I need someone to catalogue it before I can sell it; plus there are a couple of paintings that might need restoring. I'll pay you, of course.'

Miranda found it odd he hadn't told anyone his father had died until after the funeral was over. She wondered why he hadn't told her brothers, particularly Julius, who was the more serious and steady twin. Julius would have supported Leandro, gone to the funeral with him and stood by him if he'd needed back up.

She pictured Leandro standing alone at that funeral. Why had he gone solo? Funerals were horrible enough.

The final goodbye was always horrifically painful but to face it alone would be unimaginable. Even if he hadn't been close to his father there would still be grief for what he had missed out on, not to mention the heart-wrenching realisation it was now too late to fix it.

When her childhood sweetheart Mark Redbank had died of leukaemia, her family and his had surrounded her. Supported her. Comforted her. Even Leandro had turned up at the funeral—she remembered seeing his tall, silent dark-haired figure at the back of the church. It had touched her that he'd made the time when he'd hardly known Mark. He had only met him a handful of times.

Miranda had heard via her brothers that Leandro had a complicated back story. They hadn't told her much, only that his parents had divorced when he was eight years old and his mother had taken him to England, where he'd been promptly put into boarding school with Miranda's twin brothers after his mother had remarried and begun a new family. He had been a studious child, excelling both academically and on the sporting field. He had taken that hard work ethic into his career as a forensic accountant. 'I'm so sorry for your loss,' she said.

'Thank you.'

'Did your mother go to the funeral?' Miranda asked.

'No,' he said. 'They hadn't spoken since the divorce.'

Miranda wondered if his father's funeral would have brought back painful memories of his estranged relationship with him. No son wanted to be rejected by his father. But apparently Vittorio Allegretti hadn't wanted custody after the divorce. He had handed over Leandro as a small boy and only saw him on the rare occasion he'd been in London on business. She had heard via her brothers that eventually Leandro had stopped meeting his father because Vittorio had a tendency to drink to the point of abusing others and/or passing out. There had even been one occasion where the police had had to be called due to a bar-room scuffle Leandro's father had started. It didn't surprise her Leandro had kept his distance. With his quiet and reserved nature he wasn't the sort of man to draw unnecessary attention to himself.

But there was so much more she didn't know about him. She knew he was a forensic accountant—a brilliant one. He had his own consultancy in London and travelled all over the globe uncovering major fraud in the corporate and private sectors. He often worked with Jake with his business analysis company and he had recently helped Julius in exposing Holly's ghastly stepfather's underworld drug and money-laundering operations.

Leandro Allegretti was the go-to man for uncovering secrets and yet Miranda had always sensed he had one or two of his own.

'So this job…' she began. 'Where's the collection?'

'In Nice,' he said. 'My father ran an art and antiques business in the French Riviera. This is his private collection. He sold off everything else when he was first diagnosed with terminal cancer.'

'And you want to…to get rid of it?' Miranda asked,

frowning at the thought of him selling everything of his father's. In spite of their tricky relationship, didn't he want a memento? *'All* of it?'

The line of his mouth was flat. Hardened. Whitened. 'Yes,' he said. 'I have to pack up the villa and sell that too.'

'Why not use someone locally?' Miranda knew she was well regarded in her job as an art restorer even though she was at the early stages of her career. But she wouldn't be able to do much on site. Art restoration was more science now than art. Sophisticated techniques using x-rays, infrared technology and Raman spectroscopy meant most restoration work was done in the protective environment of an established gallery. Leandro could afford the best in the world. Why ask her?

'I thought you might like a chance to escape the hoo-hah here,' Leandro said. 'Can you take a couple of weeks' leave from the gallery?'

Miranda had already been thinking about getting out of London for some breathing space. It had been hell on wheels with her father's dirty linen being flapped in her face. She couldn't go anywhere without being assailed by press. Everyone wanted to know what she thought of her father's scandal. *Had she met her half-sister? Was she planning to? Were her parents divorcing for the second time?* It was relentless. Along with the press attention, she had also been subjected to her mother's bitter tirades about her father, and her father's insistence she make contact with her half-sister and play happy families.

Like that was going to happen.

This would be a perfect opportunity to escape. Besides, October on the Côte d'Azur would be preferable to the capricious weather London was currently dishing up. 'How soon do you want me?' she said, blushing when she realised her unintentional double entendre. 'I mean, I can probably get away from work by the end of next week. Is that okay?'

'Fine,' he said. 'I don't collect the keys to the villa until then anyway. I'll book your flight and email you the details. Do you have a preference for a hotel?'

'Where will you be staying?'

'At my father's villa.'

Miranda thought about the expense of staying at a hotel, not that Leandro couldn't afford it. He would put her in five-star accommodation if she asked for it. But staying in a hotel put her at risk of being found by the press. If she stayed with Leandro at his father's villa she could work on the collection without that looming threat.

Besides, it would be an opportunity to see a little of the man behind the perpetual frown.

'Is there room for me at your father's place?'

Leandro's frown deepened until two vertical lines formed between his bottomless brown eyes. 'You don't want to stay in a hotel?'

Miranda snagged her lip with her teeth, warm colour crawling further over her cheeks until her whole face felt on fire. 'I wouldn't want to intrude if you've got someone else staying...'

Who was his someone else?

Who was his latest lover? She knew he had them

from time to time. She had seen pictures of him at charity events. She had even met one or two over the years when he had brought a partner to one of the legendary parties her parents had put on at Ravensdene for New Year's Eve. Tall, impossibly beautiful, elegant, eloquent types who didn't blush and stumble over their words and make silly fools of themselves. He wasn't as out there as her playboy brother Jake. Leandro was more like Julius in that he liked to keep his private life out of the public domain.

'I haven't got anyone staying,' he said.

He hadn't got anyone staying? Or he hadn't got *anyone*?

And why was she even thinking about his love life? It wasn't as if she was interested in him. She was interested in no one. Not since Mark had died. She ignored attractive men. She quickly brushed off any men who flirted with her or tried to charm her. Not that Leandro was super-charming or anything. He was polite but distant. Aloof. And as for flirting...well, if he could learn to smile now and again it might help.

Miranda wasn't sure why she was pushing so hard for an invitation. Maybe it was because she had never spent any time with him without other people around. Maybe it was because he had recently lost his father and she wanted to know why he hadn't told anyone before the funeral. Maybe it was because she wanted to see where he had spent the first eight years of his life before he had moved to England. What had he been like as a child? Had he been playful and fun-loving, like most kids, or had he been as serious and inexpressive as he was now? 'So would it be okay to stay with you?' she said. 'I won't get in your way.'

He looked at her in that frowning manner he had. Deep thought or disapproval? She could never quite tell. 'There isn't a housekeeper there.'

'I can cook,' she said. 'And I can help you tidy things up before you sell the place. It'll be fun.'

A small silence ticked past.

Miranda got the feeling he was mulling it over. Weighing it up in his mind. Doing a risk assessment.

He finally drew in a breath and then slowly released it. 'Fine. I'll email you those flights.'

She rose from the table and began to shrug on her coat, tugging her hair free from the collar. 'Do you mind if I walk out with you? There was a pap crew tailing me earlier. I ducked in here to escape them. It'd be nice to get back to work without being jostled.'

'No problem,' he said. 'I'm heading that way anyway.'

Leandro walked beside Miranda on the way back to the gallery. He was always struck by how tiny she was. Built like a ballerina with fine limbs and an elfin face, with big tawny-brown eyes and auburn hair, yet her skin was without a single freckle—it was as white and pure as Devon cream. She had an ethereal beauty about her. She reminded him of a fairy-tale character—an innocent waif lost in the middle of a crazy out-of-control world.

Seeing her hiding in that café had tripped a switch inside his head. It was like he'd had a brain snap. He hadn't thought it through but it seemed...*right* somehow. She needed a bolthole and he needed someone to help him sort out the mess his father had left behind. Maybe it would've been better to commission someone local. Maybe he could have sold the lot without proper valuation. Hell, he didn't really know why he had asked her, except he knew she was having a tough time of it with her father's love-child scandal still doing the rounds.

That and the fact he couldn't bear the thought of being in that villa on his own with only the ghosts of the past to haunt him. He hadn't been back since the day he'd left when he was eight years old.

It wasn't like him to act so impulsively but seeing Miranda hiding behind that pot plant had made him realise how stressed she was about her father's latest peccadillo. He had heard from her brothers the press had camped outside her flat for the last month. She hadn't been able to take a step without a camera or a microphone being shoved in her face. Being the daughter of famous celebrities came with a heavy price tag. Or, at least, it did for her.

Leandro had always felt a little sorry for Miranda. She was constantly compared to her flamboyant and glamorous mother and found lacking. Now she was being compared to her half-sister. Kat Winwood *was* stunning. No two ways about that. Kat was the billboard-beautiful type. Kat would stop traffic. Air traffic. Miranda's beauty was quiet, the sort of beauty that grew on you. And she was shy in an endearingly old-fashioned way. He didn't know too many women who blushed as easily as her. She never flirted. And she never dated. Not since she had lost her first and only boyfriend to leukaemia when she was sixteen. Leandro couldn't help admiring her loyalty, even if he privately thought she was throwing her life away.

But who was he to judge?

He hadn't got any plans for happy-ever-after either.

Miranda was the best person to advise him on his father's collection. Of course she was. She was reliable and sensible. She was competent and efficient and she had an excellent eye. She had helped her brother Julius buy some great pieces at various auctions. She could spot a fraud at twenty paces. It would only take a week or two to sort out the collection and he would be doing her a favour in the process.

But there was one thing she didn't know about him.

He hadn't even told Julius or Jake about Rosie.

It was why he had gone to his father's funeral alone. Going back to Nice had been like ripping open a wound.

There'd been numerous times when he could have mentioned it. He could have told his two closest friends the tragic secret he carried like a shackle around his heart. But instead he had let everyone think he was an only child. Every time he thought of his baby sister his chest would seize. The thought of her little chubby face with its dimpled, sunny smile would bring his guilt crashing down on him like a guillotine.

For all these years he had said nothing. To anyone. He had left that part of his life—his former life, his childhood—back in France. His life was divided into two sections: France and England. Before and After. Sometimes that 'before' life felt like a bad dream—a horrible, blood-chilling nightmare. But then he would wake up and realise with a sickening twist of his gut that it was true. Inescapably, heartbreakingly true. It didn't matter where he lived. How far he travelled. How hard he worked to block the memories. The guilt came with him. It sat on his shoulder during the day. It poked him awake at night. It drove vicious needles through his skull until he was blind with pain.

Speaking about his family was torture for him. Pure, unadulterated torture. He hated even thinking about it. He didn't have a family.

His family had been blown apart twenty-seven years ago and *he* had been the one to do it.

CHAPTER TWO

'YOU'RE GOING TO FRANCE?' Jasmine Connelly said, eyes wide with sparkling intrigue. 'With Leandro Allegretti?'

Miranda had dropped into Jasmine's bridal boutique in Mayfair for a quick catch-up before she flew out the following day. Jaz was sewing Swarovski crystals onto a gorgeous wedding dress, the sort of dress for every girl who dreamed of being a princess. Miranda had pictured a dress just like it back in the day when her life had been going according to plan. Now every time she saw a wedding dress she felt sad.

'Not going *with* him as such,' she said, absently fingering the fabric of the wedding gown on the mannequin. 'I'm meeting him over there to help him sort out his father's art collection.'

'When do you go?'

'Tomorrow... For a couple of weeks.'

'Should be interesting,' Jaz said with a smile in her voice.

Miranda looked at her with a frown. 'Why do you say that?'

Jaz gave her a worldly look. 'Come, now. Don't you ever notice the way he looks at you?'

Miranda felt something unhitch in her chest. 'He never looks at me. He barely even says a word to me. This is the first time we've exchanged more than a couple of sentences.'

'Clues, my dear Watson,' Jaz said with a cheeky smile. 'I've seen the way he looks at you when he thinks no one's watching. I reckon if it weren't for his relationship with your family he would act on it. You'd better pack some decent underwear just in case he changes his mind.'

Miranda pointedly ignored her friend's teasing comment as she trailed her hand through the voluminous veil hanging beside the dress. 'Do you know much about his private life?'

Jaz stopped sewing to look at her with twinkling grey-blue eyes. 'So you are interested. Yay! I thought the day would never come.'

Miranda frowned. 'I know what you're thinking but you couldn't be more wrong. I'm not the least bit interested in him or anyone. I just wondered if he had a current girlfriend, that's all.'

'Not that I've heard of, but you know how close he keeps his cards,' Jaz said. 'He could have a string of women on the go. He is, after all, one of Jake's mates.'

Every time Jaz said Jake's name her mouth got a snarly, contemptuous look. The enmity between them was ongoing. It had started when Jaz was sixteen at one of Miranda's parents' legendary New Year's Eve parties. Jaz refused to be drawn on what had actually happened in Jake's bedroom that night. Jake too kept tight-lipped. But it was common knowledge he despised Jaz and made every effort to avoid her if he could.

Miranda glanced at the glittering diamond on her friend's ring finger. It was Jaz's third engagement and, while Miranda didn't exactly dislike Jaz's latest fiancé, Myles, she didn't think he was 'The One' for her. Not that she could ever say that to Jaz. Jaz didn't take too kindly to being told what she didn't want to hear. Miranda had had the same misgivings over Fiancés One and Two. She just had to hope and trust her headstrong and stubborn friend would realise how she was short-changing herself before the wedding actually took place.

Jaz stood back and cast a critical eye over her handiwork. 'What do you think?'

'It's beautiful,' Miranda said with a sigh.

'Yeah, well, I'm going cross-eyed with all these crystals,' Jaz said. 'I've got to get it done so I can start on Holly's. She's awfully nice, isn't she?'

'Gorgeous,' Miranda said. 'It's amazing, seeing Julius so happy. To tell you the truth, I wasn't sure he was ever going to fall in love. They're total opposites and yet they're so perfect for each other.'

Jaz looked at her with her head on one side, that teasing glint back in her gaze. 'Is that a note of wistfulness I can hear?'

Miranda rearranged her features. 'I'd better get going.' She grabbed her tote bag, slung it over her shoulder and leaned in to kiss Jaz on the cheek. 'See you when I get back.'

* * *

When Miranda landed in Nice she saw Leandro waiting for her in the terminal. He was dressed more casually this time but if anything it made him look even more heart-stoppingly attractive. The dark blue denim jeans clung to his leanly muscled legs. The rolled back sleeves of his light blue shirt highlighted his deep tan and emphasised the masculinity of the dark hair liberally sprinkled over his strong forearms. He was cleanly shaven but she could see where he had nicked himself on the left side of his jaw. For some reason, it humanised him. He was always so well put together, so in control. Was being back in his childhood home unsettling for him? Upsetting? What emotions were going on behind the dark screen of his eyes?

As he caught her eye a flutter of awareness rippled deep and low in her belly. Would he kiss her in greeting? She couldn't remember him ever touching her. Not even by accident. Even when he'd walked her back to the gallery last week he had kept his distance. There had been no shoulder brushing. Not that she even reached his shoulders. She was five-foot-five to his six-foot-three.

Miranda smiled shyly as he came towards her. 'Hi.'

'Hello.' Was it her imagination or was his voice deeper and huskier than normal? The sound of it moved over her skin as if he had reached out and stroked her. But he kept a polite distance, although she couldn't help noticing his gaze slipped to her mouth for the briefest moment. 'How was your flight?' he said.

'Lovely,' she said. 'But you didn't have to put me in first class. I was happy to fly coach.'

He took her carry-on bag from her, somehow without touching her fingers as he did so. 'I didn't want anyone bothering you,' he said. 'There's nothing worse than being a captive audience to someone's life story.'

Miranda gave a light laugh. 'True.'

She followed him out to the car park where he opened the door of the hire car for her. She couldn't fault his manners, but then, he had always been a gentleman. She had never known him to be anything but polite and considerate. She wondered if this was difficult for him, coming back to France to his early childhood home. What memories did it stir for him? Did it make him wish he had been closer to his father? Did it stir up regrets that now it was too late?

She glanced at him as they left the car park and joined the traffic on the Promenade des Anglais that followed the brilliant blue of the coastline of the Mediterranean Sea. He was frowning as usual; even his hands on the steering wheel were clenched. She could see the tanned flesh straining over his knuckles. The line of his jaw was grim. Everything about him was tense, wound up like a spring. It looked like he was in physical pain.

'Are you okay?' she asked.

He looked at her briefly, moving his lips in a grimace-like smile that didn't reveal his teeth. 'I'm fine.'

Miranda didn't buy it for a second. 'Have you got one of your headaches?' She had seen him once at Ravensdene when he had come down with a migraine.

He was always so strong and fit that to see him rendered helpless with such pain and sickness had been an awful shock. The doctor had had to be called to give him a strong painkiller injection. Jake had driven him back to London the next day, as he had still been too ill to drive himself.

'Just a tension headache,' he said. 'Nothing I can't handle.'

'When did you arrive?'

'Yesterday,' he said. 'I had a job to finish in Stockholm.'

'I expect it must be difficult coming back,' Miranda said, still watching him. 'Emotional for you, I mean. Did you ever come back after your parents divorced?'

'No.'

She frowned. 'Not even to visit your father?'

His hands tightened another notch on the steering wheel. 'We didn't have that sort of relationship.'

Miranda wondered how his father could have been so cold and distant. How could a man turn his back on his son—his only child—just because his marriage had broken up? Surely the bond of parenthood was much stronger than that? Her parents had gone through a bitter divorce before she'd been born and, while they hadn't been around much due to their theatre commitments, as far as she could tell Julius and Jake had never doubted they were loved.

'Your father doesn't sound like a very nice person,' she said. 'Was he always a drinker? I'm sorry. Maybe you don't want to talk about it. It's just, Julius told me you didn't like it when your father came to London to see you. He said your dad embarrassed you by getting horribly drunk.'

Leandro's gaze was focussed on the clogging traffic ahead but she could see the way his jaw was locked down, as if tightened by a clamp. 'He didn't always drink that heavily.'

'What made him start? The divorce?'

He didn't answer for a moment. 'It certainly didn't help.'

Miranda wondered about the dynamics of his parents' relationship and how each of them had handled the breakdown of their marriage. Some men found the loss of a relationship far more devastating than others. Some sank into depression, others quickly re-partnered to avoid being alone. The news was regularly full of horrid stories of men getting back at their ex-wives after a broken relationship—cruel and vindictive attempts to get revenge, sometimes involving the children, with tragic results. 'Did he ever remarry?' she asked.

'No.'

'Did he have other partners?'

'Occasionally, but not for long,' Leandro said. 'He was difficult to live with. There were few women who would put up with him.'

'So it was his fault your mother left him?' Miranda asked. 'Because he was so difficult to live with?'

He didn't answer for so long she thought he hadn't heard her over the noise of the traffic outside. 'No,' he said heavily. 'That was my fault.'

Miranda looked at him in shock. '*You?* Why would

you think that? That's ridiculous. You were only eight years old. Why on earth would you blame yourself?'

He gave her an unreadable glance before he took a left turn. 'My father's place is a few blocks up here. Have you ever been to Nice before?'

'A couple of years ago—but don't try and change the subject,' she said. 'Why do you blame yourself for your parents' divorce?'

'Don't all kids blame themselves?'

Miranda thought about it for a moment. Her mother had said a number of times how having twins had put pressure on her relationship with her father. But then, Elisabetta wasn't a naturally maternal type. She was happiest when the attention was on her, not on her children. Miranda had felt that keenly as she'd been growing up. All of her friends—apart from Jaz—were envious of her having a glamorous showbiz mother. And Elisabetta could *act* like a wonderful mother when it suited her.

It was the times when she didn't that hurt Miranda the most.

But why did Leandro think *he* was responsible for his parents' break-up? Had *they* told him that? Had they made him feel guilty? What sort of parents had they been to do something so reprehensible? How could they make a young child feel responsible for the breakdown of a marriage? That was the adults' responsibility, not a child's, and certainly not a young child's.

But she didn't pursue the conversation for at that point Leandro pulled into the driveway of a rundown-looking villa in the Belle Epoqué style. At first she

thought he must have made a mistake, pulled into the
wrong driveway or something. The place was like
something out of a gothic noir film. The outside of
the three-storey-high building was charcoal-grey with
the stain of years of carbon monoxide pollution. The
windows with the ragged curtains drawn were like
closed eyes.

The villa was like a faded Hollywood star. Miranda
could see the golden era of glamour in its lead-roofed
cupolas on the corners and the ornamental ironwork
and flamboyance of the stucco decorations that resem-
bled a wedding cake.

But it had been sadly neglected. She knew many
of the grand villas of the Belle Époque era along the
Promenade des Anglais had not survived urban rede-
velopment. But the extravagance of the period was still
apparent in this old beauty.

It made Miranda's blood tick in her veins. What
a gorgeous old place for Leandro to inherit. It was a
piece of history. A relic from an enchanted time when
the aristocracy had flaunted their wealth by hiring ar-
chitects to design opulent villas with every imaginable
embellishment: faux stonework, figureheads, frescos,
friezes, decorative ironwork, ornamental stucco work,
cupolas, painted effects, garlands and grotesques. The
aristocracy had indulged their taste for the exotic, with
Italian and Classic influences as well as Gothic, Eastern and Moorish.

And he was packing it up and *selling* it?

Miranda looked up at him as he opened her car door
for her. 'Leandro, it's amazing! What a glorious build-

ing. It's like a time capsule from the Art Nouveau period. This was your childhood home? *Really?*'

He clearly didn't share her excitement for the building. His expression had that closed-off look about it, as shuttered as the windows of the villa they were about to enter. 'It's very run-down,' he said.

'Yes, but it can be brought back to life.' Miranda beamed at him, clasping her hands in excitement. 'I'm so glad you asked me to come. I can't wait to see what's inside.'

He stepped forward to unlock the door with the set of keys he was holding in his hand. 'Dust and cobwebs mostly.'

Miranda's gaze went to his tanned hand, that funny fluttery feeling passing over the floor of her belly as she watched the way his long, strong fingers turned the key in the lock. Who was the last woman he'd touched with those arrantly masculine but beautiful hands? Were his hands smooth or rough or something deliciously in between? She couldn't stop herself from imagining those strong, capable hands exploring female flesh. Caressing a breast. Gliding down a smooth thigh. Touching the silken skin between her legs.

Her legs?

Miranda jerked back from her wayward thoughts as if a hand had grabbed and pulled on the back of her clothing. What was she doing thinking of him that way? She didn't think of *any* man that way.

That way was over for her.

It had died with Mark. She owed it to his memory, to all he had meant to her and she to him.

Miranda could not allow herself to think of moving on with her life. Of having a life. A normal life. Her dreams of normal were gone.

Dead and buried.

Leandro glanced at her. 'What's wrong?'

Miranda felt her face flame. Why did she always act like a flustered schoolgirl when she was around him? She was an adult, for God's sake. She had to act mature and sensible. Cool and in charge of her emotions and her traitorous needs. She could do that. *Of course she could.* 'Erm…nothing.'

His frown created a deep crevasse between his brows. 'Would you rather go to a hotel? There's one a couple of blocks down. I could—'

'No, of course not.' She painted on a bright smile. 'Don't spoil it for me by insisting I stay at some plush hotel. This is right up my alley. I want to be in amongst the dust and cobwebs. Who knows what priceless treasures are hidden inside?'

Something moved at the back of his gaze, as quick as the twitch of a curtain. But then his expression went back to its default position. 'Come this way,' he said.

Miranda followed him into the villa, her heels echoing on the marbled floor of the grand foyer. It made her feel she was stepping into a vacuum, moving back in time. Thousands of dust motes rose in the air, the sunlight catching them where it was slanting in from the windows either side of the opulently carved and sweeping staircase.

As Leandro closed the door, the central chandelier

tinkled above them as the draught of the outside air breathed against its glittering crystals.

Miranda felt a rush of goose bumps scamper over every inch of her flesh. She turned a full circle, taking in the bronze, marble and onyx statues positioned about the foyer. There were paintings on every wall, portraits and landscapes from the seventeenth and eighteenth centuries; some looked even older. It was like stepping into a neglected museum. A thick layer of dust was over everything like a ghostly shroud.

'Wow...' she breathed in wonder.

Leandro merely looked bored. 'I'll show you to your room first. Then I'll give you the guided tour.'

Miranda followed him upstairs, having to restrain herself from stopping in front of every painting or *objet d'art* on the way past. She caught tantalising glimpses of the second floor rooms through the open doors; most of the furniture was draped with dust sheets but even so she could see in times gone past the villa had been a showcase for grandeur and wealth. There were a couple of rooms with the doors closed. One she assumed was Leandro's bedroom but she knew it wasn't the master suite as they had passed it three doors back. Did he not want to occupy the room his father had slept in all those years?

Miranda felt another prickle of goose bumps.

Had his father perhaps *died* in there?

Thankfully the room Leandro had assigned her had been aired. The faded formal curtains had been pulled back and secured by the brass fittings and the window opened so fresh air could circulate. The breeze was playing with the gossamer-sheer fabric of the curtain in little billowy puffs and sighs.

'I hope the bed's comfortable,' Leandro said as he placed her bag on a velvet-topped chest at the foot of the bed. 'The linen is fresh. I bought some new stuff when I got here yesterday.'

Miranda glanced at him. 'Did your father die at home?'

His brows came together. 'Why do you ask?'

She gave a little shrug, absently rubbing her upper arms with her crossed-over hands. 'Just wondering.'

He held her look for a beat before turning away, one of his hands scoring a pathway through the thickness of his hair. 'He was found unconscious by a neighbour and died a few hours later in hospital.'

'So you didn't get to say goodbye to him?'

He made a sound of derision. 'We said our good-byes a long time ago.'

Miranda looked at the landscape of his face—the strong jaw, the tight mouth with its lines of tension running down each side and the shadowed eyes. 'What happened between the two of you?' she said.

His eyes moved away from hers. 'I'll leave you to unpack. The bathroom is through there. I'll be downstairs in the study.'

'Leandro?'

He stopped at the door and she heard him release a 'what now?' breath before he turned to look at her with dark eyes that flashed with unmistakable irritation. 'You're not here to give me grief counselling, okay?'

Miranda opened her eyes a little wider at his acerbic tone. She had never seen him even mildly angry before. He was always so emotionless, so neutral and blank...apart from that frown, of course. 'I'm sorry. I didn't mean to upset you.'

He scrubbed his hand over his face as he let out another whoosh of air. 'I'm sorry,' he said in a weighted tone. 'That was uncalled for.'

'It's fine,' she said. 'I realise this is a difficult time for you.'

His mouth twisted but it was nowhere near a smile, not even a quarter of one. 'Let me know if you need anything. I'm not used to catering for guests. I might've overlooked something.'

'Don't you have visitors come and stay with you at your place in London?' Miranda said.

His eyes were as unfathomable as ever as they held hers. 'Women, you mean?'

Miranda felt another blush storm into her cheeks. Why on earth was she was discussing his sex life with him? It was crossing a boundary she had never crossed before. She'd thought about him with other women. Many times. How could she not? She'd seen the way other women looked at him. The way their eyes flared in interest. The way they licked their lips and fluttered their eyelashes, or moved or preened their bodies so he would take notice. She had been witnessing his effect on women for as long as she could remember. He wasn't just eye candy. He was an eye banquet. He was intelligent, sophisticated, cultured and wealthy to boot. Alpha, but without the arrogance. He was everything a woman would want in a sexual partner. He was the stuff of fantasies. Hot, erotic fantasies she never allowed herself to have. What did it matter to her what he did or who he did it with?

She didn't want to know.

Well, maybe just a little.

'You do have them occasionally, don't you?' Miranda said.

One of his dark brows rose in a quizzical arc. '*Have* them?'

She held his look but it took an enormous effort. Her cheeks were on fire. Hot enough to sear a steak. He was teasing her. She could see a tiny glint in the dark chocolate of his eyes. Even one corner of his mouth had lifted a fraction. He was making her out to be a prude who couldn't talk about sex openly. Why did everyone automatically assume because she was celibate she was uptight about all things sexual? That she was some old-world throwback who couldn't handle modernity? 'You know exactly what I'm talking about so stop trying to embarrass me.'

His eyes didn't waver from hers. 'I'm not a monk.'

Miranda couldn't stop her mind running off with *that* information. Picturing him with women. Being very un-monk-like with them. Touching them, kissing them, making love to them. She imagined his body naked—the toned, tanned and taut perfection of him in the throes of animal passion.

She could feel her own body stirring in excitement, her pulse kicking up its pace, her blood pulsing with the primitive drumbeat of lust, her inner core contracting with a delicious clench of desire. She quickly moistened her lips with the point of her tongue, an electric jolt of awareness zapping her as she saw his dark-as-night gaze follow every micro-millimetre of its pathway across her mouth.

The subtle change in atmosphere made the air suddenly super-charged. She could feel the voltage crackling in the silence like a singing wire.

He was standing at least two metres away and yet she felt as if he had touched her. Her lips buzzed and fizzed. Throbbed. *Ached.* Would he kiss soft and slow or hard and fast? Would his stubble scrape or graze her? What would he taste of? Salty or sweet? Good quality coffee or top-shelf wine? Testosterone-rich man in his prime?

Miranda became aware of her body shifting. Stirring. Sensing. It felt like every cell was unfurling from a tightly wound ball. Her body stretched its cramped limbs like a long-confined creature. Her frozen blood thawed, warmed, heated. Sizzled.

Needs she had long ignored pulsed. Each little ripple of want in her inner core reminded her: she was a woman. He was a man. They were alone in a big, run-down old house with no one as buffer. No older brothers. No servants. No distractions.

No chaperone.

'I hope it won't cramp your style, having me here,' Miranda said with what she hoped was suitably cool poise.

There was little to read on Leandro's face except for the kindling heat in his gaze as it continued to hold hers. 'So you wouldn't mind if I brought some-one home with me?'

Oh, dear God, *would* he? Would he bring someone back here? Would she have to watch some gorgeous woman drape herself all over him? Would she have to watch as they simpered up at him? Flirted and fussed over him? Would she have to go to bed knowing that, only a few thin walls and doors away, he was doing all sorts of wickedly sensual, un-monk-like things with someone else?

Miranda lifted her chin. 'Just because I've sworn a vow of celibacy doesn't mean I expect those around me to follow my example.'

He studied her for an infinitesimal moment, his eyes going back and forth between each of hers in an as-sessing manner that was distinctly unnerving. Why was he looking at her like that? What was he seeing? Did he sense her body's reaction to his? She was doing her level best to conceal the effect he had on her but she knew most body language was unconscious. She had already licked her lips three times. *Three times!*

'Do you think Mark would've sacrificed his life like you're doing if the tables were turned?' he said at last.

Miranda pursed her lips. *At least it would stop her licking them*, she thought. She knew exactly where this was going. Her brothers were always banging on about it. Jaz, too, would offer her opinion on how she was missing out on the best years of her life, yadda-yadda-yadda.

'I'll make a deal with you, Leandro,' she said, eyeballing him. 'I won't tell you how to live your life if you don't tell me how to live mine.'

His mouth took on a rueful slant. 'Put those kitten claws away, *cara*,' he said. 'I don't need any more enemies.'

He had never used a term of endearment when addressing her before. The way he said it, with that hint of an Italian accent all those years living in England hadn't quite removed, made her spine tingle. But why was he addressing her like that other than to tease her? To mock her?

Miranda threw him a reproachful look. 'Don't patronise me. I'm an adult. I know my own mind.'

'But you were just a kid back then,' he said. 'If he'd lived you would've broken up within a couple of months, if not weeks. It's what teenagers do.'

'That's not true,' Miranda said. 'We'd been friends since we were little kids. We were in love. We were soul mates. We planned to spend the rest of our lives together.'

He shook his head at her as if she was talking utter nonsense. 'Do you really believe that? Come on. *Really?*'

Miranda aligned her spine. Straightened her shoulders. Steeled her resolve to deflect any criticism of her decision to remain committed to the promises she had made to Mark. She and Mark had become close friends during early childhood when they had gone to the same small village school before she'd been sent to boarding school with Jaz. They'd officially started dating at fourteen. Her friendship with Mark had been longer than that with Jaz who had come to Ravensdene when she was eight.

Along with Mark's steady friendship, his stable home life had been a huge draw and comfort for Miranda. His parents were so normal compared to hers. There'd been no high-flying parties with Hollywood superstars and theatre royalty coming and going all hours of the day and night. In the Redbank household there'd been no tempestuous outbursts with door-slamming and insults hurled, and no passionate making up that would only last a week or two before the cycle would begin again.

Mark's parents, James and Susanne, were supportive and nurturing of each other and Mark and had always made Miranda feel like a part of the family. They actually took the time to listen to any problems she had. They were never too busy. They didn't judge or dismiss her or even tell her what to do. They listened.

Leandro had no right to doubt her convictions. No right to criticise her choices. She had made up her mind and nothing he or anyone could say or do would make her veer from the course her conscience had taken. 'Of course I do,' she said. 'I believe it with all my heart.'

The humming silence tiptoed from each corner of the room.

Leandro kept looking at her in that measuring way. Unsettling her. Making her think of things she had no right to be thinking. Erotic things. Forbidden things. Like how his mouth would feel against hers. How his hands would feel against her flesh. How their bodies would fit together—her slight curves against his toned male hardness. How it would feel to glide her mouth along his stubbly jaw, to press her lips to his and open her mouth to the searching thrust of his tongue.

She had never had such a rush of wicked thoughts before. They were running amok, making a mockery of her convictions. Making her aware of the needs she had for so long pretended weren't there. Needs that were moving within that dark, secret place in her body. The way he was looking at her made her ache with unspent passion. She tried to control every micro-expression on her face. Stood as still as one of his father's cold, lifeless statues downstairs.

But, as if he had seen enough to satisfy him, he finally broke the silence. 'I'll be in the study downstairs. We'll eat out once you've unpacked. Give me a shout once you're done.'

Miranda blinked. Dining out? With him? In public? People would assume they were dating. What if someone took a photo and it got back to Mark's parents? Even though they had said—along with everyone else—she should get on with her life, she knew they would find it heartbreakingly difficult to watch her do so. How could they not? Everything she did with someone else would make their loss all the more painful. Mark had been their only son. Their only child. The dreams and hopes they'd had for him had died with him. The milestones of life: dating, engagement, marriage and children would be salt ground into an open wound.

She couldn't do it to them.

'You don't want me to fix something for us here?' Miranda said.

Leandro gave a soft sound that could have been his version of a laugh. 'You're getting your fairy tales mixed up,' he said. 'You're Sleeping Beauty, not Cinderella.'

Miranda felt a wick of anger light up inside her. What right did he have to mock her choice to remain loyal to Mark's memory? 'Is this why you've asked me here? So you can make fun of me?'

'I'm not making fun of you.'

'Then what *are* you doing?'

His gaze dipped to her mouth for a nanosecond before meshing with hers once more. 'I have absolutely no idea.'

Miranda frowned. 'What do you mean?'

He came over to where she was standing. He stopped within a foot of her but even so she could feel the magnetic pull of his body as she lifted her gaze to his. She had never been this close to him. Not front to front. Almost toe to toe.

Her breathing halted as he placed a gentle but firm fingertip to the underside of her chin, lifting her face so her eyes had no possible way of escaping the mesmerising power of his. She could feel the slow burn of his touch, each individual whorl of his blunt fingertip like an electrode against her skin. She could smell the woodsy and citrus fragrance of his aftershave—not heady or overpowering, but subtle, with tantalising grace notes of lemon and lime.

She could see the dark pinpricks of his regrowth

along his jaw, a heady reminder of the potency of his male hormones charging through his body. She could feel her own hormones doing cartwheels.

Her tongue sneaked out before she could stop it, leaving a layer of much-needed moisture over her lips. His gaze honed in on her mouth, his eyelashes at half-mast over his dark-as-pitch eyes.

Something fell off a high shelf in her stomach as his thumb brushed over her lower lip. The grazing movement of his thumb against the sensitive skin of her mouth made every nerve sit up and take notice. She could feel them twirling, pirouetting, in a frenzy of traitorous excitement.

His large, warm hand gently slid along the curve of her cheek, cupping one side of her face, some of her hair falling against the back of his hand like a silk curtain.

Had *anyone* ever held her like this? Tenderly cradled her face as if it were something delicate and priceless? The warmth of his palm seared her flesh, making her ache for him to cup not just her face but her breasts, to feel his firm male skin against her softer one.

'I shouldn't have brought you here,' he said in a deep, gravelly tone that sent another shockwave across the base of her belly.

A hummingbird was trapped inside the cavity of Miranda's chest, fluttering frantically inside each of the four chambers of her heart. 'Why?' Her voice was barely much more than a squeak.

He moved his thumb in a back-and-forth motion

over her cheek, his inscrutable eyes holding her prisoner. 'There are things you don't know about me.'

Miranda swallowed. What didn't she know? Did he have bodies buried in the cellar? Leather whips and chains and handcuffs? A red room? 'Wh-what things?'

'Not the things you're thinking.'

'I'm not thinking those things.'

He smiled a crooked half-smile that had mockery at its core. 'Sweet, innocent, Miranda,' he said. 'The little girl in a woman's body who refuses to grow up.'

Miranda stepped out of his hold, rubbing at her cheek in a pointed manner. 'I thought I was here to look at your father's art collection. I'm sorry if that seems terribly naïve of me but I've never had any reason not to trust you before now.'

'You can trust me.'

She chanced a look at him again. His expression had lost its mocking edge. If anything he looked…sad. She could see the pained lines across his forehead, the shadows in his eyes, the grim set to his mouth. 'Why am I here, Leandro?' Somehow her voice had come out whispery instead of strident and firm.

He let out a long breath. 'Because when I saw you in London I… I don't know what I thought. I saw you cowering behind that pot plant and—'

'I wasn't cowering,' Miranda put in indignantly. 'I was hiding.'

'I felt sorry for you.'

The silence echoed for a moment with his bald statement.

Miranda drew in a tight breath. 'So you rescued me

by pretending to need me to sort out your father's collection. Is there even a collection?'

'Yes.'

'Then maybe you'd better show it to me.'

'Come this way.'

Miranda followed him out of the suite and back downstairs to a room next door to the larger of the two sitting rooms. Leandro opened the door and gestured for her to go in. She stepped past him in the doorway, acutely conscious of the way his shirt sleeve brushed against her arm. Every nerve stood up and took notice. Every fine hair tingled at the roots. It was like his body was emitting waves of electricity and she had only to step over an invisible boundary to feel the full force of it.

The atmosphere inside the room was airless and musty, as if it had been closed up a long time. It was packed with canvasses, on the walls, and others wrapped and stacked in leaning piles against the shrouded furniture.

Miranda sent her gaze over the paintings on the walls, examining each one with her trained apprentice's eye. Even without her qualifications and experience she'd have been able to see this was a collection of enormous value. One of the landscapes was certainly a Gainsborough, or if not a very credible imitation. What other treasures were hidden underneath those wrapped canvasses?

Miranda turned to look at Leandro. 'This is amazing. But I'm not sure I'm experienced enough to handle such a large collection. We'd need to ship the pieces back to London for proper valuation. It's too much for one person to deal with. Some of these pieces could be worth hundreds of thousands of pounds, maybe even millions. You might want to keep some as an investment. Sell them in a few years so you can—'

'I don't want them.'

She frowned at his implacable tone. 'But that's crazy, Leandro. You could have your own collection. You could have it on show at a private museum. It would be—'

'I have no interest in making money out of my father's collection,' he said. 'Just do what you have to do. I'll pay for any shipment costs but that's as far as I'm prepared to go.'

Miranda watched open-mouthed as he strode out of the room, the dust motes he'd disturbed hovering in the ringing silence.

CHAPTER THREE

LEANDRO WORKED THE floor of his father's study like a lion trapped in a cat carrier. It had been a mistake to bring Miranda here. Here to the epicentre of his pain and anguish. He should have sold the collection without consulting anyone. What did it matter if those wretched paintings were valuable? They weren't valuable to him. Making money out of his father's legacy seemed immoral somehow to him. He didn't understand why his father had left everything to him.

Over the last few years their relationship had deteriorated to perfunctory calls at Christmas or birthdays. Most of the time his father would be heavily inebriated, his words slurred, his memory skewed. It had been all Leandro could do to listen to his father's drunken ramblings knowing *he* had been the one to cause the destruction of his father's life. Surely his father had known how difficult this trip back here would be? Had he done it to twist the knife? To force him to face what he had spent the last two decades avoiding? Everything in this run-down villa represented the mis-

ery of his father's life—a life spent drinking himself
to oblivion so he could forget the tragedy of the past.

The tragedy Leandro had caused.

He looked out of the window that overlooked the
garden at the back of the villa. He hadn't been able to
bring himself to go out there yet. It had once been a
spectacular affair with neatly trimmed hedges, flow-
ering shrubs and borders filled with old-world roses
whose heady scent would fill the air. It had been a magical place for he and his sister to scamper about and
play hide and seek in amongst the cool, green shaded
laneways of the hedges.

But now it was an overgrown mess of weeds, mis-
shapen hedges and skeletal rose bushes with one or
two half-hearted blooms. Parts of the garden were so
overrun they couldn't be seen properly from the house.

It reminded Leandro of his father's life—sad, neglected, abused and abandoned. Wasted.

How could he have thought to bring Miranda here?
How long before she discovered Rosie's room? He
couldn't keep it locked up for ever. Stepping in there
was like stepping back in time. It was painfully sur-
real. Everything was exactly the same as the day Rosie
had disappeared from the beach. Every toy. Every doll.
Every childish scribble she had ever done. Every messy
and colourful finger-painting. Every article of clothing left in the wardrobe as if she were going to come
back and use it. Even her hairbrush was on the dressing table with some of her silky dark-brown hairs still
trapped in the bristles—a haunting reminder of the last
time it had been used.

Even the striped towel they had been sitting on at the beach was there on the foot of the child-sized princess bed. The bed Rosie had been so proud of after moving out of her cot. Her 'big-girl bed', she'd called it. He still remembered her excited little face as she'd told him how she had chosen it with their mother while he'd been at school.

It was a lifetime ago.

Why had his father left the room intact for so long? Had he wanted Leandro to see it? Was that why he'd left him the villa and its contents? Knowing Leandro would have to come in and pack up every single item of Rosie's? Why hadn't his father seen to it himself or got someone impartial to do it? It had been twenty-seven years, for pity's sake. There was no possibility of Rosie ever coming home. The police had been blunt with his parents once the first few months had passed with no leads, no evidence, no clues and no tip-offs.

Leandro had seen the statistics. Rosie had joined the thousands of people who went missing without trace. Every single day families across the globe were shattered by the disappearance of a loved one. They were left with the stomach-churning dread of wondering what had happened to their beloved family member. Praying they were still alive but deep down knowing such miracles were rare. Wondering if they had suffered or were still suffering. It was cruel torture not to know and yet just as bad speculating.

Leandro had spent every year of his life since wondering. Praying. Begging. Pleading with a God he no longer believed in—if he ever had. Rosie wasn't coming back. She was gone and he was responsible.

The guilt he felt over Rosie's disappearance was a band around his chest that would tighten every time he saw a toddler. Rosie had been with him on the pebbly beach when he was six and she was three. He could recall her cute little chubby-cheeked face and starfish dimpled hands with such clarity he felt like it was yesterday. For years he'd kept thinking the life he was living since was just a bad dream. That he would wake up and there would be Rosie with her sunny smile sitting on the striped towel next to him. But every time he would wake and he would feel that crushing hammer blow of guilt.

His mother had stepped a few feet away to an ice-cream vendor, leaving Leandro in charge. When she'd come back, Rosie had gone. Vanished. Snatched from where she had been sitting. The beach had been scoured. The water searched. The police had interviewed hundreds of beach-goers but there was no sign of Rosie. No one had seen anything suspicious. Leandro had only turned his back for a moment or two to look at a speedboat that was going past. When he'd turned around he'd seen his mother coming towards him with two ice-cream cones; her face had contorted in horror when she'd seen the empty space on the towel beside him.

He had never forgotten that look on his mother's face. Every time he saw his mother he remembered it. It haunted him. Tortured him.

His parents' marriage hadn't been strong in the first

place. Losing Rosie had gouged open cracks that were already there. The divorce had been bitter and painful two years after Rosie's disappearance. His father hadn't wanted custody of Leandro. He hadn't even asked for visitation rights. His mother hadn't wanted him either. But she must have known people would judge her harshly if she didn't take him with her when she went back to her homeland, England. Mothers were meant to love their children.

But how could his mother love him when he was responsible for the loss of her adored baby girl?

Not that his mother ever blamed him. Not openly. Not in words. It was the looks that told him what she thought. His father's too. Those looks said, *why weren't you watching her?* As the years went on his father had begun to verbalise it. The blame would come pouring out after he'd been on one of his binges. But it was nothing Leandro hadn't already heard echoing in his head. Day after day, week after week…for years now the same accusing voice would keep him awake at night. It would give him nightmares. He would wake with a jolt and remember the awful truth.

There wasn't a day that went past that he didn't think of his sister. Ever since that gut-wrenching day he would look for her in the crowd, hoping to catch a glimpse of her. Hoping that whoever had taken her had not done so for nefarious reasons, but had taken her to fulfil a wish to have a child and had loved and cared for her since. He couldn't bear to think of her coming to harm. He couldn't bear to think of her lying cold in some grisly shallow grave, her little body bruised and broken. As the years had gone on he imagined her growing up. He looked for an older version of her. She would be thirty now.

In his good dreams she would be married with children of her own by now.

In his nightmares...

He closed the door on his torturous imaginings. For twenty-seven years he had lived with this incessant agony. The agony of not knowing. The agony of being responsible for losing her. The agony of knowing he had ruined his parents' lives.

He could never forgive himself.

He didn't even bother trying.

Miranda spent an hour looking over the collection, carefully uncovering the canvasses to get an idea of what she was dealing with. Apart from some of the obvious fakes, most of the collection would have to be shipped back to England for proper evaluation. The paintings needed to be x-rayed in order to establish how they were composed. Infrared imaging would then be used to see the original drawings and painting losses, and Raman spectroscopy would determine the identity of the varnish. It would take a team of experts far more qualified and experienced than her to bring all of these works to their former glory. But she couldn't help feeling touched Leandro had asked her to be the first to run her eyes over the collection.

Why *had* he done that?

Had it simply been an impulsive thing, as he had intimated, or had he truly thought she was the best one to do it? Whatever his reasons, it was like being let in on a secret. He had opened a part of his life that no one else had had access to before.

It was sad to think of Leandro's father living here on his own for years. It looked like no maintenance had been done for a decade, if not longer. Cobwebs hung from every corner. The dust was so thick she could feel it irritating her nostrils. Every time she moved across the floor to look at one of the paintings the floorboards would creak in protest, as if in pain. The atmosphere was one of neglect and deep loneliness. As she lifted each dustsheet off the furniture she got a sense she was uncovering history. What stories could each piece tell? There was a George IV mahogany writing table, a Queen Anne burr-elm chest of drawers, a seventeenth-century Italian walnut side cabinet, a Regency spoon-back chair, as well as a set of four Regency mahogany and brass inlaid chairs, and an Italian gilt wood girandole mirror with embellished surround. How many lives had they watched go by? How many conversations had they overheard?

Along with the furniture, inside some of the cabinets there were Chinese glass snuff bottles, bronze Buddhas, jade Ming dynasty vases and countless ceramics and glassware. So many beautiful treasures locked away where no one could see and enjoy them.

Why was Leandro so intent on getting rid of them? Didn't he have a single sentimental bone in his body? His father had painstakingly collected all of these valuable items. It would have taken him years and years and oodles of money. Why then get rid of them as if they were nothing more than charity shop donations? Surely there was something he would want to keep as a memento?

It didn't make sense.

Miranda went outside for a breath of fresh air after breathing in so much dust. The afternoon was surprisingly warm, but then, this was the French Riviera, she thought. No wonder the English came here in droves for their holidays. Even the light against the old buildings had a certain quality to it—a muted, pastel glow that enhanced the gorgeous architecture.

She took a walk about the garden where weeds ran rampant amongst the spindly arms of roses and underneath the untrimmed hedges. A Virginia creeper was in full autumnal splendour against a stone wall, some of the rich russet and gold leaves crunching and crackling underneath her feet as she walked past.

Miranda caught sight of a small marble statue of an angel through a gap in the unkempt hedge towards the centre of the garden. The hedge had grown so tall it had created a secret hideaway like a maze hiding the Minotaur at the centre of it. The pathway leading to it was littered with leaves and weeds as if no one had been along here for a long time. There was a cobweb-covered wooden bench in the little alcove in front of the statue, providing a secluded spot for quiet reflection. But when she got close she realised it wasn't a statue of an angel after all; it was of a small child of two or three years old.

Miranda bent down to look at the brass plaque that

was all but covered by strangling weeds. She pushed them aside to read:

Rosamund Clemente Allegretti.
Lost but never forgotten.

There was a birth date of thirty years ago but the space where the date of passing should be was blank with just an open-ended dash.

Who was she? Who was this little girl who had been immortalised in white marble?

The sound of a footfall crunching on the leaves behind her made Miranda's heart miss a beat. She scrambled to her feet to see the tall figure of Leandro coming towards her but then, when he saw what was behind her, he stopped dead. It was like he had been struck with something. Blind-sided. Stunned. His features were bleached of colour, going chalk-white beneath his tan. The column of his throat moved up and down: once. Twice. Three times. His eyes twitched, and then flickered, as if in pain.

'You startled me, creeping up on me like that,' Miranda said to fill the eerie silence. 'I thought you were—'

'A ghost?'

Something about his tone made the hair on the back of her neck stand on end. But it was as if he were talking to himself, not her. He seemed hardly even aware she was there. His gaze was focussed on the statue, his brow heavily puckered—even more than usual.

Miranda leaned back against the cool pine-scented

green of the hedge as he moved past her to stand in front of the statue. When he touched the little child's head with one of his hands, she noticed it was visibly shaking.

'Who is she?' she said.

His hand fell away from the child's head to hang by his side. 'My sister.'

She gaped at him in surprise. 'Your *sister*?'

He wasn't looking at her but at the statue, his brows still drawn together in a deep crevasse. 'Rosie. She disappeared when I was six years old. She was three.'

Disappeared? Miranda swallowed so convulsively she felt the walls of her throat close in on each other. *He had a sister who had disappeared?* The shock was like a slap. A punch. A wrecking ball banging against her heart. Why hadn't he said something? For all these years he'd given the impression he was an only child. What a heart-breaking tragedy to keep hidden for all this time. Why hadn't he told his closest friends? 'You never said anything about having a sister. Not once. To anyone.'

'I know,' he said on an expelled breath. 'It was easier than explaining.'

Why hadn't she put two and two together before now? Of course that was why he was so standoffish. Grief did that. It kept you isolated in an invisible bubble of pain. No one could reach you and you couldn't reach out. She knew the process all too well. 'Because it was too…painful?' she said.

He looked at her then, his dark eyes full of silent

suffering. 'It was my way of coping,' he said. 'Talking about her made it worse. It still does.'

'I'm sorry.'

He gave her a sombre movement of his lips before he turned back to look at the statue. He stood there for a long moment, barely a muscle moving on his face apart from an in-and-out movement on his lean cheek, as if he were using every ounce of self-control to keep his emotions in check.

'My father must've had this made,' he said after a long moment. 'I didn't know it existed until now. I just glanced at the garden when I came yesterday—I couldn't see this from the house.'

Miranda bit her lip as she watched him looking at the statue. He had his hands in his pockets and his shoulders were hunched forward slightly. Bone-deep sadness was etched in the landscape of his face.

She silently put a hand on his forearm and gave it a comforting squeeze. He turned his head to look down at her, his eyes meshing with hers as one of his hands came down on top, anchoring hers beneath his. She felt the imprint of his long, strong fingers, the warmth of his palm—the skin-on-skin touch that made something inside her belly shift sideways.

His gaze held hers steady.

Her breathing stalled. Her pulse quickened. Her heartbeat tripped and then raced.

Time froze.

The sounds of the garden—the twittering birds, the breeze ruffling the leaves, the drip of a leaky tap near one of the unkempt beds—faded into the background.

'My father wouldn't allow my mother to pack anything away,' Leandro said. 'He couldn't accept Rosie
was gone. It was one of the reasons they split up. My
mother wanted to move on. He couldn't.'

'And you got caught in the crossfire,' Miranda said.

He dropped his hand from where it was covering
hers, stepping away from her as if he needed space to
breathe. To think. To regroup. 'I was supposed to be
looking after her,' he said after another beat or two of
silence. 'The day she disappeared.'

Miranda frowned. 'But you were only what—six?
That's not old enough to babysit.'

He gave her one of his hollow looks. 'We were on
the beach. I can take you to the exact spot. My mother
only walked ten or so metres away to get us an ice-
cream. When she came back, Rosie was gone. I didn't
hear or see anything. I turned my head to look at a boat
that was going past and when I turned back she wasn't
there. No one saw anything. It was crowded that hot
summer day so no one would've noticed if a child was
carried crying from the beach. Not back then.'

Miranda felt a choking lump come to her throat at
the agony of what he had been through—the heartache,
the distress of not knowing—*never* knowing what had
happened to his baby sister. Wondering if she was alive
or dead. Wondering if she had suffered. Wondering if
there was something—*anything*—he could have done
to stop it. How had he endured it?

By blaming himself.

'It wasn't your fault,' she said. 'How can you feel
it was your fault? You were only a baby yourself. You

shouldn't have been blamed. Your parents were wrong to put that on you.'

'They didn't,' he said. 'Not openly, although my father couldn't help himself in later years.'

So many pennies were beginning to drop. This was why Leandro's father had drunk to senselessness. This was why his mother had moved abroad, remarried, had three children in quick succession and had been always too busy to make time to see him. This was why Leandro had spent so many weekends and school holidays at Ravensdene, because he'd no longer had a home and family to go to. It was unbearably sad to think that all the times Leandro had joined her brothers he had carried this terrible burden. Alone. He hadn't told anyone of the tragedy. Not even his closest friends knew of the gut-wrenching heartache he had been through. And was *still* going through.

'I don't know what to say...' She brushed at her moist eyes with the sleeve of her top. 'It's just so terribly sad. I can't bear the thought of how you've suffered this all alone.'

Leandro reached out and grazed her cheek with a lazy fingertip, his expression rueful. 'I didn't mean to make you cry.'

'I can't help it.' Miranda sniffed and went searching for a tissue but before she could find one up her sleeve he produced the neatly ironed square of a clean white handkerchief. She took it from him with a grateful glance. 'Thanks.'

'My father stubbornly clung to hope,' Leandro said. 'He kept Rosie's room exactly as it was the day she went missing because he'd convinced himself that one day she'd come back. My mother couldn't bear it. She thought it was pathological.'

Miranda scrunched the handkerchief into a ball inside her hand, thinking of the football sweater of Mark's she kept in her wardrobe. Every year on his birthday she would put it on, breathing in the ever-fading scent of him. She kept telling herself it was time to give it back to his parents but she could never quite bring herself to do it. 'Everyone has their own way of grieving,' she said.

'Maybe.'

'Can I see it?'

'Rosie's room?'

'Would you mind?' she said.

He let out a ragged-sounding breath. 'It will have to be packed up sooner or later.'

Miranda walked back to the villa with him. She was deeply conscious of how terribly painful this would be for him. Didn't she feel it every time she visited Mark's parents? They had left his room intact too. Unable to let go of his things because by removing them they would finally have to accept he was gone for ever. But at least Mark's parents were in agreement.

How difficult it must have been for Leandro's mother, trying to move on while his father had been holding back. The loss of a child tested the strongest marriage. Leandro's parents had divorced within two years of Rosie's disappearance. How much had Leandro suffered during that time and since? Estranged from his alcoholic father, shunned by his mother, too busy with her new family.

After the bright light of outdoors the shadows inside the villa seemed all the more ghostly. A chill shimmied down her spine as she climbed the groaning stairs with Leandro.

The room was the third along the corridor—the door she had noticed was locked earlier. Leandro selected a key from a bunch of keys he had in his pocket. The sound of the lock turning over was as sharp and clear as a rifle shot.

Miranda stepped inside, her breath catching in her throat as she took in the little fairy-tale princess bed with its faded pink-and-white cover and the fluffy toys and dolls arranged on the pillow. There was a doll's pram and a beautifully crafted doll's house with gorgeous miniature furniture under the window. There was a child's dressing table with a toy make-up set and a hairbrush lying beside it.

There was a framed photograph hanging on the wall above the bed of a little girl with a mop of dark brown curls, apple-chubby cheeks and a cheeky smile.

Miranda turned to look at Leandro. He was stony faced but she could sense what he was feeling. His grief was palpable. 'Thank you for showing me,' she said. 'It's a beautiful room.'

His throat moved up and down over a swallow. 'She was a great little kid.' He picked up one of the fluffy toys that had fallen forward on the bed—a floppy-eared rabbit—and turned it over in his hands. 'I bought this for her third birthday with my pocket money. She called him Flopsy.'

Miranda blinked a couple of times, surprised her voice worked at all when she finally spoke. 'What will you do with her things once you sell the villa?'

His frown flickered on his forehead. 'I haven't thought that far ahead.'

'You might want to keep some things for when you have your own children,' Miranda said.

She got a sudden vision of him holding a newborn baby, his features softened in tenderness, his large, capable hands cradling the little bundle with care and gentleness. Her heart contracted. He would make a wonderful father. He would be kind and patient. He wouldn't shout and swear and throw tantrums, like her father had done when things hadn't gone his way. Leandro would make a child feel safe and loved and protected. He would be the strong, dependable rock his children would rely on no matter what life dished up.

He put the rabbit back down on the bed as if it had bitten him. 'I'll donate it all to charity.'

'But don't you—?'

'No.'

The implacability of his tone made her stomach feel strangely hollow. 'Don't you want to get married and have a family one day?'

His eyes collided with hers. 'Do you?'

Miranda shifted her gaze and rolled her lips together for a moment. 'We're not talking about me.'

The line of his mouth was tight. White. 'Maybe we should.'

She pulled back her shoulders. Lifted her chin. Held his steely look even though it made the backs of her knees feel fizzy. 'It's different for me.'

A glimmer of cynicism lit his dark gaze. 'Why's that?'

'I made a promise.'

Leandro gave a short mocking laugh. 'To a dying man—*a boy*?'

Miranda gritted her teeth. How many times did she have to have this conversation? 'We *loved* each other.'

'You loved the idea of love,' he said. 'He was your first boyfriend—the first person to show an interest in you. It's my bet if he hadn't got sick he would've moved on within a month or two. He used your sweet, compliant nature to—'

'That's not true!'

'He didn't want to die alone and lonely,' he went on with a callous disregard for her feelings. 'He tied you to him, making you promise stuff no one in their right mind would promise. Not at that age.'

Miranda put her hand up to her ears in a childish attempt to block the sound of his taunting voice. 'No! *No!*'

'You were a kid,' he said. 'A romantically dazed kid who couldn't see how she was being used towards the end. He had cancer—the big, disgusting C-word. In an instant he had gone from being one of the top jocks to one of the untouchables. But he knew *you* wouldn't let him down. Not the sweet, loyal little Miranda Ravensdale who was looking for a Shakespearean tragedy to pin her name on.'

'You're wrong,' she said. 'Wrong. Wrong. *Wrong.* You have no right to say such things to me. You don't understand what we had. *You* don't commit to a relationship longer than a few weeks. What would you know of loyalty and commitment? Mark and I were friends for years—*years*—before we became…more intimate.'

He tugged her hands down and loosely gripped her wrists in his hands so she could feel every one of his fingers burning against her flesh. 'Am I wrong?' he asked. 'Am I really?'

Miranda pulled out of his hold with an almighty wrench that made her stumble backwards. How dared he mock her? How dared he make fun of her? How *dared* he question her love and commitment for Mark and his for her? 'You have no right to question my relationship with Mark. No right at all. I loved him. I loved him and I *still* love him. Nothing you can say or do will ever change that.'

His mouth slanted in a cynical half-smile. 'I could change that. I know I could. All it would take is one little kiss.'

Miranda coughed out a laugh but even to her ears it sounded unconvincing. 'Like *that's* ever going to happen.'

He was suddenly close. Way too close. His broad fingertip was suddenly on the underside of her chin without her knowing how it got there. All she registered was the warm, branding feeling of it resting there, holding her captive with the mesmerising force of his bottomless dark gaze.

'Is that a dare, Sleeping Beauty?' he said in a silky tone.

Miranda felt his words slither down her spine like an unfurling satin ribbon running away from its spool. Her knees threatened to give way. Her belly quivered with a host of needs she couldn't even name. She couldn't tear her eyes away from his coal-black gaze. It was drawing her in like a magnet does a tiny iron filing.

She became aware of her breasts inside the lacy cups of her bra. They prickled and swelled as if stimulated to attention by the deep, burry sound of his voice. The below-the-ocean-floor, rumbly bass of his voice—the voice that did strange things to her feminine body.

Her inner core clenched in a contraction of raw, primal need. Her blood ticked, raced, through the network of her veins at breakneck frenzied speed. Every pore of her body ached for his touch, for the sensuous glide of his fingers, for the hot sweep of his tongue, for the stabbing thrust of his body.

But finally a vestige of pride came to her rescue.

Miranda dipped out from under his fingertip and rubbed at her chin as she sent him a warning glare. 'Don't play games with me, Leandro.'

A sardonic gleam shone in his dark eyes. 'You think I was joking?'

She didn't know what to think. Not when he looked at her like that—with smouldering black-as-pitch eyes that seemed to see right through her defences. That sensually contoured mouth shouldn't tempt her. She shouldn't be wondering what it would feel like against her own. She shouldn't be looking at his mouth as if she had no control over her gaze.

He was her brothers' friend. He was practically one

of the family. He had seen her with pimples and braces.
He had seen her lying on the sofa with a hot-water bottle pressed to her cramping belly. He could have any
girl he wanted. Why would he want to kiss her unless
it was to score points? He thought her loyalty to Mark
was ridiculous. How better to prove it by having her
go weak-kneed when he kissed her?

Not. Going. To. Happen.

She bent her head and made to go past him. 'I'm
going to do something about dinner.'

He caught her left arm on the way past, his fingers forming a loose bracelet around her wrist. His
gaze drew hers to his with an unspoken command.
She couldn't have looked away if she tried. Her breath
caught as his thumb found her pulse. The warmth of
his fingers made her spine fizz and her knees tremble.
'There's no food in the house,' he said. 'I haven't had
time to shop. Let's go out.'

Miranda chewed the inside of her lip. 'I'm not sure
that's such a good idea...'

His thumb stroked the underside of her wrist in slow
motion. 'Just dinner,' he said. 'Don't worry. I won't
try any moves on you. Your brothers would skin me
alive if I did.'

The thought of him making a move on her made
the hot spill in her belly spread through her pelvis
and down between her thighs like warmed treacle. It
was hard enough controlling her reaction to him as he
stroked her wrist in that tantalising manner. Her senses
went into a tailspin with every mesmerising movement
of his fingers against her skin. What would it do to her

to feel his mouth on hers? To feel his molten touch on her breasts and her other aching intimate places?

But then, she thought: *what had her brothers to do with anything?* If she wanted to get involved with Leandro—if things had been different, that was— then that would be up to her, not to Julius and Jake to give the go ahead. 'I'm hardly your type in any case,' Miranda said, carefully extricating her wrist from his fingers.

His expression was now inscrutable. 'Does that bother you?'

Did it?

Of course it did. Men like Leandro didn't notice girls like her. She was the type of girl who was invisible to most men. She was too girl-next-door. Shy and reserved, not vivacious and outgoing. Pretty but not stunning. Petite, not voluptuous. If it hadn't been for his friendship with her brothers he probably wouldn't have given her the time of day. She wasn't just a wallflower. She was wallpaper. Bland, boring, beige wallpaper.

'Not at all,' Miranda said, rubbing at her still-tingling wrist. 'You've a perfect right to date whomever you chose.'

But please don't do it while I'm under the same roof.

CHAPTER FOUR

LEANDRO WAITED AT the foot of the stairs for Miranda. He had showered and changed and tried not to think about how close he had been to kissing her earlier. He had always kept his distance in the past. It wasn't that he hadn't noticed her. He had. He was always viscerally aware of how close she was to him. It was like picking up a radar frequency inside his body. If she was within touching distance, his body was acutely aware of her every movement. Even if it was as insignificant as her lifting one of her hands to her face to tuck back a stray strand of hair. He felt it in his body.

If she so much as walked past him every cell in his body stood to attention. If she sent her tongue out over her beautiful mouth he felt as if she had stroked it over him intimately. When she smiled that hesitant, shy, nervous smile every pore of his skin contracted with primal need as he imagined her losing that shyness with him. As soon as he caught a trace of her scent he would feel a rush through his flesh. His blood would bloom with such heat he could feel it charging through his pelvis and down his legs.

But he kept his distance.

Always.

She was the kid sister of his two closest friends. It was an unspoken code between mates: no poaching of sisters. If things didn't work out, it would strain everyone's relationship. He had seen enough with the angst between Jake and Jasmine. The air could be cut with a knife when those two were in the same room. The fallout from their fiery spat still made everyone uncomfortable even seven years after the event. You couldn't mention Jaz's name around Jake without his expression turning to thunder. And Jaz turned into a hissing and spitting wildcat if Jake so much as glanced her way.

Leandro wasn't going to add to the mix with a dalliance with Miranda, even if she did somehow manage to move on from the loss of her teenage boyfriend. She wasn't the type to settle for a casual fling. She was way too old-fashioned and conservative for that. She would want the fairy tale: the house with the picket fence and cottage flowers, the kids and the dog.

He wondered if she had even had proper sex with her boyfriend. They had started officially dating when she'd been fourteen, which in his opinion was a little young. He knew teenagers had sex younger than ever but had she been ready emotionally? Why was she so determined to cling to a promise that essentially locked her up for life? He didn't understand why she would do such a thing. How could she possibly think she'd loved Mark enough to make that sort of sacrifice?

He had always had the feeling Mark Redbank had clung to Miranda for all the wrong reasons. She be-

lieved it to have been true love but Leandro wasn't
so sure. Call him cynical, but he'd always suspected
Mark had used Miranda, especially towards the end.
He thought Mark had played up his feelings for her
to keep her tied to him. The decent thing would have
been to set her free but apparently Mark had extracted
a death-bed promise with her that she was stubbornly
determined to stick to.

But touching her had awakened something in Leandro. He had never touched her before. Not even when
he came to visit the family at Ravensdene. He had always avoided the kiss on the cheek to say hello, mostly
because she was too shy to offer it and he would never
make the first move. He had never even shaken her
hand. He had made every effort to avoid physical contact. He knew she saw him as a cold fish, aloof, distant.
He had been happy to keep it that way.

But being in that room with all those memories and
all that crushing grief had pushed him off-balance.
Something had been unleashed inside him. Something
he wasn't sure he could control. Now he had touched
Miranda he wanted to touch her again. It was an urge
that pulsed through him. The feel of her creamy skin
beneath his palm, against his fingers, her silky hair
tickling the back of his hand, had stirred his blood
until it roared through his body like an out of control
freight train. It made him think forbidden thoughts.
Thoughts he had never allowed himself to think before now. Thoughts of her lying pinned by his body, his
need pumping into her as her cries of pleasure filled
the air.

The brief flare of temper she had shown confirmed everything he had suspected about her. Underneath her ice-maiden façade was a passionate young woman just crying out for physical expression. He could see it in the way she held herself together so primly, as if she was frightened of breaking free from the tight moral restraints she had placed around herself. Kissing her would have proven it. He wanted to taste that soft, innocent bow of a mouth and feel her shudder all over with longing. To thrust his tongue between those beautiful lips and taste the sweet, moist heat of her mouth. To have her tongue tangle with his in a sexy coupling that was a prelude to smoking-hot sex.

He clenched his hands into tight fists as he wrestled with his conscience. He wasn't in a good place right now. He was acting totally out of character. It would be wrong to try it on with her. He could slake his lust the way he usually did—with someone who knew the game and was happy with his rules. He didn't do long term. The longest he did was a month or two—any longer than that and women got ideas of bended knees, rings and promises he couldn't deliver on.

It wasn't that he was against marriage. He believed in it as an institution and admired people who made it work. He even believed it *could* work. He believed it was a good framework in which to bring up children and travel through the cycles and seasons of life with someone who had the same vision and values. He was quietly envious of Julius's relationship with Holly Perez. But he didn't allow himself to think too long about how it would be to have a life partner to build a future with—to have someone to hope and dream with.

He was used to living on his own.

He preferred it. He didn't have to make idle conversation. He didn't have to meet someone else's emotional needs. He could get on with his work any hour of the day—particularly when he couldn't sleep—and no one would question him.

Leandro heard a soft footfall at the top of the stairs and looked up to see Miranda gliding down like a graceful swan. She was wearing a knee-length milky-coffee-coloured dress with a cashmere pashmina around her slim shoulders. It would have been a nondescript colour on someone else but with her porcelain skin and auburn hair it was perfect. She had scooped her hair up into a makeshift but stylish knot at the back of her head, which highlighted the elegant length of her slim neck. She was wearing a string of pearls and pearl studs in her earlobes that showcased the creamy, smooth perfection of her skin and, as she got closer, he could pick up the fresh, flowery scent of her perfume. Her brown eyes were made up with subtle shades of eye shadow and her fan-like lashes had been lengthened and thickened with mascara.

Her mouth—*dear God in heaven, why couldn't he stop looking at her mouth?*—was shiny with a strawberry-coloured lip gloss.

A light blush rode along her cheekbones as she came to stand before him. 'I'm sorry for keeping you waiting…'

Leandro felt her perfume ambush his senses; the

freesia notes were fresh and light but there was a hint
of something a little more complex under the surface.
It teased his nostrils, toyed with his imagination, tor-
mented him with its veiled sensual promise. He glanced
at her shoes. 'Can you walk in those?'

'Yes.'

'The restaurant is only a few blocks from here,' he
said. 'But I can drive if you'd prefer.'

'No, a walk would be lovely,' she said.

They walked to a French restaurant Leandro informed
Miranda he had found the day before. Every step of the
walk, she was aware of the distance between them. It
never varied. It was as if he had calculated what would
be appropriate and rigorously stuck to it. He walked
on the road side of the footpath just like the well-bred
gentleman she knew him to be. He took care at the
intersections they came to making sure it was safe to
cross against the traffic and other pedestrians.

Miranda was aware of him there beside her. Even
though he didn't touch her, not even accidently to brush
against her, she could feel his male presence. It made
her skin lift, tighten and tingle. It made her body feel
strangely excited, as if something caged inside her belly
was holding its breath, eagerly anticipating the brush
of his flesh against hers.

Miranda realised then she had never been on a
proper dinner date with an adult man. When she and
Mark went out they had done teenage things—walks
and café chats, trips to the cinema and fast-food outlets
and the occasional friend's party. But then he had been

diagnosed and their dates had been in the hospital or, on rare occasions when he'd been feeling well enough, in the hospital cafeteria. They had never gone out to dinner in a proper restaurant. They had never gone clubbing. They had never even gone out for a drink as they had been under age.

How weird to be doing it first with Leandro, she thought. It made her feel as if something had shifted in their relationship. A subtle change that put them on a different platform. He was no longer her brothers' close friend but her first proper adult dinner-date. But of course they weren't actually dating, no matter what Jaz thought about the way he looked at her. Jaz was probably imagining it. Why would Leandro be interested in her? She was too shy. Too ordinary. Too beige.

The small intimate restaurant was tucked in one of the cobbled side streets and it had both inside and outside dining. When Leandro asked her for her preference, Miranda chose to sit outside, as the October evening was beautifully mild, but also because after the dusty, brooding, shadowy interior of his father's villa she thought it would be nice to have some fresh air. For Leandro, as well as her.

The weight of grief in that sad old villa had been hard enough for her to deal with, let alone him. It pained her to think he carried the burden of guilt— guilt that should never have been laid on his young child's shoulders. She couldn't stop thinking of him as a six-year-old boy—quiet, sensitive, intelligent, caring. How could his parents have put that awful yoke upon his young shoulders?

It was a terrible tragedy that his sister Rosie had gone missing. A heart-breaking, gut-wrenching tragedy that could not be resolved in any way now that would be healing. But his parents had been the adults. They'd been the ones with the responsibility to keep their children safe. It hadn't been Leandro's responsibility. Children could not be held accountable for doing what only an adult should do. Children as young as six were not reliable babysitters. Not even for two or three minutes. They were at the mercy of their immature impulses. It wasn't fair to blame them for what was typical of that stage of childhood development. It wasn't right to punish a child for simply being a child.

How much had Leandro suffered with that terrible burden? He had shouldered it on his own for all this time—twenty-seven years. He had stored it away deep inside him—unable to connect properly with people because of it. He always stood at the perimeter of social gatherings. He was set apart by the tragic secret he carried. He hadn't even told her brothers about Rosie and yet he had asked Miranda to come here and help him with his father's collection. What did *that* mean? Had it been an impulsive thing on his part? She had never thought of him as an impulsive man. He measured everything before he acted. He thought before he spoke. He considered things from every angle.

Why *had* he asked her?

Was it a subconscious desire on his part to connect? What sort of connection was he after? Could Jaz be right? Could he be after a more intimate connection? Was that why he was challenging her over her com-

mitment to Mark? Making her face her convictions in
the face of temptation—a temptation she had never felt
quite like this before?

He thought her silly for staying true to her commitment to Mark. But then Leandro wasn't known for
longevity in relationships. He wasn't quite the one-
night-stand man her brother Jake was but she hadn't
heard of any relationship of Leandro's lasting longer
than a month or two. He moved around with work a
lot which would make it difficult for him to settle.
But even so she didn't see him as the guy with a girl
in every port.

Would Miranda's time here with him help him to
move past the tragedy of Rosie? Would he feel freer
once his father's things were packed up and sold? Once
all this sadness was put away for good?

Once they were seated at their table with drinks in
front of them Miranda took a covert look at him while
he perused the menu. The sad memories from being
in his little sister's room were etched on his face. His
dark-chocolate eyes looked tired and drawn, the two
lines running either side of his mouth seemed deeper
and his ever-present frown more firmly entrenched.

He looked up and his eyes meshed with hers, making something in her stomach trip like a foot missing
a step. 'Have you decided?' he said.

Miranda had to work hard not to stare at his mouth.
He had showered and shaved, yet the persistent stubble
was evident along his jaw and around his well-shaped
mouth. She had to curl her fingers into her palms to
stop herself from reaching across the table to touch the

peppered lean and tanned skin, to trace the sculptured line of his beautiful mouth. His thick hair was cut in a short no-nonsense style, although she could see a light sheen amongst the deep grooves where he had used some sort of hair product. Even with the distance of the table between them she could smell the hint of citrus and wood in his aftershave.

'Um…' She looked back at the menu, chewing on her lower lip. 'I think I'll have the *coq au vin*. You?'

He closed the menu with a definitive movement. 'Same.'

Miranda took a tentative sip of her white wine. He had ordered one as well but he had so far not touched it. Did he avoid alcohol because of his father's problems with it? Or was it just a part of his careful, keeping-control-at-all-times personality?

Self-discipline was something she admired in a man. Her father had always lacked it, which was more than obvious, given this latest debacle over his love child. But Leandro wasn't the sort of man to be driven by impulse. He was responsible, mature and sensible. He was the sort of man people came to for help and advice. He was reliable and principled. Which made what had happened to him all the more tragic. How hard it must be for him to come back here to the place where it all began. His life had changed for ever. He carried that burden of guilt. It had defined him. Shaped him. And yet he had kept it to himself for all those years.

'If I hadn't found Rosie's statue in the garden would you have told me about her?' Miranda said into the little silence.

His fingers toyed with the stem of his glass. 'I was planning to. Eventually.'

She watched as his frown pulled heavily at his brow. 'Leandro... I really want to say how much I feel for you. For what you're going through. For what you've been through. I feel I'm only just coming to understand you after knowing you for all these years.'

He gave her a ghost of a smile. It was not much more than a flicker across his lips but it warmed her heart, as if someone had shone a beam of light through a dark crack. 'I was a little hard on you earlier,' he said.

'It's okay,' Miranda said. 'I get it from my brothers and Jaz too. And my parents.'

'It's only because they love you,' he said. 'They want you to be happy.'

Miranda put her glass down, her fingers tracing the gentle slope on the circular base. 'I know...but it wasn't just Mark I loved. His family—his parents—are the loveliest people. They always made me feel so special. So included.'

'Do you still see them?'

'Yes.'

'Is that wise?'

Miranda frowned as she met his unwavering gaze. 'Why wouldn't I visit them? They're the family I wish I'd had.'

'It might not be helping them to move on.'

'What about your mother?' she said, deftly changing the subject. 'Does she want you to be happy?'

He gave a nonchalant shrug but his mouth had taken

on that grim look she always associated with him. 'On some level, maybe.'

'Do you ever see her?'

'Occasionally.'

'When was the last time?' Miranda asked.

He turned the base of his glass around with an exacting, precise movement like he was turning a combination lock on a safe. 'I went down for one of my half-brother's birthdays a couple of months ago.'

'And?'

He looked at her again. 'It was okay.'

Miranda cocked her head at him. 'Just okay?'

He gave her a rueful grimace. 'It was Cameron who invited me. I wouldn't have gone if he hadn't wanted me to be there. I didn't stay long.'

Miranda wondered what sort of reception he'd got from his mother. Had she greeted him warmly or coldly? Had she tolerated him being there or embraced his presence? How did his mother's husband treat him? Did he accept him as one of the family or make him feel like an outsider who could never belong? There were so many questions she wanted to ask. Things she wanted to know about him, but she didn't want to bombard him. It would take time to peel back the layers to his personality. He was so deeply private and going too hard too soon would very likely cause him to clam up. 'How old are your half-brothers?'

'Cam is twenty-eight, Alistair twenty-seven and Hugh is twenty-six.' He turned his glass another notch. 'My mother would have had more children but it wasn't to be.'

'Three boys in quick succession…' she murmured, thinking out loud.

'But no girl, which was what she really wanted.'

Miranda saw the flash of pain pass over his features. 'I'm not sure having any amount of children would make up for the one she lost. But in a way she lost two children, didn't she?'

Leandro's mouth tilted cynically. 'Don't feel sorry for me, *ma petite*,' he said. 'I'm a big boy.'

Hearing him switch to French from Italian endearments was enough to set her pulse racing all over again. His voice was so deep and mellifluous she could have listened to him read a boring financial report and still her heart would race. 'It seems to me you've always had to be a big boy,' Miranda said. 'You've spent so much of your childhood and adolescence alone.'

'I had your family to go to.'

'Yes, but it wasn't *your* family,' she said. 'You must have felt that keenly at times.'

He picked up his wine glass and examined the contents, as if it were a vintage wine he wanted to savour. But then he put it back down again. 'I owe a lot to your family,' he said. 'In particular to your brothers. We had some good times down at Ravensdene. Some really great times.'

'And yet you never once mentioned Rosie to them.'

'I thought about it a couple of times… Many times, actually.' He fingered the base of his glass again. 'But in the end it was easier keeping that part of my life separate. Except, of course, when my father came to town.'

'You were worried he would blurt something in his drunken state?' Miranda said.

He gave her a world-weary look. 'Anyone being drunk is not a pretty sight but my father took it to a whole new level. He always liked a drink but I don't ever remember seeing him flat-out drunk as a child. Losing Rosie tipped him over. He numbed himself with alcohol in order to cope.'

'Did he ever try and get help for his drinking?'

'I offered to pay for rehab numerous times but he wouldn't hear of it,' Leandro said. 'He said he didn't have a problem. He was able to control it. Mostly he did. But not when he was with me, especially in latter years.'

Miranda's heart clenched. How painful it must have been for him to witness the devastation of his father's life while being cognisant that *he* was deemed responsible for it. It was too cruel. Too sad. Too unbearable to think of someone as decent, sensitive and wonderful as Leandro being tortured so. 'It must have been awful to watch him slide into such self-destruction and not be able to do anything to help,' she said. 'But you mustn't blame yourself, Leandro. Not now. Not after all this time. Your father made choices. He could've got help at any point. You did what you could. You can't force someone to get help. They have to be willing to accept there's a problem in the first place.'

He looked back at the glass of untouched wine in front of him, his brows drawn together in a tightly knitted frown. Miranda put her hand out and covered his where it was resting on the snowy-white tablecloth.

He looked up and met her gaze with the dark intensity of his. 'You're a nice kid, Miranda,' he said in a gruff burr that made the base of her spine shiver.

A nice kid.

Didn't he see her as anything other than the kid sister of his best mates? And why did it bother her if he didn't see she was a fully grown woman? It shouldn't bother her at all. She wasn't going to break her promise to Mark. She couldn't. For the last seven years she had stayed true to her commitment. She took pride in being so steadfast, so strong and so loyal, especially in this day and age when people slept with virtual strangers.

Her words were the last words Mark had heard before he'd left this world. How could she retract them?

A promise was a promise.

Miranda lowered her gaze and pulled back her hand but even when it was back in her lap she could feel the warmth of Leandro's skin against her palm.

The rest of the meal continued with the conversation on much lighter ground. He asked her about her work at the gallery and, an hour and two courses later, she realised he had cleverly drawn her out without revealing anything of his own work and the stresses and demands it placed on him.

'Enough about me,' she said, pushing her wine glass away. 'Tell me about your work. What made you go into forensic accounting?'

'I was always good at maths,' he said. 'But straight accounting wasn't enough for me. I was drawn to the challenge of uncovering complicated financial systems. It's a bit like breaking a code. I find it satisfying.'

'And clearly financially rewarding,' Miranda said.

He gave a slight movement of his lips that might have been considered a smile. 'I do okay.'

He was being overly modest, Miranda thought. He didn't brandish his wealth as some people did. There were no private jets, Italian sports cars and luxurious holidays all over the globe; he had invested his money wisely in property and shares and gave a considerable amount to charity. Not that he made that public. She had only heard about it via her brother Julius, who was also known for his philanthropy.

Just as they were leaving the restaurant, once Leandro had paid the bill, a party of people came towards them from down the lane. Miranda wouldn't have taken much notice except a woman of about thirty or so peeled away from the group to approach Leandro.

'Leandro?' she said. 'Fancy running into you here! I haven't heard from you for a while. I've come over for a wedding of a friend. Are you here on business?'

'How are you?'

Leandro gave the young woman a kiss on both cheeks. 'Fine. You?'

The woman eyed Miranda. 'Aren't you going to introduce us?' she asked Leandro with a glinting look.

'Miranda, this is Nicole Holmes,' he said. 'We worked for the same accounting firm before I left to go out on my own. Nicole, this is Miranda Ravensdale.'

Nicole's perfectly shaped brows lifted. 'As in *the* infamous Ravensdales?' she said.

Miranda gave a tight smile. 'Pleased to meet you, Nicole.'

Nicole's gaze travelled over Miranda in an assessing, sizing-up manner common to some women when they encountered someone they presumed was competition. 'I've been reading all about your father's secret love-child in the papers and gossip mags,' she said. 'Have you met your new sister yet?'

Miranda felt the muscles in her spine tighten like concrete. 'Not yet.'

Nicole glanced at Leandro. 'So are you two…?' She left the sentence hanging suggestively.

'No,' Leandro said. 'We're old friends.'

Miranda knew it was silly of her to be feeling piqued that he hadn't made their relationship sound a little more exciting. But the woman was clearly an old flame of his, by the way she kept giving him the eye. Why couldn't he have pretended they were seeing each other? Or was he hoping for a little for-old-times'-sake tryst with Nicole? The thought of Leandro bringing someone like Nicole back to the villa made Miranda's stomach churn. Nothing against Nicole, but surely he could do better than that? Nicole seemed… hard—too streetwise to be sensitive. But maybe that was all he wanted, Miranda thought. Sex without sensitivity. Without strings. Without attachment.

'So what are you doing in Nice?' Nicole said.

'I'm seeing to some family business,' Leandro said.

Nicole's green eyes met Miranda's. 'And you're helping him?'

'Erm…yes,' Miranda said.

Nicole turned her cat's gaze back on to Leandro. 'How about we meet for a drink while you're here?'

she said. 'I'm here another couple of days. Name the time and the place. I'm pretty flexible.'

I just bet you are, Miranda thought with a savage twist of jealousy deep in her gut.

'I'll give you a call tomorrow,' Leandro said. 'Where are you staying?'

'At Le Negresco.' Nicole lifted her hand in a girlish fingertip wave as she backed away to join her friends who were waiting for her at the end of the lane. 'I'll be seeing you.'

Miranda waited until Nicole and her cronies had disappeared before she turned to Leandro with a look of undiluted disgust. *'Really?'* she said.

He looked down at her with his customary frown. 'What's wrong?'

She blew out a breath. 'I swear to God I will *never* understand men. What do you see in her? No, don't answer that. I saw the size of her breasts. Are they real? And is she really blonde or did it come out of a bottle?'

Leandro's frown softened. 'You're jealous.'

Miranda cast him a haughty glare. 'Jealous? Seriously? Is that what you think?'

'She's just someone I hang out with occasionally.'

'Oh, I understand,' she said with icy disdain. 'A friend with benefits.'

'You disapprove?'

Miranda didn't want to sound like a Sunday school teacher from the last century but the thought of him hooking up with Nicole made her insides twist into painful knots. 'It's none of my business what you do. I'd just appreciate it if you'd spare me the indignity of having to hear your seduction routine while I'm under the same roof.'

His expression didn't change. He could have been sitting at a poker tournament but she still got the feeling he was amused by her reaction. 'Don't worry,' he said. 'I never bring women like Nicole home. That's what hotels are for.'

Miranda swung away. 'I don't want to hear about it.'

He walked alongside her. 'Do you lecture Jake like this?' he said after they had gone a few paces.

'No, because Jake isn't like you,' she said. 'You're different. You have class—or so I thought.'

'I'm sorry for being such a bitter disappointment.'

Miranda flashed him a glare. 'Will you *stop* it?'

His look was guileless. 'Stop what?'

'You're laughing at me. I know you are.'

He reached out and gently tucked an escaping tendril of her hair back behind her ear. 'It's just sex, *ma petite*. No one is hurting anyone.'

Miranda's breath caught in her throat. His fingers had left the skin at the back of her ear tingling. Was he as tender with a casual lover? Did he touch that woman Nicole as if she were a precious piece of porcelain? Or was it wham, bam, thank you, mam? 'How long have you been—' she put her fingers up in air quotes '—seeing her?'

'A year or two.'

A year or two? Did that mean he was serious about her? Miranda had always got the impression he was a casual dater. But if he'd been seeing Nicole for that long surely it must mean he was serious about her? Was he in love with her? He hadn't looked like a man in love. He had kissed Nicole in a perfunctory way, and on the cheeks, not on the lips. He hadn't even hugged her. 'That seems a long time to be seeing someone,' she said. 'Does that mean you're thinking of—?'

'No,' he said. 'It's not that sort of relationship.'

'What if she falls in love with you?' Miranda said. 'What then?'

'Nicole knows the rules.'

'How often do you see her?' Miranda didn't really want to know. 'Weekly? Monthly?'

'When it's convenient.'

She could feel her lip curling and her insides tightening as if an invisible hand was gripping her intestines. 'So, how often is it convenient? Once a week? Twice a month? Every couple of months?'

'I don't keep a tally, if that's what you're asking,' he said. 'It's not an exclusive relationship.'

Miranda couldn't believe he was living his life in such a shallow manner. He was worth far more than a quick phone call to hook up. Didn't he realise how much he was short-changing himself? Didn't he want more for his life? More emotional intimacy? A deeper connection other than the physical? A casual fling every now and again might have been fine while he was young, but what about as he got older? He was thirty-three years old. Did he really want to spend the rest of his life alone? What about the women he dated? Didn't *they* want more? How could they not want more when he embodied everything most women wanted?

'Don't you have any idea of how *attractive* you are to women?' Miranda said.

His dark eyes were unreadable. 'Am I attractive to you?'

She took a hitching breath, not quite able to hold his gaze. 'I—I don't think of you that way. You're like… like a brother to me.'

He brought her chin up so she had to meet his gaze. 'I'm not feeling like a brother right now. And I have a feeling you're not feeling anything like a sister.'

Miranda swallowed. Was she *that* transparent? Could he see how much of a struggle it was to keep her gaze away from the temptation of his mouth? Could he sense how hard it was keeping her commitment to Mark secure when he looked at her like that? With that smouldering gaze burning through every layer of her resolve like a blowtorch on glacial ice? She sent her tongue out to moisten her sandstone-dry lips and saw his gaze hone in on its passage, as if pulled by a magnet.

She watched spellbound as his mouth lowered towards hers as if in slow motion. There was plenty of time for her to draw back, plenty of time to put some distance between them, but somehow she couldn't get the message through to her addled brain.

She gave a breathless, almost soundless sigh as his lips touched hers. A touch down as soft as fairy feet sent a hot wave of need through her entire body until she felt a shudder go through her from head to toe and back again. She made another helpless noise at the back of her throat as she wound her arms up around his neck, pressing closer, pressing to get more of his firm mouth before it got too far away.

His lips came down harder this time, moving over hers in a possessive manner that made her knees weaken and her spine buckle. His tongue stroked the seam of her mouth, commanding she open to him, and with another little gasp she welcomed him inside. He came in search of her tongue, exploring every corner of her mouth with shockingly intimate, breath-taking expertise. She felt the scrape of his stubble against her chin as he shifted position. Felt the potent stirring of his body against her belly. Felt her own blood racing as desire swept through her like a runaway fire.

Miranda had felt desire as a teenager but it had been nothing like this. That had been a trickle. This was a flood. A tidal wave. A tsunami. This was adult desire. A rampant, clawing need that refused to be assuaged with anything but full possession. She could feel the urgent pleas of her body: the restless ache deep in her core, the tingling of her breasts where they were pressed up hard against his chest.

Kissing in a dark lane wasn't enough. No way was it enough. She wanted to put her hands on his flesh—his gloriously adult, male *healthy* flesh—to feel his body moving over hers with passionate intent. To feel him deep inside her where she ached the most.

But suddenly he pulled away from her.

Miranda felt momentarily off-balance without his arms and body to support her. What was she doing, kissing him like some sex-starved desperado? Her whole body was shaking with the rush of pleasure his mouth had evoked—hot sparks of pleasure that reverberated in the lower regions of her body. Pulsing, throbbing sparks of forbidden, traitorous pleasure. How could she have let it happen? *Why* had she let it happen? But, rather than show how undone she was, she took refuge in defensive pride. 'Happy now?' she said. 'Proved your point?'

He stood a couple of feet away, one of his hands pushing back through the thick pelt of his hair. It should have come as some small compensation to her that he looked as shell-shocked as she felt but somehow it didn't.

Had he found kissing her distasteful? Unexciting? Not quite up to standard? A host of insecurities flooded through her, leaving a storm of hot colour pooling in her cheeks.

She hadn't kissed anyone but Mark. He had been her first and her last. Their kisses had been nice. Clumsy at first, but then nice. The sex...well, it had seemed to be okay for Mark, but she had found it hard to get her needs met. They'd both been each other's first lover so his inexperience and her shyness hadn't exactly helped.

Then the chemotherapy had made things especially awkward. She hadn't always cared for the smell of Mark's breath or the fact that he was ill most of the time. It had made her feel guilty, being so missish. After Mark's diagnosis she had shied away from sharing her body with him because in her youthful ignorance she had thought she might catch cancer. She had compensated in other ways, pleasuring him manually when he felt up to it. Her guilt over feeling like that had compounded—solidified—her decision to remain loyal to him.

But such inexperience left her stranded when it came to dealing with a man as experienced as Leandro. He was used to women who played the game. Used to hooking up for the sake of convenience before moving on. He wouldn't want the complication of tangling with a technical virgin. Had he sensed her inexperience? Had she somehow communicated it with her response to his kiss?

Leandro let out a long, slow breath as if recalibrating himself. 'That was probably not such a great idea on my part.'

Miranda pulled at her lip with her teeth. 'Was I that bad?'

His brows drew closer together. 'No, of course not. How could you think that?'

She gave a one-shoulder shrug. 'I've only kissed one person before. I'm out of practice.'

He studied her for a long moment. 'Do you miss it?'

'Miss what?'

'Kissing, touching, sex—being with someone.'

Miranda resumed walking and he fell into step beside her at a polite arm's length distance. 'I don't think about it. I made a promise and as far as I'm concerned that's the end of it.'

It wasn't the end of it, Miranda thought as she got into bed half an hour later with her body still madly craving the touch and heat of his. She put her fingers to her mouth, touching where his warm lips had moved so expertly against hers. Her mouth felt different some-how. Softer, fuller, awakened to needs she had ignored for so long.

Needs she would continue to ignore even if it took every ounce of will power she possessed.

CHAPTER FIVE

LEANDRO SPENT AN hour or two over some accounts and files he'd brought with him but he couldn't concentrate. He closed the laptop and got to his feet. Miranda had gone to bed hours ago and everything that was male in him had wanted to join her. He shouldn't have kissed her. He still didn't know why he had. He had been so determined to keep his distance and then it had just… happened. He had been the one to make the first move. He hadn't been able to stop himself from leaning down to the lure of her beautiful, soft, inviting mouth. The taste of her, so sweet, warm and giving, had shaken him. Rocked him. Unsettled him.

Miranda had seemed upset at his on-off relationship with Nicole. But that didn't mean he had the right to kiss her. She was just being protective in a sisterly sort of way.

Sisterly? There was nothing sisterly about the way Miranda had kissed him back. He had felt every tremble in her body as she'd leaned into him. Her gorgeous mouth had given back as good as he had served. The tangled heat of their tongues had made his body respond like a hormone-driven teenager. Since when did he lose control like that? What was he doing even *thinking* about doing more than kissing her?

Leandro stood at the window of the study and looked out at the neglected garden. The moon illuminated the overgrown shapes of the hedges, giving them a grotesque appearance. He couldn't see Rosie's statue from here but knowing it was there made the weight of his grief feel like an anchor hanging off his heart.

Would it *never* ease? This awful sense of guilt that plagued him day and night?

Would packing up Rosie's room bring closure or would it make things even worse? Handling the toys she had played with, touching the clothes she had worn, packing them off to where? Charity? For some stranger to use or to throw out when they were finished with them?

Leandro couldn't keep her things. Why would he? He would have no use for them and he didn't want to turn into another version of his father, making a shrine that in no way would help to heal the past.

It was time to move on.

He opened the door to Rosie's room and stood there for a moment. For the two years after Rosie's disappearance he had come to her room during the night. *Every* night. He had stood in exactly this spot in the doorway, hoping, praying, he would find her neat little shape in the princess bed. That he would see one of her starfish hands resting on the pillow near her little angel face with its halo of dark hair. That he would hear the soft snuffle of her breathing and see the rise and fall of her chest.

He remembered the last time he had stood here. The night before he had been taken to England to live with his mother. He had stood in this doorway with a tsunami of emotion trapped in his chest.

Something in him had died along with Rosie. He could feel the place where it had been. It was a hollow space inside him where hope used to be.

The moon shone a beam over the empty bed where Flopsy the rabbit had slumped forward from his propped up position against the pillows. Leandro moved across the carpet and gently straightened the toy so he was back between the pink elephant and the teddy bear.

He turned from the bed, his heart all but stopping when he saw a small figure framed in the doorway. He blinked and then realised it was Miranda, dressed in cream-coloured satin pyjamas. 'What are you doing up at this hour?' he said, surprised his voice came out so even when his heart was still thumping like a mad thing.

Even though it was dark, except for the moonlight, he could see the twin streaks of colour over her pale cheeks. 'I couldn't sleep...' she said. 'I came down for a glass of water and I thought I heard something.'

'You weren't frightened?'

She captured her lower lip between her teeth. 'Only a little.'

Leandro could feel his body calculating the distance between their bodies—every organ, every cell registering her presence like radar picking up a signal. He didn't trust himself to be near her. Not since he'd kissed her. *God, he had to stop thinking about that kiss.*

He could see every line of her slim body beneath the close-fitting drape of the satin pyjamas she was wearing. He could smell the freesia scent of her perfume. He could still taste her in his mouth—that alluring sweetness and hint of innocence that made him hard as stone. Her auburn hair was all mussed up, as if she had been tossing and turning in bed. He wanted to slide those silky strands through his fingers and to breathe in their clean, fresh fragrance. Her skin was luminous in the moonlight, her toffee-brown eyes shining like wet paint. He surged with blood when she moistened her mouth with the quick dart of her tongue. Was she remembering their kiss? Reliving it the way he had been doing for the last couple of hours? Feeling the desire licking along her veins as it had along his until he was almost crazy with it?

'Do you want a glass of milk or something?' he said, leading the way out of the room.

She screwed up her mouth like a child refusing to take medicine. 'I'm not much of a milk drinker.'

'Something stronger, then?'

'No, I'll just head back to bed,' she said. 'I'm sorry for disturbing you.'

'You weren't disturbing me.' He let out a short sigh as he closed the door behind him. 'I was just…remembering.'

Her eyes glistened as if she was about to cry. 'It must be so terribly hard for you, being here again.'

Leandro knew he shouldn't touch her. Touching her was dangerous. Touching her made it harder to keep his resolve in place. But even so his hand reached out and gently tucked a flyaway hair back behind the shell of her ear. He heard her draw in a sharp little breath, her mouth parting slightly, her eyes flicking downwards to his mouth. 'Don't tear yourself up about that kiss,' he said.

Her eyes skittered away from his. 'I'm not. I've forgotten all about it.'

He inched up her chin, holding her gaze with his. 'I can't *stop* thinking about it.'

She rolled her lips together. Blinked. Swallowed. Blinked again. 'You shouldn't do that.'

'Why not?'

'Because it's not right.'

He slid his hand along her cheek, cradling her face as his thumb moved over the silky skin of her face. 'It felt pretty right to me.' Which was the problem in a big, fat, inconvenient nutshell. It felt so damn right he wanted to do it again.

And not just kiss her. He wanted her like he had never wanted anyone. He felt it in his body now—the thunder of his blood heading south. The tingle in his thighs made him want to bring her close enough for her body to feel him. To feel the need he had for her. The hunger that would not go away now it had been awakened. Would she pull away or would she lean in like she had when he'd kissed her earlier? Would her body press urgently against his? Would she make those breathless little gasps of approval as his mouth showed her what it was like to kiss a full-blooded man?

She swept her tongue over her lips in a nervous manner. 'Just because something feels right doesn't make it right.'

Leandro moved his hand on her face to brush the pad of his thumb across her lower lip. 'Are you seriously going to spend the rest of your life being celibate?' he said.

A glitter of hauteur shone in her gaze as it held his. 'I find that imminently preferable to hooking up with people for no other reason than to slake animal lust.'

Was it just sisterly, friendly concern or was she jealous? 'Ah, so Nicole is an issue for you, then?'

Her mouth tightened to a flat disapproving line. 'It's no business of mine if you call her and sleep with her. You can call and sleep with anyone you like.'

'But you would hate it if I did.'

She stepped back from him and folded her arms across the front of her body, reminding him of a starchy schoolmistress from his childhood. 'Don't you want more out of life than that?' she said.

'Don't you?'

She pursed her lips. 'We're not talking about me.'

'No,' he said. 'Because talking about you makes you feel uncomfortable, doesn't it? You're happier dishing out the advice to everyone else while you turn a blind eye to your own needs.'

'You know nothing about my needs,' she flashed back.

He raised one of his brows. 'Are you sure about

that, Sleeping Beauty?' he said. 'I can still taste those needs in my mouth.'

Her cheeks flamed with colour. 'Why are you doing this?'

He took her by the shoulders gently but firmly. 'You're living a lie, Miranda. You know you are. A big, fat lie. You want more but you're too afraid to grow up and ask for it.'

She pulled away from him with a twist of her body, glaring at him. 'Did Julius put you up to this?'

Leandro frowned. 'Why do you say that?'

'He gave me one of his lectures recently,' she said. 'He said the same thing you said—that Mark would've moved on if the tables were turned. It's kind of telling, how you're suddenly taking an interest in me after ignoring me for all these years.'

'I haven't been ignoring you.' *Far from it*, he thought wryly. His awareness of her had been gradual, admittedly. He had always seen her as his mates' little sister. But over time he had watched her blossom from an awkward teenager into a beautiful and accomplished young woman. He noticed the way her creamy cheeks blushed when she was embarrassed, especially for some reason when he was around. He noticed her body; how it made his feel when she was in the same room as him. He noticed her slightest movement: the shy lick of her lips; the downward cast of her gaze; the nervous swallow; the sinking of her small white teeth into the blood-red pillow of her lower lip.

Leandro came to where she was standing with

her arms folded. 'I'm not ignoring you now,' he said, watching as the dark ink of her pupils flared.

She closed her eyes in a slow blink. 'Don't…'

'Don't what?'

The tip of her tongue sneaked out to moisten her lips. 'You're making this so hard for me…'

'Because you want to know what it feels like to be with a man instead of a boy, don't you?' Leandro said. 'That's why you kissed me the way you did. You didn't kiss like some shy little teenager who didn't know what she was doing. You kissed like a hot-blooded, passionate woman because that's who you really are underneath that prim and proper, twin-set-and-pearls façade you insist on hiding behind.'

Her mouth flattened to a thin line of white. 'You know something?' she said. 'I think I preferred it when you ignored me. I'm going to bed. Good night.'

Leandro muttered a stiff curse as she stalked off down the shadowed corridor until she disappeared from sight.

Miranda got to work on the collection first thing. She sorted the paintings into different sections for proper packing and shipping. She had already consulted her associates on one or two paintings that were outside her range of experience. By lunchtime she had done half the collection but that still left the other half, as well as the antiques.

She hadn't seen or heard from Leandro since late last night. She had gone to bed in a fit of temper over him pushing her to admit her needs. Needs she was perfectly happy ignoring, thank you very much. Or she had been, until he'd come along and stopped *ignoring* her. Grr! Was that why he had kissed her in the lane? Just to prove a point? To show her how it felt to kiss a man?

Well, she knew now. It felt good. It felt amazing. It felt so damn amazing she didn't know how she had managed to keep out of his arms last night. She had come close to throwing herself at him. Terrifyingly, shamelessly close. She had looked at his mouth and imagined it pressed on hers, his tongue doing all those wicked things it had done before, and the way hers had responded so wantonly.

Miranda didn't even know if he was still in the villa or whether he had left to meet Nicole. The thought of him with the other woman was like a stone in the pit of her belly.

Would he tell Nicole of the pain he held inside him? Would he share the agony of his childhood? The terrible loss he had experienced? The guilt and torment he still felt? Would he tell her about the estrangement he had suffered from his father and the distant relationship he had with his mother?

Or would they just have monkey sex without any emotional connection at all?

Miranda decided to get out of the villa for a while before she went mad over-thinking about Leandro's sex life. She bought some things for dinner and stopped for a coffee in a café that overlooked the stunning blue of the ocean. It was another mild day with soap-sud clouds gathering on the horizon. Although the late summer crowds had well and truly gone, she was surprised to see only a couple of people swimming in the sea, for the water temperature at this time of year was warmer than in many parts of England in high summer.

Miranda wondered exactly where along the shore Rosie had gone missing. The villa was only a few blocks back from the seafront. She didn't know whether she should ask Leandro to show her. Would it be too painful for him to revisit that tragic spot?

As she walked back to the villa Miranda passed a mother with a baby strapped in a pouch against her chest with a little boy of about two in a pushchair. The baby was sound asleep with its little downy head cradled against its mother's chest. The little toddler was holding a brightly coloured toy and smiled at Miranda as she navigated her way past on the narrow footpath.

Miranda resisted the urge to turn and look back at the little family. When she'd been in her teens, seeing mums with kids hadn't been an issue. Even in the weeks and months after Mark had died she had put the thought out of her mind.

But now every time she saw a mother with a baby she felt a pang, like a nagging toothache.

She would never have a baby of her own.

Somehow that had seemed like a romantic sacrifice when she'd been sixteen, sitting at Mark's bedside with his life draining away in front of her eyes. Now at twenty-three she felt as if the promise was a prison sentence—one without any possibility of parole. How was she going to feel at thirty-three? Forty-three? Fifty?

Miranda pushed the thought to the back wall of her

mind. There were other things she had to concentrate on just now. Like how to get Leandro's father's collection safely shipped to London and the villa packed up ready for sale.

The villa was quiet when Miranda came in. She put her shopping away and then went up the stairs, but instead of going to her room as she had intended she found herself turning to Rosie's instead.

She opened the door and stood there for a moment. The toys were as they had been last night. The bed was still neatly made, all Rosie's things still on the dressing table.

Leandro had intimated he wanted the room to be packed up. Should Miranda do it to save him the pain? *Could* she do it?

Miranda wandered over to the cherry-wood wardrobe and, opening it, looked at the array of neat little hangers with toddler clothes. She ran her fingers along the different fabrics, wondering how any parent could ever navigate the loss of a child. Was there any way of dealing with such overwhelming grief? No wonder Leandro's father had left Rosie's things as they were. Packing them away was so final. So permanent.

Miranda closed the wardrobe with a sigh.

Leandro could smell something delicious as soon as he came into the villa. It was such a homely smell it took him aback for a moment. It had been a long time since he had felt as if this place was anything like a home. But with the sound of dishes clattering in the kitchen and Miranda moving about he got a sense of what the villa could one day be again with the right family. He imagined children coming in from the garden, as he and Rosie had done, their faces shining with exertion and sunshine. He could picture the evening meal with the family gathered around the kitchen table or in the dining room, everyone relating how their day had gone, the parents looking fondly at their children.

His parents hadn't been one-hundred percent happy with each other but they had loved him and Rosie.

Life had seemed so normal and then suddenly it wasn't.

Leandro walked into the kitchen to see Miranda popping something in the oven. She was wearing a cute candy-striped apron around her waist and her hair was tied up in a knot on top of her head. Her cheeks were flushed from the oven but they went a shade darker when she saw him standing there.

She swiped a strand of hair back from her face. 'Dinner won't be long.'

'You didn't have to cook,' he said. 'We could've eaten out or got takeaway.'

'I like cooking.' She rinsed her hands under the tap and dried them on a tea towel. 'So how was your date with Nicole? I presume that's where you've been? Did it all go according to plan?'

'We had a drink.'

Miranda's neat brows lifted. 'Just a drink?'

He held her gaze for a long beat, watching as a host of emotions flitted across her face. 'Yes. Just a drink.'

'You must be losing your touch.'

'Maybe.'

She began to fuss over a salad she was making on the counter. 'I've packed up about half of your father's paintings. I've still got some research to do on the others. I'm waiting to hear back from one of my colleagues. 1 should have it more or less done by the end of next week, maybe even earlier. I've got the shipping people on standby but I'll need you to authorise the insurance.'

Leandro felt something in his chest slip at the thought of her leaving earlier than he had planned. Had he pushed her too far? Made her feel uncomfortable? All he had wanted to do was make her see how she was throwing her life away… Well, maybe that wasn't all he wanted to do. He couldn't get the memory of their kiss out of his head. He kept reliving it. Kept feeling the sensual energy of it in his body. Every time he looked at her mouth he felt a spark fire in his groin. Did she feel it too? Was that why she was talking so quickly and keeping her eyes well away from his? 'Do you want me to change your flight back home?'

She caught her lip with her teeth, her gaze still avoiding his as she fiddled with the salad she was preparing. 'Do you want me to leave early?'

'No, but what do you want?'

She reached for an avocado and pressed it to see if it was ripe. 'I thought I'd stay on. Help you with the clean-up and stuff.'

'You don't have to.'

'I know, but I'd like to.'

'Why?'

She still actively avoided his gaze. 'I'm enjoying being out of London and not just because of the weather. I can actually walk down the street here without anyone bothering me.'

'Always a bonus, I guess.'

Her cheeks went a faint shade of pink as she reached for some cherry tomatoes. 'Will you be seeing Nicole again before she leaves?'

Leandro couldn't help teasing her. 'For a drink, you mean?'

'For…whatever.'

'No.'

Her brow puckered as she looked at him. 'Why not?'

Leandro hadn't intended to resume his on-off relationship with Nicole in any case but he found it amusing to see Miranda struggle with the notion of him having a sex life. Was she just being a prude or was she actually jealous? Was she envisaging having a fling with him? Maybe she thought she could get away with it while she was away from home. Was that why she kept looking at him with that hungry look in her eyes? Was she rethinking her commitment to her dead boyfriend? Was she finally accepting it was time to move on and live life in the present instead of in the past? Could her fuss over Leandro's love life be a sign she was finally ready to take that first step?

The thought of exploring the spark between them was tempting.

More than tempting.

How long could he ignore the chemistry that swirled in the air when he was in the same room as her? But having a fling with her? How would he explain it to her brothers? It was a line he had sworn he would never cross. Not that he had ever discussed it with Julius or Jake. He hadn't even thought of Miranda that way. He wasn't sure when things had changed—when *he* had changed—but he had started to notice her quiet beauty. The way she moved. The way she spoke. The care and concern she expressed to those she loved. He had held back, kept his distance, not wanting to compromise his relationship with her brothers, or indeed with her.

And yet now he had kissed her. Touched her. Wanted her. How could he simply ignore the attraction he felt for her? Did he want to keep on ignoring it?

Could he ignore it?

Leandro gave a nonchalant shrug. 'It's time to move on.'

Her frown of disapproval deepened. 'So she's past her use-by date?'

'It's how it works these days.'

'I know, but it sounds pretty clinical if you ask me,' Miranda said. 'What if she was secretly hoping for more?'

He reached across for a piece of carrot. 'I make a point of never offering it in the first place.'

'But what if you change your mind?'

He gave her a pointed look. 'Like you might, do you mean?'

Her eyes fell away from his as she put the last touches to the salad. 'I'm not going to change my mind.'

'You sure about that, *ma belle*?'

Her small, neat chin came up. 'Yes.'

Leandro gave her another slanted smile. 'You're a determined little thing, aren't you?'

Miranda handed him the salad bowl. 'You'd better believe it.'

CHAPTER SIX

MIRANDA HAD BEEN asleep for a couple of hours when she woke with a sudden start. Had she heard something? She lay there for a moment, wondering if she had been dreaming that plaintive cry. Her sleep had been somewhat restless. Her visit to Rosie's room earlier that day, as well as seeing the mother with her baby and toddler, had made Miranda's slumbering mind busy with nonsensical narratives. Had she imagined that pitiless cry? Was the villa haunted by Rosie's ghost?

Miranda threw off the covers and padded to the door, listening with one ear for any further sound. Her heart was beating like a tattoo, the hairs on the back of her neck lifting as the old house creaked and groaned and resettled into the silence of the night.

It was impossible to go back to sleep. Even though in broad daylight she would swear she didn't believe in anything paranormal, it was a tough call in the middle of the night with shadows and sounds she couldn't account for. She pulled on a wrap, tied it about her waist and went out to the corridor. A shaft of pallid moonlight divided the passage. A branch of a tree scratched at the window nearest her, making her skeleton tingle inside the cage of her skin.

She tiptoed along the corridor but stopped when she got outside Leandro's room. There was a thin band of light shining underneath the door, not bright enough to be the centre light, but more like that of a lamp. There was no sound from inside the room. No sound of a computer keyboard being tapped or the pages of a book being turned.

Just a thick cloak of silence.

'Did you want something?' Leandro said from behind her.

Miranda swung around with her heart hammering so loud she could hear it like a roaring in her ears. 'Oh! I—I thought you were…someone else… I heard something. A cry. Did you hear it?'

'It's a cat.'

'A c-cat?'

'Yes, outside in the garden,' he said. 'There are a few strays around. I think my father must've been feeding them.'

Miranda rubbed her upper arms with her crossed-over hands. *A cat.* Of course it was a cat. How had she got herself so worked up? She didn't even believe in ghosts and yet…and yet she had been so sure that cry had been a small child crying out. 'Oh, right; well, then…'

Leandro looked at her keenly. 'Are you okay?'

She forced a brief tight smile. 'Of course.'

'Sure?'

Miranda licked her dry lips. 'I'd better get back to bed. Goodnight.'

He stalled her by placing a warm hand on her arm. She looked up into his shadowed face and felt her heart do another jerky somersault. She could smell the clean male scent of him, the wood and citrus blend and his own body heat that made her senses spin in dazed circles. His hair was ruffled, as if he had recently ploughed his fingers through it. It made her fingers ache to do the same, to feel those thick, silky strands against her fingertips.

His gaze was trained on her mouth. She felt the searing burn of it as if he had leaned down and pressed his sculptured lips to hers. Every nerve in her body was standing at attention, primed in anticipatory excitement.

'I thought you might be coming to tell me you've changed your mind,' he said.

She gave an involuntary swallow. 'A-about what?'

His eyes gleamed in the darkness, the moon catching the light of desire that blazed there as surely as it did in hers. 'About what you've been thinking from the moment I ran into you at that café in London.'

Miranda pulled a shutter down in her brain as she forced herself to hold his gaze. How could he possibly know what images her wayward mind kept conjuring up? How could he possibly sense the turmoil going on in her body? How could he know of the rampaging fire scorching through her veins at being this close to him? Or of the deep pulsating ache that was spreading through her thighs and pressing down between her legs? 'I'm not thinking...*that.*'

His mouth took on a sardonic slant. 'You're a terrible liar.'

Miranda forgot to breathe as he upped her chin, stroking his thumb against the swell of her lower lip until her senses were reeling. The temptation of his tantalising touch, his alluring proximity and the needs she was desperately trying to control were like a tug of war inside her body. Every organ shifted and strained against the magnetic pull of his flesh but it was too much. It was too powerful to resist. She felt her resolve collapsing like a humpy in a hurricane.

She didn't know who had closed that tiny space between their bodies but suddenly she was in his arms and his mouth was on hers in a passionate collision. The scrape of his stubble against her face made something slip sideways in her stomach. His deep, husky groan of pleasure as their tongues met and mated made her skin lift in delight.

Miranda couldn't control her response to his kiss. It suddenly didn't matter that she was supposed to be keeping her distance. Nothing mattered except tasting the warm, minty perfection of his mouth. Nothing mattered but feeling alive in his arms, feeling wanted, needed and desired. It was like a floodgate had opened up inside her. Her arms wound around his neck, her body pressed up close to the hot, hard heat of his as his lips moved with mind-blowing power on hers. She could feel the swell of his erection against her body, the exciting prospect of his potency triggering the release of intimate moisture within the secret cave of womanhood.

His tongue tangled with hers, teasing and cajoling it into seductive play with his. His arms were wrapped around her tightly, holding her as if he never wanted to let her go. Her flesh sang with the feel of him so aroused against her. It shocked her to realise how much she wanted him, how quickly it happened and how consuming it was to have the pulse of desire racing through her, skittling every sensible or rational objection out of the way.

Her mind was not in control now. Her body was on autopilot—hungry for the satiation of need. She hadn't thought herself capable of such intense passion. Of such wanton abandon that she would be breathlessly locked in Leandro's arms in a darkened corridor with her throat releasing little gasps and groans of encouragement as his mouth worked its breath-snatching magic on hers. How could one kiss do this to her? How could he have such sensual power over her?

His hands glided down her body, settling on her hips to keep her close to the throb of his arousal. All she could think was of how different he felt.

How *adult* he felt.

She could feel the swollen ridge of him against her belly, a spine-melting reminder of all that was different between them and how much she wanted to experience those differences. The intention of his body was clear—he wanted her. Her body was sending the same message back.

Miranda sent her fingers through the thickness of

his hair while her mouth stayed fused to his. One of his hands moved from her hip to settle in the small of her back, bringing her even closer to the thickened heat and throbbing pulse of his body. His blood pounded against her belly, ramping up her need until she was trembling with it. Had she ever felt such a thrill of the flesh? She had never been so aware of her body and how it reacted to the promise of fulfilment. It was like discovering a part of herself she hadn't known existed. A secret, passionate part that wanted, craved, needed. Hungered.

His mouth moved from hers to blaze a trail of fire down the sensitive skin of her neck, the sexy rasp of his stubble making her insides turn over. His tongue found the scaffold of her collarbone, dipping in and out of the shallow dish it created on her flesh. The grazing sensation of his tongue against her smooth skin made her knees loosen until she wondered if she would melt into a pool at his feet. Never had she felt such tremors course through her body. Such shudders and quakes of need that made everything inside her shake loose from its foundations.

'I want you,' Leandro said, his lips moving against her skin like a teasing brushstroke. 'But you've probably guessed that by now.'

Miranda shivered as his mouth came back up to just behind her ear. Every nerve danced as the tip of his tongue created sensual havoc. Where was her willpower? Where was her resolve? It was swamped, enveloped by a need that was clawing at her as his lips skated over her tingling flesh. How could she say no when every cell in her body was pleading for his possession?

Was this why she had hidden behind her commitment to Mark, because of the way Leandro made her feel? The way he had *always* made her feel? She had always been aware of him. Of his quiet strength. Of his heart-stopping attractiveness. Of his arrant maleness that made her female flesh shiver every time he came close.

How was she supposed to resist this assault on her senses? How was she to resist this urgent, primal call of her flesh?

'We shouldn't be doing this...' Her voice came out as a whispery thread that was barely audible. *I shouldn't be doing this.*

Leandro nudged her mouth with his lips, not touching down this time but close enough for their breaths to mingle. 'But you want to,' he said. 'I can feel it in your body. You're trembling with it.'

Miranda tried to still the tumult in her flesh but it was like trying to keep a paper boat steady in a hot tub. How could she deny it? How could she ignore the urgings of her flesh? Her whole body vibrated with clawing need. It moved through her body like a roaring tide. She could feel the pulse of lust low in her core—the hollow ache of need refused to be ignored. Her gaze went to his mouth, her belly doing a flip-turn as she thought of those warm, firm lips on her breasts, on her inner thighs. 'I made a promise...'

He pulled back to look at her. 'When you were a *kid,*

Miranda,' he said. 'You're a woman now. You can't ignore those needs. They're normal and healthy.'

Miranda had ignored those needs for so long but it hadn't really been all that hard to do so. She had never felt she was sacrificing anything. But now Leandro had stirred those needs into life, awakened them from a deep slumber. Sent them into a dizzying frenzy. How could she pretend they weren't clamouring inside her body? How could she deny the primal urges of her body when his presence evoked such a storm within her flesh? A storm she could feel rumbling through her from where his hands were holding her. Burning through her skin. Searing her so she would never be able to forget his touch. Her body would always remember. Her lips would always recall the weight and pressure of his. If she were never kissed by anyone again it would be Leandro's kiss she would remember, not Mark's. It would be Leandro's touch her body would recall and ache and hunger to feel again.

Would it be so wrong to indulge her senses just this once? He wasn't offering her a relationship. He had made it clear he didn't want the happy-ever-after. But then, she couldn't—*wouldn't*—give it to him if he wanted it.

But for this brief moment in time they could connect in a way they had never connected before.

Miranda closed the small distance between their bodies, a shockwave of awareness jolting through her at the erotic contact. She watched as desire flared in his gaze, burning with an incendiary heat that was as powerful as the backdraught of a fire. She slid her hands up the flat plane of his chest, feeling the deep thud of his heart under her palm. She knew he wouldn't take this a step further until she had verbalised her consent. But she didn't want to say the words. She didn't want to own the earthy needs of her body. That would be admitting she was at the mercy of her flesh. That she was weak, frail, human.

Leandro held her gaze with the force field of his. 'Tell me you want me.'

Miranda drew his head back down, her mouth hovering within a breath of his. 'Kiss me.'

'Say it, Miranda,' he commanded.

She stepped up on tiptoe so her lips touched his, trying to distract him, to disarm him. 'Why are we talking when we could be doing other stuff?'

He gripped her by the upper arms in a firm but gentle hold. 'I'm not doing the other stuff until I know it's what you want. That we're clear on where this is going.'

Miranda looked into his implacable gaze. Desire burned in his eyes; she could feel it scorching her through her skin where his hands were cupped around her flesh. 'It doesn't have to go anywhere,' she said. 'It can just be for now.'

His ever-present frown deepened a fraction. 'And you'd be okay with that?'

She would have to be okay. How could she say she wanted more when for all these years she had told everyone she didn't? She had taught herself not to want more. She had blocked all thoughts of a fairy-tale romance, of being married, of one day having a baby, of raising a family with the man she loved, because the man she had loved had died.

But this was a chance to live a little. To break free of the restraints she had set around herself. It didn't have to go anywhere. It didn't have to last. It *couldn't* last.

It was for the moment.

Miranda traced her fingertip over the dark stubble surrounding his mouth, her insides quivering as she felt the graze of his flesh against the pad of her finger. 'Neither of us wants anything permanent,' she said. 'This would be just something that…happened.'

'So you only want it to happen here?' he said. 'While we're in France?'

A French fling. A secret affair. A chance to play while no one was looking. No one need know. Her brothers, her parents, Mark's parents—even Jaz—didn't need to know. It would be over before it began. There wouldn't be time for things to get complicated. No one was making any promises. No one was falling in love. This would change the dynamic of their relationship, certainly, but as long as they were both clear on the boundaries then why not indulge their attraction for each other?

'That would be best, don't you think?' she said.

Leandro searched her gaze for a long moment. 'You don't want your brothers to know about us?'

Miranda bit down on her lip. 'Not just them…'

'Mark's family?'

She let out a breath. 'Look, if you're having second thoughts—'

'I'm not, but I'm wondering if you are,' he said. 'If not now, then later.'

Miranda saw the concern in his dark-as-night gaze. What was he worried about? That she would get all clingy and suddenly want more than he was prepared to give? She knew the rules. He had made them perfectly clear. She was okay with it. Totally okay. More than okay. 'I'm a big girl, Leandro. I can take responsibility for my decisions and actions.'

He brushed a strand of hair back off her face, his expression cast in serious lines. 'I want you to know I didn't ask you here to have an affair with me. The thought didn't cross my mind.'

Miranda raised one of her brows. 'Not even once?'

His mouth took on a rueful angle. 'Well, maybe once or twice.' His arms came around her to draw her close. 'I've always kept my distance because I didn't want to compromise my relationship with your family. It gets messy when things don't work out. Look at Jake and Jasmine.'

Miranda traced his mouth with her fingertip again. 'Did Jake ever tell you what happened that night?'

'No,' he said, kissing the tip of her finger. 'What's Jasmine's version of events?'

'She refuses to discuss it,' Miranda said, suppressing a shiver as Leandro's tongue curled around her finger as he drew it into his mouth. The sucking motion of his mouth made her inner core pull tight with lust.

'Someone needs to lock them in a room together until they thrash it out,' he said as he began to scorch a pathway of kisses up her neck. She shuddered as his tongue outlined the cartilage of her ear, longing coursing through her body in sweeping waves. 'Speaking of being locked in a room together...'

He gathered her up in his arms and carried her inside his room. The lamp was already on, giving the room a muted glow. He set her on her feet but not before sliding her down the length of his body, leaving her in no doubt of his need. The feel of his erection against her made her desire for him escalate to a level she had never experienced before. A restless ache pulsed deep in her body, a hollow sensation that yearned to be filled. Her breasts became sensitive where they were pressed against the hard plane of his chest. She could feel the tight buds of her nipples abraded by the lace cups of her bra. She wanted to feel his hands on her naked flesh, his mouth, his lips and his masterful tongue.

Miranda sucked in a breath as he slid his hands up under her top, the warmth of his palms against her skin sending her senses reeling. His hand came to the sensitive underside of her breast, stilling there as if to give her time to prepare for a more intimate touch. She moved against him, silently urging him to touch her.

'You're so beautiful,' he said.

Miranda had always felt a little on the small side, especially since her mother was so well-endowed. But Leandro's touch made her feel as if she was the most gorgeously proportioned woman he had ever touched.

He brought his mouth down to her right breast in a gentle caress that made her spine tingle from top to bottom. He circled her tight nipple with his tongue before he swept it over the underside of her breast where every nerve fizzed and leapt in response.

He came back to take her nipple in his mouth, drawing on her with just the right amount of suction. A frisson of excitement shot down between her legs, pooling in the warm, moist heart of her body. She had never felt desire like it. Her body had developed cravings and capabilities she'd had no idea it possessed. Never had she felt such intense ripples of delight go through her flesh.

He switched his attention to her other breast, leaving no part of it unexplored by his lips and tongue. The electric sensations ricocheted through her body, making her utter little gasping cries as he came back to cover her mouth.

His kiss was purposeful, passionate, consuming. His tongue came in search of hers, stroking, caressing and conquering, delighting her senses, stirring her passion to an even higher level.

Miranda threaded her fingers through his hair, stroking the back of his neck, going lower to his shoulders and back. She brought her hands around to the front of his shirt, undoing his buttons with more haste than efficiency. He shrugged himself out of it before helping her with her pyjama top. She watched as his eyes feasted on her naked form but, instead of feeling shy and inadequate, she felt feminine and beautiful.

He brought his mouth down to each of her breasts, subjecting them to another passionate exploration that made her insides shudder with longing. She made breathless little sounds of approval, her lower body on fire as it sought the intimate invasion of his.

Her hands glided down his chest, exploring the sculpted perfection of his toned body. She came to the waistband of his jeans, shyly skating her hand over the potent bulge below. He reached down and unfastened his jeans so her hand could go lower. Miranda took up the invitation with new-found boldness, delighting in the feel of his tautly stretched skin, thrilled by the way his body responded to her with every glide and stroke of her fingers. Moisture oozed from him as her thumb moved over the head of his penis, that most primal signal of the readiness to mate. She could feel her own moisture gathering between her legs, the deep, low ache of need throbbing with relentless urgency.

He gently eased her out of her pyjama bottoms, sliding them down her thighs with reverent care. She snatched in a hitching breath when his fingertip traced the seam of her body. His touch was so light, so careful, yet it stirred every nerve in her body into a riotous happy dance.

'I don't want to rush you,' he said.

Rush me! Rush me! Miranda silently pleaded. 'You're not… It's just…been a while.'

Leandro meshed his gaze with hers. 'I want to make it good for you. Tell me what you like.'

Anything you do will be just fine, Miranda thought. Even the way he looked at her was enough to send her senses into the stratosphere. 'I'm not very good at this…'

His brows came together. 'You *have* had sex, haven't you?'

She moved her gaze out of reach of his. 'Yes, of course…'

He gently inched up her chin so her eyes came back to his. 'But?'

Miranda moistened her lips, suddenly feeling shy and hopelessly inadequate again. What a pariah he would think her. So inexperienced she didn't know what worked for her and what didn't. How could she tell him she hadn't had an orgasm other than on her own? That she had found sex a bit one-sided? He would think her a prude, an unsophisticated Victorian throwback. She bet the women he dated—the Nicoles—would know exactly what worked for them and what didn't. They would be totally comfortable with their bodies and its needs. They would know what to say and what to do. They wouldn't be feeling gauche and stupid and useless because they had never had satisfying sex with a partner.

'Miranda?' Leandro prompted softly, his dark eyes holding hers.

Miranda drew her lower lip into her mouth, pressing down on it with her top one. 'It wasn't always good for me with Mark,' she said at last. 'It wasn't his fault. We were both inexperienced. I should've said something earlier. But then he got sick and I just let him do what he needed.'

Leandro's frown was a solid bar across his eyes. 'Did you ever come with him?'

She could feel her cheeks heating up like a radiator. 'No...'

He cupped the side of her face in one of his broad but gentle hands, his thumb moving back and forth in a slow, measured way. 'So you're practically a virgin,' he said.

Miranda lowered her gaze. 'I know you probably think that's ridiculous…that *I'm* ridiculous.'

He continued to stroke her hot cheek, his gaze soft as it held hers. 'I don't think that at all,' he said. 'It's not always easy for young women to get their needs met. Men can be insensitive and ignorant and selfish. That's why communication is so important.'

Miranda looked into the warmth of his coal-black gaze and wondered how she was going to keep her heart secure. He was so considerate, so understanding and so deeply insightful. Hadn't she always sensed he was a cut above other men? Why was he wasting himself on shallow relationships when he had so much to offer? He was 'life partner' material. The sort of man who would stand by his partner through thick and thin. He would be dependable, loyal and trustworthy. He would put his partner's needs before his own. Like he was doing now. He was taking the time to understand her. Treating her with the utmost respect and consideration.

She put her hand against his jaw, her skin tingling at the contact of his stubble. 'Make love to me,' she said in a soft whisper.

He leaned down to kiss her in a lingering exchange that made her body tremble in anticipation. His hands moved over her with tenderness but with the undercurrent of passion. Excitement coursed through her from head to toe, her breathing becoming faster, more urgent, as he stoked the fire of her desire. Sensations flooded her being, showers of them, cascades of them, great, spilling fountains of them that made her feel she had been sleepwalking through life until now.

He kissed his way from her mouth to her belly button, dipping his tongue into its tiny cave before going lower. She forgot to breathe when he came to her folds. His tongue moved down the seam of her body, tracing her without separating her. Fireworks erupted under her skin at the feel of his warm breath skating over her.

He gently separated her with his fingers, waiting for her to take a steadying breath before he put his mouth to her. A host of insecurities rushed through her brain. *Was she fresh enough? Was she waxed enough? Did she look normal? Was he comparing her to his other lovers?*

Leandro placed his hand on her belly in a stabilising manner. 'Relax for me, *cara*,' he said. 'Stop fretting. You're beautiful. Perfect.'

How could he read her mind as well as her body? Miranda wondered. But then she stopped thinking altogether as he put his mouth to her again. His tongue tasted and tantalised her, stroking and caressing her into spine-loosening delight. The tension inside her body built to a breaking point. It was like climbing a mountain only to be suspended at the edge of the precipice. Hovering there. Wavering. Teetering at that one tight, breath-robbing point, every cell in her body straining, pulling and contracting until finally she was pitched into the unknown. She felt like she was exploding into a thousand tiny fragments, like a party balloon full of glitter. Waves of pleasure washed over her, through her, tossing and tumbling her until she was spinning in a whirlpool of physical rapture.

Leandro came back over her to press a tender kiss to the side of her mouth. 'Good?'

Miranda could smell her own female scent on him. Such raw intimacy shocked her and yet somehow it felt right. She looked at him in a combination of wonder and residual shyness. 'You know it was.'

He kissed her on the lips, on the chin, on each of her eyelids and then back on her mouth. 'It'll get better when you feel more comfortable with me,' he said.

You'd better not get too comfortable, a little voice piped up inside her head.

Miranda ignored it as she moved underneath the delicious weight of his body, her senses stirring all over again at the thought of him possessing her fully. She reached down to caress him, stroking his turgid length with increasing confidence, watching as he showed his pleasure at her touch on his features and in the way he gave deep, growly groans in his throat.

He pulled back from her with a sucked-in breath. 'I'd better put on a condom.'

Miranda waited while he got one out of his wallet where it was sitting on the bedside chest-of-drawers. He sheathed himself before coming back over her, making sure she was comfortable with his weight by angling his body over hers. She stroked her hands down his back from the tops of his shoulders to the base of his spine, drawing him closer to the deep ache in her core.

He couldn't have been gentler as he entered her but

even so her breath caught at the sensation of him filling her. 'Am I hurting you?' he said, holding still.

She released a long, slow breath to help herself relax. 'No...'

'Sure?'

She smiled and stroked his lean, tanned jaw as she looked into his concerned gaze. 'You worry too much.'

He brushed her hair back from her forehead in a tender action. 'You're so tiny I feel like I'm going to break you.'

Something hot and liquid spilled and flowed in Miranda's belly. Could there be a man more in tune with a woman's sense of vulnerability? 'I'm tougher than I look,' she said, reaching up to kiss him on the lips.

He deepened the kiss as he moved within her, going in stages so she could have time to adjust to his length and width. He began to move in slow, rhythmic strokes, the gentle friction tantalising her senses, driving up her need until she was making soft little noises of encouragement in case he took it upon himself to stop. Miranda felt she would *die* if he stopped. The craving of her body rose to fever pitch. She felt it clawing at her, frantically trying to attain assuagement. She was almost there...poised to go over the edge but frustratingly unable to let go.

Leandro reached between their bodies, used his fingers to coax her and suddenly she was there, falling, falling, falling. Coming apart in a bigger and more intense way than before. Her body contracted around his, each spasm of her orgasm taking her to new even more exciting heights of pleasure.

She felt the exact moment he let go. He gave a low, deep groan and surged, his breath coming out in a hot gust against the side of her neck as he shuddered and emptied.

Miranda held him close, her hands moving over his muscled back and shoulders, massaging him, stroking and caressing him in that rare moment of male vulnerability.

She didn't know what to say so said nothing. Her senses were so dazed by the power of their physical connection it was impossible to articulate how she felt. She wondered why she didn't feel ashamed. She had broken her promise to Mark but how could she regret something so…so *magical* as Leandro's love-making? He had shown her what her body was capable of feeling. He had opened up a world of pleasure she hadn't known existed. Not like that. Not so powerfully consuming it had made her disconnect from her mind. Her body had taken over. Her primitive nature had driven her. Controlled her. Surprised her. Shocked her.

Leandro shifted his weight to his elbows to look at her. 'Hey.'

'Hey.' Her voice came out husky, whisper-soft.

He stroked his fingertip in a circle over her chin, his look rueful. 'I've given you beard rash.'

Miranda's breath caught on something. 'Just as well we're not around anyone we know,' she said lightly. 'Jaz would spot it in a heartbeat. I'd never hear the end of it.'

A frown created two pleats over his dark, serious eyes. 'You think she'd disapprove?'

Miranda recalled her conversation with her friend at

Jaz's bridal boutique. 'No,' she said. 'She thinks you've been interested in me for a while.'

Something flickered over his face like a wind rippling across sand. He moved away from her to dispose of the condom. It was a long moment before he met her gaze. 'I don't want you to think this is more than it is.'

She did her best to ignore the little jab of disappointment his words evoked. 'I know what this is, Leandro.'

He moved his tongue around the inside of his cheek as if he was rehearsing something before he said it. 'It's not that I don't care about you. I do. You're an incredibly special person to me. As are all of your family. But this is as far as it goes.'

Miranda got off the bed, dragging the sheet with her to cover her nakedness. 'Do we really need to have this conversation?' she said. 'We both know the rules. No one's going to suddenly move the goal posts.'

His expression was as inscrutable as that of one of the marble statues downstairs. 'You deserve more,' he said. 'You're young. Beautiful. Talented. You'd make someone a wonderful wife and mother.'

'I don't want those things any more,' she said. 'That dream was taken away. I don't want it with anyone else.' Even as she said the words Miranda wondered why they didn't sound as convincing as they once had. She had made that heartfelt promise just moments before Mark had died. *There will be no one else for me. Ever. I will always be yours.*

Mark's parents had been there with her at his bedside in ICU. The heart-wrenching emotion of saying goodbye, of watching as someone she loved took their last breaths, had made Miranda all the more determined to stay true to her promise. But now, as an adult, she wondered more and more if she had truly loved Mark enough to sign away her life. Or had his illness given her a purpose—a mission to follow that gave her life meaning, direction and significance?

She didn't know who she was without that mission. That purpose. It was too frightening to live without it. It had defined her, shaped her and motivated her for the last seven years.

Leandro made a sound of derision that scraped at her raw nerves. 'You're a fool to throw your life away for a selfish teenager who should've known better than to play with your emotions like that. For God's sake, Miranda, he didn't even have the decency to satisfy you in bed and yet you persist with this nonsense he was the love of your life.'

Miranda didn't want to hear Leandro vocalise what she was too frightened to think, to confront—to deal with. She drew in a scalding breath as she turned for the door. 'I don't have to listen to this. I know what I felt—*feel*.'

'That's right,' Leandro said. 'Run away. That's what you do when things cut a little close to the bone.'

She swung back to glare at him. 'Isn't that what *you* do, Leandro? You haven't been back here since you were a child. Your father died without you saying a proper goodbye to him. Doesn't that tell you something?'

His jaw clamped so tightly two spots of white appeared either side of his mouth. 'I wasn't welcome here. My father made that perfectly clear.'

Miranda dropped her shoulders on a frustrated sigh. How could he be so blind about his father? Couldn't he see what was right in front of his eyes? He was surrounded by everything his father had treasured the most: rooms and rooms full of wonderful, priceless pieces, paintings worth millions of pounds. Not to mention Rosie's things—her clothes and toys, the life-like statue in the garden—all left to Leandro's care. 'And yet he left you *everything*,' she said. 'Everything he valued he left to you. He could have donated it all to charity as you're threatening to do but he didn't. He left it all to you because you meant something to him. You were his only son. I don't believe he would've left you a thing if he didn't love you. He *did* love you. He just didn't know how to show it. Maybe his grief over Rosie got in the way.'

Leandro's throat rose and fell. He turned away to plough his fingers through his hair, the silence so acute she heard the scrape of his fingers against his scalp.

It seemed a decade before he spoke. 'I'd like to be alone.'

Miranda's heart gave a painful spasm at the rawness of his tone. What had made her speak so out of turn? She knew nothing of the heartbreak he had been through. She didn't know his father. She had never met him. She had no idea of how Leandro's relationship with him had operated. She was an armchair survivor. Leandro had every right to be furious with her. What right did she have to criticise his decision to stay away from his childhood home? He had suffered cruelly for his part in his sister's disappearance. A part he wasn't even responsible for, given he had been so young. 'I'm sorry,' she said. 'I should never have said what I said. It was insensitive and…'

'Please.' His voice was curt. 'Just leave.'

Miranda went over to him, undaunted by his terse tone. She didn't want to be dismissed. Pushed away. Rejected. She didn't want their wonderful physical connection to be overshadowed by an argument that should never have happened. What they had shared was too important. Too special to be tainted by a misunderstanding. She placed a gentle hand on his arm, looking up at his tautly set features. 'Please don't push me away,' she said. 'Not now. Not after what we shared.'

He looked at her for a beat or two before he placed his hand over hers where it was resting on his arm. He gave her hand a light squeeze, the line of his mouth rueful. 'You're right,' he said on the back end of a sigh. 'I should've come back before now.'

Miranda put her arms around him and held him close. 'You're back now,' she said, resting her cheek against his chest. 'That's all that matters.'

Leandro held her against him. 'It was hard…seeing him like that,' he said. 'Every time he came to London I had to prepare myself for spending time with him. No matter what time we agreed on meeting, he'd always been a couple of drinks down before I got there. Over the last couple of years it got progressively worse. He would sometimes be so drunk he would start crying and talking incoherently. Other times he would be angry and abusive. All I could think was it was my fault. That *I* had done that to him.'

Miranda looked up at him with tears in her eyes. 'It wasn't your fault.'

His look was grim. 'He never wanted me to come back here after the divorce. He made it clear he couldn't handle having a child around.'

'Maybe he was worried he wouldn't be able to look after you properly,' Miranda said. 'Maybe he just didn't know how to be a parent without having your mum around. Lots of divorced dads are like that, especially back then, when dads weren't so hands-on as they are now.'

'I let things slide as the years went on,' he said. 'Even as an adult it was easier to stay away than to come back and relive the nightmare. But I should've come back before now. I should've allowed my father to die with some measure of peace.'

Miranda hugged him close again. 'I'm not sure there's much peace to be had when you've lost a child. But at least you're doing what he wanted you to do— taking care of everything he left behind.'

He brushed one of his hands down the back of her head, his gaze meshing with hers. 'Don't go back to your room,' he said. 'Stay here with me.'

Miranda wondered if he was allowing her the dignity of not being dismissed now they had made love or whether he truly wanted her to spend the night with him. She didn't know what his arrangement was with other women but she hoped this invitation to sleep the whole night with him was a unique offer. 'Are you sure?' she said.

He lowered his mouth to within reach of hers. 'You don't take up much space. I bet I won't even notice you there.'

'Then I'll have to make sure you do,' Miranda said softly as his mouth came down and sealed hers.

CHAPTER SEVEN

LEANDRO HADN'T PLANNED to spend the night with Miranda but, just like when he had run into her in London, it had come out of his mouth as if his brain had no say in it at all. *So much for the rules*, he thought as he watched her sleeping. He never spent the full night with anyone. It wasn't just because he was too restless a sleeper. He didn't want to get too connected, too comfortable with having someone beside him when he woke up. He didn't allow himself to think of long, lazy mornings in bed. Not just making love but talking, dreaming, planning. Hoping.

She looked so beautiful his heart squeezed. Had he done the wrong thing in engaging in an affair with her? He had been so adamantly determined to keep his distance as he had always done in the past. But being alone with her changed everything. That first touch… that first heart-stopping kiss…had made him realise how deep and powerful their connection was. Hadn't he always sensed that connection? Wasn't that why he had respectfully kept clear of her? He hadn't wanted to start something he couldn't finish.

But now it *had* started.

He didn't want to think about how it was going to finish, but finish it must, as all his relationships did.

Her inexperience hardly put them on an equal footing. But he wanted her to realise how crazy it was to put a pause button on her life. He hated seeing her waste her potential because of a silly little schoolgirl promise that had been well meant but totally misguided. She was young—only twenty-three years old. At thirty-three, Leandro felt ancient in comparison. She was far too young to be living like a nun. Her whole life was ahead of her. She had experienced tragedy, yes, but it didn't mean she couldn't find happiness again—if in fact she had actually been happy with Mark Redbank.

The more Leandro reflected on that teenage relationship, the more he suspected how imbalanced it had been. Miranda was a sucker for romance. She had always been the type of girl who cried at soppy movies, or even at commercials with puppies or kittens in them. She had a big heart and gave it away all too easily. He didn't believe she had been truly in love with Mark. At sixteen who knew what they wanted or even who they were? She had wanted to feel special to someone and Mark had offered her that chance. Mark's parents had welcomed her into the bosom of their family and it had made her feel normal.

Normal was important to someone like Miranda. She didn't enjoy the notoriety of her father and mother and the baggage that came with it. Mark's illness had cemented her commitment to him but Leandro truly believed their relationship would not have lasted if Mark had survived.

But was sleeping with her himself going to convince her she was wasting her life?

He had crossed a boundary he couldn't uncross. Their relationship would never be the same. They could never go back to being platonic friends. The intimacy they had shared would always be between them. Would other people see it? Did it matter if they did? Her brothers might have something to say about it but only because they were protective of her. They might even be quite glad he had encouraged her to live a little.

He hadn't coerced her into sleeping with him. They were both consenting adults. He had given her plenty of opportunity to pull back. But he was glad she hadn't. Making love with her was different somehow. It wasn't just her lack of experience, although he'd be lying if he said it hadn't delighted him. It had given their union a certain quality he hadn't experienced with any other partner. Their love-making had had an almost sacred element to it. Or maybe it was because he had opened up a part of himself he had never opened before. He had never shared the pain of his childhood with anyone before. He had never shared his loss. He had never shared his guilt. He had never felt more exposed as a man, yet Miranda's gentle compassion had reached deep inside him like a soothing balm on a raw and seeping wound.

Miranda stirred in her sleep and he watched as the dark fans of her lashes flickered against her cheek. She slowly opened her eyes and blinked at him owlishly. 'What time is it?'

He brushed her mussed-up hair off her face. 'Three-thirty or so.'

She stroked one of her hands down his bare chest, making every cell in his body stand to attention. 'Couldn't you sleep?' she asked with a little frown of concern.

That was another thing that set her apart from his previous partners, Leandro thought. She genuinely cared about him. Worried about him. Put her needs and interests aside to concentrate on his. He smoothed her frown away with the blunt end of his thumb. 'I got a couple of hours.'

She lowered her gaze from his and tugged at her lower lip with her teeth. 'Is my being in your bed disturbing you?'

Leandro cupped her face, bringing her gaze back up to his. 'Only in a good way.'

Her cheeks developed a pink tinge. 'I could go back to my room if you'd like…'

He ran an idle fingertip from behind her ear to her chin, watching as she gave a little shiver, as if his touch had sent a current through her flesh. It thrilled him to think his touch did the same things hers did to him. That their bodies were so finely tuned to each other that the mere brush of a fingertip could evoke such a response. 'That would be a shame,' he said.

She licked her lips with a quick dart of her tongue, her toffee-brown eyes luminous. 'Why?'

'Because I wouldn't be able to do this,' he said, lowering his mouth to hers.

Her arms went around his neck as she gave herself

up to his kiss, her soft little sigh making his blood pound all the harder. He deepened the kiss with a stroke of his tongue against her lips and she opened on another sigh and nestled closer, her lower body searching for his. He put his hand on her naked bottom, drawing her to his straining erection. The feel of her skin on his skin made him want to break all of his rules. The condom rule in particular. But he never had unprotected sex. That was one line he never crossed. He pulled back to get one from his wallet, mentally making a note to replenish his supply.

Miranda looked at him with her clear brown gaze. 'Do you ever make love without a condom?'

'Never.'

'What about for oral sex?'

The thought of her gorgeous mouth surrounding him made him rock-hard. But he would never pressure her to do it. 'Always,' he said.

She rolled her lips together for a moment. 'Do you want me to...?'

'Not unless you want to,' he said. 'It's not for everyone.'

'But I'd like to,' she said, reaching for him, her soft little hand sending shivers up and down his spine. 'You pleasured me that way. I want to learn how to do it properly.'

'Did you do it with—?'

'No,' she said quickly, her gaze moving out of reach of his. 'I only ever used my hand.'

Leandro inched up her chin again. 'You don't need to feel bad about that. You should only ever do what you're comfortable with. No one should force or pressure you into doing something that doesn't feel right.'

She stroked her hand down the length of his shaft. 'I want to do it to you.'

His heart rate soared. His blood quickened. His skin peppered with anticipatory goose bumps. 'You don't have to.'

'I want to,' she said, sliding down his body, her warm breath teasing him as she positioned herself.

He drew in a sharp breath as she sent her tongue down him from the tip to the base. Her warm breath puffed over him as she came back up to circle her tongue around the head, her lips closing over him and then drawing on him. Even with a condom the sensations were electrifying, the sight of her so stimulating he had to fight hard for control. He tried to ease away to give her the chance to take a break but she hummed against him and held on, her mouth taking him over the edge into mind-blowing bliss.

He disposed of the condom once he could move again. His body was so satiated he felt like someone had undone every knob of his spine. Waves of lassitude swept through him, making him realise how long it had been since he had truly relaxed.

His sexual relationships had been pleasurable in a clinical, rather perfunctory way. He always made sure his partners got what they needed but sometimes he felt as if he was just going through the motions: drink, dinner, sex. It had become as simple and impersonal as that. He didn't linger over deep and meaningful conversations. He didn't spend the whole night with anyone.

He didn't allow himself to get that close. Close enough to want more. Close enough to need more.

But looking at Miranda beside him made him realise how much he was missing. His life was full of work and activity and yet…and yet deep down he felt something was missing. He had thought financial security would be enough. He had thought career success would satisfy him. But somehow it just made the empty space inside him seem bigger.

There was a canyon of dissatisfaction inside him. It echoed with the loneliness he felt, especially during the long hours of the night. He knew what would bridge it but he dared not risk it. He couldn't be part of a long-term relationship because he couldn't allow himself to risk letting someone down the way he had let Rosie and his parents down. How could he ever envisage a life with someone? A life with children was out of the question. How could he ever trust himself to keep them safe? He would always live with the gut-churning fear he might not be able to protect them. He had been responsible for so much heartache.

He couldn't bear to inflict more on anyone else.

Miranda lifted her fingertip to his face, tracing the line of his frown. 'Did I disappoint you?'

Leandro captured her hand and pressed his mouth to it. 'Why would you think that?'

'You went so still and quiet and you were frowning… I thought I must've done something wrong…'

He stroked his fingertip down the length of creamy cheek. 'You blew me away, literally and figuratively.'

Her eyes brightened and a smile tilted up the corners of her mouth. 'I did?'

He pressed her back down on the bed, hooking one of her legs over his. 'And now it's my turn to do the same to you.'

Miranda woke to bright sunlight pouring through the windows of Leandro's bedroom. She turned her head to the pillow beside her but, apart from the indentation of where his head had been, the space was empty. She sat up and brushed her sleep- and sex-tousled hair out of her face. When she swung her legs over the bed she felt a faint twinge of discomfort. Her inner muscles had experienced quite a workout last night. Leandro's love-making had been passionate and breathtakingly exciting and her body was still humming with aftershocks of pleasure.

It occurred to her it might not be so easy to put her fling with Leandro to one side when she returned to England. Would she blush every time she saw him, knowing he had pleasured every single inch of her body? That he alone knew exactly what made her cry out with ecstasy? That he alone knew what she looked like totally naked?

Would *he* look at her differently? Would he treat her differently? Would others notice? How on earth would she keep it a secret from Jaz? Or would Jaz guess as soon as she saw her?

Miranda went back to her own room to shower and dress. When she came downstairs she found Leandro in the study working on his laptop. He was so deep in concentration he didn't notice her at first. But then he looked up and his heavy frown was replaced with a brief smile. 'Sleep okay?' he said.

'Yes, but clearly you didn't.'

He stood and rubbed the back of his neck with one of his hands. 'I had some accounts to go through. It's a big job I'm working on for Jake. I need to get it sorted as soon as possible.'

Miranda slipped her arms around his waist and nestled against his tall, lean frame. 'You work too hard.'

He rested his chin on the top of her head as he drew her closer. 'How are you feeling?'

'Fine.'

He eased back to search her gaze with the intensely dark probe of his. 'Not sore?'

Miranda felt her cheeks heat up. 'A little.'

He stroked her cheek with a gentle fingertip, his expression rueful. 'I'm sorry.'

She pressed closer to link her arms around his neck, her pelvis flush against the hardness of his. 'I'm not.' She stepped up on tiptoe to brush her lips against his. 'You were wonderful.'

He looked down at her with that persistent frown between his brows. 'You don't regret getting involved like this?'

'Do you?'

He let out a long breath. 'I'm worried it will change our relationship,' he said. 'In a negative way, I mean.'

'We've always been friends, Leandro,' Miranda said. 'That's not likely to change just because we took it to a new level for a week or two.'

He continued to look at her in a contemplative manner. 'Do you think you'll date someone else when you get back?'

Miranda frowned. 'Why would I do that?'

'Because now you've broken the drought, so to speak.'

She slipped out of his hold and folded her arms across her middle, throwing him a hardened glance. 'So, I suppose you'll call Nicole once we're done?'

His eyes took on a flinty edge. 'I'm not sure why that should be such a sticking point for you.'

Miranda let out a whooshing breath. 'How can you settle for someone who just uses you to scratch an itch? How can you use her? Don't you want more than that?'

'Don't you?'

'I *hate* how you do that,' she said. 'You always shift the focus onto me because you're not comfortable talking about what it is you really want. You think you don't deserve to be happy because of what happened to your sister. It's. Not. Your. Fault. You didn't do anything wrong. Sacrificing your life won't change the past.'

His top lip curled. 'Will you listen to yourself? How about we play a little game of "it's hypothetical"? If I were to ask you to commit to a long-term relationship with me, would you do it?'

Miranda stared at him for a dumbstruck moment. 'I don't— I'm not— You're not—'

He gave a bark of cynical laughter. 'The answer is no, isn't it? You're too invested in living the role of the martyr. I bet you won't even tell your best friend what you got up to with me.'

Jaz will probably guess as soon as she sees me, Miranda thought. 'But you would never ask me to commit to you… Would you?'

'No.'

A sharp pain jabbed her under the ribs. Did he have to be so blunt? So adamant? 'Wow,' she said with a hint of scorn. 'You really know how to boost a girl's self-esteem.'

He swung away to stand with his back to her as he looked out of the window. He drew in a deep breath and let it out in a halted stream. 'I knew this would be a mistake. I have this amazing ability to ruin every relationship I enter into.'

Miranda couldn't bear to see him so tortured with such guilt and self-blame. Her heart ached for him. He was so torn up with regret and self-recrimination. He was so alone in his suffering, yet she wanted to stand by him, to help him work his way through it to a place of peace. She stepped up to him and stroked her hand down the tightly clenched muscles of his back. He flinched as if her touch had sent an electric shock through him. 'You haven't ruined our relationship,' she said softly.

He put an arm around her and drew her close to the side of his body, leaning down to press a soft-as-air kiss to the top of her head. 'I'm sorry, *ma petite*,' he said. 'None of this is your fault. It's me. It's this wretched, bloody house. It's all the stuff I can't fix.'

Miranda looked up at him with compassion. 'Have you told Julius and Jake about your sister yet?'

'I emailed them a couple of days ago.'

'Did that help? Explaining it to them?'

'A bit, I guess,' he said. 'They were good about it. Supportive.'

A little silence passed.

'What about us?' she said. 'Did you tell them we were…?'

'No,' he said. 'Have you?'

Miranda shook her head. 'It's not that I'm ashamed or anything… I just don't feel comfortable discussing my sex life with my older brothers.'

'Fair enough.'

She waited another beat or two before asking, 'Will you take me to the place where Rosie went missing?'

His frown carved a deep trench in his forehead. 'Why?'

'Because it might help you get some closure.'

He turned his gaze back to the view outside the window but his arm was still around her. She felt it tighten momentarily, as if he had come to a decision inside his head. 'Yes…'

Leandro could feel his heart banging against his chest wall like a church bell struck by a madman. A cold sweat was icing down between his shoulder blades and his stomach was pitching as he walked to the place where Rosie and he had been sitting. The beach wasn't crowded like that fateful day in summer but the memories came flooding back. He could hear the sound of children playing—the sound of splashing and happy shrieking—the sound of the water lapping against the shore and the cracking sound of the beach stones shifting under people's feet.

Miranda slipped her arm through his, moving close to his body. 'Here?' she said.

'Here.' Leandro waited for the closure she'd spoken of but all he felt was the ache. The ache of loss, the noose of guilt that choked him so he could barely breathe. He could see his mother's face. The horror. The fear. The dread. He could see the ice-creams dropping from her hands to the sun-warmed stones on the shore. Funny how he always remembered that moment in such incredible detail, as if a camera lens inside his head had zoomed in at close range. One of the cones had landed upside down, the other had landed sideways, and the scoop of chocolate ice-cream had slid down the surface of a dark blue stone.

He could still see it melting there.

He could hear the shouts and cries. He could feel the confusion and the panic. It roared in his ears like he was hearing everything through a distorting vacuum. He could hear the shrieking sirens. He could see the flashes as police cars and an ambulance came screaming down the esplanade.

If only the ocean could talk. If only it could tell what it had witnessed all those years ago. What secrets were hidden below that deep blue vault?

'Are you okay?' Miranda's soft voice brought him back to the present.

Leandro put his arm around her shoulders and

brought her close to his side as they stood looking at the vastness of the ocean. 'My father used to come down here every day,' he said after a moment or two of silence. 'He would walk the length of the beach calling out for her. Every morning and every afternoon and every night. Sometimes I would go with him when I wasn't at school. I don't know if he kept doing it after Mum and I left. Probably.'

She slipped her arm around his waist and leaned her head against his upper arm, as she couldn't quite reach his shoulder. She didn't say anything but he felt her emotional support. It was a new feeling for him, having someone close enough to understand the heartbreak of his past.

'I left a part of myself here that day and I can't get it back,' he said after another little silence.

Miranda turned to look up at him with tears shining in her eyes. 'You will get it back. You just have to stop blaming yourself.'

Easier said than done, Leandro thought as they walked back the way they had come.

CHAPTER EIGHT

A COUPLE OF days later, Miranda had finished packing up the last of the paintings ready for the shipping people to collect when she got a phone call from Jaz. Miranda gave her a quick rundown on Leandro's tragic background.

'Gosh, that's so sad,' Jaz said. 'I thought he was a bit distant because of his dad being a drunk. I didn't realise there was more to it than that.'

'Yes, I did too, but I think it's good he's finally talking about it,' Miranda said. 'He even took me to the place on the beach where his sister went missing. I was hoping it would give him some closure but I know he still blames himself. Maybe he always will.'

'Understandable, really,' Jaz said. 'So how are you two getting along?'

Miranda was glad she wasn't using the video-call option on her phone. 'Fine. I've sent off the paintings. Now we're sorting through his father's antiques. Some of them are amazing. His dad might have had a drinking problem but he sure knew how to track down a treasure or two.'

'Has Leandro made a move on you yet?'

Miranda thought of the moves Leandro had made on her last night and that morning. Achingly tender moves, on account of her soreness. It had made it harder to keep her emotions in check. He was so thoughtful and caring; how could she not begin to imagine them having a life together? 'You have a one-track mind,' she said. 'Did you get the dress done?'

'Yep. I'm working on a design for Holly as we speak,' Jaz said. 'Now, tell me all about it.'

Miranda frowned. 'All about what?'

'What you and Leandro have been getting up to apart from sorting out dusty old antiques and paintings.'

'We're not getting up to anything.'

'Hey, this is me—your best friend—you're talking to,' Jaz said. 'We've known each other since we were eight years old. You would've at least hugged him. You wouldn't be able to help yourself after he told you about his little sister. Am I right, Miss "Compassion and Tears at the Drop of a Hat" Ravensdale?'

'Anyone would do the same,' Miranda said. 'It doesn't mean I'm sleeping with him.'

'Aha!' Jaz said. 'Methinks more than a hug. A kiss, perhaps?'

Miranda knew it would be pointless denying it. Jaz was too astute to be fobbed off. 'We kissed and…stuff.'

'Stuff?'

'It's not serious,' she said. 'It's just a thing.'

'A thing?'

'A fling…sort of, but I hate that word, as it sounds so shallow.'

'Seriously?' Jaz said. 'You're *sleeping* with Leandro?'

Miranda frowned at the incredulity in her friend's tone. 'Isn't that what you thought I was doing?'

'You're actually doing the deed with Leandro Allegretti?' Jaz said. 'Oh. My. God. I think I'm going to pass out with shock.'

'It's just sex,' Miranda said. 'It's not as if we're dating or anything.'

'But what about Mark?' Jaz said. 'I thought you said there was never going to be another—'

'I'm not breaking my promise to Mark,' she said. 'Not really.'

'Listen, I never thought much of your promise in the first place,' Jaz said. 'Mark was nice and all, and it was awful that he died, but Leandro? *Seriously?* He's ten years older than you.'

'So?' Miranda shot back. 'Jake was ten years older than you when you had that silly little crush on him when you were sixteen.'

There was a tight little silence.

Miranda knew she shouldn't have thrown Jaz's crush on her brother in her face. She knew how much it upset Jaz to have been so madly infatuated with Jake back then. Even though Jaz had never told her what had actually happened in her brother's bedroom that night, it had obviously been something she wanted to forget. 'I'm sorry,' she said. 'That was mean of me.'

'Are you in love with him?' Jaz said.

'No.'

'Sure?'

The thing was, Miranda *wasn't* sure. She had always cared about Leandro. He was part of the family, a constant in her childhood, someone she had always respected and admired. She had loved him like a brother. Now her feelings for him were different. More mature. More adult.

But *in* love?

Or was it because of the amazing sex? She had read somewhere that good sex was deeply bonding. The more orgasms you had with a lover, the more you bonded with them. She wouldn't be the first woman to mistake physical compatibility for love.

'We're friends as well as lovers,' Miranda said.

'What's going to happen when he breaks it off?' Jaz said. 'Will you still be friends?'

'Of course,' Miranda said. 'Why wouldn't we be?'

'What if you want more?'

Miranda had already starting day-dreaming them as a couple—as a permanent couple. Becoming engaged. Getting married. Going through life as a team, building a future together. Having children and raising them in a household with love and security—all the things he had missed out on.

But then there was her promise to Mark to consider. She would have to tell Mark's parents she was ready to move on with her life. She would have to stop feeling guilty for being alive when Mark was not. She would have to confront the fact that maybe she hadn't loved Mark the way she had thought. That they hadn't been soul mates but just two teenagers who had dated. 'I don't want more.'

'What if Leandro does?' Jaz asked.

'He doesn't,' she said. 'He's not the commitment type.'

'That could change.'

'It won't,' she said. 'He only ever dates a woman for a month or two.'

'So you're his Miss October.'

Miranda didn't care for her friend's blunt summation of the situation. But that was Jaz. She didn't sugar-coat anything—she doused it in bitter aloes. 'Stop worrying about me,' Miranda said. 'I know what I'm doing. But I'd appreciate it if you didn't let it slip to my brothers, okay?'

'Fine,' Jaz said. 'I only ever speak to one of your brothers, in any case. But are you going to tell Mark's parents?'

Miranda bit down on her lip as she thought about that poignant ICU bedside scene seven years ago. Her promise to Mark had comforted his parents. They still got comfort from having her call on them, spending time with them on Mark's birthday and the anniversary of his death. How could she tell them she was falling in love with someone else? It would shatter them all over again. It would be better to let this short phase in her life come and go without comment. She couldn't bear to hurt them when they had been so loving and kind towards her. They needed her. She saw the way their faces lit up every time she called in. She lifted their spirits. She gave them a break from the depressing emptiness of their life without their son. 'Why would I tell them?' Miranda said.

'What if someone sees you with Leandro?' Jaz said. 'He's been photographed in the press before. He's one of London's most eligible bachelors. You and him being linked would be big news, especially right now, with your dad's stuff doing the rounds. Everyone wants to know what the scandalous Ravensdales are up to.'

Miranda groaned. 'Did you have to remind me?'

'Sorry, but you guys are seriously hot property just now,' Jaz said. 'Even I'm being targeted on account of being an adjunct to the family.'

'Really?'

'Yeah. I'm thinking I might meet up with this Kat chick,' Jaz said. 'She sounds kind of cool.'

'Why do you think that?' Miranda said, feeling a sharp sting of betrayal deep in her gut.

'I like her ballsy attitude,' Jaz said. 'She's not going to be told what to do no matter how much money your family's hot-shot lawyer, Flynn Carlyon, waves under her nose.'

Miranda couldn't bear the thought of Jaz kicking goals for the opposition. Jaz was an honorary family member. She was the sister she had always longed for. Ever since Jaz's mother had dropped her off for an access visit at Ravensdene and never returned, Miranda and Jaz had been a solid team. When the mean girls had bullied Miranda at boarding school, Jaz had stepped up and dealt with them. Jaz had been there for her when Mark had got sick and had been there for her when he died. Jaz had been everything and more that a blood sister would be. The prospect of her becoming friendly with Miranda's father's love child was unthinkable. Unpalatable. Unbearable. 'Well, I *don't* want to meet her,' she said. 'I can't think of anything worse.'

'I can,' Jaz said. 'Leandro lost his little sister and here you are pushing away what you've always wanted. It doesn't make sense. The least you could do is make the first move. Be the bigger person and all that.'

Miranda frowned. 'I don't need a sister. Why would I? I have you.'

'But we're not blood sisters,' Jaz said. 'You shouldn't turn your back on blood. Only crazy people do that.'

Miranda knew there was a wealth of hurt in Jaz's words. Jaz put on a brash don't-mess-with-me front but deep down she was still that little bewildered eight-year-old girl who had been dropped off at the big mansion in Buckinghamshire and had watched as her mother drove away from her down the long driveway into a future that didn't include her. Miranda had heard Jaz cry herself to sleep for weeks. It had been years before Jaz had told her some of the things her mother had subjected her to: being left in the care of strangers while her mother had turned tricks to feed her drug habit; being punished for things no child should ever be punished for. Jaz had suffered horrendous neglect because her mother had been too busy, or too manic, or off her face with drugs, to care about her welfare.

But Miranda didn't want to meet the result of her father's infidelity to her mother. If she met Katherine Winwood she would be betraying her mother. Elisabetta was devastated by Richard's behaviour. How could she not be when at the time of his affair with Kat's mother he had been reconciling with her?

Miranda had spent most of her life trying to please her mother, living up to the unreachable standards of her beautiful, talented and extroverted mother. This was one way to get the relationship with her mother she had yearned for. If she met with her father's love child it would undo everything she had worked so hard to achieve.

Besides, Kat Winwood hadn't expressed any desire to meet her half-siblings. She was apparently doing her level best to avoid all contact with the Ravensdales.

Long may it continue, Miranda thought.

Leandro had just finished talking on the phone to an estate agent when Miranda came into the study. 'I think I've got a buyer for the villa,' he said, putting his phone down on the desk. 'Hey, what's wrong?'

She came and perched on the edge of the walnut desk, kicking one of her slim ankles back and forth, her mouth pushed forward in a pout. 'Jaz thinks I should meet Katherine Winwood. She thinks I should make the first move.'

He took her nearest hand and stroked the back of it with his thumb. 'I think that would be a really good thing to do,' he said.

'But what about Mum?' she said, frowning. 'She'll think I'm betraying her if I become best buddies with her husband's love child. God, this is such a mess. Why can't I have normal parents?'

'Your mother will have to deal with it,' Leandro said. 'None of this is Kat's fault, remember.'

Miranda let out a long breath. 'I know, but I hate how Dad wants everything to be smoothed over as if he didn't do anything wrong. He doesn't just want his cake and eat it too, he wants to decorate it and hand out pieces to everyone as well.'

'People do wrong stuff all the time,' Leandro said. 'There comes a time when you have to forgive them for it and move on. For everyone's sake.'

She brought her gaze back to his. 'Is that what you're doing? Forgiving yourself as well as your father?'

Am I? Leandro thought. Was it time to accept some things were outside his control and always had been? He hadn't been able to protect his sister. He hadn't been able to save his parents' marriage. He hadn't been able to protect his father from self-destructing. He hadn't come home in time to say goodbye to his father, but he was here now, surrounded by the things his father had treasured. Being here in the place where his father had spent so many lonely years had given Leandro a greater sense of who his father was. Vittorio Allegretti hadn't planned to live alone. He hadn't planned to drink himself into an early grave. He had once been a young man full of enthusiasm for life, and then life had thrown him things that had made him stumble and fall and he simply hadn't been able to get back up again. 'Maybe a little,' Leandro said.

A little silence passed.

Miranda looked down at their joined hands. 'I hope

you don't mind, but I kind of told Jaz we're seeing each other…'

Leandro frowned. 'Kind of?'

She met his gaze, her cheeks a faint shade of pink. 'It's impossible to keep anything a secret from Jaz. She knows me too well. She put two and two together and… well… I confessed we're having a thing.'

Is that what we're having? he thought. *A thing?* Why did it feel much more than that? It didn't feel like any other relationship he'd had in the past. It felt closer. More meaningful. More intimate. He felt like a different person when he was with her. He felt like a whole person, not someone who had compartmentalised himself into tidy little boxes that didn't intersect.

Why did it make him feel empty inside at the thought of bringing their 'thing' to an end?

'I don't like calling it a fling,' Miranda continued. 'And given what my father did I absolutely loathe the word affair. It sounds so…so tawdry.'

Leandro didn't like the words either. He didn't like using the word 'affair' or 'fling' to describe what he was experiencing with Miranda. As far as he was concerned, there was nothing tawdry or illicit about his involvement with her. He had always had a relationship with her—a friendship that was distant but polite. He had always cared about her because she was a sweet girl who was a part of the family he adored. Even her parents—for all their foibles—were very dear to him. Miranda's brothers were his best mates. He didn't want his involvement with her to jeopardise the long-standing mateship he valued so much.

But defining what he had with her now was complicated. The more time he spent with her, the more he wanted. Her gentle and compassionate nature was soothing to be around. But she deserved to have all the things girls her age wanted. He couldn't commit to that sort of relationship. It wouldn't be fair to her to allow her to think he could. He had been honest with her. Allowing their involvement to go on when they returned to England would be offering her false hope. Postponing the inevitable. It would make it harder to let go if he held on too long.

Once her family found out they were seeing each other, there would be pressure from them to take things to the next level. There would be pressure from the public because everyone loved a celebrity romance. The press had already taken an avid interest in Julius's engagement to Holly. What would they do with the news of Leandro and Miranda's involvement?

'Miranda...' He gave her hand a gentle squeeze. 'I know I've said this before, but you do realise we can't continue this when we go back home, don't you?'

She didn't quite meet his gaze. 'Are you worried what Julius and Jake will say?'

Leandro raised her chin so her eyes met his. 'It's not about what your brothers think. It's about me. About what I can and can't give.'

'But you'd make a wonderful partner,' she said with an earnest expression. 'I know you would. You're so caring and kind and considerate. How can you think you wouldn't be happy in a long-term relationship?'

'But you don't want a long-term relationship,' he said, watching her closely.

Her eyes went back to his chin as if that was the most fascinating part of his anatomy. 'I wasn't talking about me per se... It's just I think you'd be a great person for someone to spend the rest of their life with. To have a family with and stuff.'

He let out a heavy sigh. 'It's not what I want.'

She pressed her lips together for a beat or two of silence. 'I suppose you think I've fallen madly in love with you.'

'Have you?'

Her eyes still didn't quite make the full distance to his. 'That would be rather fickle of me, given this time last week I was in love with Mark.'

Leandro brushed her cheek with his fingertip. 'You're twenty-three—still a baby. You'll fall in love with dozens of men before you settle down.' The thought of her with someone else made his chest ache. What if they didn't treat her right? She was an incredibly sensitive person. She could so easily be taken advantage of. She was always over-adapting to accommodate other people's needs and expectations. Even the fact that she'd settled for his 'thing' with her was evidence of how easily she could be exploited.

Not that he was exploiting her...or was he? He had been as honest as he could be. He hadn't given her any promises he couldn't keep. She had accepted the terms and yet... How could he know for sure what she had invested in their relationship? She acted like a woman in love, but then anyone looking in from the outside would think he was madly in love with her. Being physically intimate with someone blurred the boundaries. Was it lust or love that motivated her to be with him?

How could he tell the difference?

His own feelings he left in the file inside his head labelled 'Do Not Open'. It served no purpose to think about the feelings he had for Miranda. He would have to let her go. He couldn't hold her to him indefinitely. Over the years he had taught himself not to think of the things he wanted—the things most people wanted. He had almost convinced himself he was happy living the single-and-loving-it life. Almost.

Miranda slipped off the desk and smoothed her hands down her jeans. 'I should leave you to get on with your work…'

Leandro captured her hand and brought her close to his body, watching as her pupils flared as his head came down. 'Work can wait,' he said and pressed his mouth to hers.

Desire rose hot and strong in him as her mouth flowered open beneath his. He stroked his tongue against hers, a shudder of pleasure rocketing through him when her tongue came back at him in shy little darts and dives. He spread his hands through her hair, cupping her head so he could deepen the kiss, savouring the sweet, hot passion of her.

Her small dainty frame was pressed tightly against him, her mouth clamped to his as her fingers stroked through his hair. Her touch sent hot wires of need through his body. The slightest movement of her fingers made the blood surge in his veins.

He wondered if he would ever forget her touch. He wondered if he would ever forget her taste. Or the way she felt in his arms, like she belonged there and no-where else. He wondered how he would be able to make love to someone else without making comparisons. Right now he couldn't envisage ever making love to anyone else. How could someone else's touch make his flesh tingle all over? How could someone else's kiss stoke a fire so consuming inside him he felt it in every cell of his body?

'Make love to me here,' Miranda said, whisper-soft, against his mouth.

Leandro didn't need a second invitation. He was fighting for control as it was. Every office fantasy he had ever had was coming to life in his arms. Miranda was working her way down his body, her hands shaping him through the fabric of his jeans, then unzipping him and going in search of him. The smooth, cool grasp of her fingers around his swollen heat made him stifle an animalistic groan. She read his body like a secret code-breaker, stroking him, caressing him, taking him to the brink, before pulling back so he could snatch in another breath. 'Let's even this up a bit,' he said and started on her clothes.

She gave a soft little gasp as he uncovered her breasts. He brought his mouth to each tightly budded nipple, rolling his tongue around each one. He drew on each nipple with careful suction, delighting in the way she responded with breathless sounds of delight. He moved to the underside of her breast where he knew she was most sensitive. He trailed his tongue over the creamy perfection of her flesh, his groin hard with want as he felt her shudder with reaction.

Miranda wriggled her jeans down to her ankles but he didn't give her time to step out of them. Leandro didn't step out of his either. He eased her back against the desk, deftly sourcing a condom before he entered her with a deep, primal groan of satisfaction. Her tight little body gripped him, milking him with every thrusting movement he made within her. He had to force himself to slow down in case he hurt her or went off early. But she was with him all the way, urging him on with panting cries. He worked a hand between their hard-pressed bodies to give her the extra stimulation she needed. It didn't take much. She was so wet and swollen he barely stroked her before she came hard around him, making it impossible for him to hold on any longer.

He shuddered, quaked, emptied. Then he held still while the afterglow passed through him like the gentle suck and hiss of a wave.

Miranda's legs were still wrapped around him as she propped herself on her elbows to look at him, her features flushed pink with pleasure, a playful smile curving her lips. 'Should I have told you first I was a desk virgin?'

He pressed a kiss to the exposed skin of her belly, letting his stubble lightly graze her flesh. 'I would never have guessed.'

She shivered as he went lower. 'I haven't done it outdoors either.'

Leandro thought of the timeframe on their relationship with a jarring sense of panic. There wasn't time to do all the things he wanted to do with her. In a matter of days they would go back to being friends. There would be no making love under the stars. No making love on a remote beach or in a private pool. No making love on a picnic rug under a shady tree in a secluded spot. He hadn't done those things with anyone else for years. Some of those things he had never done. How had he let his life get so boring and mundane?

The sound of his phone ringing where it was lying on the desk confirmed how much he had hemmed himself in with work. It rang day and night. He had forty emails to sort through, ten text messages to respond to and fifteen calls to make before he missed the time zone differences.

Miranda reached for his phone to hand it to him and then blushed as she glanced at the screen. 'It's Jake,' she said in a shocked whisper, as if her brother could hear without the phone even being answered.

Leandro took the phone off her, turned it to silent and put it back on the desk. 'I'll call him later.'

She slipped off the desk and pulled up her jeans. Her teeth were savaging her bottom lip, her eyes avoiding all contact with his as she went in search of her top and bra.

He pulled up his own jeans before he took her by the hand and drew her close. 'There's no need to feel ashamed of what we're doing.'

Miranda glanced at him briefly before lowering her gaze to his chin. 'I'm not... It's just that... I don't know...' She slipped out of his hold and ran a hand through her hair like a wide-toothed comb. 'What if he finds out?'

'He won't unless you tell him.'

She gave him a worried glance. 'But what if Jaz tells him?'

Leandro gave her a wry look. 'Jaz talking to Jake? You seriously think that's going to happen any time soon?'

She chewed at her lip again, hugging her arms around her body. 'Will you tell him or Julius?'

That was the other file inside Leandro's head—the 'Too Hard' file. The conversation with her brothers about his thing with Miranda wasn't something he was looking forward to. It would have to happen at some point. He couldn't hope to keep it a secret for ever and nor would he want to in case they heard about it later via someone else. He suspected Jake and Julius would guess as soon as they saw him and Miranda together at a Ravensdale gathering.

Like at Julius and Holly's wedding next month. He couldn't get out of going as he was one of the grooms-men, along with Jake, who was best man. Miranda was one of the bridesmaids. Maybe he would have to decline all future invitations. But then that would only increase speculation. 'They'll have to know eventually,' he said. 'I've kept enough secrets from them as it is.'

Her brow was still puckered with a frown. 'I know, but…'

Leandro rubbed his hands up and down her upper arms in a soothing motion. 'But you're worried what they'll think? You don't need to be. I reckon they'll be happy you're finally moving on with your life.'

The trouble was she would be moving on with her life with *someone else*, he thought with another sharp dart of pain in his gut. He would have to stand to one side as she walked up the aisle to some other guy. He would have to pretend it didn't matter because it *shouldn't* matter.

Miranda lifted her toffee-brown gaze to his. 'But what about you?' she said. 'Will you move on with yours?'

Leandro gave her a crooked smile. 'I already have. You've helped me with that.'

'I have?'

'Sure you have,' he said. 'You've helped me understand my father a little better.'

She touched a gentle hand to his face. 'I'm sure he loved you. How could he not?'

Leandro captured her hand and pressed a kiss to the middle of her palm. 'I'd better call your brother back. You want to hang around and say hi to him?'

Her eyes widened in alarm as she started to back away. 'Not right now… I—I think I'll have to take a bath.'

'Leave some hot water for me, okay?'

She nodded and scampered out of the room.

Leandro let out a breath and pressed the call button on his phone. 'Jake, sorry I was busy with something when you called.'

'So, what's this about you doing my little sister?' Jake said.

Leandro felt a chill tighten his skin. 'Where'd you hear that?'

'Joke, man,' Jake laughed.

'Right...'

'You okay?'

'Sure,' Leandro said. 'Been busy sorting out my father's stuff. Now, about this Braystone account—'

'So have you introduced Miranda to any hot French or Italian guys over there?' Jake said.

'No,' he said, trying not to clench his jaw. 'Not yet.'

'Not that it'd work,' Jake said. 'But it's worth a try.'

'I'm sure when she's ready to date again she will,' Leandro said. 'You can't force people into doing stuff until they're ready emotionally. You and Julius shouldn't be giving her such a hard time about it. It's probably why she's been pushing back for all this time. Give her the space to recognise what she needs and stop lecturing her. She's not a fool.'

'Whoa there, buddy,' Jake said. 'No need to take my head off.'

'I'm just saying you need to back off a little, okay?'

'Okey dokey,' Jake said. 'Point taken. Now, about this Braystone account. It's a humdinger of a puzzle, isn't it?'

Leandro mentally gave a deep sigh of relief. *Work*. Now that was something he was comfortable talking about.

CHAPTER NINE

THERE WERE ONLY two days left before Miranda was to fly back to London. How had the last few days gone so quickly? It seemed like yesterday when she had arrived and walked into the villa with Leandro to all the dusts and secrets inside. Now the villa was all but empty apart from the kitchen, the bedroom they'd been sharing and Rosie's room. He hadn't done anything about that yet and Miranda didn't want to push him. She knew he would do it when he was ready. He had a couple more days here after she left before he flew on to Geneva for a meeting over the big account he was working on for Jake.

Miranda looked at the date on the flight itinerary on her phone with a sinking feeling. Forty-eight hours and it would all be over. She and Leandro would go back to being friends. Platonic friends. They would no longer touch. No longer kiss. No longer make love. They would move on with their lives as if nothing had happened. She would have to interact with him at Julius and Holly's wedding, maybe even dance with him and pretend they were as they had been before—distant friends. How was she going to do it? Wouldn't everyone see the chemistry they activated in each other? She didn't think she would be able to hide her emotions or her response to his presence. She had no control over how he made her feel. He had only to look at her and she felt her body tremble with need.

He wasn't in love with her. She was almost sure of it. He certainly acted like it but he had never said the words. Every kiss, every caress, every time he made love to her, she wanted to believe he was doing it out of love instead of lust. But if he loved her why hadn't he changed his mind about the time frame of their involvement? He hadn't even mentioned it since the evening in his office. Had it been her imagination or had he been distancing himself since that night? She knew he was worried about the account he was working on. There were lawyers involved and a court hearing scheduled. Every spare minute when he wasn't sorting out his father's stuff he worked on his laptop with a deep frown etched on his forehead. She had tried to give him the space he needed to work in peace, even though it had been more than tempting to interrupt him and have him make love to her the way he had before.

But at night when he finally came to bed he would reach for her. His arms would go around her; his mouth, hands and deliciously male body would pleasure her until she was tingling from head to foot. She would sometimes wake and see him lying on his side looking at her, one of his hands idly stroking her arm or the back of her hand.

How could that just be lust?

The date blurred in front of Miranda's vision. How could she leave without telling him how she felt? But how could she tell him when he had warned her from the start about moving the goal posts? She was supposed to be an adult about this. Do what everyone else her age did—have flings and 'things' with no strings. She wasn't supposed to fall in love. Not with Leandro. He had always been so honest with her. He hadn't made any promises or misled her in any way. She knew what she had been signing up for and yet she had broken the first rule.

The love she felt for him felt completely different from what she had felt for Mark. More adult. More mature. She loved him with her body and her mind. She couldn't separate the two, which was part of the problem. She couldn't separate her desire for him from her love of him. They were so deeply, inextricably entwined, like two parts of a whole.

Something about that date on her phone calendar began to niggle at the back of her mind.... She was as regular as clockwork. She should have had her period two days ago. She couldn't be pregnant...could she? But they had used protection. Condoms were fairly reliable, weren't they? She wasn't on the pill because she hadn't needed to be.

Surely it was too early to be panicking? Periods could be disrupted by stress and travel—not that hers had ever been disrupted before. They were annoyingly, persistently regular. She could set her watch by when the tell-tale cramps would start.

Miranda put a hand on her abdomen. Could it be

possible? Could Leandro and her have made a tiny baby? The thought of having her very own baby made the membrane around her heart tighten. How could she have thought she could go through life without experiencing motherhood? Of course she wanted a baby. She wanted to be a mother more than anything. She wanted to be a wife, but not just anyone's wife. She wanted to be Leandro's wife. How could she live the rest of her life without him beside her? He was everything to her. He had shown her what she was capable of feeling as a woman. He had unlocked her frozen heart. He had awakened the needs she had suppressed. He was The One. The Only One. How could she not have realised that before now? But maybe a part of her had always been a little bit in love with him.

Would the prospect of having a baby change his mind about them having a future together?

Miranda gnawed at her lip. It would be best to make sure she was actually pregnant first. She would have to slip out and get a test kit and take it from there. There was no point in mentioning it until she was absolutely sure. Her mind ran with a spinning loop of worry. How would he take it if the test was positive? She couldn't imagine how she was going to find the courage to tell him. *'Hey, guess what? We made a baby.'* Like that was going to go down well. How would she explain it to her family? Or Mark's family?

Leandro was tied up with the gardening team who were sorting out the garden in preparation for selling the villa. Miranda told him she was going to do some shopping for dinner, which was fortunately partially true. She was the world's worst liar and didn't want to raise his suspicions. Luckily he was preoccupied with the gardeners, as he simply kissed her on the forehead before turning back to speak to the head gardener.

Inside the pharmacy there were two young mothers. One was buying nappies; the other was looking at nursing aids. Their babies were under six months old. Miranda couldn't stop staring at them sleeping in their prams. In a few months' time she would have one just like them. Would it be a girl or a boy? Would he or she look like her or Leandro or a combination of them both? One of the babies opened its mouth and gave a wide yawn, its little starfish hands opening and closing against the soft blue bunny blanket it was snuggly wrapped in.

Miranda felt a groundswell of emotion sweep through her. How had she managed to convince herself she didn't want to be a mother? She wanted to be just like these young mothers—shopping with their babies, doing all the things mothers do. Taking care of their little family, loving them, nurturing them, watching them grow and mature. Taking the good with the bad, the triumphs with the tragedies, because that was what made a full and authentic life.

Miranda came home with three testing kits and quickly took them upstairs to the bathroom off her suite. Not that she had slept another night in her suite. She had spent every night with Leandro in his. Could that mean he wanted her to be in his life more permanently? Hope lifted in her chest but then it deflated like a pricked balloon. She was in his room because

the furniture had been packed up in hers. It was a convenience thing, not an emotional one.

Her heart was in her throat as she waited for the test
to work. She blinked when the results came through.
Negative? How could it possibly be negative? She
snatched up the packaging and reread the instructions.
Maybe she hadn't followed the directions. No. She'd
done exactly what she was supposed to do. Maybe it
was too early to tell. She was only a couple of days past
her period time. Maybe she didn't have strong enough
hormonal activity yet.

But she *felt* pregnant.

Or was it the hope of it she was feeling? The hope of
a new life growing inside her—a life that would bond
her and Leandro together for ever. A little baby boy
or girl like those she had seen in the pharmacy. The
little baby who would be the first child of the family
she had always wanted.

Miranda did another test and another one. Each one
came up negative. The disappointment was worse each
time. She held up the first test for another look and
her heart stopped like it had been struck with a thick
plank when she saw Leandro reflected in the mirror
in front of her.

'What are you doing up here?' he said. 'You know
you can use my bathroom.'

She turned to face him, hiding the test stick behind
her back. 'Erm…nothing…'

His eyes went to the pile of packaging on the marble
top near the basin to the right of her. Miranda's heart
felt like it was going to pound its way out of her chest.

She could feel it hammering against her breastbone as Leandro stepped into the bathroom. It wasn't a tiny bathroom by any means but now it felt like a shoebox. She watched in scalp-tingling dread as he picked up one of the packages.

He turned and looked at her with a deep frown. 'What's going on?'

Miranda licked her tinder-dry lips. 'I thought I was pregnant, but I'm not, so you don't have to panic. I did a test. Three times. There were all negative.' Tears were close. She could feel them building up behind her eyes. Stinging, burning. Threatening to spill over.

'Pregnant?' His voice sounded hoarse.

'Yes, but it's all good,' she said, swallowing a knotty lump of emotion. 'You don't have to change your brand of condoms. They've done the job.'

His frown was so tight his brows were joined over the bridge of his nose. 'Why didn't you tell me earlier?'

'I only just realised I was late,' Miranda said. 'I'm never late. I wanted to make sure before I told you. I didn't see the point in telling you if there was nothing to worry about. And there's nothing to worry about, so you don't have to worry.'

He put the package down and raked a hand through his hair with a hand that wasn't steady. His face was a strange colour. Not his usual olive tan but blanched, ashen. 'So...you weren't going to tell me unless it was positive?'

'No.'

He studied her for a moment. 'Are you relieved it was negative?'

'I...' Miranda couldn't do it. She couldn't tell another white lie. It was time to face up to what she had been avoiding for the last twelve days—for the last seven years. 'I'm bitterly disappointed,' she said. 'I want a baby. I want to be a mother. I want to have a family. I can't pretend I don't. I *ache* when I see mothers and babies. I ache so deep inside it takes my breath away. I can't do this any more, Leandro. I know you don't want what I want. I know you can't bear the thought of having a child in case you can't keep them safe. But I want to take that risk. I want to live my life and take all the risks it dishes up because locking myself away hasn't made me happy. It hasn't brought Mark back and it hasn't helped his parents move on. I'm ready to move on.' She took a deep breath and added, 'I want to move on with you.'

A flicker of pain passed over his face. 'I can't. I told you before. I can't.'

Miranda's heart sank. 'Are you saying you don't love me?'

His jaw worked for a moment. 'I'm saying I can't give you what you want.'

Miranda fought back tears. 'You love me. I know you do. I see it every time you look at me. I feel it every time you touch me. We belong together. You know we do.'

He turned to grip the edges of the marble counter, his back turned towards her as if he couldn't bear to look at her. Self-doubt suddenly assailed her. Could she be wrong? Could she have got it horribly wrong? Maybe he didn't love her. Maybe all this had been for him was a 'thing'. Maybe she was just another one of his casual flings that didn't mean anything.

'Leandro?'

He pushed himself away from the counter and turned to look at her, his expression taut, his posture stiff as if every muscle was being drawn back inside his body. 'It was wrong of me to get involved with you like this. I'm not the right person for you. I'm not the right person for anybody.'

'That's not true,' Miranda said. 'You're letting the past dictate your future. That's what I was doing. For the last seven years I've been living in the past. Clinging to the past because I was too frightened of loving someone and losing them. I can't live like that any more. I'm not afraid to love. I love you. I think I probably always have loved you. Maybe not quite as intensely as I do now, but the first time you touched me it changed something. It changed me. You changed me.'

'You're in love with the idea of love,' Leandro said. 'You always have been. That's why you latched onto Mark the way you did. You're doing it now to me. You like to be needed. You like to fix things for people. You couldn't fix things for Mark so you gave him the rest of your life. You can't fix me, Miranda. You can't make me into something I'm not. And I sure as hell don't want you to give me the rest of your life so I can ruin it like I've ruined everyone else's.'

Miranda took a painful breath. 'What if that test had been positive?' she said. 'What would you have done then?'

He looked at her with his mouth tightly set. 'I would have respected your decision either way.'

But he would have hated it, she thought. He would have hated her for putting him through it for she could never have made the decision to terminate. Not when she wanted a baby more than anything. Why had it taken her this long to see the lie she had been living? Or had she lived like that because everyone had kept telling her what she should do for so long, she had dug her heels in without stopping to reflect on what she was actually giving up? But if Leandro couldn't give her what she wanted then there was no point in pretending and hoping he would some day change his mind.

She was done with pretending.

She had to be true to herself, to her dreams and hopes. She loved Leandro, but if he couldn't love her back then she would accept it, even though it would break her heart.

But life was full of heart-breaking moments.

It was what life was all about: you lived, you learned, you hurt, you healed, you hurt and healed all over again.

'I know you warned me about changing the rules,' Miranda said. 'But I couldn't control my feelings. Not the way you seem to be able to do. I want to be with you. I can't imagine being with anyone else. I know we only have two days left, in any case, but it would be wrong of me—wrong *for* me—to stay another minute knowing you can't love me the way I want and need to be loved.'

Nothing showed in his expression to suggest that

he was even remotely upset by her announcement. She could have been one of the gardeners outside telling him she had finished for the day. 'If you feel you must leave now, then fine,' he said. 'I'll bring your flight forward.'

Do you need any further confirmation than that? Miranda thought. He couldn't wait to get rid of her. Why wasn't he reaching for her and saying, *don't be silly, ma petite, let's talk about this*? Why wasn't he holding her close and resting his chin on the top of her head the way he so often did that made her feel so treasured and so safe? Why wasn't he saying he had made a mistake and that *of course* he loved her? How he had *always* loved her and wanted the same things she wanted. Why was he standing there as if she was a virtual stranger instead of the lover he had been so intimately tender and passionate with only hours earlier?

Because he doesn't love you.

'If you don't mind, I'll make my own way to the airport,' Miranda said. 'I hate goodbyes.'

'Fine,' he said and pulled out his phone. 'I'll order a cab.'

Miranda didn't waste time unpacking her bag when she got home to her flat. She went to her wardrobe and pulled out the drawer that contained Mark's football jersey. She unwrapped it from the tissue paper she kept it in and held it up to her face but all she could smell was the lavender sachet she had put in the drawer beside it. She gently folded the jersey and put it in a cardboard carrier bag.

Mark's parents greeted her warmly when she arrived at their house a short time later. She hugged them back and then handed them the carrier bag. 'I've been holding onto this for too long,' she said. 'It belongs here with you.'

Mark's mother, Susanne, opened the bag and promptly burst into tears as she took out Mark's jersey and pressed it to her chest. Mark's father, James, put a comforting arm around his wife's shoulders while he fought back his own tears.

'I'm not sure if I've helped or hindered your grieving of Mark,' Miranda said. 'But I think it's time I moved on with my life.'

Susanne enveloped Miranda in a warm motherly hug. 'You helped,' she said. 'I don't know what we would've done without you, especially in the early days. But you're right. It's time to move on. For all of us.'

James stepped forward for his hug. 'You've been marvellous,' he said. 'I'm not sure Mark would've been as loyal if things had been different. Susanne and I are looking into fostering kids in crisis. We're ready now to be parents again, even if it's only in temporary bursts.'

Miranda smiled through her tears. 'Wow, that's amazing. You'll be fantastic at fostering. You're wonderful parents. Mark was so lucky to have you. *I've* been lucky to have you.'

'You'll still have us,' Susanne said, hugging Miranda again. 'You'll always have us. We'll always be here for you.'

Miranda waved to them as she left, wondering if she would ever see them again, but then decided she would.

They would always have a special place in her life, just as Mark would.

Leandro couldn't put it off any longer. He had to pack up Rosie's room. Everything else had been seen to: the paintings had gone; the antiques were sold—apart from a few things he couldn't bear to part with. His father's walnut desk and the brass carriage clock that sat on the bookshelves nearby and gave that soothing tick-tock of time passing steadily by. The villa was an empty shell now everything had been taken away. The floors and corridors echoed as he walked along them. The rooms were like cold caves.

All except for Rosie's room.

He opened the door and the memories hit him like a tidal wave…not of Rosie so much, but of Miranda standing in there with him. Of her standing with him, supporting him, understanding him. Loving him.

His eyes went to Flopsy. The silly rabbit had fallen over again. Leandro walked over and picked the toy up but, instead of putting it back against the pillows, he hugged it against his chest where a knot of tightly bound emotion was unravelling.

He had let Miranda leave.

How could he have done that when she was the only one he wanted to be with? She was the only one who understood his grief. The only one who understood how hard it was to move on from the past.

But at least she'd had the courage to do so.

He had baulked at it.

Seeing those pregnancy tests on the bathroom counter had thrown him. It had thrown him back to the past where he hadn't been careful enough, not diligent enough, to protect his little sister.

But Miranda was right. It was time to move on. He hadn't done anything deliberately. He had been a child—a small, innocent child.

He finally understood why his father had left him his most treasured possessions. His dad hadn't been able to move on from the past but he had known Leandro would have the courage to do so.

He had the courage now. He had it in spades.

He was an adult now and he wanted the things most adults wanted. He wanted to love and be loved. He wanted to have a family. He wanted to build a future with someone who had the same values as he did.

Miranda was that person.

He loved her. He loved her with a love big enough to overcome the past. He loved her with a love that could withstand whatever life dished up. How could he have let her leave? Why had it taken him this long to see what was right before his eyes? Or had he known, always known, but shied away from it? Hadn't he felt it the first time they kissed? The way her mouth met his, the way her arms looped around his neck, the way her body pressed into his, the way she responded to him with such passion and generosity.

He had been a fool to let her go. He had hurt her and the very last thing he wanted to do was that. Her pregnancy scare had thrown him. Terrified him. Shocked him into an emotional stasis. He had locked down. He hadn't been able to process the enormity of his feelings. All the hopes and dreams he had been suppressing for all those years had hit him in the face when he'd seen that pregnancy test. It had been like a carrot being dangled in front of his nose: *this is what you could have if only you had the courage to take it.*

Speaking of carrots… Leandro smiled at the floppy-eared rabbit in his hands. 'I think I've just found the perfect home for you.'

Miranda was on her way out to her car to meet Jaz at the boutique when she saw a dark blue BMW pull up. Her heart gave a little leap when she saw a tall figure unfold from behind the wheel. Leandro was carrying something in a bag but she couldn't see what it was. She wondered if she had left something behind at the villa, as she had packed in rather a hurry. She didn't allow herself to think he was here for any other reason. Her hopes had been elevated before and look how that had turned out.

She opened the door before he pressed the buzzer. 'Hi. I thought you were going to Geneva?'

He smiled at her. An actual smile! Not a quarter-one. Not a half-one, but a full one. It totally transformed his face. It took years off him, made him look even more heart-stoppingly gorgeous than ever. 'I postponed the meeting,' he said. 'Is now a good time to talk?'

Miranda hoped Jaz wouldn't mind her being a few minutes late. Even if he was just returning a stray pair of knickers it would be worth it to see him smile again. 'Sure,' she said. 'Come in.'

He stooped as he came inside and her belly gave a card-shuffling movement as she caught the citrus notes of his aftershave. She had to restrain herself from reaching out and touching him to make sure she wasn't imagining him there. *Why* was he here? He'd said he wanted to talk but that might be about how to keep the news of their 'thing' a secret from her family, especially with Julius' and Holly's wedding coming up. She didn't dare hope for anything more.

Miranda glanced at the bag in his hand. 'Did I leave something behind?'

He handed it to her. 'I want you to have this.'

Miranda opened the bag to find Flopsy the rabbit inside. She took him out and held him close to her thrumming chest. 'Why?'

'Because I want our first baby to have him,' Leandro said.

She blinked and then frowned, not sure she'd heard him correctly. 'But we're not pregnant. I told you, the tests were all negative. You don't have to worry. It was my mistake. I worked myself up into a panic over nothing.'

He stepped closer and held her by the upper arms, a gentle, protective touch that made her flesh shiver in delight. His dark brown eyes were meltingly warm, moist with banked-up emotion. 'I want you to marry me,' he said. 'I want you to have my babies. As many as you want. I love you. I don't think it's possible to love someone more than I love you.'

Miranda's heart was so full of love, joy and relief, she thought it would burst. Could this really be happening? Was he really proposing to her? '*Really?*' she said. 'Did you really just ask me to marry you?'

'Yes, really.'

'What made you change your mind?'

'When you left I kept telling myself it was for the best,' he said. 'I convinced myself it was better that way. I was annoyed with myself for crossing a boundary I'd always told myself I'd never cross. But when I finally worked up the courage to pack up Rosie's room it made me realise what I was forfeiting. I think that's why I was so shocked at seeing that pregnancy test. It was like being slammed over the head with the truth. The truth of what I really wanted all this time but wasn't game to admit. I *want* to risk loving you and our children. I can't promise to keep you and them safe, but I will do everything in my power to do so. No one can offer more than that.'

Miranda threw her arms around his neck, Flopsy getting caught up in the hug. 'I love you,' she said. 'I want to spend the rest of my life with you. I can't imagine being with anyone else.'

Leandro kissed her tenderly before holding her slightly aloft so he could look down at her. 'You know what's ironic about this? That night I returned Jake's call, I lectured him about hassling you all the time about moving on with your life. I told him all you needed was some space to sort it out for yourself. But then I realised that's what I needed. When you left I could finally see what I was throwing away. I didn't want to end up like my father, living alone and desperately lonely, with only liquor for comfort. He knew I would eventually get past the grief and guilt. That's why he left me what he loved most. He knew I would reclaim my life. I want to be with you while I do it, *ma petite*. No one else but you.'

Miranda wrapped her arms around his waist. 'I wonder what my brothers are going to say.'

'I think they'll be pleased,' Leandro said. 'In fact, I'm wondering if Jake's already guessed.'

She looked up him with a twinkling smile. 'You think?'

'I got a bit terse with him when he asked if I'd introduced you to any hot French or Italian guys.'

'Ah, yes, jealousy is always a clue.' Miranda gave a little laugh. 'Or so Jaz says. She'll be so thrilled for us. She's been itching to make me a wedding dress since we were kids. Now it's going to happen for real.'

Leandro brushed an imaginary hair away from her forehead. 'You will be the most beautiful bride. I can't wait to see you walk down the aisle towards me.'

'How long before we get married?'

'I'd do it tomorrow, but I think we shouldn't steal Julius's and Holly's thunder.'

Miranda loved how thoughtful he was. It was one of the reasons she loved him so much. 'I can wait a few months if you can.'

'It'll be worth the wait,' he said. 'We have the rest of our lives to be together.'

Miranda touched the side of his face with her hand, looking deep into his tender gaze. 'I don't care what life throws at us. I can handle it, especially if I've got you by my side. Which is kind of where you've always been, now that I think about it.'

Leandro smiled as he held her close, his head coming down to rest on top of her head. 'It's where I plan to stay.'

* * * * *

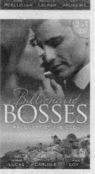

'The perfect Christmas read!' - Julia Williams

Jewellery designer Skylar loves living London, but when a surprise proposal goes wrong, she finds herself fleeing home to remote Puffin Island.

Burned by a terrible divorce, TV historian Alec is dazzled by Sky's beauty and so cynical that he assumes that's a bad thing! Luckily she's on the verge of getting engaged to someone else, so she won't be a constant source of temptation... but this Christmas, can Alec and Sky realise that they are what each other was looking for all along?

Order yours today at
www.millsandboon.co.uk

MILLS & BOON®

Man of the Year

Our winning cover star will be revealed next month!

**Don't miss out on your copy
– order from millsandboon.co.uk**

Read more about Man of the Year 2016 at

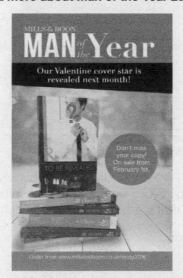

www.millsandboon.co.uk/moty2016

**Have you been following our
Man of the Year 2016 campaign?
🐦 #MOTY2016**